EVERYTHING IN PROSPERITY

Judy Hannigan

"Seriously, darlin', what gave me away?" Jackson asked.

"I just knew you were there," she replied. "You're the one who claims I'm a witch, so you shouldn't be surprised I'd know your whereabouts." Seeing a corner of his mouth twitch before he caught it, she dipped her head, hiding her eyes and unknowingly exposing the column of her throat. She'd never confess her stallion had recognized Jackson's presence and signaled it to her.

"But I'm teasing when I say you're a witch," Jackson confessed with a hint of laughter in his tone, disguising the waves of relief and tenderness flooding through him. Another slight tilt of Sam's head had him imagining his lips nibbling and licking the delicate arch of the ivory skin she was innocently offering.

Sam was reminded of how Jackson had searched for her after they'd been tossed from the stage. He'd found her half-conscious, legs dangling over a fifty-foot drop to the ravine bottom. He'd pulled her to safety, held her, and cared for her—not knowing she didn't recognize him. Her memory, as blank as a schoolroom slate washed clean in the rain, had her thinking he was a kind stranger. Because she'd felt safe with him, trusted him, she hadn't protested when he'd kissed her. Ignoring propriety completely, she hadn't had the willpower to deny him—or herself—the pleasure. And she'd wanted more—more warmth—more kisses. She felt the same longing for pleasure pulsing through her now.

"Have you considered this may be my way of conceding?" Sam teased, her question an obvious jest, though she'd expressed it in a seductive tone she hadn't intended to use.

Each word of Sam's inquiry traced a line of fire on Jackson's skin, awakening a need only she could extinguish. *You may not be a witch, but there's magic between us.* He knew her powers—her spirit, her scent, her taste, her soft warmth—the inner and outer heat of every inch of her.

Everything in Prosperity

Judy Hannigan

Book 2—Prosperity Series

ISBN: 979-8-9909624-2-2 (Print)
ISBN: 979-8-9909624-3-9 (eBook - EPUB)

Library of Congress Control Number:
2024920381

Cover Design: Judy Hannigan/Cheryl Perez

Copy & Line Editor: Maggie Fenton:
www.maggiefenton.com

Author Photo: Waters Photography LLC:
www.waters-photos.com

Interior Design: Cheryl Perez:
https://yourepublished.wixsite.com/youre-published

DEDICATION

To my husband, Richard, who doesn't tell me what to do and believes that if I say I will do something—I do it. And he never doubts that I will do it well.

He's given me a lifetime of kindness and love that would make my heroines envious.

COMING SOON

BOOK 3

PROSPERITY SERIES

Acknowledgments

Thank you to my Beta readers for your enthusiasm, encouragement, and feedback: Sue Bevard, MaryAnn Hayden, Beth Kuhn, Jennie Masche, Michelle Moser, April Pickering, Sara Stevenson.

A special thank you to Ray Ortiz and Matt Stevenson for patiently explaining the organization of shooting contests. (They didn't roll their eyes even once.) If not for their help, I'd still be drafting those related chapters.

Another special thank you to David Frost, Beta Reader Extraordinaire! He not only provided invaluable feedback, he treated me to a four-hour "lunch" to explain it—and I loved every minute and every word.

He even recognized the "inside" joke about Peter Jack's hating cooked carrots.

Prologue

Occasionally, after accepting Sam Hilliard Stone Knight had been christened with a man's name, a new acquaintance would ask how it felt not having memories. Sam didn't mind the question as much as she minded not knowing the complete answer.

Ordinarily, she offered the same short response, comparing it to being born fully grown, already immersed in a life in which she was cognizant of only the present. She didn't bother explaining the doubts and uncertainty of wondering what her place in life was—or the anxiety she suffered from worrying about past events influencing the future.

In the first weeks after the stage wreck that caused her amnesia, the question had concerned her more than it did now. But as she adjusted to her condition, she came to understand not remembering wasn't such a bad thing—especially when she acknowledged the future was all any person could count on—for however long a person's future might last. When she thought of memory in that context, its importance diminished—its significance reduced to the simple ability to trace the path a person traveled to get to the next moment in life. She found a modicum of solace in that concept.

She also garnered comfort from people in the present sharing their memories with her. And, when God allowed her a glimpse of her past—the bad and the good—the people who loved her helped her bear the pain or celebrate the joy.

But during the times when the confusion and isolation of having no memory threatened to overwhelm her, she forced herself to think of the twenty-six years of her life in terms of *before* and *after*. *Before* was the life she couldn't remember because of being catapulted from a sabotaged stagecoach and hitting her head on a granite ledge suspended over a fifty-foot drop to a boulder-strewn ravine. *After* were the seven months since the crash in which she'd learned to live without the memories from the *before*.

And Jackson Knight, the man she'd loved *before* she forgot how she came to be the woman she was, was the man who still loved her *after* she lost that awareness. In the *before*, hampered by her past, she'd held a piece of herself from him, believing she was unworthy to be his wife because her body was unable to carry a child.

But in the *after*, she'd discovered a different truth. She saw it in Jackson's eyes when he looked at her—felt it in his lips when he kissed her—sensed it in his touch when he loved her. His body made promises each time they joined; and in return, she gave him *everything* she had to give.

Together, they had *everything* that mattered.

And when they'd married, she'd vowed they would find their way forward—because *he was everything*—the present and the future.

Not once did she consider the possibility *everything* could disappear.

Chapter 1

March 1876, Wyoming Territory

Struck by a sudden longing to remain home—near his wife—Jackson Knight paused on his front porch while pressing the flat of his hand against his belly as if it could calm the unease pooling there since rising at dawn.

Until the discomfort began plaguing him, he'd been looking forward to accompanying some of the ranch's cowhands and his foreman, Davis Wilson, to Trinity's south range to check on how the cattle were wintering. Though only early March, a stretch of mild weather, unusual for a Wyoming winter, was providing a welcome opportunity to see the chore done ahead of schedule.

Clad in a thin wrapper, her feet bare, his wife launched herself out the door he'd purposely left open and stepped into him, raising her arms to twine them behind his neck. Bending to cover her lips with his, he savored her kisses while wrapping his arms around her and pulling her closer to feel her breasts against his chest.

"Hmm, but you're tempting," she purred, parting her lips, inviting his tongue to sweep past her teeth in a tantalizing glide to tangle with hers. He growled, low in his throat, and tightened the embrace, lifting her against him so her toes barely touched the boards beneath her feet. She was tall, but he was more than half a head taller than she. He slanted his mouth over hers to take the kiss deeper. Her lips clung, and her tongue enticed.

Hot, supple skin burned Jackson through the silk of Sam's wrapper. She tasted of sweet tea and sultry seduction. They both were breathing fast. He wanted to carry her into the house, part the sides of her wrapper, run his hands over her bare skin, keep her safe… *Wait. Keep her safe?* The unexpectedness of the thought had him wrenching his mouth from Sam's to search her eyes. But nothing in her return gaze explained his sudden need to protect her.

"Jackson?" Sam questioned, tilting her head and raising delicate eyebrows. With her swollen breasts and tight nipples pressed against his hard-packed chest, he knew he had her body craving his. *Why had he withdrawn from her so unexpectedly?*

Realizing he'd been staring, Jackson brushed a honey-gold curl from Sam's cheek. But the warmth of her skin beneath his fingertips supplanted his protective concern—persuading him to focus on his senses—to taste the rich nectar of her soft lips, rub his chest against her pebbled peaks, press his arousal into the cradle of her thighs. His eyes moved back to her lips, where a corner of her mouth lifted.

"Are you thinking of telling Wilson something has come up that needs your attention?" she asked, laughter in her voice, and beneath that—seduction.

The muscles of his abdomen clenched, stirring his already hard cock. "Something *has* come up, darlin'. *Should I tell him to go without me?*"

"No," Sam murmured, resisting the sexual need tempting her to say otherwise. "But you can expect I'll do whatever it takes to make sure it *comes up* again when you return."

"I like when you plan my work for me, darlin'."

"And I like it better when you do the work. However, I warn you, I may not be satisfied with it coming up only once."

"Jesus, Sam. Are you trying to kill me?"

"Think of it as an incentive to hurry home," she purred.

Wilson and the other cowpokes were mounted and waiting. Jackson hesitated, recognizing the internal struggle she waged convincing herself to let him go. Then one of the men's horses stamped impatiently, and she stepped back. But Jackson didn't turn away. The desire flaring between them had him hard and aching, not a condition compatible with beginning a two-hour ride—in a saddle, that is. The men could wait a little longer.

"Christ, I need a minute, Sam," he murmured, huskiness raw in his voice. He shifted his gaze to the door standing open behind her. "I should have kissed you while we were on the other side of the door where it wouldn't have mattered if things got out of hand."

She was smiling when his eyes came back to her. "We've provided enough entertainment for the morning," she replied. "Tonight's performance will be private. You'd better go."

But he still hesitated. The unease in his gut hadn't lessened. "Sam, is everything all right? I have this feeling—" Her fingers came up to rest lightly on his lips, stopping his words.

"I'll miss you. That's all," she admitted. "Truly," she added softly, lowering her hand.

Holding her gaze, he pushed down his doubt and turned reluctantly. As he descended the porch steps and strode to his mount, he concentrated on regaining control over his body and his apprehension. After swinging up onto his saddle, he picked up the reins and nudged the sides of his horse. The sooner he left, the sooner he'd return.

When he reined in next to his foreman, Davis Wilson shot him a knowing look before abruptly turning to follow the other riders who'd begun climbing the hill overlooking the ranch. The trail to the south range began at its base on the other side.

Halfway up the hill, Jackson looked back. Sam hadn't moved from the porch. He suppressed a wild urge to race back and haul her up onto the saddle with him.

At the top of the hill, he twisted in his saddle again, his gaze tunneling past the main house, where his partner, Parker Evans, lived with his daughter, Becky. Sam's white wrapper was visible in the heavy shadow cast by the porch roof. Why didn't she go inside? She must be freezing. Hell, she hadn't bothered with shoes or a shawl when she'd followed him for that goodbye kiss. Something didn't feel right, and he couldn't help worrying.

Sonofabitch.

***

"What's the matter, Jackson?" Wilson teased after noticing his boss turning for a second time to peer behind him. "Afraid Sam will get into trouble while you're gone?"

Damn, if that wasn't exactly what he was thinking. Jackson pinned Wilson with a scowl that would make most men leap from their saddle and run for cover. Unfortunately, it was wasted on the cowman. Wilson knew him too well to be intimidated.

Chuckling softly, pleased his guess had been spot on, Wilson raised a leather-gloved hand to the crown of his hat to shove it forward, effectively concealing the amusement twinkling in his eyes. Knowing from experience it wouldn't be wise to take another poke at the man when he was worried about his wife, he made a clucking noise to urge his mount to pick up its pace. "If you're not going to be any friendlier than the look you singed me with, Jackson, I'll leave you in the company of your horse. Maybe he won't mind you acting like a riled polecat."

While riding to catch up with the other cowpokes, Wilson's thoughts stayed with his boss. Though few knew it, Jackson's first name was Providence. But any man bold enough to have used it to his face was living the remainder of his life wishing he'd been born mute. Personally, Wilson thought the exalted moniker fit. After all, Divine Providence hadn't only blessed Jackson with good looks, intelligence, confidence, and a cool head, but also with opportunities to use those gifts to amass a fortune and win the heart of a remarkable woman.

While Jackson's wife might be considered unconventional, willful, and impulsive by a few no-account, pious hypocrites, her goodness and fair nature won over most folks. It was true she had a temper, but she usually had a good reason for displaying it. It was also true she wasn't good at doing traditional wifely things, like cleaning house, mending, or cooking an edible meal. But to make up for those deficits, she could ride like the wind, shoot faster and truer than a body could believe, deal cards like a dream, and nearly blind a man if he forgot himself and stared at her for more than ten seconds at a time. Yessiree, Sam Hilliard Stone Knight was an extraordinary woman. And Jackson lived and breathed for her.

***

Having crested the hill, the ranch no longer visible, Jackson kept his eyes glued to Wilson's back while struggling to review the day's chores instead of wallowing in the dread gnawing his insides. Two hours later, his mount again alongside Wilson's, it was all he could do to pay attention to his foreman giving out assignments to the men. Then it was his turn to point out the hills and gullies in which the beeves were most likely sheltering. After that, each man turned his mount and headed to his designated area.

While canvassing a grove of cottonwoods and losing count for the second time, Jackson gave a frustrated growl, admitting defeat. He could no longer ignore his gut. His intuition was rarely wrong, and it was telling him Sam needed him. His men could do this job without him.

***

When Wilson noticed Jackson signaling from the edge of the cottonwood grove that he was returning to Trinity, he wasn't surprised. Raising an arm in acknowledgment, he muttered a prayer under his breath asking Divine Providence to continue to ride at his boss's side. With Sam's gift for trouble, Providence Jackson Knight would need all the help he could get.

***

With the warmth of Jackson's goodbye kiss fading from her lips, the fear Sam had been repressing since she'd first awakened began testing her strength, a little push here and a little prod there, so by the time Jackson mounted his horse, she could think of little else. Arms wrapped across her chest for warmth, she stood as if frozen, watching the distance grow between them. When he disappeared, her fear doubled in strength.

To keep emotion from overwhelming her, Sam reminded herself Jackson would return by sunset. And though his presence wouldn't force the fear into hiding, it would lessen its power. But suddenly, the fear took on an unexpected sharpness—an edge she hadn't experienced before. Was it getting stronger or was she sensing some other danger?

Having tiptoed across the cold floorboards of the porch to the door, Sam stepped over the threshold and eased the door shut. Resting her back and shoulders against its heavy planks, she considered barring it. A tremor moved through her, not a chill from the outside air, but rather an inner one, whispering the depraved sexual taunts of the stalker who'd once hidden within the house watching her and imagining a dark and erotic purpose for her every gesture. His twisted mind had likened her movements to a siren's call performed to arouse his lust. He'd interpreted even so innocent a thing as smoothing a wrinkle in her skirt as a silent invitation—no, that wasn't right—as a silent command—demanding he come to her to satisfy unnatural, wanton needs. Though her stalker was dead, whenever she was alone in the house, she felt his presence. Remnants of his depraved lust reverberated from wall to wall, filling each room, seeking to capture and violate.

With Jackson away, Sam invented a plausible reason to flee the house. No one would suspect she fabricated the excuse to conceal her cowardice. Only she knew the truth.

***

Dressed for riding and headed to the barn, Sam wasn't especially surprised when Cal Ennis, the young owner of the Double Bar ranch, arrived with a telegram he'd picked up while doing errands in Prosperity. Though she greeted him warmly, she suspected whatever the missive contained wouldn't be welcome.

Because she was uncommonly tall for a woman, Cal barely needed to lean from his saddle to press the telegram into the open palm of her outstretched hand. After straightening, he sat quietly, reins held loosely in one gloved hand, studying her face as she scanned the paper. When she

9

looked up, her gaze shot to the top of the hill as if she expected to see Jackson approaching. When she brought her eyes back to Cal, it was to ask a favor.

"Jackson is on the south range with Wilson. It's a two-hour ride, but I'd be beholden to you if you took him this telegram and a note from me."

Though Sam didn't voice it, the worry in her slate blue eyes must have communicated her concern because he nodded his willingness to do the favor without asking questions. Though, he had his own ranch to run, he must have judged her errand more important.

Grateful not to be asked for an explanation, Sam disappeared inside to pen a quick note. Back outside, Cal reached from his saddle to take the envelope she offered. "I'll ride as fast as I can, Sam," he promised. But his words didn't lift the furrow she knew was pinched between her arched brows.

"I know you will, Cal. Thank you—and please tell Jackson I said not to worry."

Cal flashed a grin. "I'll tell him, but you know I might as well tell a coyote to stop howling at the moon. Jackson will worry."

Though Sam wasn't aware of it, her answering smile was so faint it barely registered as one. Pulling the reins to turn his horse south, Cal touched the edge of his hat in farewell as he started out on his way.

Rather than watch Cal, Sam strode purposefully toward her house and, once inside, paused to rub the annoying ache pulsing in her temple. The telegram that summoned her and Jackson to an unexpected meeting had been delayed because a storm northwest of Prosperity had taken down wires. The meeting place was to be the Webster ranch, now owned by Holt Webster.

Martin Webster, Holt's father, had become an enemy after she'd rejected his sexual advances. In retaliation, Webster had sabotaged their stage, sure they'd die in the crash. When that failed, he'd hired assassins in Chicago to murder them in what was to resemble an attempted robbery. Webster's bid for revenge ended when he'd snatched up the gun Sam had shot from his son's hand in a gunfight and turned it on Sam. Her bullet killed Webster before he could pull the trigger.

Because Webster's son, Holt, had been a victim of his father's bullying and abuse, he was sentenced to serve one year probation under Sheriff Price Hardin's supervision for his participation in his father's crimes. Remorseful and grateful, Holt pledged his friendship and buckled down to the business of running the prosperous ranch he'd inherited.

The meeting Price communicated in the telegram was tonight, and Sam knew no matter how fast Cal rode, it would take two hours to reach Jackson, then another two for Jackson to return home, assuming Cal had no difficulty finding him. She couldn't wait for Jackson's return if she were to arrive anywhere near the meeting time specified.

After changing her clothes and gathering her bedroll and other supplies, Sam searched for Old Charlie, the hand who'd know about the bull, Hercules, that she and Jackson had delivered to Martin Webster's ranch last fall. Under the pretense Jackson had a potential buyer for another of Trinity's bulls, Sam questioned Charlie about the arrangements for transporting Hercules. From Charlie's rambling answers, Sam managed to extract sketchy directions to the Webster ranch. Lord knew, because of her amnesia, she didn't *remember* how to get there.

Having mounted her black stallion, Hooker, Sam huffed a frustrated oath while skillfully controlling Hooker's playful prancing. Jackson would soon follow—but he'd be angry—because of his worry. And Sam couldn't help feeling sorry about that.

With miles to Laramie stretching ahead of her, Sam's thoughts returned to the message. When she'd first examined the telegram's remittance and saw it was from the Chairman of the HQ Lee Stock Corporation, she'd expected it to be from her stepfather, Mac. But seeing "bylaws" precede the word "meeting" had shifted her thinking, leaving no doubt in her mind Price Hardin, the sheriff of Laramie, was the sender. Price wasn't a man who casually called in favors.

***

Three quarters of an hour from home, Jackson was surprised to see Cal Ennis making a beeline for him. Cal was a frequent visitor at Trinity because he was courting Becky Evans, his partner's daughter. Well, maybe courting was too strong a word since Becky wasn't yet sixteen. Though only twenty, Cal was mature beyond his years and patient enough to wait for Becky to finish growing up. He was also confident about his feelings and what he wanted. When he'd declared his intentions to Becky's father, he'd told Parker Evans he'd delay making a formal proposal for the year or two he needed to ensure the financial success of his ranch.

Certain only a matter of urgency would send Cal racing in his direction, the dread burgeoning in Jackson suddenly felt as if it were a shovel full of cow dung hitting him dead center in the chest. Reining in and snatching the envelope Cal held out to him, Jackson barely heard Cal tell him Sam said not to worry. He read the telegram first.

IMPORTANT SAM AND JACKSON ATTEND BYLAWS MEETING FOR HQ LEE STOCK AT HOME OFFICE 7 PM MARCH 13 STOP

It was obvious something delayed the wire. No amount of hard riding would enable him or Sam to arrive on time for the meeting. But Jackson would've bet the percentage of profit he earned from the gold mining of his South Pass gold claims that Sam would disregard the dangers of traveling alone and leave without him.

Skimming Sam's note, he saw it offered her interpretation of the telegram and confirmed she'd leave for the rendezvous before he returned. She also wrote their friend, Price Hardin, had sent the wire, but Jackson had already figured that out. The "Home Office" was Holt Webster's ranch, near Laramie, easily recognizable because "HQ Lee" was the code name they'd used in the past for Hercules, the prize bull they'd sold to Martin Webster. The fact Price used code warned of danger and the need for secrecy.

Without a word of explanation to Cal, Jackson shoved the papers in his shirt pocket and spurred his horse to race the remaining distance to the ranch. He couldn't waste a second if he were to have a prayer in hell of catching Sam.

Sonofabitch.

***

Having visited JB, Trinity's cook at the main house, to pick up grub, Jackson strode to his and Sam's partner's office. Parker Evans was a man he and Sam respected and trusted.

Years ago, after Jackson's mother died from pneumonia in South Pass a few short weeks after his father was murdered, Jackson began a relentless hunt for the two brothers who'd left his father's broken body wedged between two rocks in the stream running through his family's claims. After three months of following leads and sightings, bribing disloyal outlaws, and scouring hideouts and gold fields through the Colorado and Wyoming

13

territories, Jackson traveled full circle back to South Pass, where his quarry, Jeremy and Colter Brogan, ambushed him from the protection of a played-out mining tunnel.

Fortunately, the brothers didn't check to make sure Jackson was dead from the bullet they'd drilled into his back because he'd had enough life in him to crawl to the mine entrance, jam a fuse into a dynamite keg, light it, and use his legs to roll it into the tunnel. He didn't stay conscious long enough after that to hear the explosion.

When he woke the next day, he was surprised to learn his nurse was the wife of one of the men who shot him. Jessa Nolan Brogan, also a victim of the brothers, grateful to Jackson for making her a widow, had done everything in her power to keep him alive.

After Jackson recovered, he drifted here and there, even traveling to New York and Chicago to experience the sights and investigate investment opportunities. He was rich, but money couldn't make him forget—couldn't provide a true purpose. Restless and missing the openness of the land and country he loved, he returned to Wyoming Territory and began taking temporary jobs as a cowhand, not for the money but because he enjoyed the work, and it kept him from thinking about what he'd lost.

Like other ranches he'd worked, Jackson hadn't planned to stay at Trinity more than a few months, but Parker and his young daughter, restarting their lives after Parker's wife died, needed him as much as he needed them. So, when Parker offered him a partnership in the ranch, he couldn't turn it down, believing it was a chance to start over. Until Trinity, none of Jackson's business concerns had appealed to him enough to entice him to put down roots—or let people he could care for into his life. Later, when Sam came to Prosperity, Parker and Becky warmly absorbed her into their family, just as they had Jackson.

Before his father had uprooted him and his mother to search for gold in South Pass, Jackson had dreamed of owning a spread of his own. His experience with ranching and horse breeding exceeded Parker's, so Jackson becoming a partner was a natural fit. At Parker's side, Jackson could fulfill his dream of ranching, yet have the freedom to pursue other enterprises, such as the hotel he'd built in Prosperity next to Sam's gambling parlor.

Shrewdly recognizing surface gold would run out long before a big investment, equipment, and mining experience would be needed to extract it, Jackson had had the foresight to sell his two claims to a large mining corporation. Rather than sell outright, he'd opted to accept a modest share of the profits, which he wisely poured into other investments.

Worried about Sam and anxious to be on his way, Jackson handed Parker a sealed envelope containing the wire and Sam's note. "Sam and I are running an errand. If anyone asks, say we're in Eden Ridge with Mac and Grace." Jackson knew their visiting Sam's stepparents wouldn't seem out-of-the-ordinary to anyone curious enough to inquire.

"If you don't hear from one of us in the next forty-eight hours, read this, then wire Mac where to start looking for us." Should they need help, Jackson had confidence Sam's stepfather would be able to find them. Mac and Price Hardin had been partners in their younger days.

"You'll know what to tell Mac after you read the contents. Then find Morgan and come after us." Sam's stepbrother was six years older than Sam. Guided by his mother, Grace, proprietress of the Golden Crown gambling salon, and Sam's stepfather, Morgan had grown into an intelligent, level-headed man, as capable of chairing a big city boardroom as he was of trail bossing beeves to railheads. He could track, rope, and shoot as proficiently as he negotiated contracts. And he'd do anything for Sam.

"Give Sheriff Cooley a heads up about what's transpired if you need to come after us, but don't tell anyone else, at least not until you've investigated enough to know how deep in trouble Price Hardin has sunk us."

The faint creases in Parker's forehead deepened as he listened to Jackson's instructions. "But, Jackson, I saw Sam ride out two hours ago."

"I know, Parker," Jackson replied. "I can't explain more now. I've got to catch up with her."

"Well, get going then. You can trust me to follow your instructions. Sam's amnesia makes it too dangerous for her to be out there alone. Too many people from her past, not to mention yours and Mac's, could catch her unaware."

Jackson agreed. "If this is one of Price Hardin's jokes and one hair on Sam's head is harmed because of it, friend, or no friend, I swear it'll be the last prank he plays."

Sonofabitch.

Chapter 2

Sam wasn't making good time, and the minor ache in her temple had turned into a persistent, dull throbbing that added to the physical strain of the ride. Though she had fewer headaches now than after the stage crash, they tended to strike when she was overtired or anxious—or when memories were trying to surface. After seven hours in the saddle, the muscles in her back and legs were protesting. She'd thought her stamina would have been better but had to acknowledge she hadn't bothered to test it until today. What troubled her most were the prickles of unease traveling up and down her spine from the feeling she was being watched. This was the first time she experienced it away from her house. Checking behind her for what felt like the hundredth time, she wished mightily there had been time to wait for Jackson.

Whenever she heard the rattle of a wagon or the clomp of hooves approaching, Sam left the road, concerned she'd encounter someone who meant her harm or would ask too many questions about her destination. With no memory, she'd have no idea who was friend, foe, or curious stranger. And no matter how she tried, she couldn't rid herself of the feeling someone watched her.

Intending to see to her personal needs when she once again had to duck off the road to avoid an approaching rider, Sam headed for a grove of trees. Dismounting, she caught

Hooker's bridle to lower his head. Stroking down the slope of his forehead, she stopped at his mouth, resting her fingers on his upper lip and made a quiet shushing noise, the signal she'd taught him for silence. Hooker ducked his head once in acquiescence before nudging her shoulder, expecting payment for his compliance. Affectionately rubbing his powerful neck, Sam uncurled the fingers of her other hand to offer a chunk of dried apple.

Wiping her palm on her trousers, she held her breath while listening to clomping hooves on the road draw parallel. When they continued without hesitation and began to recede, she resumed normal breathing. With that danger avoided her senses recognized the unmistakable sound of flowing water, reminding her of the need to relieve the pressure in her bladder. Stepping away from Hooker, her eyes moved to a row of bushes bordering the bank. Since they were thick enough to hide the water, they'd perform the same service for her.

As she vanished into the foliage, the murmur of the water, occasionally interrupted by a rippling burble, soothed Sam's troubled thoughts. If her understanding of the directions old Charlie had provided was correct, she was more than halfway to her destination. And though Jackson would be angry when he arrived, he'd calm down and forgive her soon after he saw she was safe. While giving a final tug to adjust the waistband of her trousers, her optimism disappeared as quickly as it had risen—because that's when she noticed the sound of the stream was louder—because everything else was quiet—too quiet.

Bent at the waist to make a smaller target, Sam moved silently to shelter behind the thick trunk of a nearby tree, her gun hand automatically moving to release the leather thong securing her Colt.

She could see Hooker standing quietly with his ears cocked forward. Then his tail rose and lowered. "I know you're there," Sam called, moving from the protection of the tree she'd been hiding behind. "Come out where I can see you." Her stance was relaxed with her right elbow resting on the butt of her gun, her thumb hooked behind her belt buckle. As she expected, Jackson stepped from the shadows into the open.

What she didn't expect was the appearance of another man doing the same thing twenty feet from where Jackson stood. The stranger and Jackson were reaching for their guns.

Sam was faster, her arm a blur of motion that ended with her Colt cocked, aimed, and finger tightening on the trigger.

A fraction of a second away from blowing a hole in the stranger's chest, Sam saw him hesitate and raise his hands in the air. With one palm turned in Sam's direction and the other to Jackson, the man—more boy than man now that she had time to study his features—spoke to her.

"Don't shoot, ma'am. I was only meanin' to keep that varmint," he paused to wave faintly at Jackson, whose Colt was also trained dead center on his chest, "from gettin' the drop on you." Though his voice betrayed embarrassment at being outdrawn, the angle of his jaw said he was making no apology for going for his gun. Sam admired his courage, but not enough to influence her to redirect the angle of her gun barrel.

"How did you know I was here?" Sam had nearly added "son," but stopped herself, recognizing a male his age would consider it an insult. Though he was as tall as a full-grown man, she doubted he could be much more than sixteen or seventeen.

"I caught a glimpse of you leavin' the road, ma'am, which ain't all that unusual of a thing for a lady to do when she rides on her own. I heard my ma tell my sister plenty of times a smart woman knows to do that, so I didn't pay no mind. I reckoned a lady as pretty as you would naturally practice the rule."

Sam saw a pink flush creep up the boy's neck and onto his cheeks as he realized he'd said she was pretty. From the corner of her eye, she thought she saw Jackson's gun barrel lower a bit. Giving her full attention back to the boy, she asked, "What made you come after me?"

The boy's eyes darted to Jackson before answering. "I didn't trust that fellow over there, ma'am. I met him where you left the road, and he took his time givin' me a good once-over before throwin' me a neighborly nod. Can't say it made me trust him, so I kept my eye on him. Thought he might be the type to double back and rob me or somethin'. Folks ain't always good, you know."

Sam's perfunctory nod acknowledging the irrefutable wisdom of his statement encouraged the young philosopher to offer further explanation.

"Naturally, bein' suspicious of the way he was acting, I wasn't none too surprised to see him follow you. That's when I knew he'd been interested in you the whole time he was lookin' me over. I thought you might need help, so I followed him." Dropping his eyes to her gun, he shook his head in wonder. "I can't hardly believe a gun could leave a holster as fast as yours did. I'll allow that big fellow over there's fast, but I'd bet if you'd wanted to, you could've got both of us. Guess that's when it came to me you were aiming at me, and I pulled back on drawin'."

Despite hearing a low chuckle from Jackson, Sam kept a straight face. The young man's concern was to be admired. Lowering her barrel to point at the ground, she released the hammer and nodded her thanks. "*That varmint,* as you referred to him, is my husband, and I can understand how a person might think he was up to no good. Have to admit, I thought the same until I figured out he only looks mean."

Jackson, who hadn't let his eyes wander from the boy, declared, "You must've decided my looks were pleasing enough, or you wouldn't have married me, darlin'."

Sam didn't respond, but a hint of amusement curved her lips. To her delight, the boy didn't hesitate to comment.

"My ma says pretty women marry ugly men so they don't need to worry about them dallying with other women."

Sam's lips stretched into a genuine smile, and though she knew it wasn't proper, she couldn't resist replying, "Well now, your mother might have the right of it. Truth is, I'm rather partial to his dallying, and I'm not a woman that would tolerate sharing." Her tone sounded as if she'd given the matter a great deal of consideration.

Jackson was no longer paying a bit of attention to the boy. Instead, he turned to face Sam, legs braced apart, shoulders wide, projecting every bit of the male possessiveness he was feeling. "And I have less tolerance for sharing than you." His voice reminded Sam of the snapping growl a male wolf makes when warning a sexually aggressive rival away from its mate. Sam's eyes locked with his.

The boy's voice cut between them. "Well, I reckon if you can outdraw him, ma'am, you ain't afraid of him, so I'll be takin' my leave. My ma and sister will worry if I'm late to supper." After making his excuses, her would-be rescuer began inching away. Sam didn't miss the knowing smile on his lips. Maybe he wasn't as young as she thought.

Without a word, Jackson followed the boy. When he returned, Sam was perched on a fallen log. Though she looked composed, he didn't miss the fact her left thumb absently stroked the lightning bolt scar near the curve of her thumb on the back of her right hand—something she did when she was upset. It also meant she preferred he not make a fuss over what had nearly happened. With eight feet between them, he halted his approach.

"Sam?" he called, letting the quiet inflection of saying her name tell her what he needed. Then exhaling a breath, he waited, recognizing they both needed a moment to calm their emotions. With a bit of reassurance from her, he could be patient.

Understanding, she raised her head, allowing him to see the answer in her eyes before she said, "I'm fine, Jackson."

For the first time since dawn, Jackson felt free of the dread dogging him. A minute of silence passed before he ventured a question mainly from idle curiosity. "Tell me, Sam, how did you know I was there?"

The log beneath Sam's backside, still warm from the rays of the waning afternoon sun, helped quell the tremors passing through her as adrenaline drained from her blood. The boy's surprise appearance had been such a shock she'd feared not being fast enough to prevent a tragedy. Erasing a horrifying image of the boy and Jackson sprawled on the ground with bloody, gaping holes in their chests, Sam forced herself to concentrate on answering Jackson's question.

"You blocked the breeze I was enjoying," she teased, her voice light and flippant.

"Seriously, darlin', what gave me away?" Jackson asked.

"I just knew you were there," she replied. You're the one who claims I'm a witch, so you shouldn't be surprised I'd know your whereabouts." Seeing a corner of his mouth twitch before he caught it, she dipped her head, hiding her eyes and unknowingly exposing the column of her throat. She'd never confess her stallion had recognized Jackson's presence and signaled it to her.

"But I'm teasing when I say you're a witch," Jackson confessed with a hint of laughter in his tone, disguising the waves of relief and tenderness flooding through him. Another slight tilt of Sam's head had him imagining his lips nibbling and licking the delicate arch of the ivory skin she was innocently offering.

Sam was reminded of how Jackson had searched for her after they'd been tossed from the stage. He'd found her half-conscious, legs dangling over a fifty-foot drop to the ravine bottom. He'd pulled her to safety, held her, and cared for her—not knowing she didn't recognize him. Her memory, as blank as a schoolroom slate washed clean in the rain, had her thinking he was a kind stranger. Because she'd felt safe with him, trusted him, she hadn't protested when he'd kissed her. Ignoring propriety completely, she hadn't had the willpower to deny him—or herself—the pleasure. And she'd wanted more—more warmth—more kisses. She felt the same longing for pleasure pulsing through her now.

"Have you considered this may be my way of conceding?" Sam teased, her question an obvious jest, though she'd expressed it in a seductive tone she hadn't intended to use.

Each word of Sam's inquiry traced a line of fire on Jackson's skin, awakening a need only she could extinguish. *You may not be a witch, but there's magic between us.* He knew her powers—her spirit, her scent, her taste, her soft warmth—the inner and outer heat of every inch of her.

"Does that frighten you?" Sam challenged, aware they both were feeling the stirrings of something carnal.

"No." Jackson's voice had dropped a notch, openly conveying the need she'd awakened in him. "It just makes me want you more."

"The way you said that has me wondering why you aren't already kissing me." Sam's eyes were openly appreciating the long, muscular length of his body. When she raised them to his lips, she stopped to linger. *God, but he was handsome.*

Jackson had once explained fights with bullies, provoked over his name, had forced him to develop his body. Childless for years, his mother, Lucy, decreed his name, Providence, a homage to God's goodness for giving her a fine son. Though his mother had been kind and loving, she chose to ignore the battles her son fought over the outrageous moniker. Jackson thanked his father for having the foresight to choose "Jackson" for his middle name and to insist all within his hearing, except Jackson's mother, use it. Working the family ranch and South Pass gold claims had chiseled Jackson's body into muscled iron. And when his earth-toned eyes smoldered with passion, his maleness melted Sam's center to liquid wanting.

"And the way you're looking at me, darlin'," Jackson replied, "has me wondering why you don't come here so I can kiss you." It was amazing how easily she heated his blood—but more gratifying that he did the same to her.

"I want to, but I'm tired," she replied, aware her admiring eyes and come-hither tone said differently. Patting the spot next to her, she invited him to sit. "Why don't you come here?"

Jackson wondered if she comprehended the cruelty of tempting him when they needed to exercise self-restraint. "Have you forgotten this morning? One kiss would lead to something coming up and I doubt either of us would be able to resist." His voice held more than a touch of regret. Reluctantly he pulled his thoughts from what he knew they both wanted and took a steadying breath. "Soon, we'd need *more*—and we're already late."

Sonofabitch.

Rising to her feet, Sam willed strength to her legs to traverse the short distance to her horse. As she was about to lift her foot into the stirrup, she felt her cheeks heat from the wicked thought Hooker wasn't the stallion she wished she were mounting. Then Jackson was behind her, hands at her waist, strong arms lifting her. From her saddle, she reached down to cradle the side of his face in her palm.

"You look weary, Jackson."

"I was worried, Sam."

"I know, and I'm sorry."

"I'm angry with you," Jackson retorted.

"I can see that. And I'm grateful you could overlook it to come find me so soon."

"I was nearing home when Cal came with your message. I had a feeling you needed me before I even left the ranch this morning."

"I'll always need you, Jackson."

"And I'll always come for you, darlin'."

Chapter 3

Something had delayed Sam and Jackson's arrival. Well after midnight, Price Hardin paced in the narrow confines of a line shack on Holt Webster's ranch. While waiting, he couldn't help grinning over the fact they'd married. Despite her beauty and intelligence, Sam was the closest he'd come to encountering a female hellcat. Blessedly, Jackson possessed the rare combination of confidence, patience, and tenderness to win her. In Price's opinion, they were perfect for each other.

Price was known for his sense of humor and mocking wink; however, no one, especially the outlaws and miscreants he brought to justice, would mistake either trait as a sign of weakness. A man of high integrity, keen judgment, uncommon skill, and unwavering commitment, Price Hardin not only symbolized the ideal of a faithful, vigilant, and resourceful officer of the law; he was also the man from whom the ideal was fashioned. And though he downplayed his reputation, had all his deeds been known, he would have stood taller than other legendary men of his day.

Though climbing the steeper slope of his fifties, the power packed in Price's six-foot frame and one hundred seventy pounds of lean muscle commanded respect from men and admiring glances from women. Except at his temples, it was difficult to distinguish the gray hair hiding among the tawny strands bleached gold by the sun. His back was straight, reflexes lightning quick, and jaw square and determined. Folks who didn't know him were often surprised to see his pale blue eyes sparkling with warmth and humor instead of the cold reality he regularly dealt with as a lawman.

Born on an Ohio dirt farm, the youngest of six boys, Price had dreamed of adventure from the day he entered the world. At eighteen, he left home to follow the legion of gold seekers who believed dipping a screened pan into a stream, washing out the sand, and picking out the gold nuggets would be all the effort required to make them rich.

He hadn't been looking for gold himself, but rather for adventure and a way to make a living. And he'd found it, or rather, his gun skills did. There were plenty of opportunities for a man who knew how to use a gun to protect the claims and the men who owned them. Most miners knew little about handling guns, dealing with claim jumpers, or preventing unscrupulous mining companies from taking over claims when the surface gold gave out.

During those gunman days, Price and his friend Mac Covington, Sam's stepfather, rode together. Unlike most of their peers, he and Mac used their guns to protect clients with legitimate claims—and they were well paid for their services. They often fulfilled their contracts without firing a shot. Their reputations persuaded adversaries to think twice about facing their guns, so most of the time, the job they performed was negotiating equitable agreements. Believing notoriety attracted bullets to a man's back when least expected, Price and Mac had been careful not to grow their reputations too large.

When Price decided to turn his hand to the law, Mac partnered with Chase Stone, Sam's father. After Chase married Sam's mother, Mac settled in to help the young couple manage Highbreeze, their ranch. Unfortunately, Chase's wife died giving birth to Sam. Three years later, Chase remarried the kind, angelic-looking widow who owned the Golden Crown gambling salon in Eden Ridge. After Chase was killed, Mac consoled Grace, Sam's stepmother, and helped her raise Sam and Grace's son, Morgan.

In those early years, it was the sworn duty of the Laramie County Sheriff to enforce the law. Not only Laramie but the whole Wyoming Territory needed civilizing. A month before Price arrived, two low-down horse thieves murdered the former Laramie sheriff near Fort Collins. Instead of waiting to be offered the job, Price simply assumed the duties. Never lacking confidence or hesitating to use his fists, weapons, or wit, he waded in to stop trouble wherever he found it.

Since a vigilance committee was administering the law instead of a sheriff, they welcomed Price's efforts because he supported their goals. The committee's acceptance contributed to the populace's perception Price was the new lawman. Consequently, citizens began tipping their hats and calling him sheriff. Then one day, hoping to make it official, the town council authorized payment of back wages for his services.

Keeping the job wasn't as easy as assuming it. In subsequent years, Price was forced to campaign to keep his badge. And though he didn't mind kissing babies and pretty women, those were the few activities associated with politicking he enjoyed. When ballots were tallied in the last election, he'd won by a mere fifteen votes, the count so close his opponent, more politician than gunman, contested the outcome in court. Of course, no one took the case seriously, and after a few weeks, everyone decided a hearing was too much trouble, so the vote stood and Price remained sheriff.

But duties that included collecting taxes, serving legal papers, and attaching and selling property by order of the Court, soon started Price questioning whether sheriffin' was a good fit for him. The job was beginning to feel too law-abiding, making him wonder what kind of man he was for preferring to deal with murderers, thieves, and confidence men. Though Laramie still had its share of thugs, they were blending with the law-abiding citizens so well that it was difficult to distinguish the criminals. Consequently, Price's dissatisfaction with the job was the main reason he was here in the line shack waitin' on Sam and Jackson.

***

"What do you mean you aren't the sheriff of Laramie anymore?" Sam repeated Price Hardin's words, stunned disbelief evident in her tone's volume. Hungry, cold, tired, worried, and aching in places she wished she could ignore, she was in no mood for Price's jokes. Despite riding hard, she and Jackson hadn't only missed the meeting time by several hours but learned on their arrival they'd another hour's ride to reach the line shack where Price waited. Sam was even more disgruntled when she discovered Price had picked the meeting time arbitrarily to make the telegram sound legitimate. Locking eyes with him, she couldn't appreciate the humor in his calling the eyesore of a rough-hewn shack, fit with a latch-string door and a crumbling fireplace in which they were standing, HQ Lee Stock Corporation's home office.

Thumbs hooked in his gun belt, looking as if he hadn't a care in the world, Price lifted his shoulders in a nonchalant shrug and winked at her. "I gave up sheriffin', darlin'," he announced, in an exaggerated drawl. "I guess you could say for the present, I'm an outlaw." Then he abruptly turned from her to confront Jackson, whose angry eyes and tightly clenched jaw warned his mood was blacker than Sam's.

Price's eyes, normally as warm as a summer day, narrowed to an intimidating cold hardness. "Too many church-goin' moralists and ladies' societies think they can run the town better than me. A man can't hardly breathe, let alone sheriff, with all that civility chokin' him."

Jackson's response was a sharp skyward lift of one dark eyebrow warning the end of his patience would coincide with the introduction of his fist to the former lawman's firm jaw.

Fearing that outcome, Sam stepped in. "What in hell are you going on about, Price?" Familiar with his jokes, she'd expected him to break into a grin and admit he was funning them. "Even before you were a sheriff, back in your gunman days, you stayed on the right side of the law." But as she finished the statement, she noticed Price wasn't wearing his badge. His clothes were rumpled, and he needed a shave and haircut. Though thirty years her senior, Price was still a handsome man who took pride in his appearance. It was hard to believe he'd turned outlaw. Was he being forced? Had someone threatened someone for whom he cared? She couldn't think of another reason for Price acting against his nature.

"Are you protecting someone? If it's money you need, Jackson and I will—"

Price interrupted. "Aw, Sam. It's nothing like that." He'd taken his joke too far. Though he was no longer Laramie's sheriff, he hadn't turned outlaw. Sam's offer was downright humbling. He must've borrowed a mule's backside to replace his brains when he'd concocted this ruse.

Recognizing a change in Price's expression, Jackson felt relief and anger. But it was the anger he vented. "You're acting like a mangy coyote yapping for no other reason than no one's bothered to shoot straight enough to put you down. Sam was worried you'd get yourself killed if one of us didn't show up on time, so she left the ranch without me. Dammit,

Price, you know she wouldn't recognize the devil if he popped up out of the fires of Hades right in front of her, let alone an enemy hellbent on vengeance. If you put her in jeopardy for no good reason, I won't bother killing you before I throw you in a hole and cover you."

Imagining Sam riding alone and some lowlife getting a jump on her made the color drain from Price's face and softened his voice with apology. "And I wouldn't harbor any hard feelings for you doing it, Jackson. I guess I'd even help you out by jumpin' in on my own."

He reached out to take Sam's hand in his. "I'm sorry, sweetheart. I had no idea the wire would be delayed. And I didn't mean to take my joke so far. Instead of usin' good sense, I fooled myself into thinkin' humor would take the embarrassment from asking for a favor."

Sam's eyes softened for a split second before hardening and threatening murder if he didn't come clean. Price saw it and talked fast. "I'm not the sheriff of Laramie anymore, but I'm still a lawman—Deputy U.S. Marshal—pretending to be an outlaw so I can run with the Brigham Gang."

Seeing the puzzled look in Sam's eyes, Jackson explained. "Brigham's gang has been on a rampage for over four years, and the law hasn't been able to do a thing to stop them. Their leader, Colson Brigham, is as ruthless as he is shrewd. Those who cross him or talk too much end up dead. His gang is good at holing up in their hideout where the law can't follow."

Giving the stubble on his jaw a thoughtful scratch, Price disagreed with Jackson's latter statement. "Well, it's not exactly true the law can't follow. Any man representin' the law who tried storming the place would be committing suicide. The entrance is narrow and easy to defend, making the law and any unwelcome visitors sitting ducks. 'Course,

Mac's welcome, and I am, too, so long as I ain't flashin' my badge. I never did it before now because Brigham didn't commit any crimes in Laramie where I did my sheriffin'."

Listening to Price, Jackson had to agree. While hunting his father's murderers, he'd wheedled his way in with a group of outlaws. But after ascertaining the Brogan brothers weren't there, he'd discovered leaving could be as difficult as entering. Price's voice interrupted Jackson's thoughts.

"Now that I gave up sheriffin' for Deputy U.S. Marshal, I got the idea to use my gunman past to catch the Brigham Gang," Price Hardin announced. "Everyone knows gunmen work both sides of the law. They earn a living by pinning on a star when opportunities are scarce, but when a big payday crops up, they go back to their outlawin' ways.

"I joined up with Colson Brigham's gang two months ago. It weren't much of a stretch for him to accept my returnin' to my old profession. But the man ain't stupid. He has his men watched whenever they go out on their own. I had to shake one before I sent you that telegram and arranged with Holt Webster to meet you here. If Brigham finds out about this meetin', I won't be seein' daylight again."

"And the same is true for Sam and me!" Jackson barked. "Your promotion certainly hasn't boosted your intelligence!"

Moving between Jackson and Price, Sam pressed her palms to her husband's broad chest and spoke softly, "We owe Price—and he wouldn't call in a favor if he didn't need our help. I know you haven't forgotten he backed Mac and me in that shootout with Martin Webster last autumn and helped rescue us at Ryder's place when Ruth Kensington and Reed Ferguson would have killed us."

Jackson remembered, and if it weren't for Price involving Sam, he would've followed him into outlaw hell, guns blazin'. But Price wanted Sam's help, too, so he started to argue. "I know, darlin', but—"

Sam rose on her toes and brushed her lips across his. "I know you're afraid it's too dangerous. I love you for wanting to keep me safe, but I won't step aside when a friend needs help—so we'll listen to what Price has in mind."

***

What Price planned was a trap baited with a reward so enticing no outlaw craving fame, fortune, or power could resist it. But to succeed, it needed renowned marksmen. Sam and Jackson Knight and Sam's stepfather, Mac Covington, fit the bill.

Though Wyoming was still a territory, its populace would celebrate the United States' hundredth year as if it were a state, and its Centennial birthday would provide the perfect pretext for promoting a local shooting competition. Brigham wouldn't be able to resist the opportunity to win the prize money and acquire the fame. The victory would boost the notoriety of his gang's reputation. He'd also use the occasion to clean out Prosperity's bank.

Price asked Sam and Jackson to explain the stratagem to Mac and enlist his expertise before returning to Trinity. Mac, because of his gunman past and friendship with Price, would act as the go-between to coordinate events and details.

The conspirators agreed they'd selectively advertise to limit the entry of other unsavory competitors. If they did otherwise, every outlaw within two hundred miles of Prosperity would crawl out of his den to compete. Nor did they want any of their enemies showing up to settle old scores. Capturing Brigham and his gang was a big job. They couldn't handle more than that. Price would work with Mac to arrange for a few trusted lawmen friends to pick off any undesirables who might inadvertently learn of the contest before they could get within twenty miles of town.

Having infiltrated Brigham's gang, Price would talk up the Independence Day shooting contest to steer Brigham, unsuspectingly, to their trap. In short, his job was ensuring the participation of the targeted prey and favorably pulling strings from the inside to increase the odds of success.

Besides participating in the contest, Sam and Jackson would volunteer to donate the cash prizes and awards and pay for the improvements and materials required to ready the town's venue. Their generosity would easily overcome any objections Prosperity's town council might raise against sponsoring the competition and allow them to assume the power to control decisions and establish rules.

Their plan was clever but full of danger.

Chapter 4

May 1876

Two months later, no one except Sam's stepparents and Parker Evans knew about her and Jackson's meeting with Price. Since then, she and Jackson had won enthusiastic agreement from Prosperity's Centennial Committee, the town mayor, and the city council to incorporate the shooting contest into the town's Independence Day celebration. Because the contest's addition would attract more visitors and business to Prosperity and because she and Jackson were committing their time and money, all concerned had quickly recognized the rewards.

Work was progressing nicely to ready the shooting range, as were the organization and staffing for conducting and managing the event. Of course, she and Jackson had responsibilities and details to address between now and the contest, but none were particularly worrisome. When Brigham's gang arrived, they'd worry in spades.

Sam's energy had shifted to a more immediate and personal issue—one she intended to approach with care to prevent Jackson from becoming suspicious of her motives for broaching it.

***

Upon waking early in the morning in their ranch house, a week before Jackson would leave for a business trip to

Cheyenne, Sam snuggled close to her husband's side, putting off the discussion she planned to have with him. A little disappointed in herself for stalling, she finally willed herself to just get it done.

"I don't know much about the timber business, do I?" she asked. She hated that she didn't remember and that she was using the fact to segue to the real issue she wanted to resolve.

"No, darlin'," Jackson answered, disliking the uncertainty he heard in her tone. "You weren't at Trinity the last time we sold timber, and none of your other business concerns deal with it, at least none I've heard you or Morgan mention. Are you worrying it's something you should know?"

"Not worrying—wondering. Whenever you and Parker discuss it, nothing comes to mind. Then I start speculating about what other things I've forgotten—until I remind myself it doesn't matter." She allowed herself a dismissive shrug and reminded herself to keep her tone even.

"Must you go to Cheyenne next week about the timber deal?" she inquired, carefully modulating her tone to reflect mild curiosity, hoping Jackson wouldn't detect how much his answer would affect her peace of mind. Fear is a difficult emotion to disguise.

She didn't want him to go.

"I do, Sam," Jackson replied, as he propped himself up on his elbow to see her face. While her beauty always stunned him, it was the trust shining in her unblinking gaze that moved him. He recognized a shadow of vulnerability in her eyes—one that hadn't been there before the stage crash, though she did a good job hiding it most of the time.

While immersed in his thoughts, in an unconscious gesture of comfort, Jackson had been stroking Sam's bare thigh. But as awareness returned, his caress changed to conscious seduction—his palm moving higher to skim over the gentle swell of her naked hip. Relishing the warmth and silkiness of her bare flesh, he edged closer to explore the rounded curves of her buttocks. Dipping the tips of his fingers into the soft dimples at the base of her spine, he followed the shallow indent in the center of her back to her nape beneath the long tresses of her honey-gold hair. As she arched in response to his touch, the tips of her breasts sent rippling pulses of pleasure over the flat muscles of his midsection, down to his hardening sex.

Rising on her elbow, Sam saw her reflection in Jackson's chocolate brown, green-flecked pupils. She watched his fingertips round her neck, trace her collarbone, dip into the hollow of her throat, and linger on the firm mounds of her breasts. The combination of touch and sight was so erotically arousing she briefly forgot she'd asked a question.

"Do you want to talk about Cheyenne or finish what we started, darlin'?" he asked, circling a dusty pink nipple with his index finger.

"You mean, finish what *you* started," she corrected, pretending indifference.

Staring into her eyes, Jackson imagined her slate blue irises darkening with passion could set a man aflame. Teasing her, he expelled a disappointed huff and rolled away. "I guess that means you prefer talking to loving."

"You make me sorry I asked," she pouted, feeling as though her favorite treat had been snatched away before she could taste it. Not waiting for a response, she leaned over to glide the tip of her tongue across his bottom lip before delving inside his mouth to twine her tongue passionately with his.

Groaning deep in his chest, Jackson roughly hauled her against him and rolled to spread her beneath him, reveling in how perfectly she fit against his six-foot-two length, her supple curves cushioning his hard-muscled ridges.

"My mistake was letting your attention wander long enough to ask the question," Jackson murmured as he threaded his right hand into her sleep-tousled hair and kissed her with the full potency of the passion she'd stirred in him.

"You don't make mistakes when it comes to loving me. That's one of the reasons I married you." Though playful, her voice was a whisper as she shifted to align the apex of her legs to cradle his erection against her softness—she wanted him.

Tenderness enveloped Jackson. It had taken so much for them to find their way. There had been times he'd despaired she would ever agree to marry him. But *she was his wife now*.

"You so bewitch me, Sam, I sometimes imagine this is all I need to subsist." His hand swept up her inner thigh to find the bud within the soft petals of her sex while his tongue laved one nipple, then the other.

"*Only this*, Jackson?" Sam managed to ask. His thumb, massaging her pleasure spot, alternating between slow and fast rotations, turned her mind to mush. Swallowing a sob, she rocked against his hand. "You don't have any need for food…for water…for air?" Between pauses, she demonstrated *this* with rhythmic thrusts against his hand. "Then being apart for five days while you go to Cheyenne will be as torturous for you as it will be for me." Wanting him inside her, she reached between them to guide him to her.

Jackson surged into her. Hot and quivering, she took all of him. "God, what you do to me, darlin'." Moving together, slowly at first, his thrusts evoking swells of sensation, they ascended a sensory scale soon demanding harder, quicker strokes. Poised on the edge, desperately straining to crest the pinnacle, Sam ground against him.

Crying his name, the powerful contractions of her climax closed around him. Thrusting deep, the engorged head of his shaft against her womb, he climaxed in hot, forceful bursts.

Unable and unwilling to separate or speak, they clung to each other, the power of their joining leaving them replete, their breathing slow to return to normal.

When able to raise her face from the curve of Jackson's shoulder, Sam brushed a damp lock of ebony hair from his forehead. She loved his looks, dark and handsome. The chiseled lines of his jaw had a rugged symmetry, his eyes a rich, caring warmth, and his lips a sensual quality.

Rolling, Jackson turned Sam's body with his to rest on their sides. No longer joined, but unwilling to release her, he pulled her in close to settle against him.

Passions slaked and mental faculties recovered, Sam resumed her original campaign. "I'm glad we have this week before you go, but it will be a busy one," she murmured.

"Mmm," Jackson responded, sounding drowsy.

"We have several engagements in Prosperity, beginning Wednesday evening," Sam stated, her tone insistent, pitched to keep Jackson awake. "We can stay in town until Sunday morning. Since Parker and Becky are staying until then too, I offered them your hotel suite. Then you'll leave for Cheyenne on Monday."

"That's fine, Sam," Jackson muttered, recognizing sleep wasn't an option. Hoping to shorten the conversation, he summarized the list of obligations. "I know there's a Centennial Committee meeting Thursday afternoon. Friday we're supposed to review specifications for the special targets you designed for the contest. The civil engineer Morgan hired to ensure the berms are adequate to protect spectators from stray bullets wants us to approve his plan for configuring the backstops. Saturday, the glass balls Adam Bogardus wants you to test will arrive on the train, as will the replacement parts for the ranch's main house windmill."

"The Winchester rifles and workers' payroll are arriving, too," Sam reminded him. "The sheriff agreed to provide an escort to the bank. The workers and merchants are counting on that money. We're storing the rifles and prize money in McKinley's bank vault with the payroll."

"I remember. That's a wagonload of temptation," Jackson replied, with an undertone of unease in his voice. Though he didn't say it, he feared an enterprising outlaw would try to rob the prize and payroll money. He didn't want Sam riding shotgun and planned to enlist Morgan's help with convincing her to let them guard it. But now wasn't the time to argue the point, so he steered the conversation back to their plans. "I don't recall Wednesday's engagement."

"You forgot the dinner party at your hotel—the one Wade Harper convinced Hank Bainbridge's wife to arrange so he could escort the new schoolteacher. The gossips say Wade's sweet on her. I'm not certain of the guest list, but Alexa told me she and Morgan are invited. Parker will escort Laurel Ennis, Cal's mother. And, of course, Becky and Cal will attend."

"You'd think I'd remember that invitation, especially since I'm beholden to Charity Rawlins for taking a romantic interest in Wade. For once, I won't need to throttle him to keep him away from you. Now that he's courting the schoolmarm, I can enjoy his company."

"Your jealousy doesn't become you, Jackson. I'm not interested in Wade."

"I know you don't encourage him, or any other man, Sam, but they all act as if you do." Early in his courtship, he'd both witnessed and experienced the icy, distancing gaze she used as a weapon to discourage men's overtures. Unfortunately, her beauty and the pleasure men imagined while brazenly appraising her attributes transcended their fear. "It's hard to feel nothing when another man, especially one as handsome and prosperous as Wade, boldly seduces *my* woman."

Sam punched his arm. "That jealous streak of yours isn't worthy of you. And you make me sound like property. I'm not, you know."

Jackson thought about that for a moment. "Before I met you, I lost my family. You're my wife and my family and my world. You mean more to me than anything or anyone, and for as long as I breathe, I won't allow anyone to harm you or take you away from me. Face it, darlin', you're *mine*, and I'm *yours*—and it's all nice and legal. Our feelings have nothing to do with ownership—but everything to do with love."

Though touched by the sentiment, Sam bated him. "Marriage contracts can be dissolved. Although, you do have one or two attributes I'd miss."

"Such as?"

"You're kind."

"And?" he prompted.

"And what?"

"You said one or two things, Sam. What else?"

"Perhaps I shouldn't tell you."

Jackson grinned. "You don't need to because I know."

"Oh?" she probed, daring him to say it.

Wearing a smug smile, he leaned close, his breath kissing her lips. "The way I—*dally*—drives you crazy."

Sam wrinkled her nose, showing her displeasure. "You've figured it out then, haven't you?" she grumbled, her tone conveying she thought it no great achievement.

"I have," Jackson affirmed. He captured her hand and held it against his chest over his heart. "The way *you dally* does the same to me, darlin'."

"Well, there is that," Sam murmured, a little out of breath. Distracted by the heat of his skin and the tingling of her nerve endings, her response was more a witless retort than a glib parry. Lord, they'd *dallied* only minutes ago, and he already had her mind turning to mush.

Chuckling, Jackson shifted fractionally closer. "It's good we've settled that."

"It is," she agreed. Distracted by the press of his body, she took a few seconds to marshal her thoughts. "Perhaps I could accompany you to Cheyenne," she suggested, believing it the perfect solution to her problem. "I know lots of men don't prefer to take their wives on business, but it's not that way with us." If she went with him, she wouldn't need to battle her fear of being in the house alone. Later, after they returned, she'd tell him why she was afraid.

"I'd take you with me if Grant Johnson hadn't stipulated he won't do business with Trinity if you're involved. Before you lost your memory, Parker and I discussed it with you."

Jackson had watched her face while explaining and noticed she raised her chin, something she did to give herself courage. He resisted asking why she needed it. He'd also felt the slight tension in the softness of her body pressing against his and the barely perceptible tightening of her arm at his waist. He knew she was afraid of something, although he didn't press her about it, respecting her right to keep her fear private. Though difficult, he'd wait for her to tell him.

"Grant Johnson wouldn't need to know I was with you," Sam replied.

"It won't work, because I'll be staying at his home. He and his son will be meeting me at the train station." Jackson could feel her disappointment. "Do you recall after the crash asking why we lived together instead of marrying?"

Nodding, Sam answered, "You said I'd refused proposals from powerful men and thought they'd hurt you. Those men didn't care about me. They wanted to control my fortune."

"Yes, and at least one of them wanted you to marry his son for the same reason—Grant Johnson wanted you to become his son's wife."

"Oh." She hadn't realized that. Having no personal memories—not even remembering her name—she'd turned to Jackson for answers. From him, she learned her father named her Sam Hilliard because he believed women should be respected the same as men. He'd also gently explained her mother died in childbirth and bank robbers killed her father. She depended on Jackson, her family, and a few trusted friends to tell her the things she couldn't recall. But not recognizing people and not knowing about her life sometimes made her feel as if she were a ship adrift in a vast sea.

Besides her memory loss and the uncertainty of her feelings for Jackson, she'd had to deal with Reed Ferguson, the son of the man who'd raped her. Although he was dead now, he was at the root of her fear—the reason she didn't want Jackson to go to Cheyenne—the reason she was afraid to stay home alone. At ten, three years younger than Sam, Ferguson had watched his father brutally rape her. He'd also witnessed his father fall to his death from the loft when she fought him. Years later, Ferguson had stalked her, waiting for the opportunity to repeat his father's abuse.

Some memories should be forgotten—buried.

"I've put off this trip to Cheyenne for months, Sam," Jackson explained, wishing he could take her with him. "It's not fair to Parker to postpone it any longer. We need to sell the timber in the grove east of the river. It will take a couple of months to set up the operation once we make the deal because of our conservation plan and forging a logging road to the Landis mill. If we don't start soon, Johnson's crew won't be able to harvest the trees before the snow starts flyin'. Parker needs the revenue to carry his part of the ranch through next winter." Sam knew Parker was financially sound but not as wealthy as she and Jackson.

Sam gave in gracefully, consoling herself with thoughts of escaping to their Gracelyn Palace suite if she couldn't conquer her fear. With her brother, Morgan, and his wife, Alexa, living in the gaming house's twin suite, she wouldn't be alone.

"I understand," Sam murmured, her voice soft with acceptance, all too aware understanding wouldn't expunge her fear of being watched or make the days pass quickly.

Chapter 5

Price Hardin, former sheriff of Laramie, now, by all accounts, outlaw, knew if he weren't careful playing the game in which he was presently engaged with the thieves and murderers keeping him company, he'd be the next dead man fed to the scavenger birds circling their hideout. Only a few officials and select friends knew of his mission. If he failed, none outside that small circle would know he'd died fulfilling the duties of Deputy U.S. Marshal.

The hideout was more than a day's ride from the nearest town. Though many a posse and lawman had tracked outlaws to the hideout, they were forced to halt their chase and swear in frustration as they watched their quarry disappear up twisting narrow paths. They couldn't follow because the sentries posted on the high walls guarding the paths into the sanctuary would pick them off like clay targets in a shooting gallery. Consequently, no lawman had entered the hideout—at least not until Price Hardin pretended to turn from the law to crime.

Rustlers and outlaws had been using the hideout since the early 1860s. Some sought its protection temporarily when the threat of capture was high, while others, like Colson Brigham's gang, used it as their main base of operations.

Hideout inhabitants were expected to obey rules and contribute to its upkeep. Over the years, they'd built cabins for protection from the harsh winters and extreme climate, as well as storage chambers for provisions and stables and pens for livestock. Disputes were settled according to an established, mutually agreed-upon code. Ironically, stealing from another gang was against the rules; however, gang members were allowed to ride with a different gang if they deemed an opportunity lucrative. There was no official leader, though some gang leaders were more powerful than others. Presently, Colson Brigham was the leader most feared, as he had no conscience. He'd do, say, torture, or kill to get whatever he wanted and, now that Hardin had thrown in with him, he had six skilled brigands to back him up.

When Colson Brigham overheard a conversation between Price Hardin and Sedge Cannon, his gang's chief lieutenant, discussing the merits of pulling a bank robbery in Prosperity while the town reveled in Independence Day festivities, he paid little attention. He didn't doubt Hardin's ability to identify a good opportunity.

He'd taken the lawman into his fold because he was smart, cool, and fast—and age hadn't shaved a fraction of anything off the man's stamina, speed, or accuracy. Brigham's lack of interest was because he'd been planning a bold, two-pronged robbery under cover of Cheyenne's celebration. Three of his men would hold up a Union Pacific train carrying a Wells Fargo shipment when it was within a few miles of the city the day before the official celebration. Then, with the law chasing that diversionary contingent, he and the rest of his men would rob the Cheyenne National Bank—while citizens oohed and aahed over the fireworks display. The plan was brash and dangerous. He'd be a legend if they succeeded or stone-cold dead if one little thing went wrong.

Only half listening, Brigham's ears burned when Price explained there'd be a shooting competition and mentioned

Jackson Knight's sponsorship and participation. Though Hardin couldn't possibly know it, Knight's name was a compelling reason for Brigham to change targets. He had a personal score to settle with Knight.

Besides getting even with Knight, the Prosperity job would net huge profit for less effort and risk than his Cheyenne plan. The fact Knight's wealth was deposited in the bank, along with that of his wife, who, according to Hardin, dripped with money from an inheritance, a profitable gaming house, and various other enterprises, made the job irresistible. The rich cattle country around Prosperity meant the bank would be full of money, not to mention the extra dollars deposited because of the celebration and contest cash prizes. The Winchester rifles being awarded to the winners were worth more than their purchase price. He knew several rich desperados who'd pay at least twice their cost. There would be less expectation of crime and fewer lawmen present in the smaller town, so less risk of failure. And should anything go wrong, the gang would be closer to their hideout.

Chapter 6

"Are you going to eat those pancakes or stab them to death?" Jackson asked setting his coffee cup down on the table in the hotel's dining room where they were eating their breakfast.

Sam glanced at him before her eyes returned to her plate, where the tines of her fork were embedded in a stack of pancakes. Using the thumb and index finger of her left hand to hold the stack down, she yanked the fork up and waved it over two sausages on a side plate before dropping it unceremoniously onto the white tablecloth. Sighing, she swept the napkin from her lap, snapped it to straighten its folds, and released it to shroud the mutilated orbs.

Jackson lifted his left eyebrow. "I thought you were hungry. At least that's what you claimed when you pulled the covers off me this morning and insisted I bring you here for breakfast."

"I *am* hungry." Sam sighed in exasperation. "I yanked the covers to make it clear the breakfast you had in mind wasn't being served, at least not until after I have a pancake smothered in maple syrup."

Jackson's green-flecked brown eyes flicked to the shrouded plate before returning to Sam's pouting lips. "So, why aren't you eating?"

Sam swept the tip of her tongue along her lower lip. The delicate muscles at her throat undulated as if she were swallowing a delectable morsel. "Maple syrup. There isn't any—only molasses. In my opinion, pancakes with molasses are hardly fit for pigs."

Jackson rolled his eyes.

"Last night at the dinner party, Hank Bainbridge bragged he would be the first guest this morning to order pancakes because a case of maple syrup for the hotel restaurant came in at the freight office. I want maple syrup, Jackson. Hell, I dreamed about maple syrup last night."

"I'm disappointed, darlin'. I thought all those soft sounds of pleasure I heard last night were because you were dreaming about me," he remarked, his voice low and suggestive.

"Those sounds *were* about you—*before* we went to sleep. *After*, they were about maple syrup." Damned if the man wasn't almost making her forget about the syrup— almost, but not quite. Affected by his tone, not to mention the spark of desire flaring in his eyes, she lowered her lashes and raised the tip of her satin slipper to stroke his upper thigh.

White tablecloths, reaching half the distance to the floor, draped the dining tables, yet Jackson couldn't stop his eyes from darting to the other diners to ensure they weren't witnessing Sam's wicked titillation. Already, his blood was racing hot in his veins. Shifting to relieve the pressure of an inseam pressing against his swelling erection, he caught her ankle and pulled her foot closer, gliding the satin tip of her slipper along the hard ridge of what she was doing to him.

Startled, Sam slid to the edge of her chair. If he raised her foot any higher, she'd disappear under the table. To recover lost ground, she braced her other foot on the floor, gripped the chair seat with both hands, and jerked upward while scooting forward to put more wood than air beneath her bottom.

Unexpectedly, a small, sticky hand cradled the side of Sam's face, and she found herself staring into the earnest, chocolate-brown eyes of a five-year-old boy whose dark, tousled hair looked as though he'd waved a comb over it instead of through it.

"Missus Sam, didn't you hear me call you?"

The boy had called her *Miss* Sam before she'd married Jackson. Addressing her as *Missus* Sam was his solution to how he thought it proper to address her now that she was a married woman. She thought the form of address was charming.

Leaning forward to tweak the boy's nose with her index finger, Sam was unaware her foot, still in Jackson's lap, flexed. "No, I'm sorry, Peter Jack, I didn't hear you. Jackson was teasing me about something."

With the ache in his groin growing with each reflexive caress of her slipper, Jackson had but two choices—drop Sam's foot from his lap to gain control over his lust or allow it to remain until she stroked him to completion. He chose the former because the latter was a fantasy. Unfortunately, her shinbone cracked against the table's center post when he thrust it from his lap. Her startled eyes flew to him while emitting a soft, wounded, "Ow." Then, ducking her head to table level, she reached to massage the hurt. When she straightened, her eyes, filled with suspicious accusation, immediately shot to his.

Sam's reaction told Jackson she was more surprised than hurt. It truly had been an accident. Besides, if honest, she'd admit she was more responsible than he. Nevertheless, he was sorry, so he returned her gaze with an apology-filled one.

Peter Jack's innocent curiosity was piqued. "What's the matter? Did Miss Kitty nip at you? She prob'ly wants to rub her head on your foot. She likes your satin slippers." Peter Jack's calico cat, Miss Kitty, wasn't supposed to be in the hotel dining room, but she flagrantly ignored the rule most of the time. Rarely did she get in trouble for it.

When Mister Jackson tossed back his head and laughed, Peter Jack wondered what was so funny. He swiveled his head from Missus Sam to Mister Jackson, then back to Missus Sam. Unable to solve the mystery, he dropped his eyes to Missus Sam's plate covered with the napkin. Guiltily glancing over his shoulder to see if his mother was nearby, he thrust a creamer of syrup into Missus Sam's hands. "I'm sorry. I should've brung this before now. Mama told me not to dawdle, but I got to talkin' to Sheriff Cooley about the shootin' contest on In'pendence Day and forgot."

He peeked at Missus Sam's expression to see if she was disappointed in him. She hardly ever was, but he'd been a long while comin' to her. He knew she liked maple syrup. He'd heard his mama say she'd drink a bottle of it and leave the pancakes behind if she thought no one would notice. He'd do the same but figured if she couldn't get away with it, neither could he.

Seeing a soft smile on Missus Sam's lips, Peter Jack breathed a sigh and watched her swivel her lower body toward him and pat her knee in invitation. Though he thought himself too old, he anchored his bottom against her knee and let her lift him onto her lap. He was more than willing to lose dignity for a chance to share her pancakes. He knew Missus Sam rarely ate more than one.

Recognizing an opportunity, Peter Jack lifted the napkin draped over Missus Sam's pancakes before she finished settling his bottom in her lap.

"How'd those holes get poked in the middle of those 'cakes?" Peter Jack asked, certain his mama hadn't served them like that because she was the best cook Mister Jackson ever had at his hotel. Everybody said so. Everything his mama made, except carrots, looked good and tasted even better. Even his mama couldn't make carrots taste good.

Peter Jack thought that Missus Sam's eyes looked like they were laughing when she turned away from Mister Jackson just before answering. "Jackson tried to steal half the stack from me, Peter Jack. He stabbed his fork in the middle of them before I could lift mine from the table. Not a pancake in Wyoming Territory is safe when he's around. I don't know why I put up with him."

Peter Jack trained disapproving eyes on Jackson. "Mama says it ain't polite 'havior. You ought not take Missus Sam's pancakes." Resting the back of his head against a pillowy breast, he warned, "She's the softest and purtiest girl in town. If you don't give her enough to eat, she'll lose her nice soft spots, though I reckon she'll still be purty."

Suppressing her laughter and an impulse to kiss the top of Peter Jack's head, Sam moved the top pancake to the plate with the sausages. Fascinated, Peter Jack watched her drizzle maple syrup in squiggly lines over the pancake and sausages. When she looked at him for approval, he nodded. Smiling, she handed him the creamer of syrup. "The rest is yours, Mr. Peter Jack Nolan. Don't get a tummy ache, or your mama will swat some soft spots on both of us."

Peter Jack giggled. "Mama won't swat you. She likes you."

Jackson and Sam watched Peter Jack devour the pancakes. Strangely, he didn't pour the syrup over them. Instead, he tore off small pieces and dunked them in the syrup before stuffing them in his mouth, licking his fingers as he went. It was amazing how not a drop of syrup found its way to his clothes or the tabletop. When he finished, he leaned back, his head again cushioned on Sam's breast.

One sticky hand rested on the table and the other on his rounded belly.

Sam absently brushed a lock of dark hair off his forehead.

Expecting Peter Jack's eyelids to droop closed, Jackson lifted his gaze from the boy's face to Sam's. Recognizing a hint of sadness in her expression, he experienced a momentary stab of longing. He and Sam would never have a child of their own because of the damage caused by her being raped. Refusing to wallow in things he couldn't change, he engaged Peter Jack's attention. "So, what did Sheriff Cooley say about the shooting contest?"

Peter Jack puffed out his chest and wrapped a hand around a drooping suspender. "He said I could help put up the posters. If any go missin', I'm to report it right away. It's a real 'portent job. The sheriff said I'm jus' the man for it now that I've turned five."

Listening to Jackson and Peter Jack, Sam recognized he would be a good father. He was sincerely interested in what the child had to say, and Peter Jack was basking in his attention. Suddenly, she found herself having to swallow around a lump of sorrow forming in her throat. Nathanial McBride had taken more from her than her virginity when he violated her. He'd taken her ability to carry a child.

Having noticed Jackson's sad expression earlier, Sam guessed he'd been thinking about not having a son of his own. Though he'd told her after she'd lost her memory that it didn't matter, she felt he had regrets. Not for the first time, she wondered if it had been a bigger factor for their not marrying sooner than he'd intimated. Had she done the right thing letting him convince her otherwise?

Sam knew people thought Peter Jack was Jackson's son. Since Jackson had been instrumental in bringing Jessa Nolan and her young son to Prosperity, folks gossiped Jessa wasn't a widow and Jackson was her child's father. The winsome boy's eyes were the same color as Jackson's, but his hair wasn't as dark. However, as children matured, hair color tended to darken. Sam could easily imagine Peter Jack's rich, brown locks deepening to raven black. Although no one could predict whether Peter Jack would be as tall or as broad-shouldered as Jackson, his sturdy, well-proportioned frame didn't rule out the possibility.

If Peter Jack were Jackson's son, he'd been conceived long before Sam met Jackson. Sam believed Jackson's code of honor would have demanded he tell her about Jessa Nolan before pledging himself to her. *Yet, what did it matter now?* Confident of his love, she'd married him, and they were happy.

Glancing toward the hotel lobby, Sam spotted Parker Evans approaching. Nearing forty, Parker was distinguished. His six-foot frame didn't carry any extra weight, despite his spending considerable time behind the desk in his office. He had a full head of wavy brown hair, touched with gray at the temples. Laugh lines perpetually hovered at the corners of his mouth and his soft hazel eyes twinkled more often than not. He was a kind and loving father to his daughter, Becky, and a good friend and business partner to her and Jackson.

Parker's eyes flitted from Sam's welcoming smile to her empty plate, to the small boy languishing in her arms, to the restaurant's front window where a young, tall cowboy impatiently paced, and finally, back to the table, where he noticed the pancake and sausage on Sam's side plate. Leaning down, he hefted Peter Jack from Sam's lap. "You'd better eat your breakfast, Sam, before this pudgy little pancake beggar gets hungry again and devours what's left."

Then he pulled out a chair and sat while playing at controlling the struggles of the boy he was tickling. "Don't you know it's not polite to slurp up all the lady's syrup and pancakes and fall asleep in her arms?"

Peter Jack grinned up at him. "I didn't slurp her syrup and pancakes, I dunked 'em."

Grinning back, Parker patted Peter Jack's tummy. "I see you did a right admirable job of it. That belly of yours is sticking out like you swallowed a watermelon." Then he plucked one of Peter Jack's suspenders and set him on his feet. "Run along to the kitchen and tell your mama she has three hungry customers who need a stack of her pancakes."

Peter Jack ran to do his bidding, knowing Miss Becky, Mr. Evans's daughter, was likely good for a pancake or two.

Sam cleared her throat to get Parker's attention. "So where *is* Becky, and why order three stacks of pancakes?" Parker nodded toward the restaurant's front windows.

Looking in the direction Parker indicated, Sam recognized Cal Ennis's handsome face and gave Parker a sympathetic smile.

Parker grumbled, "I suspect he's the reason Becky is taking twice as long to get ready this morning." Having a pretty, young daughter, who caught the eye of every mother's son in the Territory, wasn't easy, especially since he was a widower. He did like Cal. However, what man was prepared for his daughter to be courted? Sighing, Parker rose. "I'll invite Cal to join us. I hate to see a man sufferin' this early in the morning. Then I'll make sure Peter Jack gives our order to Jessa."

Sam noticed Jackson's eyes following Parker as he made his way to the front entrance to wave Cal in before turning to weave through tables and vanish into the kitchen. Then just as she was about to enjoy her second bite of pancake, Jackson said, "What Parker meant to say was that since he can't keep his daughter from falling in love, he'll do whatever he can to make sure Becky is happy."

Sam nodded, pleased Parker recognized true love couldn't be thwarted, even by a loving father. "Parker's a special man. From what you've explained, he did the same for us. You said when you came to Prosperity, you'd made a fortune in the South Pass gold fields but had been drifting because of having no family or direction in your life. Parker welcomed you to Trinity, and you found a home with him and Becky.

"When I moved here to build Gracelyn Palace, he took me under his wing, too. Because he's a widower and Becky acts as if I'm her stand-in mother, he pretends he needs my help. He didn't need another partner for the ranch. He took me on because of you, so we could build our house. He's even endured the barbs and criticism of the moralists who spoke out about our living together without the benefit of marriage. Hell, in some towns, folks would condone lashing a woman with my morals to a stake and burning her for being a whore or a witch." Grinning, she added, "Now that I think about it, I wonder why I didn't fall in love with Parker instead of you."

"I've told you before, darlin'—you couldn't resist me any more than I could you. It's just the way it is." Jackson retorted. Then, she watched him slide onto the chair next to hers. Because she assumed he was making room for Cal, she was surprised when he hauled her onto his lap and kissed her breathless. It wasn't the first time he'd done it in public. When he broke the kiss, he chuckled—probably because she hadn't resisted.

In a low whisper, she asked, "Is this your way of getting even with me for what I did earlier with my slipper?"

"No."

Sam recognized something in the decisiveness of his curt answer. Before she could ask, he nodded toward her barely touched pancake. "Finish your breakfast, darlin'."

Sam pulled back to search his eyes. "Are you ordering me?"

"No, of course not," he replied.

Though Sam was fairly certain his tone said the opposite, Jackson confirmed it when he added, "We came downstairs early because you were craving—pancakes and syrup. But it doesn't appear you find them satisfying. Would you prefer something else?" When she looked into his hooded eyes, they were asking, *Like me?*

Swiping her tongue to moisten suddenly dry lips, she began scooting the soft mounds of her buttocks across his hard thighs to return to her chair. "Nooo. I want—the pancake." She slanted Jackson another glance. *For the love of God, was he grinning?* Feeling a warm flush move through her body, she lifted her fork and attacked the remnants of her breakfast.

Much later, she couldn't recall whether she tasted what she ate.

Chapter 7

Jessa Nolan normally cut through the alley behind Gracelyn Palace and the Prosperity House Hotel when going to or coming from work. But today was Friday, the day she baked the pies, cakes, and pastries served over the busy weekend in the hotel dining room and visited McKinley Trust and Savings Bank before work.

Though she had two options to reach the hotel when leaving the bank, neither bypassed the Fortune Queen saloon, which sat on the opposite corner of Main Street from Gracelyn Palace. It posed a mild threat to unescorted women. However, Sheriff Cooley and his deputy were conscientious about locking up drunks and sending loitering men on their way, so she was wary rather than afraid.

In Jessa's experience, avoiding men meant preventing trouble, the best strategy a woman could employ to ensure gossips gained no fuel to fire their tongues. Jessa was aware some folks assumed a young widow with a son settling in a town where no one knew her or her family had likely fabricated her marriage and a deceased husband to hide the fact her child was a bastard. Worse, the more malicious scandalmongers believed a woman who'd experienced "carnal pleasure" would continue to seek it, so any encounter or word spoken with a male, any age or marital status, was suspect. And while the gossips watched for evidence, they never tired of whispering about how Jackson

Knight had been instrumental in bringing Jessa and Peter Jack to Prosperity, how fortunate it was Jackson employed her as the hotel's pastry chef and breakfast cook, and how coincidental it was her son's dark hair and eyes favored Jackson's. Consequently, any trouble Jessa avoided with the clientele of the saloon was worth sidestepping.

All manner of men patronized the Fortune Queen, and though against town ordinance, a fair number slipped through the saloon's back door to visit the bawdy house directly behind it, *if* they had the money and *if* there were enough sportin' women to keep up with demand. Women, decent and indecent, weren't abundant in the Wyoming Territory. Of course, when compared to South Pass, the rough mining town from which Jackson Knight had rescued them, Prosperity was tame.

Stepping up to the boardwalk from Third Street, Jessa saw Sam Knight studying the public announcements board outside the hotel. Something about the way Sam stood, back straight, hands limp at her sides, head not moving, bothered Jessa. Expecting to see Jackson nearby, she scanned the boardwalk on both sides of the street. No sign of Jackson, but two men, each with a shoulder braced against the wall of the Fortune Queen saloon across the street, necks craned forward, keenly interested in Sam, made Jessa's pulse jump. Surprisingly, Sam, who normally noticed everything, was unaware the two half-drunken drifters were eyeing her as if she were spread naked beneath them.

Hurrying forward, Jessa wondered what had captured Sam's attention so completely she didn't notice the leering men or Jessa's approach. Jessa touched Sam's arm hoping to break whatever spell suspended her friend's awareness, but she didn't react. Moving into Sam's line of vision, Jessa was startled to see unfocused slate blue eyes. "Are you all right, Sam?"

Sam didn't answer. Darting her gaze from Sam to the men, Jessa saw they had moved to the edge of the boardwalk, more interested now that she'd joined Sam. While throwing hungry, heated looks at her and Sam, they were arguing. And from the few words her ears caught, the bastards were fighting over who would bed Sam while the other settled for her.

"C'mon, Sam, there's gonna be trouble." Jessa tugged at Sam's arm, certain the men would soon cross the street.

Sam moved barely an inch.

The sound of the men's boots grating against the lip of the boardwalk propelled Jessa to action. Flaring her skirt to hide her movements, she slipped Sam's Colt from her holster. Then as if pushed to the brink of a temper tantrum, she stomped her foot to disguise the click from cocking the hammer—twice. Though not good with a gun, she knew the first chamber would be empty. Sam would never risk an accidental discharge from a weapon loaded with six bullets.

Burying the gun in the folds of her skirt, Jessa tugged on Sam's arm with her other hand and deliberately spoke in a loud voice. "Come along, dear. The doctor is waiting to give you your treatment." She stomped her foot again to show her patience had run out.

In her side vision, she saw the men halt, their boots clomping to a dead stop in the packed dirt of the street. They were big men—dark and threatening, with broad, powerful shoulders. Dressed in rough clothes, clearly in need of washing, their gazes openly devoured her and Sam's curves. The combined male strength of them was unnerving.

Jessa sucked in a controlled breath to fortify her courage. Why was there never a decent man around when a woman truly needed one? Well, she'd handle the situation on her own. She'd faced dangers plenty of times since her father had been railroaded into prison. Left alone, she'd fended for herself. Though she hadn't always made the best decisions or been successful, she'd learned from her mistakes, which made her more capable than most. She had to be because of Peter Jack.

Turning to the men, Jessa beamed a radiant smile, as if welcoming good Samaritans sent directly from the Lord to assist her in her time of need. Her smile wasn't returned, but Jessa didn't let it deter her.

"Gentlemen, would you be so kind as to help me with my sister?" Gesturing toward Sam, she added, "She slipped out while I was talking with the doctor about her—uh—mercury treatments." Pausing, Jessa pretended embarrassment over letting that last piece of information slip out while she studied the men's expressions from beneath her lashes, praying fervently they knew mercury was used to treat the pox, a dreaded venereal disease.

One man took a hesitant step forward. Hearing the other one bite back a curse, Jessa watched him grab his companion's arm and yank him back to his side. Jessa wanted to clap for joy but pretended puzzlement.

"Her mind gets confused because of her—uh, affliction." Jessa used her most confidential tone to erase any remaining doubt her sister was a victim of syphilis, a disease common to those who traded in pleasures of the flesh. "The doctor comes twice a week to check on her—uh, condition." Waving her free hand in front of Sam's face, she said, "As you can see, it's begun to affect her mind."

The man who'd grabbed his companion's arm earlier began tugging his friend in the reverse direction. Then, after exchanging a few low, terse words, the men did an about-face.

Jessa held her breath, watching until they disappeared through the saloon's doors. Exhaling, she released the cocked hammer. Thank God the trick worked, because even when near enough to touch it, she couldn't hit the broad side of a barn.

Sidling to the hotel entrance, Jessa peeked inside, hoping to find help. Only one person was in the deserted lobby, cowering in the shadows near the front windows. One of the maids had witnessed the encounter. Though Jessa doubted the woman had been able to hear everything she'd said, she could feel her cheeks flame, horrified she'd all but labeled Sam a diseased whore.

"Have you seen Jackson Knight?"

"No, ma'am."

"Well, Morgan's likely in Alexa's office. Run and get him. Sam needs help."

Less than a minute later, Morgan Garner, Sam's brother, hurried to the open door. Catching sight of Jessa holding Sam's Colt with both hands, barrel pointing at his chest, he halted as if he'd hit an invisible wall and took a cautious step back. Glancing to his left, he saw Sam. Since she was standing and there was no blood, Jessa became his priority.

"Jessa, you'd better give me that," he said, nodding toward the gun, "unless you're planning to shoot me for that crack I made the other day about your rhubarb pie."

Seeing Jessa's gaze move from his face to Sam's gun, he realized she'd forgotten she was holding it. Lowering the barrel to point at the ground, she stepped nearer to allow him to take it from her grasp. "You hate everyone's rhubarb pie, Morgan. I didn't take it personally." She swiveled her head toward Sam. "Something's wrong with Sam. She's hardly moved a muscle since I came up on her."

Before Morgan could comment, a voice from behind Jessa caused her to whirl around.

"It happens sometimes when a memory takes her over," Jackson remarked, his eyes assessing Sam. Quickly covering the distance to his wife, he recognized the vacant emptiness in her eyes. Realizing they'd soon draw the attention of curious residents, he swept Sam up in his arms and carried her inside, making straight for the kitchen. Jessa and Morgan followed.

After settling Sam onto a chair, Jackson squatted in front of her, rubbing one of her hands between his, as if the friction would ignite a spark to revive her.

Morgan disappeared into the pantry and came out with a bottle of bourbon.

Jessa hurried to a cupboard for a glass. The tender look in Jackson's eyes as he cared for Sam made her feel a little breathless. He was a fine man. Why hadn't she been able to find a man who would love her like that?

Frowning at Morgan, Jackson accepted the bottle. "You know she thinks bourbon is medicine."

"Regardless, given the circumstances, it's the appropriate libation."

The corner of Jackson's mouth quirked up. "I'm not Sam, Morgan, so how about saving your wisecracks for her?" His soft drawl removed the sting from the words. He understood Morgan's response was his way of dealing with his worry. Verbal sparring was how Sam and her brother expressed their affection for each other.

Rising to his full height, Jackson poured two fingers of alcohol into the glass Jessa passed him and moved to Sam's side. Cradling the back of her head, he raised the glass to her lips and tipped it forward. The barest amount of liquid passed between her lips and trickled down her throat. Swallowing reflexively, she bent forward, first coughing, then drawing in a great wheeze of air before her head came up, a hand clutching the base of her throat, her eyes watering.

Dragging in another breath, Sam searched for and found Jackson's face. Blinking to focus, she saw his dark brown eyes were filled with worry, studying her as if she'd appeared suddenly from thin air. In a way, she supposed she had.

"Take another sip," Jackson urged, supporting her arm.

Sam tried to say she hated bourbon, but her voice wouldn't work because of the coughing spell, so she gave her head a little shake to decline. Jackson's expression turned sympathetic as if he understood what she'd been unable to say.

"I know you don't like it, darlin', but take another swallow. Jessa's getting you some water to chase it with." He kept his hand steady on her arm, guiding the glass back to her lips. After she swallowed, he replaced the bourbon with the water glass, letting her take a few sips on her own.

"You remembered something," Jackson said, prompting her to explain what had happened when she lowered the glass.

Sam nodded, her mind working furiously to orient itself to the present. "I—I remembered the shooting contest after we met, when—" Pausing, she turned and tipped her head up to look at Morgan. "I remembered I should have won. Jackson hit the last target because he was lucky." Even to her ears, her tone sounded resentful. Heat rushed to her cheeks as she felt Jackson's eyes studying her.

Morgan shrugged and one corner of his mouth quirked up. "And now that you remember it, you're mad?"

She'd been angry at the time. But not now. Shame was the reason she was avoiding Jackson's gaze. She felt shame over what she'd done after the judges declared the tie.

Dropping her eyes, she waved a hand, dismissing her brother's question and signaling it too ridiculous to waste breath answering. Puzzled as to how it got there, she let herself be distracted by the Colt tucked in Morgan's waistband. Until this moment, she hadn't noticed her weapon was missing from her holster. "Why do you have my gun?"

Morgan and Jessa exchanged looks.

Massaging her fingertips against the little stab of pain throbbing at her temple, Sam pressed for an answer. "How did you get my Colt, Morgan?"

"Jessa gave it to me, Sis. I don't know why she had it. I didn't have a chance to ask her before Jackson arrived."

All eyes turned to Jessa.

Though she wasn't the sort to fall apart over unwanted advances or even outright abuse, Jessa had to admit at this moment she physically needed the support of the chair back she was gripping so fiercely. "There were two men— drifters, I think. I didn't recognize them. They were—well, they looked to have been drinking—and they had—uh— something on their minds—and I couldn't get Sam to go inside—so I took her gun—in case I couldn't trick them into leaving us alone." Her stuttered explanation suffered from the faint tremor she hadn't been able to control in her voice and the facts she'd deliberately glossed over. Confident she'd said enough for her audience to fill in the details, she dragged the chair closer, crushing her skirts, needing its support to stay on her feet.

Moving to Jessa's side, Morgan gently uncurled her fingers from the chair and helped lower her onto another that Jackson held for her opposite Sam.

Jackson wrapped one of Jessa's hands around the bourbon glass and poured liberally. "Steady, Jessa. Drink that. All of it." While she gulped the fiery liquid, he carefully ran his eyes over Jessa and Sam. "Did they hurt you?"

"No. I—pretended Sam was suffering from an—ah, illness—the doctor was treating with—mercury—so they wouldn't want to risk—ah—catching anything from her." Her words dropped into shocked silence as the listeners worked out what her explanation implied. *Christ, from where had she gotten the idea to fool the men into believing Sam had a whore's disease?*

As the silence lengthened, Jessa thought it probable Sam was not only insulted but deeply embarrassed. Avoiding Sam's gaze, she peeked at Jackson's face, hoping to find understanding. Instead, she saw shock and anger. The green flecks in his brown eyes flashed lightning. She cringed, expecting a deluge of swear words that didn't come.

Well, she'd done what she'd done, and she couldn't undo it. And because of it, she and Sam were sitting here safe and unharmed. That didn't mean she was too proud to tell Sam she regretted it. Jessa reached out to rest her hand on Sam's arm. "I'm sorry, but there wasn't anyone around to help, and you know I'm no good with a gun, so I—well, what I said made them leave. That was all I was thinking about at the time."

Sam's hand covered Jessa's. "What you did was brave and smart. There's no need for an apology. I'm grateful to you." A mischievous smile playing on her lips, she added, "Hell, I wouldn't care if you'd claimed I copulated with the devil and was rotting from the inside out."

Jackson and Morgan stared at the two women, a disturbing light in their eyes. As if a unit, they headed for the back door.

Sam jumped up. "Come back here!"

When neither man heeded her command, Sam snatched up the bourbon glass and hurled it past them to explode against the door. They spun to face her.

Now that she had their attention, she lowered her volume. "Let it go. They didn't *do* anything. Besides, you don't know what they look like. How many strangers do you think you can beat into a bloody pulp before the sheriff throws you in jail?"

"But, Sis—" Morgan started to argue but abruptly shut his yap when he saw Jackson, jaw still set, begin to turn back to the door. Grabbing a handful of Jackson's shirt, he said, "You know she's right."

Jackson's eyes swept past Morgan to stare deep into the swirling emotion of Sam's eyes. His anger drained, and Morgan let go of his shirt and stepped away.

Relieved, Sam swallowed around a lump of shame stuck in her throat. She needed to talk to Jackson about what she'd remembered—but not in front of Jessa and Morgan. "Jackson, you said you'd go with me to the firing range to check the contest targets. I was waiting for you out front. And I—well—I think we should clear out of here so Jessa can do her baking."

Knowing his sister, Morgan was sure what she'd recalled had affected her more than she was comfortable saying in front of an audience. Giving Jackson a light jab in the ribs with his elbow, he made an excuse to leave. "Alexa and I need to finish putting an order together, so we'll see you tonight at supper."

Sam dipped her head acknowledging Morgan's comment as Jackson clasped her elbow. "I'd forgotten about the targets, Sam," he replied. "Now's still a good time." Waiting for her to precede him through the door, he turned to Jessa. "I see Eddie's stacking crates out here. I'll ask him to come help you." He didn't want her working alone.

The danger Jessa had faced when she'd tricked those men to protect Sam chilled him. Long ago, in South Pass, she'd saved his life. And today, she'd risked herself for Sam. He owed her more than he could repay, and he'd do almost anything to keep her and Peter Jack safe and happy.

***

As Jackson walked with Sam to the shooting range, he didn't speak. Aware Sam was upset over the memory she'd had of the shooting contest they'd entered soon after she'd moved to Prosperity, he thought it best to be patient. While he held his silence, he let his mind wander to their first meeting.

Sam had been standing in front of her partially built gambling salon after learning he'd thwarted her plans to build a hotel next door by purchasing the property from under her beautiful little nose. She'd been hopping mad, her eyes flashing like blue steel in sunlight and her tone resembling ice-glazed cream chipped from a snowdrift. He knew right then she was the only woman for him. He'd stared into the emotion-filled depths of her eyes and recognized she was experiencing the same attraction. He also saw she didn't understand what she was feeling.

After that, whenever they met, which he'd been diligent to ensure happened frequently, Sam would act as if she could barely tolerate him. On her more forgiving days, she'd throw him a cool glance or utter a veiled insult. She'd delivered her rebukes bluntly, conveying succinctly she didn't return his feelings. Much later, she confessed her behavior hadn't been because she disliked him. It sprang from the near-paralyzing fear she had of men because of the brutal assault she'd survived when she was a young girl.

When Jackson had learned a shooting match was to be one of the events held at the Prosperity Fall Festival, he'd goaded Sam into participating for no other reason than wanting to spend time near her. Though he was better than good with a gun, he'd heard Sam's skill was superior to his and felt certain she wouldn't back away from proving it.

Sam had taken the bait, intending to trounce him so thoroughly he'd be too embarrassed to continue pursuing her. And she would've won except Lady Luck stood by his side to guide his bullets with more accuracy than his skill warranted. With their scores even, the match came down to one final round. Sam's bullet had pierced the bullseye dead center. Jackson had been sure he couldn't make the shot—but by some miracle he did.

When the judges announced the tie, a gracious competitor would've pasted on an insincere smile and offered her hand in congratulations. Instead, Sam had decided to administer a public dose of embarrassment. Capturing the crowd's attention with a devilish grin and broad wink, she'd pressed her body to his, and with her arms around his neck, she'd kissed him with a passion that still got him hard whenever he thought about it. But before she'd released him, he'd felt her tremble. And when she'd stepped back, he'd glimpsed a confused, frightened expression on her lovely face. Then, recovering quickly, she'd turned to the enthralled audience with a triumphant smile and executed a curtsy, for which she'd received raucous whoops and wild applause.

***

Walking at Jackson's side, Sam was having difficulty associating her memory with the woman she was now. It had so captured her senses that she'd lost awareness of the present. And when it released her, it left behind shame—for it revealed a side of her character she wished she hadn't seen.

Beneath her hand in the crook of Jackson's arm, she felt his strength. He was confident and self-assured—qualities she admired as much as she did his kindness. Keeping her eyes straight ahead, she tried to work out how to ask him to forgive her, but nothing seemed right. When she finally spoke, her words were more confession than apology. "I remembered I kissed you—and I didn't do it for the right reason."

Jackson had been expecting her to say something like that—because when taken out of context, she wouldn't understand how miraculous it was she'd found the courage to kiss him under any circumstance. Nor would she recognize her kiss was the beginning of the healing she'd needed to find her way to trusting him, loving him.

Though Sam saw Jackson was about to say something, she didn't give him the chance. "I haven't told you not remembering our first kiss is one of the memories I've most regretted losing. A woman should remember her first kiss with the man she loves."

Jackson stopped and pulled her against him. She came reluctantly into his arms. "And now that you've remembered, you wish you could forget it."

Sam heard Jackson's statement as a question. Her head moved up and down in a quick bob. He lifted his hand to stroke her cheek with two fingers before positioning them beneath her chin, urging her to look at him.

"I'm glad you remembered, darlin'."

"How can you say that when we both know I kissed you to hurt you? I told you I remembered—I saw how my temper flared. I didn't care about your feelings, so I did my best to kiss you like a woman inviting a man to her bed. I did it for revenge, and—and it makes me ashamed. I'm sorry." Her eyes, shining with moisture, dropped from his.

"But, Sam, think about the memory. Did you remember how the kiss affected you?"

"What do you mean? I just told you," she replied.

"You told me you remembered how you wanted to make *me feel*—not how the kiss made *you feel*."

Sam blinked. "Oh!" The syllable sounded as though it were expelled with the last bit of air in her lungs. "It didn't—feel—how I expected it would."

Jackson remembered every nuance of that kiss—her lips covering his, her tongue tasting, then settling in to provoke, tease, excite—no—promise sexual gratification like none he'd ever known. Her body had strained intimately against his, filling him with a desire for more. Taking Sam's hand in his, he brought the backs of her fingers to his lips.

"That kiss still makes me half-crazy when I think about it," he admitted. "But more importantly, it gave me hope because I felt it unleash a surge of desire you had no idea you could feel. Because of—of what McBride did to you, the first kiss couldn't have come from me. Can you understand that?"

Had she understood? She must have, because instead of the punishment she'd intended, it had sparked a torturous craving for something she'd thought she'd never want.

"I did feel—something—like flames fusing our bodies. I—I didn't—understand.*" But she'd wanted it—desperately.* Her hand opened to flatten against his chest, absorbing his heat.

"I knew it frightened you, Sam. But it also piqued your curiosity. You began wondering whether pleasure between us was possible—whether your denial hurt more than your fear of pursuing it." Recognizing a flicker of uncertainty in her eyes, he softened his tone. "That kiss was our beginning. It told me you could love me. Please, don't feel sorry about it."

"And if I were to kiss you now, what would it tell you?" she asked.

"I'm not certain, darlin', but I know how we could find out."

Her mouth lifting to his, Sam couldn't deny herself the pleasure of learning the answer.

Chapter 8

Saturday afternoon, dressed in chambray shirts and breeches, gun belts buckled at their waists, and Winchesters lying crosswise on the nearest table, Sam and Morgan stood companionably at the end of Gracelyn's bar. Once Jackson and Parker arrived, they'd walk over to the railroad freight dock together.

When Parker came in through the hotel entrance, they did little more than nod at him as he darted past them to slip into Alexa's office, presumably to arrange for her to keep a watchful eye on Becky while he helped Jackson and Wade Harper move building materials and ammunition to the firing range. They knew he'd also promised Jackson he would inspect the replacement blades arriving for the ranch's windmill repairs before allowing Wilson, Trinity's foreman, to cart them to the ranch.

Though Jackson hadn't convinced Sam to let him handle the transport of the contest prize money to McKinley's bank, she'd consented to accept the sheriff's offer to provide an armed escort and post guards at critical vantage points should some outlaw be crazy enough to attempt a holdup in the middle of town.

Morgan was impatient to get started. "Sis, did you remember to send Eddie to the bank to remind Mr. McKinley the extra bank guards need to be on duty when we arrive?"

"Yes, and I asked Eddie to take Peter Jack with him."

"I thought Widow Chambers looks after Peter Jack when Jessa works in the afternoon?" Morgan commented.

"Mrs. Chambers isn't feeling well today, so Jessa kept Peter Jack with her. But a busy kitchen isn't a good place to play. He was getting underfoot—well, *underfoot* is misleading. When I arrived, he was under the table, emitting meows, high-pitched shrieks, and yowls—playing a game called *Cat Eats Rats*. The second time he bumped the table leg and Jessa's rolling pin gouged the pie crust she was rolling out, I suggested Peter Jack run errands with Eddie."

Morgan could imagine waging a war with wooden soldiers but not a game in which a feline hunted rats. "How is the game played?"

Sam's eyes sparkled with mischief. "The little thief had helped himself to some piecrust scraps and used them to sculpt game pieces. He shaped the dough into oblong and rounded parts to make the animals' bodies and broke lengths of discarded matchsticks for legs. He pulled straws from the kitchen broom for cat whiskers and stuck tuffs of Miss Kitty's fur to the cat figure. He dusted the rats' bodies in ashes and filled their eyes with tiny pieces of a cherry. Ugh! Those red eyes were downright disgusting. During the battle, if the rats slip by the cat, they hide in one of two empty tins Peter Jack set up as safe houses. Trust me, I rooted for the cat."

Morgan laughed. "I suppose doing battle with wooden soldiers pales in comparison."

Sam nodded. "Anyway, after visiting the bank, Eddie and Peter Jack are delivering a letter of credit from the mercantile to the orphanage. The children need new shoes and lighter clothing for this warmer weather. Wade's offering everything at cost. By the time they return, Jackson and I will be done with our deliveries, so we'll watch Peter Jack while Jessa freshens up before joining us for supper. After all, she fell behind with her baking because of helping me with those two drifters yesterday." Breaking off to glance at the front entrance, she added, "Jackson should be here soon. He went to Jessa's to get clean clothes for Peter Jack because he'll need a good scrubbing before he can sit at a proper supper table. Since he's complained that he's too old to allow a 'girl' to bathe him, Jackson will oversee his bath."

"Won't be many years before Peter Jack discovers the flaw in that logic," Morgan mumbled, picturing his wife Alexa's soapy hands sliding over his naked skin.

Correctly guessing the images flitting through Morgan's mind, Sam swatted his arm. "Shame on you for having carnal thoughts of your wife in front of your sister."

"You and Jackson are just as wicked," Morgan accused.

Widening her eyes in her best imitation of virginal innocence, Sam gave him a prim toss of her head. "I'm sure I don't know what you mean. I'm always a lady."

"You are, Sis—when you aren't doing whatever the hell you please."

"Well, I don't recall your manners always emulating those of a gentleman."

"Of course, you don't. You have no memory." Morgan enjoyed hearing Sam's snort of indignation before he continued. "I'm enough of a gentleman to know it's bad manners to pull my wife onto my lap and kiss her in a public restaurant—unlike my sister's improper husband."

"Perhaps you should consider it. It's—exciting."

Well, that certainly wiped the grin from his face. How the hell had she drawn him into this conversation? Morgan cleared his throat. "I suggest we change the topic."

"Are you having trouble keeping up, Brother?"

Morgan responded with his quick, easy smile. The same one he'd teased her with when he'd returned from Chicago after the stage crash and found her barely able to sit on a chair without losing her balance. Though her condition shocked him, he'd proceeded to tease her with his wry wit, accepting her as he'd found her: damaged, different, but undeniably his cherished sister, leaving no room for doubting the strength of his fidelity or the bond between them.

"Oh, I can keep up, Sis," Morgan assured her. "But what's the point?"

He had her there. Sam couldn't imagine having a better brother.

Morgan drew Sam's thoughts back to their current mission. "How'd you convince Mr. McKinley to let us keep the rifles in the bank's vault?"

A smug smile settled on Sam's lips. "I made up a story about your proposing we open our own bank. I said you've always had an interest in banking and had been trying to convince Jackson and me it would be good for the town to have an alternate lending institution. Then, I assured him I had doubts and preferred to rely on him and his bank."

Morgan's expression changed from mild curiosity to astonishment.

"Why do you look like that, Morgan?"

A second clicked by while he considered his answer. "What you told McKinley is true. I *have* always wanted to open a bank. Before your amnesia, we were well into the work needed to make the bank a reality. The unoccupied red brick building next to City Hall is where we planned to open the Commerce Bank of Prosperity. We even purchased and installed a vault salvaged from the 1871 Chicago fire. The work is nearly complete, but we halted renovations after you were hurt."

"Why?"

"Opening the bank requires more financial commitment from you than from me and Jackson. I thought it important to give you time to know me—and I hoped your memory would return. We didn't want you to wonder if we were taking advantage of you and your wealth. Then with Martin Webster and Reed Ferguson threatening our lives, it seemed best not to pursue it. And since then, we've both been busy settling into our married lives."

"But, Morgan, I trusted you from the moment you pretended you weren't shocked by my amnesia and teased me about my equilibrium. Why, I even confided my feelings for Jackson that same night. I've never once doubted what's between us."

"I think some part of your mind must remember about the bank, Sis, or you wouldn't have thought of using that threat— especially when you could secure McKinley's cooperation by hinting we'd transfer the bulk of our funds to a bank in Laramie. Your memories are trying to surface—just yesterday, you remembered the shooting match with Jackson."

"I'm concentrating on living in the present—not worrying about the past," Sam replied, refusing to raise his expectations. "Back to the bank start-up, I think we should go ahead with it. I'm sure Jackson will feel the same. He's leaving for Cheyenne on Monday about the timber contract. While he's away, you can show me the building and explain the financing and plan for operation: overhead costs, risks, daily management, employees. I'd also like to understand what it would take to make the building ready for business."

"I'd like that—if you're sure you want to go ahead with it."

"I rather like the idea of my niece or nephew having a bank president for a papa." *And I'm thrilled to discover the soon-to-open Commerce Bank of Prosperity will help capture Colson Brigham's gang.*

Chapter 9

Alone with Price Hardin in the cabin he claimed for himself whenever his gang took refuge in their remote hideout, Colson Brigham was hellbent on devising a plan to get rid of Jackson Knight.

"Who do we know that could win a place on Knight's team to compete in that shooting contest?" Brigham asked. Revenge was one of the few laws in the universe he respected, and the Prosperity competition was a perfect opportunity for him to catch his old enemy unaware.

"Well, Knight would be glad to have me on the team, but if I did that, I couldn't shoot on yours." Pausing, Price rubbed his jaw while considering candidates. Then locking his gaze with Brigham's, he said, "Next to me, the best long-range man is Mac Covington. I reckon if he was offered the right incentive, he'd consider proving it. Knight would be a fool to pass on him."

Sabotaging the contest was only one of the punishments Brigham intended for Jackson. "What would tempt Covington?"

"Mac runs Highbreeze for Chase Stone's daughter. She married Knight and is wealthier than he is. If she and Knight were out of the picture, Highbreeze would be Mac's—something Mac's always wanted. Mac and the daughter have some baggage. She blames him for not protecting her when she was a young girl—letting a neighbor ruin her."

"What does that mean?"

"It means the neighbor was a pervert and used the girl as if she were a knot in a tree at pecker height while his young son watched him do it. Though Mac's tried to make up for it, she won't forgive him. Last year, the son tried to do the same as the father. Mac and I helped rescue her and Jackson from the pervert and a crazy woman. Mac killed Ferguson, but even that wasn't enough for Sam Knight to forgive him. She and Mac pretend to have feelings for each other, but things will never be right between them. But Sam will do anything for her husband, so if Jackson wants Mac on their team, the daughter will accept it. Promising to rid Mac of the daughter and Knight would seal the deal for Mac's agreein' to join up." Price explained.

Suspicious, Brigham asked, "If you helped Mac rescue them, why are you sellin' them down the river now?"

"She's a beauty and rich. But her being raped put her off men. Before she met Knight, I was angling for her to marry me for the protection of havin' a husband who wouldn't demand his conjugal rights. Had her convinced because I'm thirty years her senior, I wouldn't care about beddin' her. She's known me all her life and has a soft spot for me. But Jackson Knight ruined my plan. I don't know if he has nothing between those long legs of his or if it's something extra special Sam can't resist, but he stole her clean away. Like Mac, I'd enjoy making them hurt—but when all is said and done, I want her alive. With Jackson out of the picture, I'll marry her—both the woman and the ranch will be mine. 'Course Mac won't like bein' cut out, but I'll deal with him later. It's nothin' you need to worry over."

Brigham nodded. No one understood a double cross better than he did. "Tomorrow, you and Sedge ride for Highbreeze to feel Mac out. Bring him here to talk if he's willing to buy in."

"Why send Sedge? Price asked. Mac would agree in a heartbeat if you do the askin' personally."

"He might agree quicker, but you can convince him without my help. And while you handle Covington, I'll visit Prosperity to collect a few facts and make some plans."

Brigham's bold, aggressive leadership was a good match for a band of men with no morals or conscience. They needed his brains. Without a strong leader to guide them, none of them would've lived long enough to profit from their crimes. Nor in a town where most adult males carry guns would they be able to rob a bank and escape with more loot than they'd ever scored before.

***

At the Prosperity train station's loading dock, three buckboards were lined up, but only one was ready to pull out. Jim Ryder, on the Trinity wagon, second in the queue, watched Davis Wilson, Trinity's foreman, and young Cal Ennis fastening the tarpaulin spread over their heavily laden wagon. Before returning to Trinity, Wilson and Ryder would help unload Cal's supplies before Ryder went home to his wife, Jenny, and their Double-J ranch. Before marrying, Jenny had been Gracelyn Palace's manager and Ryder, Trinity's foreman.

A patient man, Parker Evans, reins in hand, waited in the driver's seat of the third conveyance for Jackson to assist Sam up onto the first wagon, bound for the bank. Neither Parker's wagon nor the Trinity wagon could leave until Sam's moved out, but Jackson's last-ditch effort to convince Sam to trade places was delaying everyone.

Despite harboring the same concerns as Jackson, Parker was anxious to return to Becky. Gracelyn Palace and the hotel were hubs of activity on the weekend, and Alexa could easily encounter a situation that would pull her watchful eye away from his daughter. Parker exchanged a knowing look with Wade Harper, owner of the mercantile, who was perched on an ammunition box stowed in the wagon bed.

Like Parker, Wade hoped Jackson would capitulate or bodily carry his stubborn wife to their wagon and dump her curvy bottom next to Parker. Wade wanted to return to his store before Prosperity's new schoolmarm arrived to make her weekly purchases. She always shopped late in the afternoon on Saturdays after helping in her aunt's millinery shop.

Charity Rawlins, a prim, twenty-eight-year-old spinster with golden eyes hidden behind glasses, strawberry blonde hair fashioned into a severe coronet, and a lush figure disguised under plain, shapeless frocks, had replaced the former teacher, who'd resigned when her mother took ill. Though Charity's attempts to hide her attributes fooled others, Wade had been quick to recognize the beauty inside and out. He intended to be the man for whom she removed those glasses, loosened her silken hair, and revealed the contours of her figure.

Parker and Wade heaved a relieved sigh when they saw Jackson give up the argument with Sam about riding shotgun. They watched him kiss his wife and then help her up to sit next to Morgan. When Jackson finally climbed aboard their wagon to sit beside Parker, his eyes stayed on Sam. "I don't like it, but I'll have to live with it," he grumbled.

Parker shrugged. "If you want to keep her, you don't have much choice."

Behind him, Parker heard Wade swallow a chuckle.

***

Having guided the horses to the town's main thoroughfare, Morgan shifted the Winchester lying across his lap and glanced at his sister. "I thought Jackson was never going to let you come aboard," he teased, not bothering to conceal his amusement.

Sam shot him a heated glare. "Jackson doesn't control me. I make my own decisions."

"It didn't look that way," Morgan goaded, deliberately trying to fire her temper. She didn't disappoint.

"Then your eyesight is going bad," Sam snapped. "You'd better get it checked." As soon as the words left her lips, she regretted them. "He's worried something will happen between here and the bank. If Alexa were sitting in my place, you'd feel the same."

Morgan's face paled at Sam's words. He would've hog-tied Alexa and locked her in a jail cell before allowing her to join him on this wagon, especially now she was carrying their child. He wouldn't admit it to Sam, though, so he clamped his jaw shut and concentrated on the horses.

Sam watched the streets, her hand never far from her Colt. Sheriff Cooley caught her eye and nodded, sending the message he wasn't seeing anything suspicious. She didn't let it relax her vigilance.

In her side vision, she saw Morgan scanning storefronts, recessed doorways, and alleys looking for signs of an ambush. They'd covered a third of the distance to the bank.

"Offering the rifles and prize money will undoubtedly bring trouble to town," Morgan commented. "Half the criminals west of the Mississippi would give their left…ah…nostril for the chance to go against you, Jackson, and Mac—even without the lure of prize money and custom rifles."

"You're inflating our reputations," Sam said, while internally acknowledging he was right.

Morgan risked a glance at Sam's face before returning his gaze to the street. "No, I'm not. You and Jackson are uncharacteristically enthusiastic about this event." As he said it, he realized he'd been thinking that for quite some time—since they'd returned from visiting their parents in Eden Ridge. He was certain there was something odd about that visit.

"What fun would it be to limit our competition to ranchers, cowboys, and soldiers?" Sam asked, intending to distract Morgan, but it didn't work.

"It's not normal for you or Jackson—or Mac, for that matter—to draw attention to yourselves—especially you."

Deliberately, Sam kept her reply vague. "Let's say we decided to make an exception for this occasion." *And that was the understatement of the decade.* "Promoting Prosperity is good business and we'll raise money for the orphanage, thanks to Alexa's idea to raffle two rifles and ask merchants to pledge contributions. The 1873 Model Winchester rifles Mac recommended we award to each of the shooters on the three placing teams are highly coveted because Winchester used the best barrels the company produced to make them. The flat of each rifle's top barrel is engraved in script letters with *One in One Thousand*. The three team members winning first place in the Rifle Shoot Contest will split six thousand in prize money. Second-place winners will split three thousand in prize money. And third place winners will split fifteen hundred in prize money. Each person on the three winning teams will receive one of the rifles. Those prizes should be incentive enough to make the competition entertaining."

Morgan whistled. "Not counting the cost of the rifles, that's more than ten thousand cash in prize money."

"That's why Jackson's worried about a robbery."

Recognizing Sam had gotten him off track, Morgan returned to his probing. "Jackson said Frank Butler and Annie Oakley sent a letter to sign up for the rifle shoot but need a third marksman." When Sam didn't comment, he prodded her arm with his elbow. "C'mon, Sis. Jackson said you promised to provide someone. Who'd you talk into it?"

"I haven't told them his name—just said it was all set and they'd be glad to get him."

Morgan chuckled. "You must've convinced Price Hardin to turn over the Laramie sheriff job to his deputy so he can join their team. You, Jackson, and Mac aren't a sure bet to win if he enters."

"No, Price isn't available. But there's someone here in Prosperity that's good enough. In fact, he's almost as good with a rifle as I am." After dropping that bomb, she waited.

Less than a second passed before Morgan exploded. "No, Sis! I don't want any part in this. I don't want your reputation."

Laughter in her voice, Sam quipped, "You don't need to worry about that. You're good—just not as good as the rest of us." She caught and held Morgan's gaze and her voice lost its mirth. "You are an expert, Brother—Mac taught you the same as me. If you, Annie, and Frank were to win, Mac, Jackson, and I could live with it. You don't need to worry about gaining a reputation. Since you aren't a professional and your name isn't known, people will soon forget about a third team member. Annie and Frank will garner all the attention. It will be good for their careers."

Morgan was about to ask more when he noticed the town's mayor, Windom Bagley, raise a hand to wave them over. The man was well liked but long winded. Morgan once joked that by the time the mayor finished commenting on an average sunny day the sun would be setting. Though Mayor Bagley sincerely cared for his constituents and worked diligently to improve Prosperity, people couldn't resist fondly shortening his name to "Windbag," though never within his hearing. The long rectangular shapes beneath the tarp covering the buckboard must have caught the politician's eye. Since he'd donated the acreage for Prosperity's gun club, he certainly had the right to see the rifles. He'd also been instrumental in convincing the town council and several prominent businessmen to contribute funds to build the grandstand and speaking platform, as well as commission a community fairground and picnicking area.

Seeing where Morgan's eyes were directed, Sam pasted on a smile, shook her head at Windbag, and gestured with her rifle to the sheriff and deputy while holding the watch pendant she wore around her neck, indicating they couldn't spare the time or risk their cargo's safety.

The mayor waved them on, and Morgan blew out a heavy breath. "Good thinking, Sis. We don't need Windbag or McKinley slowing this mission."

Sam jabbed Morgan's side with her elbow. "Perhaps not now, but make no mistake, we will need McKinley's help."

Morgan's body stiffened. "I'm beginning to understand, Sis. This whole shooting match is a set-up, isn't it? You'd better have a good reason it needs doing and a plan to keep everyone safe if you want my help."

"I do, Brother," she said, thinking of the new bank and an article describing a patent Jackson had shared with her in an issue of *Scientific American*. She needed to discuss both with him before he left for Cheyenne.

"You're talking mighty bold, Sis, but I'll give you the benefit of the doubt until you can explain later." Drawing back on the reins, he pulled the horses to a stop in front of the bank's double doors and set the wagon's brake. "Right now, let's get this loot and those rifles safely stored in the vault."

Chapter 10

On the same day Jackson Knight boarded the train for Cheyenne, Storey Deale stepped from the gentlemen's smoking car onto the Prosperity rail station platform. Noting the town's growth, he shrugged away a moment of regret for having let too much time pass between visits. Then, after making arrangements to have his bags sent to the Prosperity House Hotel, he set out to visit Gracelyn Palace.

***

"Sweetheart, even from your backside, I can see you're a beauty," Storey proclaimed upon entering Gracelyn Palace's main gaming room. "How's about a kiss for your ol' uncle?" Placing a hand on each side of the waist of the shapely, honey-golden-haired woman standing with her back to him, he spun her around to face him, expecting to receive a warm hug and kiss. Instead, he faced an angry woman he didn't recognize.

Under the circumstances, Storey conceded he deserved the slap she delivered to the side of his face. Dropping his arms to his sides and retreating two steps, he hoped she'd understand his behavior was mistaken identity rather than drunken lechery. "Please forgive me, ma'am. I meant no offense. I mistook you for my goddaughter, the proprietress of this establishment."

Alexa Garner ran her eyes coolly over the well-dressed man and concluded he was a professional gambler. Seeing him warily eye her hand hovering near the front of her jacket, from which she was anticipating having to draw the derringer Sam gave her for her birthday, she conceded he must be an intelligent one. Deeming his apology sincere, she lowered her hand. "Ah, so you thought I was Sam, did you?"

Staring at the classical features of the tall, self-possessed woman appraising him, Storey Deale was amazed by her remarkable resemblance to his goddaughter. Allowing his gaze to flit over her again, he concluded she had Sam's height, figure, bone structure, and coloring, although Sam's gray blue eyes were more slate-colored than this woman's. He also noticed she blinked normally, whereas Sam rarely blinked—much to the discomfort of most people—especially men.

"I must also apologize for staring," Storey murmured. "Your resemblance to my goddaughter is uncanny." Extending his hand, he added, "I'm Storey Deale, Sam Stone's and Morgan Garner's godfather."

Alexa put her hand in his. "Mr. Deale, it's a pleasure meeting you. I'm Alexa Garner, Morgan's wife. Morgan has mentioned you many times. Sam is my second cousin. Perhaps that explains the resemblance. I understand you've been away for several years. From your expression, I suspect the news of Morgan's marriage and other events in recent months haven't reached you."

Storey lifted the back of her hand to his lips. He recognized the diamond-encircled ruby ring Drake Garner, his former partner, gave to Grace, Morgan's mother, on her wedding day. Smiling, he released Alexa's hand. "Do I detect from the amusement I hear in your tone you enjoy my ignorance?" Not expecting an answer, he added, "I don't suppose you'd take pity on an old family friend and enlighten me?"

Alexa instantly warmed to him. She liked how his mouth naturally fell into a smile as if he found something pleasant in most things. "You *are family*, Mr. Deale. Of course, I will. Would you care to join me in my office?"

"My pleasure, and please call me Storey."

Alexa nodded. "And I'm Alexa."

Stepping back, Storey waited for her to precede him. Following her through the room, he admired how welcoming and charming she was to patrons. He thought her particularly adept at keeping men at a distance with little more than a tactful word. He supposed conducting herself as the lady she so obviously was deterred most unwanted overtures. The men acted as if it were a privilege to be in her presence.

Seated companionably in her office, Storey with a snifter of brandy and she with a glass of lemonade, Alexa recounted the details of how she'd come to Gracelyn Palace to meet Sam without revealing they were second cousins, had become her trusted assistant and friend, and fell in love with Morgan.

She broke the news about Sam's amnesia gently, beginning with Martin Webster's engineering the stage crash and ending with how Reed Ferguson, the son of Sam's rapist, and Ruth Kensington, an enemy of Sam and Jackson, had tried to murder them. During that time, she and Morgan had admitted their feelings for each other, as did Sam and Jackson, and married.

By the time Alexa concluded her recitation, Storey was finishing his second brandy. Now he understood why Sam had ceased writing. It was doubtful she remembered him or his son, Deacon. Learning Sam was married eased some of his concern over her amnesia. Storey had met Jackson once before and judged him to be a man worthy of his goddaughter. Briefly, he wondered what his son would think about Sam's marriage.

Before parting, Storey asked for and received Alexa's promise not to tell Sam he was in town, explaining he wanted the opportunity to witness how her amnesia affected her. What he didn't divulge was his hope that surprising her would unlock a memory. He was aware it was a foolish hope—one almost certain to disappoint, but hope wasn't such a bad thing to have.

***

Alone in the ranch house after Jackson left for Cheyenne, Sam made herself wait a full ten minutes before barring all the doors and windows. In the bedroom Reed Ferguson had used to sneak into the house to stalk her, she examined the two-inch screws sunk deep into the thick wood of the window frame and sill.

Reassured by her inspection, she withdrew to her bedroom to change into a split skirt and blouse, thankful riding supplied a credible excuse for escaping the house. She put no thought into the destination. In her present state of mind, "anywhere" was a good enough direction.

She returned in the midafternoon to work in her office. She thought of Jackson while studying the rough diagram he'd drafted after she'd explained her idea to use their bank and William E. Wharton's improved robber trap to capture Brigham's gang with no gunplay.

Jackson had considered her idea for brief seconds before deciding. "I think it might work, Sam." He'd then moved to the built-in bookcases lining the wall from the hall and began scouring the shelves to identify titles, looking for back copies of *Scientific American.* "I'm surprised you remember me showing you that article, darlin'."

Watching him search, she'd replied, "I remember because the joy you felt in sharing it with me vanished from your face the second you saw my puzzled reaction. It was only a week or so after we married, and I knew my amnesia was the reason."

Jackson's hands stopped sorting as he turned toward her. "In my enthusiasm, I'd forgotten you didn't know anything about our bank plan. When I realized what I'd done, I didn't want you to feel bad, so I mentioned Wharton's trap might be a good investment."

Sam raised her gaze to meet Jackson's. "And I accepted your explanation because—well—admitting it was about a memory I no longer had was superfluous." She'd allowed herself a sigh before gesturing for him to resume his search.

A few seconds later, Jackson located the correct volume and began flipping through it as he moved to her side. The article was only two pages. The first described the improved trap and frequently referred to three diagrams on the second page. William E. Wharton, of Lawson, Missouri, had filed the patent application on August 10, 1875.

While reviewing the article, Jackson had turned frequently to the three diagrams. Minutes later, his eyes shining, his head nodding, he said, "I'm certain Morgan and I, with help from a few trusted friends, can install a larger version of this trap. We'll need sturdier materials: thicker planks, larger rollers and hinges, a heavier weight, three times as many braces, and higher tensile-weight rope. We'll set iron bars in the basement's concrete floor to construct a holding cell. Anyone standing beyond the two feet of stable flooring directly in front of the vault door will fall into the cell below when the floor drops open. We'll space the bars the same as a prison cell and install a door with a key lock."

Opening the page to Wharton's diagrams, Sam spent more than an hour deciphering the design and jotting down a few notes for herself and Morgan. Jackson had left a list and asked her to give it to Morgan to begin purchasing construction materials. Anything they couldn't buy locally, he was to order with expedited shipping, regardless of cost.

Next, she inspected the bank floor plan and architect's drawings. While bright sunlight filtered through the windows, her focus was good. But as the day waned and shadows collected in corners the light couldn't reach, unease began creeping in. Taking several calming breaths, she reminded herself her fear wasn't reasonable—no one was watching. But reassurances did little to alleviate anxiety.

As the shadows deepened, claiming more and more of the light, the room seemed to narrow, creating an illusion of walls moving inward, forcing oxygen out, threatening suffocation—perhaps entombment was a better description. Sam rubbed her arms, an appropriate action for smoothing away the bumps raised by a passing cold shiver but laughably insufficient to defeat her budding terror.

She knew fear was tricking her, but she couldn't ignore the dark particles gathering into disparate patterns in the gloom—beginning to resemble a spectral shape. Though the form had no discernible features, it appeared to be watching, as if waiting for darkness to endow it substance to pull her into its dominion.

Motionless at her desk, Sam's alarm inexorably climbed an invisible inner scale. Already beyond uneasy, it barely paused at anxious before spiking to full-blown terror. Her eyes darted to the windows again to measure the light. It was nearly gone.

Recognizing panic would soon become paralysis, she made herself draw a calming breath. If she could deny the spirit's presence, convince herself her mind conjured the apparition, she could free herself.

But the power to vanquish it eluded her, and the certainty she was in mortal danger threatened to immobilize her. As her inner protective wall of reason crumbled, so did her resolve to stand and fight. Cautiously, she rose and inched toward the front door. Once there, she half expected a ghostly hand to seize her arm and stop her from lifting the bar.

But nothing interfered.

The door swung inward, shepherding fresh air, still warm from the sun, to penetrate—aerate—the thick oppressive atmosphere at her back, thinning its viscosity, loosening the fear, encouraging forward movement. Stepping onto the porch, she attained the first milestone on the path to safety. Pulling the door closed, blocking the watcher's pursuit, she barely heard the latch click as it caught in the frame.

With eyes locked on the main house, she crossed the porch and stepped down to the walkway: two more milestones gained. Resolutely, one step accomplished, then another and another, she fled, refusing to feel shame for surrendering her house to the malevolent watcher.

***

In the last of the day's light, Parker Evans looked up from the corral near Trinity's barn to watch Sam trudge up the drive to the main ranch house. He wasn't surprised.

Later, when he entered his study, he found her settled behind the desk pretending to review accounts, the thumb of her left hand stoking the jagged lightning bolt scar near the curve of her thumb on her right hand. Distracted, she glanced up and gave him a fleeting half-smile.

Although he wasn't old enough to be her father, Parker loved Sam as if she were his daughter. Having thought it best not to interfere, he regretted not offering council before Jackson left for Cheyenne. "When Jackson comes home, will you tell him what's bothering you, Sam?" he asked, certain his directness surprised her; though, she didn't show it.

"I don't know what you're talking about," she answered coolly, her eyes remaining on the ledger.

Parker wouldn't be put off. "I've figured it out, Sam. You don't need to pretend."

Raising her head, she challenged him. "Really? What do you think you know?"

Parker held her gaze. He wasn't bluffing, and she needed to understand that. "You've done a good job of concealing your feelings, especially around Jackson. But you've been less vigilant around me, and since I have an almost sixteen-year-old daughter, I'm inclined to see things other men might miss. You and Becky are good at using diversionary tactics to focus people's attention away from yourselves. I admit it took several months, but I've figured it out. You're afraid of being alone in your house, but I don't understand why."

Angry Ferguson still had a hold on her, Sam eyed the study door as if contemplating escape. She didn't want to admit her weakness. Mac killing Ferguson should have freed her.

Parker stepped closer to the desk. "You haven't spent one night alone in your house since Ferguson kidnapped you and Jackson. You work there during the day, but come nightfall, if Jackson's not home, you find a legitimate reason to leave. Jackson has noticed, too, but hasn't figured it out yet." Parker paused before adding, "Talk to me, Sam."

Sam took a steadying breath. "I didn't want you or Jackson to worry. I thought it would pass, but it hasn't." She waited while Parker settled in the chair facing the desk.

"Being alone doesn't bother me. The feeling someone is watching me is what I can't get over. I've let that pervert get in my head. Before Jackson, Mac, and the others came to rescue me, he taunted me with how he'd hidden in the house and watched me. He—believed I knew he was there and deliberately did—ah, certain things to—arouse him. He thought I wanted him to—to bed me." Dropping her gaze from Parker's, she added, "Sometimes, he even watched when Jackson and I were—together."

"Good God, Sam, no wonder he haunts you. Why didn't you say something?"

"I was shocked and embarrassed I hadn't known what he'd been doing. Although he's dead, I can't get over the sensation that he, or someone like him, is still watching."

Parker wanted to put his arms around her to offer comfort but didn't, because she'd interpret it as a sign he thought her weak. "Sam, contrary to your maiden name, you aren't made of stone. You wouldn't be human if you weren't affected by what Ferguson said and did. But don't let it come between you and Jackson. He knows something is wrong and is thinking all kinds of things—even wondering if you regret marrying him."

Sam had no regrets about marrying Jackson, other than she couldn't carry his child. "I nearly told him last week but decided to wait until he comes home. I didn't want him putting off the trip to Cheyenne again."

Parker nodded. "He'll understand when you tell him. Meanwhile, you can stay here with Becky and me. She won't think anything about it."

"I'll stay here tonight, but tomorrow I'll go to town."

"Are you sure, Sam? If you prefer to sleep in your house, I could check on you every couple of hours or ask Wilson or one of the other hands to stand watch."

"Thank you, but tomorrow, when Wilson goes for supplies and the mail, I'll ride with him. Now that I've learned about the bank, we've decided to push for a mid-July opening. And last night, Jackson and I discussed a modification we need Morgan to begin while Jackson's away. Jackson made a rough drawing and I need to give it to Morgan. On Wednesday, the workers will begin wallpapering and painting the lobby and offices. Morgan has so much to do, I promised to oversee anything that has to do with decoration and furnishings."

Lifting her chin, she managed a smile. "I'll get over this watcher thing, especially once I talk to Jackson. I was foolish to wait so long. I'll gather a few things from the house. Then I'll talk to Wilson about tomorrow."

Parker followed her to the front porch, where he reached for a lantern. "Give me a second to light this, and I'll walk with you."

Relieved, Sam waited. "Thank you, Parker. You always know just the right thing."

Chapter 11

Late in the afternoon on the day after Jackson left for Cheyenne and Storey Deale arrived in Prosperity, Morgan Garner cautiously raised his arms when the steel of a gun barrel prodded the center of his back. A hand clapped down on his shoulder and a low, gruff voice ordered him to retrace his steps in the hotel's second-floor hallway. As he approached an open door, the voice behind him barked, "Step into that room, *hermano*, and take a seat."

Angry he hadn't heard or sensed the man approaching, Morgan followed orders. As he eased down onto a chair near the bed, he tried to get a look at the man holding him captive. Beginning at the floor, Morgan took inventory—expensive black boots; sharply creased black trousers encasing powerful legs and thighs; silk maroon vest; white, ruffled shirt custom tailored to fit wide, well-developed shoulders. About six feet. The man's hair, so dark brown it resembled blackstrap molasses, touched his open collar. The silver-banded, black Stetson on his head was angled to hide the features beneath it. Leaning to see under the brim, Morgan was surprised to recognize the sparkling, emerald-green eyes of an old friend.

The gun trained on Morgan disappeared into the fancy black leather holster strapped to a lean thigh and a hand reached out to him. Morgan rose from his chair and clasped it in warm welcome. "It's good to see you, Deacon."

Grinning, Deacon Storey chucked Morgan's chin. "It's good to see you, too, Morgan, though I was disappointed you let me get the drop on you like that. I guess that beautiful, legs-up-to-heaven blonde you married must've emptied your head of everything Mac taught you. I reckon Mac and Sammy will have plenty to say when I tell them how easy this was."

Smiling broadly, Morgan quipped, "If you promise not to mention it, I'll introduce you to my wife."

Deacon laughed. "Since I've already seen her, I know she's a woman to tempt any man. You have my promise."

"What's it been, Deacon, five years?" Morgan asked, hardly believing his childhood friend was standing there in front of him. "I've missed you like hell. We heard rumors of some trouble, but Storey told us not to worry. Mac and I tried to check with you, just in case, but you always managed to stay one step ahead of us. We finally concluded you did it intentionally, so we backed off. You all right?"

Deacon held Morgan's concerned gaze for a long moment before answering. "Yeah, I'm fine." *Only his father knew he worked as a special agent for the Pinkerton agency.* "If you don't mind, could we leave all that alone? I'm in no trouble."

Satisfied, Morgan nodded. If Deacon needed him to back off, he had no problem letting it drop. Changing the direction of the conversation, Morgan asked, "Does Storey know you planned to visit? He's here."

Deacon nodded. "Yeah, I wired Dad after receiving his letter with the date he expected to arrive."

"You wouldn't be able to describe Alexa unless your father introduced you," Morgan commented.

"I haven't seen him yet," Deacon replied. "On my way from the livery, I was stunned to see a beautiful blonde I mistook for Sammy. She was crossing Main Street on her way to Gracelyn Palace. Your town doctor, Roy Baxter, caught me staring and warned me off. Told me to put my eyes back in my head because the lady had a husband and sister-in-law who'd make short work of me if I didn't mind my manners. A sister-in-law able to take on a desperado made me suspicious, so I asked a few questions that the good doctor didn't mind answering—after I explained we were raised as one big, happy family. That's how I learned you'd gone and got yourself hitched. Doc said you're a lucky man, Morgan. I'm happy for you."

"Thanks, Deacon," Morgan replied while contemplating whether to inquire about his plans. Deciding not to pry, he joked, "So rather than find your father, you opted to play a prank on me?"

Deacon chuckled. "That's right. Consider it payback for you helping Sammy sneak up on me when you were kids. I paid a boy to pass your barkeep a message saying an old friend was visiting town and wanted to see you. I deliberately gave the wrong room number."

"Hell, Deacon, you know those were kid games. Sam loved practicing what Mac taught her. You're two years older than I am and eight years older than Sam. It's no secret you let her ambush you. I saw the laughter in your eyes when she bragged about it. She trailed after us like a puppy." He paused, chuckling to himself. "A year after her papa died, I heard her tell Grace that since Mac lived at Highbreeze managing the ranch, would Grace ask Storey to marry her so she'd have another brother and Storey could be our papa too."

"I never knew that," Deacon said, careful to keep the emotion from his voice. Though he'd known it wasn't in the cards, he would have liked his father to marry Grace, but— mostly, it had been something nice to wish for—somewhat like wishin' on a star. The fact he and his father were thought of and treated like family was what was important.

It wasn't often Deacon thought about living with his mother in a room above the saloon where she'd worked or how unhappy she'd been before she died. When his mother learned how ill she was, she wrote Storey asking him to come for him.

The day before his mother passed away, Deacon watched Storey climb the stairs to his mother's room. When he reached the landing, he smiled kindly, patted Deacon's shoulder, and gave him some coins, telling him to go along to the mercantile for some peppermint sticks while he talked to his mother. Deacon had never asked Storey exactly what he and his mother discussed. But when Deacon returned, Storey and his mother explained about her having to go away. That's when Storey told Deacon he was his father and would take care of him—if Deacon was agreeable to it. His mother assured him Storey was a good man and would be a kind father. Deacon didn't question what she said because he trusted her and was certain she loved him. Besides, he hadn't had another choice, unless he'd wanted to fend for himself, so he'd accepted what he couldn't change.

His mother died the next day. After Storey saw to her being buried decently with a preacher saying words over her grave, he took Deacon away on the stage. They traveled for days. When they reached Saint Louis, they boarded a riverboat on the Mississippi River. That trip was the first of many, for wherever Storey went, he took Deacon with him.

Drake Garner, his father's partner, traveled with them. Grace, already married to Drake, took to mothering him. Her pale hair and kind eyes reminded him of a beautiful angel he'd once seen in the stained-glass window of a fancy church. Storey was godfather to Drake and Grace's son,

Morgan. And as far as Deacon was concerned, Morgan was his younger brother. After Drake died in a riverboat accident, he and Storey moved with Grace and Morgan to Eden Ridge to help Grace run her gaming salon, the Golden Crown.

Though different from the childhoods of most children, Deacon's had been full of adventure. And thanks to his mother, Storey, and Morgan's family, Deacon had known plenty of love. Storey was a good father, and it had been a good life, the kind that freed a young man's thinking to discover there were as many ways to live as there were people.

"How about having supper with me and Alexa tonight, Deacon?" Morgan suggested. "I'll arrange for something special from the hotel restaurant. We live in a suite above Gracelyn Palace. You can spend some time with your father this afternoon, then bring him with you tonight."

Surprised Morgan hadn't mentioned their sister, Deacon asked about her. "What about Sammy? Doesn't she live at Gracelyn Palace, too?"

Morgan nodded. "We'll invite her. Most of the time she lives at her ranch house, but luck is with us because she arrived earlier today to stay for the week. She bought into Trinity Ranch a year after we moved here to open Gracelyn Palace."

Deacon was surprised because she owned Highbreeze, one of the richest ranches in the Territory. Mac ran it for her. Her father, Chase, had arranged for Mac, his partner, and his second wife, Grace Garner Stone, Morgan's mother, to raise Sam and manage her inheritance until she reached legal age.

Morgan cleared his throat. "I hate being the one to tell you this, Deacon, but Sam doesn't remember you, and she married last November."

Deacon looked away from Morgan before crossing to the table where he picked up a half-full bottle of bourbon and poured some into the glass. As he sat on the bed, he motioned Morgan to the chair and offered him the glass. Then he took two long draws straight from the bottle while waiting for Morgan to sit. After swiping his lips with the back of his hand, he said, "I'm not as shocked that Sammy is married as I am that she doesn't remember me. I think you'd better explain." He brought the bottle back to his lips and took another long draw.

After tossing back the liquor in his glass, Morgan replied, "Sam and I came to Prosperity to open Gracelyn Palace. Soon after, she met Jackson Knight and they fell in love. But they didn't marry until recently." Morgan went on to describe the crazed events perpetrated by Reed Ferguson, the son of Sam's rapist, who had drugged and abducted the couple, intending to murder them. Fortunately, Jackson had been able to convince Ferguson's accomplice, Ruth Kensington, that Ferguson had murdered her daughter and was planning to double-cross Ruth. When Ruth turned on Ferguson, it gave Morgan, Mac, and Price Hardin the opportunity they needed to rescue Sam and Jackson, but not before Ferguson killed Ruth.

Reaching the end of the tale, Morgan said, "Mac drilled a bullet through Ferguson's skull. And through all the trouble, Jackson stood by Sam—loved and protected her. And Sam figured out her refusing to marry him was hurting them both." He paused before finishing the last of it because he knew it would be the most hurtful. "They're good together, Deacon, and she's happy. I don't think that would be true with any other man—not even you."

Deacon drained the last of the bourbon. If he had another bottle, he would have started on it. After carefully setting the empty bottle on the nightstand, he stretched out on the bed. "I'll pass on supper tonight, Morgan. I need to sleep the bourbon off. Will tomorrow night work? I'll see Storey in the afternoon and bring him to your place for whatever time you say."

Coming to his feet, Morgan stared down at Deacon, who already had his eyes closed. At the door, he turned to answer. "Sure, Deacon. Tomorrow's fine, say about six o'clock."

Pulling the door closed, Morgan took a deep breath. He had his doubts whether Deacon would show up for supper. On his way back to Gracelyn Palace, he'd find Storey and they'd come up with a plan to make sure Deacon didn't leave town too soon.

***

Deacon stared at the ceiling of his hotel room after Morgan left. So, Sammy didn't remember him—and she was married. Same as Mac and Morgan, Deacon would've killed the neighbor who raped Sammy if the bastard hadn't died in the fire that burned down his barn. He'd thought the fire was an accident, but Morgan said the man's son started it. Of all the memories lost to her, why must that terrible day be what came back in her dreams? Life could be such a bitch.

What seemed a lifetime ago, Deacon planned to marry Sammy when she turned sixteen. He'd loved her for years. Though she was young, especially when compared to his twenty-four years, he would have been gentle and patient, careful not to pressure her to accept more than she was ready for. It wouldn't have taken many years for the age difference not to matter. But he'd never proposed because she hadn't been able to overcome her fear of being with a man. And who could blame her? Certainly not him, not when he knew she'd been taken with brutality and in more ways than most women knew existed—hell, some whores weren't even that experienced.

Sam's sixteenth birthday came and went, while Deacon's love and need for her grew stronger with each passing day. When she turned eighteen, he knew he had to leave because his frustration and physical need scared the bejesus out of her. He couldn't stop seeing the woman she

104

could be if she'd trust him. Between her fear and his need, he was driving them both crazy. When he decided to go, he promised himself he'd come back every year. And he'd done just that—for a while.

He hadn't intended to stay away so long. Work was one excuse. But the primary reason was he'd begun to believe Sammy would never heal. So, while he stayed away, she'd moved to Prosperity, fell in love with a good man, and lost her memories. How was it he'd always had such good luck with cards and such bad luck with the woman he loved?

Since reconnecting with his family wasn't the only reason Deacon had come to Prosperity, he couldn't invent an excuse and leave. He had a job to complete. With Sammy not remembering him, it might not be so bad. After all, she wouldn't know anything about his feelings for her. He had to accept the dream he'd chased for half his life could never be.

It would be good to see his father and spend time with Morgan. Hell, maybe with his dream crushed, he could learn to think of Sammy as a sister again. He'd try because he wished her happiness, even if it were with another man.

Chapter 12

Moving to their Gracelyn Palace suite dulled the sharp edge of Sam's apprehension but didn't eradicate it. Her fear yesterday had jettisoned her from her house quicker than a coward fleeing a battlefield at the first boom of a cannon. Her stepfather would've likened the length of time her courage lasted to water draining from a bucket with a rusted-out bottom. Restlessly pacing from desk to window—concentrating on work or anything else was impossible.

Her stomach rumbling, Sam realized she'd been too keyed up to eat since the dry toast and coffee she'd choked down at breakfast. However, when the food ordered from the hotel dining room arrived, she'd lost her hunger. Not bothering to remove the covers from the dishes, she relegated the tray to the hallway to be taken away.

Unable to work, eat, or sleep, she decided to seek refuge in the gaming salon. From her wardrobe, she chose a lilac taffeta skirt, matching jacket, and ivory blouse. After changing her clothes, she assessed her appearance in the full-length mirror. The blouse's square neckline was low but rescued from immodesty by three rows of narrow lace. The expert tailoring of her over jacket concealed her derringer.

***

Having made his way to Gracelyn Palace's gaming salon, Deacon propped himself comfortably against the doorjamb of what he presumed was an office door while searching for his father. After sleeping off the bourbon, he'd become increasingly impatient with his inability to keep his thoughts from turning to Sam. He'd considered getting another bottle but knew distraction was a better solution. His father had a way of grounding him when he was in a black mood. Though late, if Storey were present, Deacon would benefit from his company. If not, he'd seek out a card game.

Lazily scanning faces, Deacon's eyes no sooner met his father's than he saw him nod toward the stairs at the far end of the bar. Deacon cast his gaze in that direction and followed the staircase to the top, where the vision of a honey-haired beauty nearly stopped his heartbeat. Sammy was breathtaking. He couldn't take his eyes from her. Nor could at least half the other men in the room who stared boldly, captivated by her loveliness—something he knew she abhorred.

***

Sam paused on the stair landing, scanning the gaming floor, appreciating the familiar sounds of spinning roulette wheels, shuffling cards, and clinking glasses. The salon's elegance and welcoming atmosphere soothed her senses and calmed her nerves. She and Morgan had designed Gracelyn Palace to cater to a well-behaved clientele. Unlike most gaming establishments, men and women were welcome. Drinking was encouraged, but in moderation—no rotgut served. Mild cursing was acceptable, but outright crudeness was grounds for banishment. Gracelyn Palace games weren't rigged, nor did its dealers cheat. Hostesses provided congenial company and served drinks but didn't sell their bodies.

Sam's eyes searched for Alexa, expecting to see her moving about the room, overseeing business and chatting with guests, but she wasn't there. Shifting her gaze to the door of Alexa's office, she encountered the piercing green eyes of a dark-haired stranger.

Returning the man's stare, Sam gauged his interest to be more than casual, but not necessarily lascivious. Reminding her of a sleek predator, he looked all lean muscle. He was tall, but not as tall as Jackson. His shoulders, wide and well developed, signified strength and confidence—giving the impression he was a man who feared little. A few seconds passed before Sam dropped her eyes. The mild throbbing of her headache picked up its pace. Dismissing the stranger from her thoughts, she raised a hand to massage her temple.

As she began her descent, Sam's eyes were drawn to two men playing poker near the front entrance. The deliberate nonchalance of the older player in the face of the open dislike of the other warned of trouble brewing. At the bottom of the stairs, she reached beneath her jacket, adjusting her derringer's angle. It wasn't that she planned to use the gun, she simply needed reassurance she could react quickly if circumstances warranted it.

While approaching the two players, Sam admired the elegant appearance of the older gentleman. The woven texture of his black jacket and vest made the white silk of his shirt appear whiter. The gold studs in his cuffs flashed when they caught the light. The fit of his coat emphasized the smooth line of his shoulders. Evidence he'd passed his fiftieth year was visible in the gray at his temples and the lines engraved at the outside corners of his eyes. Belying his slim build and average height, he looked toned and fit—a man to whom a woman would naturally gravitate because of his distinguished features and confident demeanor.

The object of Sam's attention tracked her progress as she crossed the room. His open interest and a raised eyebrow suggested he was a bit of a rogue—though Sam judged it probable he was more titillating than dangerous. Yet, if provoked, she had no doubt he'd be capable of holding his own.

Though he pretended indifference, the younger player also watched her. He appeared to be in his mid-thirties, although it was difficult to be certain because his well-groomed pencil mustache and anchor-shaped goatee, which faintly resembled a Luciferian image, partially disguised his chin and jawline. Despite the draw of obsidian eyes, the cruel line of his mouth marred what most women would've otherwise described as darkly handsome. From the fine-cut and tailored fit of his charcoal-gray suit, with its understated silk vest, he sported an air of sartorial elegance and the arrogant disdain often assumed by the affluent. He held his body at attention as if expecting a need to escape danger. Why such a man was passing through Prosperity was a puzzle.

Upon reaching the men's table, Sam inclined her head, first acknowledging the older gentleman, who'd risen politely to his feet. She saw his eyes flick to her wedding band as he proffered a slight bow in her direction. "Good evening, Mrs. Knight," he said in greeting, his voice warm and welcoming.

Sam wasn't surprised he knew her name. This man would make it his business to be informed, a practice that had probably saved his life on many occasions. She offered her hand. "Since you know my last name, I assume you also know my first. Please call me Sam." She paused to raise a questioning eyebrow and flash an apologetic smile. "I do confess you have the advantage, though, Mr.—?" Breaking off, she waited expectantly for him to provide his name. He didn't disappoint.

"Deale. My name is Storey Deale." Gesturing toward the other player who'd remained seated, Storey added, "And this gentleman is Colby Briggs." Turning to Briggs, Storey completed the introduction. "Mr. Briggs, this is Sam Knight. She and her brother, Morgan Garner, own Gracelyn Palace."

Sam nodded to acknowledge Storey's graciousness for making the introductions before pinning a cool gaze on Briggs, who under her scrutiny reluctantly rose to his feet. His eyes boldly assessing her figure lingered on her neckline. "Pleased to make your acquaintance, ma'am." The flatness of his tone belied the sincerity of his words, confirming for Sam what truly pleased him was the swell of her breasts.

"If you have no objections, I'd like to join your game," Sam said, gesturing toward the deck of cards on the table.

***

While his father made introductions, Deacon sidled closer. Hearing Sam's request, he impulsively decided to join their game. He had no concerns his father would give him away. Storey had the best "poker face" in the business. A person could ascertain Storey Deale's thoughts only if Storey wished for that person to know them. So, when Deacon materialized at his father's side, playing the ill-mannered opportunist, Storey's face merely reflected amused curiosity.

"I, like the lady, am looking for a friendly game," Deacon stated, his gaze resting on Sam. "I was standing nearby and overheard the introductions. My name is Deacon." He purposely omitted his surname to prevent Sammy and Briggs from learning his and Storey's father-son filiation. Then, assuming his inclusion was welcome, he held a chair for Sam and took the one to her left. "Gentlemen, please join us," Deacon invited, waving a hand at the empty chairs in front of his father and Briggs as if he were the host and they the interlopers.

Sam gave no indication she noticed the omission of Deacon's last name or recognized him from earlier. Now that she was close to him, she understood why he'd captured her attention. Dark, broad-shouldered, with intelligent green eyes that missed nothing, he radiated masculine sensuality, leashed for the moment, only because he wished it so. She doubted whether she'd ever met a man, other than Jackson, who appealed to her more.

Though her intuition told her he was pretending to be something he wasn't, it didn't put her off. She had no idea of his motive, but so long as he didn't endeavor to embroil her in whatever deception he was planning, she expected she'd enjoy watching his machinations.

Aware of Sam's scrutiny, Deacon picked up the cards and shuffled expertly. Though Morgan had told him about her memory, he was finding it difficult to cope with the deep disappointment he felt over her interacting with him as she would any stranger. He sensed a turbulent river of speculation and emotion flowing beneath the cool, self-possessed calmness she projected.

After gesturing to the cards in Deacon's hands, Sam addressed all three men. "So, what'll it be, gentlemen, five-card draw?"

Without looking to the other two men for a response, Deacon agreed. "Excellent choice. I suggest table stakes."

Storey glanced across the table at the cards in Deacon's hands and motioned toward Briggs seated to his right. "It was Briggs's turn to deal."

Deacon leaned to his left and placed the cards in front of Briggs, who with a half-mocking smile drawled, "Ladies first," before extending his arm to offer Sam the deck. As he placed it in her open palm, the pads of his fingers lingered to caress the curve of her thumb.

Repressing the shiver of revulsion his touch evoked, Sam controlled her distaste by telling herself his lack of subtlety meant he'd have little talent for bluffing—something she'd use to her advantage. She suspected he was a man driven by a need for cruelty and domination, both physical and sexual. She wouldn't make the mistake of underestimating him.

Conducting his own appraisal, Briggs found much to admire. Though her outward coolness belied it, he had no doubt she was a woman of passion. His eyes rested on her lips before moving to the honey-gold tresses spilling in soft waves over her shoulders. From there, his gaze moved to her breasts. His fingers itched to squeeze the tender flesh mounded so temptingly beneath a few thin layers of fabric. He wanted to make her scream when he put himself in her—and preferred her cry be induced from pain rather than pleasure. It made him hard just thinking about it.

She ignored him as she shuffled the cards with dazzling speed. He saw Deacon and Storey watching her hands. But his own gaze didn't wander from her breasts quivering from the motion.

She slapped the deck down in front of Deacon and waited for him to cut. Without looking down, he lifted half the cards and laid them on the table. She picked up the remainder of the deck and placed it on top of Deacon's cut.

Barely registering the distinct swish and splat sounds the cards made as they landed on the table facedown, Sam's mind weighed the disadvantages of drawing her derringer against Brigg's Colt Peacemaker should he push things too far. She concluded, at this range, she'd likely hold her own. However, were he able to get her alone, she'd be in trouble. She'd need to guard against that happening. Setting down the deck, she picked up her cards and was disappointed the only card of interest was a jack. The others were slated for the discard pile.

Deacon was considering the possibilities of a pair of eights. He'd won fortunes on less, but not when playing with his father. He opened with a modest bet, signaling Storey he had little faith in his hand.

Holding a potential straight—deuce, tray, four, and five—Briggs raised, planning to discard a ten of clubs in hopes of receiving an ace or six. If he drew neither card, he'd retrieve the ace hidden in the hem of his trousers. Preparing for the switch, he trapped a few greenbacks under his elbow and slid them precariously near the table edge. He saw no shame in cheating—only in losing.

When it was Storey's turn, he raised the stakes. Sam had dealt him two fives, two queens, and a deuce. If he received a five or a queen when he discarded the deuce, he'd hold a full house. Two pairs could be a winning hand, but a full house would be better.

After calling, Sam dealt each man whatever number of cards he requested before dealing herself four cards and sweeping the discards to the side. Permitting herself a quick glimpse of each man's face, she saw Briggs was the only player who looked concerned. His greenbacks near the table edge hadn't escaped her notice, and though their faces didn't indicate it, she was confident Storey and Deacon were aware of what Briggs intended. It wasn't a particularly clever way to cheat.

When Briggs didn't receive the card he needed, his elbow nudged the greenbacks off the table, and Sam was ready. Her gasp and the open hand pressed to her chest were so convincing not one person witnessing it was surprised her startled reaction launched three of her gold eagles into the air.

On the pretext of recovering Briggs's greenbacks along with her gold pieces, she darted around Storey's chair and sank to her knees next to Briggs. She was careful to put herself between him and the card he intended to pull. The pose she assumed was deliberate, for it presented a tantalizing view of her cleavage while allowing her skirt to drape around his calf.

Reaching for greenbacks, Sam plucked the card concealed in the hem of Briggs's trouser leg with her free hand and slipped it beneath her skirt, tucking it under a garter securing her silk stocking. To distract Briggs while making the transfer, she rested the hand with his cash on his inner thigh—higher than she'd intended. Now that it was there, she took satisfaction in feeling a tremor pass beneath her hand. She felt another when he loosened her fingers to take possession of the money.

Pretending not to notice, Sam turned her hand palm down to use his thigh to stabilize her balance as she leaned to thread her free arm through the rungs of Storey's chair to retrieve one of her gold eagles. When her gaze collided with Storey's, she winked. Then straightening, she jubilantly held up the gold piece and flashed Briggs a dazzling smile. Briggs, his eyes hungry, looking as if he could taste the creamy skin exposed to his view, slowly brought her hand from his thigh to his lips.

Feigning shyness, Sam lowered her gaze and hesitantly began inching away. When she finally scooped up the two remaining gold pieces and returned to her chair, she murmured a pretty apology for her clumsiness, her expression giving nothing away of the triumph she felt over her performance.

Briggs used the distraction of Sam Knight purring her apology to retrieve his hole card. Under the pretense of straightening his trouser leg, he discovered its theft and knew immediately Sam had duped him. A flame of fury ignited in his veins and surged to his cheeks. She'd made a fool of him, but she hadn't exposed him for a cheat. He had no choice but to suppress his rage, promising himself she'd pay dearly later.

Though Storey had taught Sammy the transfer countermeasure, he'd never seen it executed with such precision and innocent guile. By God, she had ice in her veins, and he'd never been prouder.

Once Sammy returned safely to her chair, Deacon wanted to throw his head back and laugh. Instead, he pretended to study his cards. He still had only a pair of eights. Shrugging, he folded, certain his father held the winning hand.

Briggs had no choice but to fold.

Shifting her gaze to Storey's face, Sam admired how nothing in his expression, eyes, or body tension hinted at the contents of his hand or his feelings about it. He was good. He was so good that a player less experienced than she might be fooled into believing he wasn't a professional gambler. She was pleased he would win.

Though he expected Sam to fold, Storey threw a twenty-dollar gold piece onto the center of the table, raising the stakes as if he believed Sam held a viable hand. He hadn't drawn the five or queen to make his two pairs a full house but was certain it didn't affect the game's outcome. Sam had telegraphed she held nothing of significance when she'd given him that brazen wink while reaching for the gold eagle.

When Sam folded, she sent a congratulatory smile in Storey's direction. Then after waving a hostess to the table, she ordered a brandy and a bottle of good bourbon. While waiting for the drinks, they played an uneventful hand, which Storey also won.

Sipping her brandy, Sam felt the tension at the table rising. It was Briggs's turn to deal. His anger seething, but contained for the moment, he'd resumed his lascivious perusal, letting his eyes travel over her as if she were a broodmare, and she didn't like it.

Clenching a cigar in his teeth, Storey struck a Lucifer with his thumbnail and raised the flame to his cigar. His eyes narrowed to peer through the smoke and to make a slow turn around the room before stopping to rest on Sam.

"Have we met before, Sam?"

"Not that I recall, Mr. Deale, but then my memory is a little faulty because of an injury I suffered several months ago." Sam smiled inwardly. She was developing quite a talent for understatement.

"Please, first names, Sam. I'm sorry to have reminded you of your injury. I trust you suffered no other ill effects?"

"Only the occasional headache when some odd remembrance or other tries to break through." Because she was preoccupied with another thought, she'd answered his question more honestly than she'd intended. Though she hadn't voiced it, she thought she recognized something familiar about Storey's voice. She rubbed her temple to ease the nagging throb of her headache.

"Are you two going to exchange pleasantries all evening or play cards?" grumbled Briggs. He intended to teach the bitch a lesson. Later, he'd teach her an even more painful one. With one gulp remaining in his second glass of bourbon, his tone was more belligerent than before.

Storey remarked, "Nothing wrong with polite conversation, friend, but I take your point." Nodding at the deck in Briggs's hands, he added, "Please proceed."

Tight-lipped, Briggs shuffled and dealt, while entertaining the thought of shooting Storey in the back. He resented the gambler's affability.

Studying her cards, Sam wondered if Briggs believed her fool enough to draw to an inside straight. He'd manipulated the cards, though he hadn't done it well. She was sure Deacon and Storey saw him do it. Since he'd made the effort, Sam supposed Briggs did believe she was that stupid. Recklessly, she decided to give him rope to hang himself.

Storey chose to play the cards he was dealt.

Seeing Briggs's hold on the deck in his hand relax when she requested one card told Sam that he believed she'd fallen for his trick. He dealt her card from the bottom of the deck before again gluing his heavy-lidded gaze on the modest cleavage peeking from the neckline of her blouse.

Enunciating carefully, her voice low and cool with menace, Sam challenged him. "Move your eyes up, Briggs. I don't have any cards where you're looking."

Briggs didn't lift his eyes when he said, "Your expertise in playing cards makes me wonder what other talents you have."

In her side vision, Sam saw Deacon shift on his chair, putting the butt of his six-gun near his hand. Storey casually brushed his jacket lapel, within easy reach of his derringer.

Sensing a shift in atmosphere, onlookers eased away from the table. As if sound was sucked temporarily from the room, silence settled around the players. The barkeep's assistant sidled around the end of the bar and darted through the connecting archway to the hotel, presumably to get the sheriff.

Sam's expression didn't alter as she smoothly drew her derringer and pointed it at Briggs's chest. "Since you bring it up, Mr. Briggs, you should know I'm also a marksman of some reputation. I prefer targets to cardsharps, though, so I suggest you return that card you dealt me to the *bottom* of the deck then deal me the one on the top. I advise you not to give me a reason to demonstrate how good I am, but I will if you insist."

"What if I decline, Mrs. Knight?" Gesturing toward her gun, Briggs added, "That derringer may be nothing more than a clever bluff on your part."

Sam smiled, though nothing in it conveyed pleasantness. She angled her head to make sure Briggs saw the cold glint in her eyes. "Cleverness isn't a substitute for skill, Mr. Briggs—I never bluff when it comes to a loaded gun." A muscle in Briggs's cheek pulsed.

Gripping the table edge with his left hand, Briggs set the deck of cards in the center of the table. His right hand slid to join his left. She saw no fear or uncertainty in his dark eyes, only anger. Nothing irritated Sam more than a man too stupid to feel fear. She didn't blink once as she waited him out.

Briggs, however, blinked twice before leaping to his feet and using both hands to ram the marble-topped table into her rib cage. With the table edge positioned beneath her left breast, he angled the slab's weight, trapping her against the chair back until the chair's balance succumbed to gravity and went flying out from under her, slamming her head, shoulders, and back forcefully to the floor. The overturned table followed, effectively pinning her in place, its weight concerted to the section resting on her rib cage.

The table top shielded Briggs from Sam's view. Though she couldn't see him, she was certain Briggs was either stepping in to administer more injury or reaching for his Colt to fire its cartridges into her body. And she couldn't do a damn thing about it. Her bullets couldn't penetrate marble.

Her lungs, constricted from the crushing weight, could barely take in air. She almost welcomed a bullet. It would be an easier way to die than suffering slow suffocation.

Sam heard a soft click—followed by another. Then Deacon was ordering Briggs to freeze.

Storey's voice commanded, "Unbuckle your gun belt and lower it to the floor real gentle like, Briggs. I get skittish when I'm holding a gun, and you wouldn't like what happens should my finger jerk this trigger."

In the ensuing silence, Sam heard Briggs drop his rig as instructed, followed by boot soles slapping the floor. When the footsteps halted, she recognized the sheriff's voice.

"Put your guns away gentlemen. Deputy Springer and I will take over from here."

Though she wouldn't like to admit it, Sam was relieved Sheriff Cooley took control of the situation. When his head popped around the edge of the table, he released a hiss between his teeth and passed his hand over his eyes as if he couldn't believe what he was seeing. Then, as quickly as he'd appeared, he was gone. A moment later, he barked an order. "Sam's turning blue. I suggest you gents get that table off her."

Sam might have appreciated the amusement in Rem's voice if her ribs weren't crushing her lungs. As it was, her condition was too damn close to matching his description.

When Deacon appeared at her side, she rolled her head in his direction. On her right, she felt Storey gently pry her derringer from her hand. Her gaze stayed on Deacon's face. "The table—please, I can't breathe."

His mouth set in a grim line, Deacon nodded curtly. Eyes locked with two customers standing nearby, he pointed to the other side of the table. "On the count of three, you men lift the pedestal while Storey and I lift the top." Gesturing to a spot above Sam's head, he added, "We'll set it down there. Everyone understand?"

The men must've nodded their heads because the next thing Sam heard was Deacon counting.

When she was free of the weight, Alexa knelt by her side. Taking shallow sips of air, Sam concentrated on keeping her voice calm. "Alexa, please trust me. There's no reason for me to stay on the floor, and you don't need to send for Morgan or Doc Baxter. I'm fine." Managing a grin, she gestured toward the table. "Look, even the table's not damaged." A smattering of weak laughter from onlookers broke out.

Despite her joke, the worried and disapproving expressions on Alexa and Storey's faces didn't alter. Deacon's mouth was set in a hard line as he boldly moved his hands over her rib cage and the back of her head. Not allowing herself to react to his touch or her pain, Sam ended his probing by taking hold of one of his arms, intending to pull herself up. To her surprise, he gripped her wrists and moved her hands to his shoulders.

After Deacon eased an arm under Sammy's shoulders and another under her knees, he lifted her. When he put her down, he tipped her feet to the floor and held her braced against him until he felt sure she could stand on her own.

Though Sam's lungs cried for air, she resisted taking a deep breath, convinced she'd trigger pain that would send her back to the floor. Willing herself to stand as if pausing while getting her bearings after being helped from a carriage, she glanced up at Deacon's face, then over his shoulder to see Sheriff Rem Cooley rolling his eyes heavenward as if asking the Almighty for strength. Sam swallowed hard, preparing for a scolding.

"Of course, the table's not damaged," Rem barked. "It's made of marble and iron. When are you going to use the brains the Lord gave you, Sam, and admit you're made of flesh and blood? Daggnabbit, woman—I hope Jackson ain't gonna be gone long." He sucked in a breath before moving closer to wag a finger in her face. "We'll discuss this in my office tomorrow morning." Gesturing to Storey and Deacon, he added, "Make sure you bring your two new friends with you." Then he did an about-face and marched out behind Briggs and his deputy.

Sam turned to Deacon and Storey. "Thank you for your help. No need to worry about the sheriff. I assure you I can handle Rem. Could you meet me there at nine?"

Without waiting for an answer, Sam reached for Alexa's arm. "Come on, Alexa, I need a brandy." Striding to the bar, she concentrated on keeping her back straight and head high. Having left her dignity on the floor, she attributed the ability to act as if nothing happened to the little bit of pride she had left. She'd visit Doc Baxter later when things calmed down.

Chapter 13

"What were you thinking to confront Colby Briggs that way?" Alexa asked. "Are you sure you're all right?"

Standing with a glass of brandy suspended in her hand and her back to Gracelyn Palace's bar, Sam gave Alexa a brusque nod. "I'm fine. There wasn't much damage—mainly my pride and a few shattered glasses." Her mouth turned up in a fleeting smile. "You don't need to worry, Alexa. I won't stir up more trouble tonight. I just want to finish my brandy."

Alexa didn't return Sam's smile. "You're pale, and you've been massaging your temple. Maybe I should send for Doc Baxter."

"I don't need Doc Baxter. I do have a slight headache, but it's because I haven't been sleeping well since Jackson went to Cheyenne." It was a plausible excuse.

Alexa didn't believe a word, except for the headache part. Sam admitting her head ached meant it was painful; otherwise, she'd have denied its existence. But Alexa let it drop. "Angie's taking over for me soon. Maybe you should stay with me and Morgan tonight."

Savoring the last swallow of her brandy, Sam glanced over to the empty staircase, half expecting to see her brother descending. Thankfully, no one had thought to rouse him. Taking advantage of the oversight, she decided it was time to make her excuses. After setting her empty glass on the bar, she gave Alexa a brief hug. "No need to stay with you when I'm just across the landing. You go on up to bed. I need some fresh air. I'll see you in the morning."

Alexa watched her stubborn cousin walk away and disappear through the archway to the hotel lobby. She intended to tell Morgan everything and insist he bully Sam into seeing Doc tomorrow. With Jackson out of town, Morgan was the one person who had a prayer in hell of making Sam listen to reason.

***

Outside, on her way to Doc Baxter's, Sam paused next to the hotel's side door to steady herself. When Alexa had asked about her headache, she'd known she couldn't deny it, so she'd downplayed the severity. Besides, it was a minor annoyance when compared with the pain from her ribs. She was certain a couple were cracked but doubted any were broken.

Dizzy from breathing shallowly, Sam pressed her palms against the wall behind her for support. Experimentally, she forced herself to inhale deeply, only to be rewarded with sharp daggers spearing her side, leaving her weak and trembling.

Deacon had followed Sam outside. The weak light shining from the lantern mounted above the hotel's side door didn't penetrate the shadows in which he'd taken refuge. The fact she hadn't heard or sensed his presence said all he needed to know about the severity of her injuries. She was worse off than he'd suspected. Stepping into the dim light, he approached her.

"Sammy, it's Deacon. I didn't mention it earlier, but I'm a friend of your family. I've known you since you were little, from before your father married Grace. Morgan told me you wouldn't remember me because of the stage wreck.

Would you let me escort you to Doc's office? I can see you're hurting."

Sam turned toward him, surprised to hear his voice. She hadn't known anyone was nearby. Though Deacon and Storey had stood with her against Briggs, she wasn't all that comfortable with accepting his help. Rather than answer, she took a step closer to the side door. That's when her legs turned to jelly. Desperate, her fingertips scrambled to find a hold on the smooth boards lining the wall. Unfortunately, the wall turned out to be a slower, less forceful path to the ground.

Deacon sprang forward, catching her before her backside settled in the dirt. With his arms wrapped low around her waist, he pulled her up so her head rested on his shoulder.

To Sam, Deacon felt like a wall of muscle. He had no trouble repositioning her against him and lifting her in his arms. The pain screaming at her, she pressed her free arm to her side and her mouth to the cloth of his coat to keep from groaning.

"Can you hear me, Sammy?" Deacon asked, believing she was about to pass out. She nodded, but not convincingly.

"Good. I'll take you to my room. I'll send someone to get Doc Baxter and go for Morgan and Alexa. I'm telling you, so you won't take it in your head that I mean you harm and pull your derringer. Do you understand?"

"Yes, but—"

Impatient, Deacon interrupted. "There's always a 'yes, but' with you, Sammy. We'll do things my way." He'd said the words kindly though and with a hint of amusement in his voice. It had never been in her nature to answer with a plain "yes." Even as a little girl, she said "yes, but" because in her mind *everything* was a negotiation. She needed to control things.

"Deacon?" Her voice was soft and hesitant. A memory had flickered, and she needed to tell him about the two voices she'd recalled from the past. One of the voices belonged to her stepfather, Mac. The other voice was Deacon's. "I remembered hearing you tell Mac the only three words I knew were 'no' and 'yes, but.' Then you said when I turned ten, I learned 'hell no.' It wasn't fair you told Mac—not when you were the one who taught me to say that. I was angry."

Deacon's arms involuntarily tightened around Sam. Yeah, she'd been angry. Later, finding him alone by one of the corrals, she'd kicked him in the shin and told him to go to hell. He'd limped for two days afterward. "Morgan said your memory is gone, so how in the devil did you remember that?"

She couldn't explain. When a memory came, it just came. "I don't know. Was it because I loved you?" She was asking if he was someone she loved because he'd been an important person in her past life.

But Deacon didn't understand. Turning her question over in his mind, he thought it odd she should ask—because damned if it weren't the same one he'd been asking himself ten times a day since falling in love with her.

All these years later, he still didn't know the answer.

***

When Morgan let himself in Sam's suite the next morning, Deacon was enjoying the last sip of coffee sent with breakfast from the hotel kitchen. Before he could finish swallowing and offer a greeting, Morgan crossed to the table and jerked him to his feet. Guessing what was on Morgan's mind, Deacon raised his palms signaling he didn't intend to fight.

After grabbing a handful of shirt collar and raising his fist within inches of Deacon's jaw, Morgan thrust his face near Deacon's. "What the hell are you doing in Sam's suite?"

125

Worried the commotion would wake Sammy, Deacon put a finger to his lips. "Be quiet. She's sleeping. Neither of us got much rest last night."

Morgan's fist plowed into Deacon's jaw and sent him staggering back. As Morgan moved in to hit him again, Deacon shoved an ottoman in his path. Then he rolled forward to break Morgan's fall and flip him, effectively pinning him on his back. "Sonofabitch, Morgan, it's not what you think." He could feel Morgan's muscles contracting to buck him off. "Give me a chance to explain, will you?"

The two men glared at each other for several seconds before Deacon took the risk of loosening his hold and lifting some of his weight. He felt a ripple of powerful muscles beneath him as Morgan slowly relaxed. When Morgan nodded, Deacon stood and extended his hand to help him up.

Eyeing Deacon warily, Morgan accepted Deacon's hand. Back on his feet, he flung himself into a chair and folded his arms over his chest. "You need to talk fast, Deacon, because I can't let go of this feeling I should be pounding your head through the floor. I don't care if you are like my brother, I'll cripple you if you touched Sam."

Deacon's eyes darted to the bedroom door before he responded. "Calm down, Morgan. I'm here because Doc Baxter told me to stay with Sammy last night and because I let her talk me into promising not to go for you and Alexa."

Morgan uncrossed his arms. "Why was Doc Baxter here?"

"Doc said her ribs are bruised." Sweeping his fingers horizontally beneath the slab of his left pectoral muscle, he added, "These two ribs are cracked. She's in a lot of pain, especially when she tries to take a normal breath."

Morgan let out an exasperated huff. "Alexa told me about Colby Briggs cheating and overturning the table on her. When she mentioned you and Storey backed Sam, I thought it couldn't have been as bad as Alexa said, so I decided to wait until this morning to talk to her."

"Well, Alexa was right. She put everybody off, pretending she wasn't hurt. She'd intended to go to Doc Baxter's on her own but ran out of steam outside in the alley by the hotel's side entrance. Knowing Sammy, I wasn't convinced she'd been truthful, so I kept my eye on her. When I saw she was in trouble, I stepped in. She didn't like it much."

When Deacon paused, he saw Morgan was studying him closely, making no effort to pretend he was doing otherwise. Shrugging off his disappointment, Deacon continued his explanation. "I knew she'd have a fit if I took her through Gracelyn Palace, so I told her I'd let her rest in my room while I went for you. I figured once you were with her, I could go for Doc Baxter. Of course, she started to argue with me. I told her I wouldn't listen to any of her 'yes, but' arguments, but, damn me, if I didn't give in to her. She swore the dizziness had passed and that she could walk if I helped her. She was struggling so hard to make me put her down, I was afraid she'd hurt herself more if I didn't give in."

Morgan derisively waved a hand in the air. "Sam rarely does what's good for her."

Deacon didn't disagree. "She insisted we go to Jackson's suite. Then she fished a key from behind a painting in the hall and let us in. Damn if there isn't a door hidden in the bedroom behind a full-length mirror that opens into her bedroom here."

Deacon suspected that Morgan knew about the secret doorway. Sam not marrying until recently would explain why the door existed. He guessed they probably used it now as a convenient route for leaving and returning to Gracelyn Palace unnoticed.

"When Doc arrived, he wouldn't let her spin any stories. She fessed up about her ribs right away. When he questioned her about the bump on the back of her head, she admitted she had a headache. But she blamed it and her dizziness on not sleeping or eating well since before Jackson left on business. Doc was stern with her and insisted she take laudanum. She didn't argue."

"Doc does have a way with her," Morgan acknowledged. "She trusts him."

Though Morgan's response was unexpected, Deacon accepted it. "I would have left, but she mumbled something to Doc about someone watching her. She didn't mean for me to hear." Deacon passed his hand wearily over his eyes. "She sounded afraid, so Doc Baxter shoved me over to where Sammy could see me and told her I would stay with her. He glared at me while saying it, looking as if he'd hog-tie me if I refused. Of course, I didn't argue."

Morgan's eyes had narrowed again and were searching Deacon's face. Deacon waited, giving his adopted brother time to assess his explanation. When he sensed Morgan's acceptance, he continued, "While Sam slept, Doc said he'd order breakfast and have it sent up early because Sam would wake by then and need food. Then he left orders to insist she eat a slice of toasted bread and half the oatmeal before giving her the laudanum he measured for her."

Deacon watched Morgan's face as he added, "I mentioned yesterday I met Doc Baxter, so I knew you trusted him. I swear I did exactly as Doc said and nothing more."

Morgan refused to give Deacon too much credit for his good behavior because he understood the depth of Deacon's feelings for Sam. Nevertheless, in this circumstance, he'd jumped to a wrong conclusion. "I'm sorry I slugged you. Thanks for seeing to Sam."

Rubbing his jaw, Deacon replied dryly, "In your place, I would've done the same, so thank you for stopping when you did." Recalling more instructions from Doc, Deacon said, "Doc Baxter said to remind you he's catching the morning train—something about visiting family in Nebraska. The mayor's brother-in-law is the physician filling in while he's away. Doc said to warn you Sammy won't like him, so think twice about calling him to attend her."

"I forgot about Doc's trip. Alexa isn't comfortable with the substitute doctor either. Let's hope we don't need him in Roy Baxter's absence."

"The sheriff ordered Sammy to his office this morning and told her to bring me and Storey with her. Dad and I will go, but I don't think Sam is up to it. Will the sheriff understand?"

"Don't worry about Rem Cooley, Deacon. He's a reasonable man. By now, he will have questioned witnesses. He knows if Briggs hadn't been cheating, Sam wouldn't have forced the issue. He's upset because she didn't wait for him to handle things. And his real problem will be what to do with Briggs since he won't be able to prove he cheated. He worries Sam's temper will get her into a situation where she'll get hurt worse than this. He prides himself on running a peaceful town. On the other hand, he can't keep someone in jail with no proof."

Morgan plowed a hand through his hair and let out an exasperated sigh. "Damn, I should have been keeping a closer watch on her. But since she married Jackson, she's been less inclined to get into trouble."

"She didn't make the trouble," Deacon responded. "She sensed things heating between Briggs and Dad and initially approached to keep it from boiling over. Briggs liked her looks. And when he learned who she was, he decided to take things to another level."

"Understandable," Morgan conceded, looking unconvinced. "Did she say anything more about being watched after Doc left?"

"Since she was more comfortable on the chaise longue, I slept on the bed so I'd be close should she need something. Despite the laudanum Doc gave her, she did wake up a couple of times, confused and afraid. Once she called for you, begging you to make the watcher go away. But mostly she asked for Jackson. I calmed her by saying you and Jackson sent me to keep her safe and wanted her to rest easy so she'd mend."

"Thank you for that. Did she say anything else?"

"No. She woke early, like Doc said she would, and ate half her breakfast. When I gave her the laudanum, she apologized for being a bother and thanked me for helping her." Deacon grinned then, probably because he knew Morgan would appreciate the humor in his next statement. "She didn't utter even one 'but' before she fell back to sleep."

Chapter 14

Relieved to relinquish Sammy's care to Morgan, Deacon released a measured breath as he quietly eased the suite door closed. Caring for her had awakened too many memories—feelings—he didn't care to examine. It was ironic Sam would probably trade her fortune to unearth her buried memories while he was desperate to expunge his.

At the end of the hall, squatting on his haunches in the dim shadows cast by the wide and ornately carved landing railing, Peter Jack Nolan watched Deacon with more than a bit of wariness. What with living in town and being in and out of the restaurant all the time, he thought he knew most everyone. But he didn't know this man. A stranger wearing a gun, leaving Missus Sam's room at this time of morning, worried him.

Preoccupied with thoughts of Sam and his impending visit to the sheriff's office, Deacon didn't notice the boy. As he neared the staircase, he stopped to run his hand along his jaw. Though he'd shaved before visiting the gambling salon the night before, the rasp dragging against his fingers told him he needed another. And the deep wrinkles in his jacket and the wilted cling of his shirt confirmed he must look as rumpled and disheveled as he felt. Worse, he realized there wasn't time to do anything about his appearance if he intended to be punctual, not that he believed it would matter to a man like Rem Cooley. If Deacon had read the lawman's character correctly, being well groomed wouldn't sway Rem's opinion—or add any credibility to his rendition of what happened between Sam and Colby Briggs.

As Deacon took another few seconds to adjust his cuffs and smooth his jacket, his eyes caught a furtive movement at the far end of the landing. Instinctively, his hand dropped to his Colt but relaxed when he recognized the form hiding in the shadows was that of a child.

Shifting his shoulders to release the tension bunched there from sensing danger, Deacon nodded a silent greeting in the child's direction. But something in the stiff line of the pint-size spy spurred him to take a better look. The child was a young boy. His dark hair and eyes framed a face communicating his displeasure at being discovered.

Amused and curious, Deacon repressed an impulse to smile at the boy. Keeping his face impassive as his gaze met and held the boy's, he wondered why the kid was hiding. Maybe it was as simple as not wanting his mother to find him so he wouldn't have to do chores.

After a few seconds of silent staring, Deacon shrugged, deciding it wasn't his responsibility to question the boy's presence or interfere with his business. But as he was about to turn away, his conscience prodded him. The boy was younger than he'd first estimated—maybe five or six—too young to be hanging about alone in a gambling salon, even one as respectable as Gracelyn Palace. Perturbed by feeling a duty to ensure the boy didn't need help, he called out a friendly greeting. "Hello, son. You blend so well with the wall I almost didn't see you. Are you waiting for someone?"

Peter Jack hadn't meant for the man to see him, but now that he had, he wouldn't show fear. Stalling while deciding how to answer the man's question, he rose from his crouch and took a couple of cautious steps forward. Sweeping his eyes up the length of the stranger, he was impressed his height was almost equal to Mister Jackson's. He was also respectful of the gun belt resting comfortably on the stranger's thigh. It was tied down—like a gunman would wear it. Mister Jackson and Missus Sam wore their guns like that, too.

Deacon waited while allowing the boy, who had moved closer, to look his fill. Because his silence continued, Deacon tried another approach. "Do you need help, Son?"

Peter Jack's head swiveled from side to side. "No, sir. I work here."

Deacon was more puzzled than before. The boy acted as if his answer explained his presence, but it made no sense to Deacon. "You mean you work here at Gracelyn Palace?"

"No, sir. I work at the hotel with my mama. She cooks breakfast and makes the cakes and pies for the hotel dining room." The pride in the boy's tone was unmistakable.

"I see. So, it was your mama who prepared my breakfast this morning. Her pancakes are the best I ever ate."

Peter Jack's chest puffed out and his wary scowl was quickly replaced with a wide grin that lit up his face. He was a handsome boy. The compliment must've reassured him because he fearlessly moved a few steps closer while nodding toward Sam's door. Then his words tumbled out in a rush. "Missus Sam wishes she could cook even half as good as my mama. But I don't guess it matters because she's awful purty and can draw a gun as fast as lightning strikes." After gulping air, he concluded with, "My mama can shoot, too, but she don't hit much of what she points at. Missus Sam can hit anything."

Deacon swallowed the laughter rising in his throat. As boys, he and Morgan had teased Sammy about her bad cooking because it was the one insult she couldn't refute. She was a natural at most everything she did and took pride in besting them whenever she was given the chance, especially when it came to showing off her shooting and riding. Though Deacon and Morgan's abilities were a close second to Sam's—she never let them show her up. So, when retaliating, they used her pathetic cooking ability as their favorite weapon.

Leaning down, Deacon replied, "Sam is about the best marksman God ever put on this earth, but she and a stove have never been comfortable in the same room—for some reason, they just naturally don't seem to understand each other."

His eyes sparkling with mirth, Peter Jack clamped a hand over his mouth to stifle his giggles. Then as if expecting Sam to step into the hallway and catch them gossiping, he moved closer to Deacon. "Mister Jackson says she can't even boil water unless it's over a campfire."

Deacon didn't swallow his laugh this time. And he would've voiced his appreciation of Jackson's comment if suddenly the mischievous sparkle in the boy's eyes hadn't evaporated. When he lifted his face to Deacon's, genuine concern was furrowing his forehead. "You won't say anything to Missus Sam about it, will you? It'd hurt her feelings real bad—and I'd feel awful if she was to cry or somethin'."

The boy looked so distressed at the thought of hurting Sam's feelings that Deacon rushed to reassure him. "I give my word. This will be between us." As an afterthought, he added, "Though I sympathize with her husband regarding her lack of culinary skills."

The boy cocked his head to the side and looked at Deacon from beneath thick, dark lashes. "What's culin—whatever it was you said—got to do with Missus Sam's cookin'?" His face wore a scrunched frown of pure puzzlement.

"Culinary skills—it's a fancy way of saying cooking," Deacon explained.

"Seems like you should've said that the first time, mister."

Deacon chuckled. "You make a good point. I apologize."

"No need for that. I was just pointin' it out."

The boy was so engaging that Deacon offered his hand. "By the way, my name's Deacon. What's yours?"

"I'm Peter Jack Nolan." Ignoring Deacon's hand, Peter Jack put his hands on his hips, puffed out his chest, and announced, "I look after Missus Sam when Mister Jackson ain't here."

Deacon nodded. "I guess that explains why you're camped in this hall. I'm pleased to know she's under your protection." So, the little warrior was guarding Sammy. Damn, if she didn't inspire admiration in almost every male she met, regardless of age.

Deacon's comment reminded Peter Jack of his self-appointed duties. It wouldn't be right to overlook the fact this man had called on Missus Sam very early when Mister Jackson was away. "I seen you leavin' Missus Sam's. I don't think it right you should be bothering her."

Although Deacon respected the boy's courage in speaking up to an adult, the youngster's rebuke rankled. Putting his irritation aside, he kept his tone friendly. "Well, Peter, Sam's an old friend—" That was all Deacon could get out before the boy interrupted.

"My name is Peter *Jack*—and my mama says it's not proper for a gentleman to call on a lady this early in the mornin'." The young rapscallion spoke as though he had the size and strength to do something about it.

Patiently, Deacon offered enough of an explanation to satisfy a child's simple understanding of right and wrong.

He chose his words carefully. "Your mama has the right of it, *Peter Jack*. Under normal circumstances, I wouldn't visit a lady at this time of day, but you see, the lady isn't feeling well and asked me to sit with her until her brother arrived."

***

Listening from the foot of the stairs, Jessa Nolan smiled. Deacon Storey's kind answers to her fierce little boy tugged at her heartstrings. The man had a voice that inspired trust and confidence. And she fancied she could hear a smile in it, which made her wonder if he were as quick to laugh as his father. She admired a man who could recognize the humor in things.

From her vantage point, Jessa noticed Deacon's fine clothes were rumpled, which reminded her the main topic of conversation in the hotel dining room had been about Sam and the cardsharp. Jessa had already known Storey Deale's son was caring for Sam because Doc Baxter left a note for her in the kitchen explaining and asking that she send up breakfast.

Jessa knew other things, too. In a small town, the exchange of gossip was as popular as discussing the weather; consequently, the whispers about Deacon had started to circulate before he'd even signed the hotel register. And from Storey Deale's regular visits to the hotel kitchen, Jessa had learned his son was a professional gambler—same as Storey.

Before meeting Storey, Jessa didn't know itinerant gamblers could be ethical and successful. She'd believed there were but two types of gamers. The less offensive were down-on-their-luck drunks. The others were unscrupulous cheats who didn't think twice about their victims or crossing to the wrong side of the law. From the friendship Jessa had formed with Storey, she'd discovered the rare third type—men who followed their conscience, competed ethically, and enjoyed exercising charm and intelligence to make a comfortable living. Because Jessa already felt an uncommon fondness for Storey, it was easy to see those same qualities in Deacon.

Assessing Deacon's looks, Jessa thought his broad shoulders set well on his lean frame. And though the planes of his face were sharper than his father's, they were pleasing—no, striking was a better word. From this distance, she couldn't tell the exact color of his hair and eyes. As she started up the stairs, she speculated about what Jackson would say when he heard Deacon spent the night alone with Sam. Though Deacon was supposedly the equivalent of Sam's brother, Jessa would bet her last dollar Jackson would have a problem with it.

Midway up the stairs, Jessa confirmed the gambler's thick hair was a rich walnut brown, his eyes vibrant green. She'd never seen a real emerald, but she imagined its sparkle couldn't be half as arresting as Deacon's gaze. Her body gave a thrum of appreciation that made her wonder what it would be like to lay with him. Taking the next steps with little notice, she told herself entertaining such a thought wasn't wicked. Most females, regardless of marital status, would have similar thoughts were they to cast eyes on such a fine male specimen. After all, the man could probably tempt a reverend mother.

Her mind paying no heed to her place on the stairs, Jessa's foot sought the next step, only to discover, too late, that there was no next tread. A startled gasp accompanied her sudden pitch forward.

"Mama!" Peter Jack cried, reaching for her.

Deacon caught Jessa's elbow and wrapped an arm around her waist, easily able to rescue one hundred and thirty pounds of soft woman from colliding with the landing and pull her to his chest. Her hands, trembling, clutched the bunched muscles of his biceps.

Arms feeling like roped steel surrounded Jessa—her pulse raced, not so much from the fright of falling but more from the sensual response of her body crushed against the hard ridges of masculine power supporting her. Seconds passed. Heat flared low in her abdomen. She should step back and thank him. Instead, she clung tight and inhaled the bourbon and cigar smoke clinging to his clothes.

Deacon wasn't unaware of what she was feeling. With her breasts molded to his chest, belly pressed to his hips, and scent stirring his senses—a blend of maple syrup and spiced cinnamon—he repressed a sudden urge to drag his tongue along the exposed column of her neck to test if her skin tasted as delicious as her fragrance. But weak male that he was, he didn't resist the impulse to pull her closer, position his lips near the delicate curve of her ear, and murmur, "Good morning." His tone was seductive, reminiscent of a lover awakened from a sensual dream to find his arms filled with the woman of whom he'd been dreaming.

"Good—m-morning," Jessa stuttered, perturbed to feel the hot flush of embarrassment climb from her chest to her cheeks. His voice and the morning stubble on his chin grazing the tender skin beneath her earlobe sent a warm shivery sensation straight to her core. From somewhere, she dredged the courage to look up at him. "I mean, excuse me, I thought there was—a-another step," she said in a small voice. A raised eyebrow and knowing smile told her he was enjoying his effect on her.

Keeping her close, Deacon took a moment to admire a few dark, curling tendrils escaped from the braided coronet framing a face with high, delicate cheekbones and pert nose. Though her son's face was sprinkled with freckles, hers was flawless. The pink stain on her cheeks enhanced her beauty. And, Lord, he was all but drowning in the deep pools of her gray eyes.

Jessa was all too aware she needed to regain her composure. She couldn't allow a surge of lust for a man—even one as compelling as Deacon Storey—to jeopardize her hard-won respectability. Summoning the remnants of her self-discipline, she moved her hands from Deacon's arms to his chest and pushed gently.

His embrace tightened rather than loosened. It made her breathless. Uncertain what to do, she looked away and down, only to be further discomposed by the curious wonder on her son's face, his eyes wide, darting between her and Deacon.

Deacon's eyes followed the woman's gaze. Registering her son's interest, he let her go, though his fingertips traced her rib cage to the swell of her hips as he did it. Diverting attention from what had flared between them, he teased, "Not much experience climbing stairs, I take it?"

Jessa's eyes flew back to his face. In a hundred years, she wouldn't have expected him to say that. The upward curves at the corners of his mouth definitively said he was jesting. She couldn't help smiling in response.

Quick to give as good as she got, she replied, "Odd, before this, I would've said stairs were no more problem than whipping up a batch of pancakes." Pausing a fraction of a second, her smile relaxed and she added, "I was listening to you and Peter Jack. I'm flattered you enjoyed the breakfast Doc Baxter ordered for you and Sam."

Unfortunately, his mind still lingering on certain parts of her anatomy and pleasure, Deacon mumbled, "I very much enjoyed your, ah—pancakes—and I'm certain your pastries would be just as delectable." His statement, at surface level, was merely a polite response, meant to compliment. However, the low huskiness of his voice betrayed another meaning—a most improper one.

Jessa commanded her expression to show no evidence she recognized sexual innuendo when she heard it. With her conscious control concentrated on mastering facial muscles, the remainder of her body, unsupervised, responded in a natural feminine manner to sensual provocation. Leaning away, her bust lifted, and she glided her palms over the curve of her hips and around to her backside.

Deacon's eyes traced the intriguing path her palms caressed—traveling down, over, and around lovely, fascinating, tempting places—as if she'd peeked into his head and couldn't resist demonstrating what he'd pictured. Desire made him hard in an instant.

Desperate to redirect blood flow, he clapped a hand on Peter Jack's shoulder and drew him forward. "Y-Your son and I were just getting acquainted." He paused to take a breath. "I'm Deacon Storey. My father and I are visiting Sam and Morgan. We grew up together—I-I mean, I did—n-not my father, of course."

Assuming embarrassment was the reason for his flustered speech, Jessa offered a smile and friendly nod. "It's a pleasure meeting you, Mr. Storey. I'm Jessa Nolan. As you know, this is my son, Peter Jack. Your father visits my kitchen frequently, claiming he can't resist the temptation of cinnamon rolls."

"Or the company of a beautiful woman," Deacon tacked on. "Trust my father to have introduced himself to the best cook and prettiest woman in town." *From where had that come?* Even to his ears, the comment sounded half resentful.

Jessa laughed. "I refuse to believe you could resent such a charming parent."

"Please, it's Deacon, and may I call you, Jessa?" Taking her consent for granted, he plowed on. "He's a wonderful father, Jessa. But his considerable charm makes it difficult to garner attention for myself."

Jessa was confident charm wouldn't have a prayer of winning even a minor skirmish, let alone a woman's affections, were it to do battle with Deacon Storey's roguish smile and quick wit. He was not only compelling but dangerous. He possessed the kind of danger that made thirty-year-old mothers stumble on stairs and think wicked thoughts about pleasure. Though shaken by her thoughts, she murmured, "Oh, I imagine you garner more than your fair share."

Deacon countered, "And I'm sure you're admired for more than cooking." Several other analogies came to mind, but he managed not to voice them. *Where were his manners?* He knew better than to say things like that to a lady—especially in front of her son.

Jessa knew she should discourage him and end this—whatever *this* was. After all, he was just visiting. And the gossips said he was in love with Sam. When Jackson returned from Cheyenne, he'd put a quick end to any hopes Deacon fostered for winning Sam. And if Jackson let him live, Deacon would leave town—pronto. She wasn't interested in being second choice. She firmly dismissed her body's response to him, labeling it a natural reaction—perfectly normal for a woman who hadn't experienced sex since conceiving her son.

Sighing, she scolded herself to quit dwelling on pleasure when she had a kitchen to put in order and a boy to care for. Taking Peter Jack's hand, she made their excuses, suddenly eager to escape the speculation in Deacon Storey's appraising eyes. She was certain she'd benefit from some cool, fresh air.

Remaining on the landing, Deacon watched mother and child descend the stairs and disappear through the arch into the hotel. Had he been privy to Jessa's thoughts, he would've been surprised they were similar to his—though fresh air wouldn't do much to reverse the need she'd roused in him. Hell, in his present state, it would take an icy plunge into a pond to ease the ache in his groin.

Yet, something more than sexual desire had passed between them.

Holding Jessa in his arms had awakened something— something that made him think about protecting and caring for a woman—something that felt like the unfurling of a blossom's first petal. Was the binding protecting his heart from the pain of Sammy not being able to return his love loosening?

Was that the—*something*—he was feeling?

Deacon navigated the staircase as if speed could outrun his unsettling thoughts. But they followed relentlessly. By the time he reached the bottom step, he'd conceded those thoughts were *something* he needed to think more about.

Chapter 15

Sheriff Rem Cooley ran his hand around the iron ring holding the keys to the Prosperity jailhouse's three cells while listening to Storey and Deacon explain how the altercation with Briggs started. Storey sat on a straight-backed chair across from the sheriff's desk, while Deacon studied the Wanted posters on the wall to Rem's right and twice offered brief clarifications to supplement his father's recitation of events.

Finally, satisfied with their answers, Rem placed the key ring on his desk. "I heard the same facts from other witnesses. Sam was lucky you backed her. She's as capable as they come but gets reckless when her temper overcomes her good sense." Then, directing his gaze to Storey, he asked, "Does Sam know you're her godfather?"

Storey shook his head. "I haven't told her." Turning to Deacon, he asked, "Did you mention it?"

"No. I said enough to convince her to accept my help. She mostly slept because of the laudanum Doc Baxter prescribed so there wasn't an opportunity to explain anything. When she woke this morning, she choked down a few bites of breakfast. I left Morgan with her."

"Is there anything else you want to know, Sheriff?" Storey asked, rising to his feet.

"When's Jackson Knight coming home from Cheyenne?"

"Morgan said three days," Deacon replied.

Rem Cooley scratched his jaw before speaking. "Scant time to decide about Briggs but too much to keep an eye on Sam." A resigned grunt and sag of his shoulders spoke volumes about the long-suffering responsibilities of a lawman. "She's taken ten years off my life. Thankfully, she's less trouble when Jackson's home." Pausing to direct a stern eye at Deacon, Rem added, "Jackson takes up most of her attention, and vice versa, if you catch my meaning."

Annoyed, Deacon ignored the implied warning. He didn't need to be reminded Sammy belonged to another man.

"What *are* you going to do about Briggs?" Storey asked, endeavoring to break the tension mounting between the sheriff and his son.

Rem shrugged. "I don't know yet, gents." He forgot whatever else he planned to say when the office door banged into the wall, heralding the arrival of Peter Jack, who barely managed to skid to a stop before colliding with Rem's knees.

Deacon winked at the boy. Then, as if sensing her closeness, he looked up to lock eyes with Jessa, who stood in the open doorway cradling a cloth-covered basket.

"Please excuse us for bursting in, Sheriff," Jessa said, dropping her eyes from Deacon to frown at her son. "Peter Jack and I are on our way to the mercantile, so we decided to drop off the prisoner's lunch, although it's a little early. We didn't mean to interrupt. Isn't that right, Peter Jack?"

Taking his cue from his mama, Peter Jack did his best to look apologetic. "Sorry, for bangin' your door, Sheriff. The handle kinda got away from me."

Rem reached out to ruffle Peter Jack's hair. "I reckon I'll forgive you if you make restitution by closin' what you opened."

Peter Jack tipped his head to the side. "I understand about closin' the door, but what's the *rest-too-son* part mean? Do you expect me to take a nap or somethin'?"

Rem blinked. "Why no, son. I said *restitution*, meaning you can make up for banging my door by setting things back to the way they were."

"Well, the door was closed," Peter Jack said, puzzling it out. "Then I opened it—so the way to set it back would be to close it—right?"

"Yup."

"Why didn't you just say so 'stead of confusin' a fella?"

"I guess I wasn't thinkin' about it that way, son. Now then, let me see if I can do a better job making introductions." Gesturing to include Jessa, Rem's head nodded toward Storey and Deacon. "This is Mrs. Nolan and her son, Peter Jack. Mrs. Nolan is breakfast and pastry cook over at the hotel, and Peter Jack is my deputy in charge of guarding Centennial signs and Wanted posters."

Jessa interrupted. "We've already met, Sheriff." Turning eyes brimming with mischief on Storey, she remarked, "So, this is where you went after raiding my kitchen for cinnamon rolls. If I'd known you were planning to visit the sheriff, I'd have asked you to deliver this hamper."

Holding back a smile, Storey pretended interest in the basket. "Good thing you didn't trust me with it, Jessa. As wonderful as its contents smell, I'm afraid I would've given in to temptation and it would've arrived empty. No doubt, the sheriff would've arrested me for thievery."

"More like gluttony," Rem muttered.

"Or outrageous flirtation," Deacon grumbled.

Jessa glared at Deacon. "Are you aware you sound envious of your father? I thought we agreed earlier that you needn't be concerned about your ability to capture a lady's attention."

The sheriff and Storey exchanged glances.

"Perhaps I'm envious," Deacon retorted, oblivious of their audience.

"Well, what do you expect me to do about it?" Jessa shot back.

Kiss me. "Nothing. Absolutely nothing," was what Deacon made himself reply.

"Then it seems we agree because that's exactly what I intend to do." But intent was far different from want—and what Jessa wanted was to kiss him. And, despite his pretend scowl, she saw he could barely keep the corners of his mouth turned down. Good thing. She knew from experience what his smile did to her.

In the silence that fell, Peter Jack tugged on the crease of Rem's pant leg. "Are you keepin' the cardsharp in jail because he has to see the judge or so Mister Jackson don't shoot him for hurtin' Missus Sam?"

Arms folded across his chest, Rem could hardly drag his eyes from Jessa and Deacon, let alone formulate an answer for Peter Jack. The youngster, accustomed to grownups ignoring his questions, plunged on, confidently offering his opinion before asking another question. "If the judge lets him go, I don't put much truck in his bein' able to leave town in one piece. Can I look at the sharpie, Sheriff?"

Without waiting for Rem's permission, Peter Jack scrambled through the open cell block door separating the jailhouse's office from the cages. Jessa sprang after him, grabbing for his arm but missed. Lifting her skirts to step into the corridor running the length of the cells, her eyes naturally followed Peter Jack's gaze. Sickness washed up into her throat, but she contained it.

The prisoner resembled the devil he served. Bone-chilling evil glared at Jessa from familiar black eyes. She saw the features masked by the pencil mustache, goatee, and black hair, thick and oiled, slickly smoothed away from his forehead. The disguise was effective, but she was the one person who'd see through it—despite the fact he was supposed to be dead. *Oh, God, he looked as if Satan had puffed air into his chest to resurrect him.* Her mind flashed an image of a man's body lying broken and unrecognizable, except for the familiar gold wedding band on his finger.

Her husband was dead—*only he wasn't*. Whose body had he used to fool everyone? Somehow, he'd escaped death—because he was sitting right there in that cell looking every bit as cruel as he'd always been.

When his eyes moved to Peter Jack, Jessa threw herself in front of her son—shielding him from the man she'd believed, until this moment, was burning in hell. *Where had he gotten the idea to call himself Colby Briggs?* Slowly backing away, she pulled Peter Jack after her.

The shock on Jessa's face gave "Briggs" a great deal of pleasure, although her darting in front of the kid signified she was more afraid for the boy than for herself. He'd heard talk, but now seeing the boy, he understood why the gossips believed the brat was Knight's son. The boy, Jessa, and Knight's wife could all be formidable weapons if he used them to his advantage. After all, once Knight discovered he was alive, it would be kill or be killed.

Positioned to see the corridor running the length of the cells, Deacon witnessed Jessa's shock and defensive behavior. *Does she know Colby Briggs?* Disappointment swept through him. He didn't want her or Peter Jack to have any link to Briggs. Though not her fault, she already had a past. But he couldn't discount what he was seeing, and it signified a dangerous connection to Briggs.

Jessa willed the tentacles of fear tightening her chest to loosen so she could breathe and speak normally. She took hold of Peter Jack's hand and hauled him back in front of the sheriff before thrusting the prisoner's lunch into Rem's hands. "We must be going, Sheriff. Give Eddie the basket when he brings supper." Despite her effort to appear calm, she heard the waver in her voice. Capturing Peter Jack's hand again, she steered him to the office door.

Deacon was already there, the door open, waiting for her. She gave him a perfunctory nod and in an over-bright voice managed, "Good day, gentlemen." She tried to rush her steps once her feet were on the boardwalk.

Not bothering with words of farewell or pulling the door shut behind him, Deacon followed Jessa.

While Storey's speculative gaze remained on his son, Rem turned to Storey. "For a man who makes his living playing cards, I'd say your son forgot himself and flashed his hand."

Nodding in thoughtful agreement, Storey recalled his first passion-filled night with Deacon's mother. "When it comes to falling in love, Sheriff, the men in my family don't believe in gambling. Playing cards is for winning money— not a woman—at least not the one you love."

***

After a few long strides along the boardwalk, Deacon caught up to Jessa. Peter Jack had skipped several paces ahead. "May I escort you? I need to stretch my legs, and I could carry your packages."

Jessa didn't bother turning her head. Her eyes followed Peter Jack. "No, thank you. Your presence will start tongues wagging and cause nothing but trouble."

"Then will you meet me later and explain what happened in the jailhouse?"

"Nothing happened, and even if it did, why would I tell someone I barely know?"

"Because I can help you if you let me. You don't need to be afraid of me."

"Maybe I do and maybe I don't, but one thing *you* can wager on, Mr. Storey. I care about my son too much to gamble on you." The tremor was back in her voice.

"If not me, then who would you ask for help if you needed it, Jessa?" Deacon's voice was firm but not forceful.

"Jack—" she began before biting back the rest of the name. *Jackson would help—if he were here.* But it could be dangerous for him—for Sam, too. Oh God! Sam had already been hurt. Had Colter Brogan, or Briggs as her husband called himself now, come to Prosperity looking for her or Jackson and found Sam? Jessa drew a ragged breath to calm her nerves.

Jackson. Deacon silently completed the name that Jessa almost let slip. Interesting that her first instinct was to seek help from Sammy's husband. Were the rumors true? Was Jackson Peter Jack's father?

Jessa felt light-headed, stunned. For years, she'd believed she and Peter Jack were safe. A sudden suspicion gripped her, bringing her to a full stop in the middle of the boardwalk. "Am I part of the business that brought you to Prosperity, Mr. Storey? Are you a boun—I mean, d-did someone hire you to find me?"

"Find you?" Deacon questioned, feigning bafflement despite recognizing she'd nearly said bounty hunter, which wasn't far from what he was, depending on how one looked at it. "You know my relationship with Morgan and Sam, and I haven't seen my father for nearly a year. Why would I come here looking for you?"

Although Jessa was a wanted fugitive, Deacon was almost certain she'd been framed, just as her father had been. He wondered if before dying, her vengeful husband had buried her in other misconduct Deacon's investigation hadn't discovered yet. Pushing the thought aside, he attempted to reassure her. "Come on, Jessa, a woman like you could hardly be a criminal, unless it's a crime to break men's hearts. Though you're projecting a rather mysterious persona, I doubt it's because of an unsavory past." Even as he spoke, he knew she heard his words for what they were— a lame attempt to calm her fears.

He tried again. "Jessa, if before Jackson returns, or at any time you feel the need, please come to me or my father. Ask Morgan about us if you're unsure. He'll tell you we can be trusted. I haven't met Jackson, but I grew up with Morgan, and from what he's told me, I'd wager Jackson would advise you to consign your care to me and Dad in his absence."

The sag of Jessa's shoulders and the uncertainty in her eyes told him she was at least considering his offer. He'd press her no further—at least not now.

"Thank you, Mr. Storey."

"It's Deacon," he reminded her gently. "I know you have doubts, but when you're ready to trust me, I'll be here." He wanted to pull her into his arms, hold her, protect her, and make her fears vanish. But he knew those thoughts sprang from feelings rather than practicality. The mere fact he'd been escorting her and they'd stopped in plain view of everyone on Main Street to conduct this conversation, not to mention the dialog they'd had in front of the sheriff and his father, guaranteed Jessa would be whispered about over shop counters and in parlors.

Touching two fingers politely to his hat brim, Deacon turned from Jessa to return to the hotel. He didn't like seeing her living in fear. He was certain the woman he'd held in his arms earlier that morning was no criminal. He needed to learn who Colby Briggs was to Jessa and why she was afraid of him, as well as find evidence to lift the trumped-up robbery and murder charges her dead husband had fabricated to control her.

Back in his room, Deacon dug out his satchel of drawing materials. One of the talents that made him a good gambler was his ability to read faces and mannerisms. He also had the ability to draw those faces. His sketches had helped solve several investigations over the years he'd worked for Pinkerton.

Before leaving to collect his father for their supper engagement with Morgan and Alexa, Deacon completed three sketches of Briggs. Later tonight, he'd trace copies to produce two more sets of the drawings. He'd keep the original set, send the second set to Pinkerton headquarters in Chicago, and the third to Pinkerton's Denver division. The first drawing showed Briggs's full face, in typical Wanted poster style; the second was a profile; the third was another full face, but clean-shaven, depicting what Briggs might look like without the facial hair and his hair parted to the side. As he'd worked on the third sketch, Deacon had the odd sense he'd seen the bare-faced features before. But the more he tried to recall where or when, the less certain he was he'd had the experience. Perhaps the sense of familiarity came from capturing the likeness on paper.

Regardless, he'd send a set of the three drawings and a physical description to the Chicago and Denver offices. The Pinkerton National Detective Agency had amassed a vast collection of criminal faces and descriptions for identifying criminals. The agency clipped and filed newspaper stories to use for reference in investigations. Along with noting suspects' distinguishing marks and scars, agents gathered and linked information to generate fact sheets detailing previous arrests, known associates, and areas of expertise. The collection of Wanted posters, photographs, drawings, and case histories provided agents with an impressive criminal research library called the "Rogues Gallery." Because much of the gallery content had been lost or damaged in the Chicago fire of '71, agents regularly checked files stored in division and branch offices spread across the country. Deacon expected a response from Denver in a week or less. Chicago would take twice as long, but he could do nothing to speed the mail.

While waiting, it would be no hardship to spend time with Jessa.

***

That evening, soon after Sheriff Cooley and his deputy began their first set of nightly rounds, Jessa slipped into the jailhouse. Since moving to Prosperity, she'd vowed not to waste one moment thinking of Colter Brogan, her former husband, or his cruelty. Now, here she was about to face the man she believed dead for more than five years. Standing with her back pressed flat against the wall across from her husband's cell, as far from his reach as the width of the space allowed, it took every bit of courage Jessa could summon to confront him.

"If it ain't the little wife dropping by for a visit. Discovering your beloved husband is alive must've filled you with so much joy you couldn't wait to enjoy a conjugal reunion."

Shocked, Jessa's stomach heaved. But now was not the time to retreat. She needed answers. "Wh—Why aren't you dead? I saw your body. Your brother's, too."

"Did you now? Well, I'm sorry to confirm my brother is dead, but the other corpse was one of my men wearing my ring. His build and coloring were the same as mine so with his head crushed under tons of debris, no one questioned his identity."

"Why have you come here after all this time?"

"I came to reunite with my grief-stricken wife and son." It wasn't true, but it would keep her fearful. "And now that I've seen the boy, I want him—a son should know his father." Also not true, but it would double her fear.

Suppressing a shudder at the thought of her gentle-hearted son in this devil's hands froze the blood in Jessa's veins. "You can't be serious. No child needs a father who's a murderer and a thief." Suffocating fear was making rational thought difficult.

"What have you told the boy about his father?" Briggs asked. Although his main reason for asking was to add to Jessa's terror; he was also mildly curious.

"I've told him the truth. His father died before he was born."

"But the kid doesn't believe it, does he? He thinks Jackson Knight is his father."

Jessa gasped, surprised he'd heard the gossip. "That's not true. Peter Jack doesn't think that."

"The boy favors Knight's looks and receives special treatment from him. That's all the evidence people need to think the worst. Hell, folks love talking about how Knight moved you and the boy to live in the same town as he and his rich wife. Besides, it doesn't matter what you told the kid. What he believes is what counts. It surprises me, though, that the hellcat Knight married tolerates you and the brat. Pretending to be friends with a woman who's spread her legs for her husband and bore him a bastard son ain't exactly normal behavior."

"Leave us alone, unless you want me to tell Jackson you're alive. We're happy. I have a good job. We've made a place here, and we have friends."

"Yes, you have friends—rich friends. Knight and his wife are wealthy. But if you don't want the boy hurt, you'll do whatever I say."

"I'll—I'll go to the law," Jessa stammered. He was scaring the wits out of her. Was it a coincidence he'd found her and Peter Jack here or had he already known where they were? Had he come to embroil them in a crime he wasn't presently willing to divulge?

A cold, hollow bark of a guffaw accompanied by a vicious sideways slash of his hand in the space between them dismissed her threat. "No, you won't go to the law because it will come out that you're wanted. And they'll believe me when I tell them details of your participation in the stage holdup. Or I could order one of my men to do a small job here in Prosperity and leave evidence casting suspicion on you. Even if you eventually prove you weren't involved, people won't forget. You'll never be trusted."

"I won't bargain with the devil. You'll stay dead and away from us, or I'll do what I said. Jackson and Sam, as well as other influential people here in Prosperity, will back us." Jessa had gone so pale Briggs thought she'd faint before finishing the threat. Her words were all bravado.

Unaware she'd inched close enough for Briggs to reach her, Jessa almost screamed when he grabbed her wrist and held it, slowly applying pressure, forcing her up against the iron bars separating them. Unable to pull from his grasp, she averted her face, leaving him access to whisper in her ear in a low, threatening rasp. "Ah, but will Knight help you after

I tell him you knew I was alive and lied to protect me? He won't forgive you for that, wifey, dearest."

"Jackson won't believe you. He knows I didn't love you—that you mistreated me—framed my father."

"Certain of that, are you?" Briggs sneered, gratified to feel her trembling. "What'll Knight think of you when I inform him the brat isn't mine? I'll make sure he knows I never took you to my bed, and it won't be a lie. You were ruined before I ever laid eyes on you—already carrying the seed your sodbuster lover planted in you. And since Knight hasn't seen your Wanted poster, I'll show him that, too. After that, you'll be lucky if you're allowed to say goodbye to your son before Knight turns you in to the sheriff."

"Nothing on the poster is true. You and your men held up that stage and killed the driver. You forced me to go with you. I was your captive and knew nothing about your plan."

"But you don't have any proof of that, so you'll do whatever I order you to do." He knew the key to controlling Jessa was to control her son. And once he used her and the boy to get what he wanted, he'd get rid of them. Accidents were easy to arrange.

***

"Why do I get the feeling your reason for visiting Prosperity isn't solely to enjoy the company of your family?" Storey asked, studying the smoke pattern wafting from his cigar rather than his son's face. After dining with Alexa and Morgan, he and Deacon had retired to the Prosperity House's second-story, L-shaped veranda to enjoy a cigar. Their chairs sat back from the street-side balustrade on the inner corner of the L, making them nearly invisible to passersby, while providing a view of the street that included the Fortune Queen saloon and jailhouse.

155

"You read people better than anyone I've ever met, Dad," Deacon replied. "Why not confess you know I have an assignment and ask if it's family I'm investigating?"

"Because I doubt it's family, although I'm not sure what your intentions are regarding Sammy. It did occur to me that discrediting Jackson Knight might be to your advantage."

"I have no intentions regarding Sammy. She's my sister and anything else I felt for her no longer matters. I'm glad she's recovered from what that perverted neighbor did to her and that she's made a marriage that hasn't destroyed her spirit. Falling in love has made her even more beautiful. It's odd, though, talking to her, knowing and remembering things she doesn't."

"I'm sorry things didn't turn out as you hoped, Deacon."

"No reason for pity, Dad. I lost Sammy a long time ago, though I realize I haven't been able to admit it before now. I believe what you, Morgan, and Alexa tell me about Jackson Knight being a good man who makes Sammy happy. And," he added drolly, "if the sheriff can be believed, he keeps her out of trouble, too."

Storey chuckled. "I thought you might lose your temper over that comment. I'm glad to see your sense of humor is intact." Raising a questioning eyebrow, he segued to Jessa. "I wondered, though, why Jessa Nolan rattles you."

"You don't wonder. You know I'm attracted to her."

"I do, but I wouldn't like to think you're looking for a dalliance or anything else that might cause her trouble."

Deacon locked eyes with Storey. "I'll tell you straight out. Jessa's my assignment. I've been looking for her for several weeks. She has a past, and though her husband is dead, he was a criminal who got her into trouble with the law. He also framed her father so that he's spent years in prison. Jessa doesn't know it, but her father was proven innocent and released. He married a rich widow and hired Pinkerton to find her. Well, I've found her, but I need to free her from the charges on her Wanted poster and whatever other trouble she's in. You saw how she acted after seeing Briggs at the jail."

Just then the object of their discussion caught Deacon's attention while cautiously checking the street before leaving the jailhouse. Motioning Storey to his side, they watched Jessa furtively move from shadow to shadow.

"Hmm. Didn't we see the sheriff and deputy leave there twenty minutes ago?" Storey asked.

"You know we did, Dad. They won't return from their rounds for another hour."

"So, what reason would Jessa have for visiting the jail when the sheriff's not there?"

"I guarantee it's not to bring the prisoner a freshly baked pie. Colby Briggs scares the bejesus out of Jessa. I don't know how they know each other, but there's no question they do. Jessa started to say she'd trust Jackson Knight to help her, but cut off before finishing his name. I asked her to trust us, but she denied needing help. Her response makes me wonder how deep a relationship Sammy's husband had or still has with Jessa. I've heard the town gossip that her boy is Jackson's son."

"I don't believe it, Deacon. But if Jackson is the boy's father, it happened long before Sammy met Jackson. And while I don't doubt that he cares about Jessa and the boy, I can't believe they have that sort of relationship. Once you meet him and see him with Sammy, you won't believe it either. But I do know Jackson killed Jessa's husband and his brother after they shot him in the back and left him for dead."

"I've been to South Pass, Dad, and know all about that. I also know if Jessa hadn't taken him in and nursed him, Jackson Knight would have died." Deacon pitched his cigar in a nearby spittoon and started for the stairs to the street. "Sorry to abandon you, but I think I'd better keep an eye on our little widow."

"Good idea, Son. I've grown quite fond of her cinnamon rolls, you know."

Deacon grinned. "Her pancakes are damn good, too."

***

Hurrying back to the house, Jessa barely altered her stride when the tip of her shoe caught on a bowed boardwalk plank. Several steps later, she slowed her pace to chance a quick look over her shoulder. She didn't want anyone questioning where she'd been or why she was out alone after dark—especially Sheriff Cooley. Thankfully, she saw only a few citizens walking in the other direction, seemingly oblivious to her presence. Why then did she have a crawling feeling at the back of her neck? Inwardly she groaned at the absurdity of that question. She'd be an idiot not to be nervous. Discovering her outlaw husband alive and threatening to harm Peter Jack made her wish that she could flee the country.

Spying the lamplit window in her front parlor drained a portion of the tension fueling her brisk steps. Thank God Alma Chambers had agreed to watch Peter Jack while she went to the jailhouse. In her mid-sixties, widowed for ten years, Alma was energetic, nurturing, and nonjudgmental. She and her husband Albert had raised a fine son, who'd married long ago and lived on a nearby ranch. In their late teens, her two grandsons, Alton and Jessup, visited Alma every other Sunday. Alma cooked and baked for two days before their visits for the pure pleasure of watching them stuff themselves at her table. The cheery widow adored Peter Jack; he made her feel as though she were helping raise a third grandson.

Though Alma had studied Jessa's face with concern-filled, hazel eyes when Jessa asked her to watch Peter Jack while she went out on an errand, she hadn't asked questions or voiced any well-meaning cautions. In Jessa's mind, Alma was a paragon among women.

About to mount the porch steps, Jessa's energy lagged. She was past tired and her nerves were raw. She exhaled an exhausted breath and straightened her shoulders. The welcoming light and comforting greeting from Alma and her son gave her the strength to curve her lips in a pleasant smile and pretend nothing was out of the ordinary.

***

With Doc Baxter on his way to Nebraska, it was easy for Deacon to slip into the shadows beneath the portico of his house to spy on Jessa. He watched her bend to kiss her son before following the boy and the older woman inside. Five minutes later, he was still watching when the elderly woman scurried to the house next door. Shortly after that, the lamps in Jessa's house were extinguished, signifying mother and son had retired for the evening. Deacon kept watch for another half hour before starting back to the hotel.

***

In her parlor's quiet darkness, Jessa spent the next hour pacing, determining the best solution for protecting Peter Jack. Though her first impulse was to run and hide, she knew it wouldn't guarantee their safety—especially Peter Jack's. Colter Brogan was smart and ruthless. The better strategy would be to bind Peter Jack to a man who'd give his life to protect her son's.

If she had the strength to put Peter Jack in such a man's care, her odds of successfully hiding from her husband increased. If he couldn't get to her boy and couldn't find her, he wouldn't be able to use them as weapons. Of course, if he found her, he'd make her suffer, but it was a risk she was willing to take. She wouldn't allow Colter to use them to murder Jackson, hurt Sam, or endanger anyone else standing between him and whatever goal he sought, for Jessa had no doubt he'd make good his threats.

She had some money, but not enough to hide indefinitely. And she couldn't bear to go far from Peter Jack. Wearily she settled onto the cushions of the settee to formulate a plan. Whatever solution she devised would need to be a good one.

Chapter 16

When Jessa emerged from her house the next morning, Deacon was leaning casually against the whitewashed slats of her gate. She deplored that he appeared to be calm and patient—something she was not, and might never be again. Of course, abusive husbands resurrected from the grave tended to do that to a woman.

Yet, even as she demanded Deacon leave, and added for emphasis he wasn't wanted or needed, Jessa couldn't ignore the attraction arcing between them. She'd always wanted a man to love, a man who was capable, kind, honest—a man who'd love her and her son with all his heart.

Deacon understood Jessa's rejection wasn't personal. He had no doubt she felt the same *something* he did. She was denying the budding possibility they might be right for each other because of her secrets and fear. He'd always wanted a home with a woman who loved him. That's what he'd hoped to have with Sammy. Now, examining that *something* he'd begun feeling for Jessa, he wondered if fate had known Jessa was the woman he needed.

Deacon didn't interrupt while Jessa said her piece. He was there because she needed help and he intended to provide it—regardless of her rejection. To that end, he turned his attention to the house next door, where a heavyset, sharp-featured woman pretended to sweep her porch while endeavoring to memorize his and Jessa's every expression and gesture. He tipped his hat to the shameless eavesdropper in polite acknowledgment of her presence. He took no satisfaction in dealing Jessa such a low card, so when he heard her strangled gasp of embarrassment, he felt a sharp pain uncomfortably close to his heart.

Smothering another gasp, Jessa showed no other outward reaction—except for the telltale heat burning in her cheeks. Well, there was nothing to be done other than paste on a pleasant smile and deal with it—what she always did when her life went out of control. The speculative gleam in Delvinia Dalrymple's eyes was unmistakable. Some people knew how to make things, even innocent things, seem sordid. And Delvinia was one of those people. No one in or around Prosperity escaped her scrutiny, judgment, or acid tongue.

"Good morning, Mrs. Dalrymple," Jessa trilled. "It certainly looks as if it will be a lovely day, doesn't it?" Casting a glance to the sky, she gave a regretful shrug. "I do wish I had time to enjoy it and a visit with you, but I mustn't be late for work." She wiggled her fingers in a weak farewell. Plucking her hand from the air as she turned away, she dropped it to clutch at the base of her throat.

Though the mean-minded snoop didn't deserve respect, Deacon raised two fingers to his hat brim before turning to grasp Jessa's elbow and steer her toward the center of town, acting as if he performed the same service each morning.

Jessa cut her eyes at him. "You've done it now," she hissed. "Delvinia's a malicious gossip. By tonight she'll have told half the town that you spend wicked nights in my bed and are trying to fool everyone by slipping out my window and traveling a full circle to escort me as if you've just come from the hotel."

"Hmm—a clever idea. I don't suppose you'd consider making Delvinia's fantasy our pleasure. After all, if she's as influential as you claim, we've already been judged guilty of the crime."

"That isn't funny, Deacon. Is your need to satisfy your curiosity so perverse you don't care how difficult you make things for me and Peter Jack?"

"I care, but you're in trouble," he replied, regret in his tone. "Your refusing my help wounds me almost as much as your denying the attraction between us."

Acting on her attraction would endanger her son, Deacon, and her friends. Besides, Jessa doubted his feelings were so strong they'd drive him to seriously pursue a past-her-prime widow with a five-year-old boy whose father was rumored to be the husband of his adopted sister.

***

Storey Deale paused the game of solitaire he'd begun shortly after breakfast to watch his goddaughter descend Gracelyn Palace's staircase. Though Sammy didn't look fit to be out of bed, it didn't surprise him she was doing her best to act as if she were. He assumed she was on her way to talk to the sheriff.

Hesitating at the bottom of the stairs, Sam tapped the brim of the black Stetson she carried against her leg while resting the elbow of her right arm on the butt of her gun and hooking her thumb behind her belt buckle—a pose Storey had seen her stepfather, Mac, strike a thousand times. Dressed in a white cotton blouse and belted, navy-blue skirt, her gaze darted from the gaming parlor's front entrance to Storey's table, apparently undecided about which direction to traverse. Indecision was not behavior he expected to see her exhibit.

Finally deciding, she turned and marched to Storey's table. Slipping onto a chair, she placed her hat in front of her and met his gaze. "You know me, don't you? I don't mean from playing cards with Briggs—from before—the past I can't remember. Am I right?"

Storey nodded. "Yes, you're right. I didn't mention it before this because it didn't seem proper to do it in front of Briggs. I've known you since you were a little girl, from before your papa married Grace. You and Morgan are my godchildren."

Sam had sensed Storey was familiar—perhaps that was why the severity of her headache worsened when she was around him. Was her subconscious stirring her memory?

Storey watched Sam press the fingers of her right hand against her temple, something he'd noticed her do while playing cards with Briggs. He was curious whether the severity of her headaches increased in his presence. He suspected his voice stirred something in her because she tended to cock her head and dart a puzzled glance in his direction when he spoke.

"You're Deacon Storey's father," she stated. Morgan had told her Deacon's surname. Now that she knew, the likeness was undeniable. Both men were unquestionably good-looking. This one was mature, with deep laugh lines and gray at his temples, while the younger one had the same coloring and features but was taller and wider in the shoulders.

Storey nodded. "Yes."

"Why is your first name Storey when your son uses it as his surname?"

Storey grinned. "Some things don't change, Sammy. You're still direct and to the point." Holding her gaze, he explained. "I changed my name when I left home. My real name is Deacon Patrick Storey. I was the youngest of three children and a true disappointment to my father, which is saying a lot because my older siblings are female. My father loved my sisters but held the opinion daughters were given to a man to adore, spoil, and bear grandsons. Out of respect for him, whom I loved but couldn't emulate, I changed my name by taking my last name as my first name and replacing the last three letters of my first name, Deacon, with an *l* and an *e*, thus creating the surname of Deale. Besides saving my father embarrassment, I thought it a clever name for a man who chose to make his living dealing cards."

Sam smiled. "It is a clever name, and from what I've observed, you're good, perhaps more skilled than I am. Did you teach me?"

"I'd say between me and your stepmother, Grace, we taught you pretty much all there is to know about gaming, Sammy." He was surprised to see Sam's smile fade and a quizzical furrow appear on her forehead.

"'Sammy,'" she repeated, "that's the second time you've called me that—Deacon called me that too. Why 'Sammy?'"

"Deacon had a friend named Sam Caldwell who worked at the livery, so 'Sammy' was Deacon's way to distinguish between the two of you. You didn't like it. But whenever you complained, Deacon would tug your braid and threaten to call you 'Honey,' which is what his other friend, Johnny Perkins, called you. Does the nickname bother you?"

Sam raised her eyes to meet Storey's. "I don't mind it, except—" She trailed off before adding, "There's something about the way you say it. It tugs at me—as if you're about to reveal the answer to an important question. When the answer doesn't come, my headache gets worse." For a moment, she envisioned her memories as scattered pieces of paper weaving in wild currents of wind.

Storey understood it was too soon to wrap his arms around her in loving comfort. Perhaps sharing his memories was the safest path to reestablishing a bond.

"I was a protégé of Drake Garner, your stepmother's first husband. We mainly worked riverboats. Drake was handsome, educated, and damn successful. Morgan favors him—in looks and temperament—same black hair, build, and smile. Nothing much could ruffle Drake Garner's confidence, and Morgan is much the same."

"Except his wife," Sam mumbled.

Storey's face split into a grin. "Yes, I've met Alexa. As it happens, I mistook her for you. Once she understood it was an honest mistake, she took pity on me and kindly explained about your memory loss and some other—er—recent events."

Seeing a quizzical expression on Sam's face, Storey quickly cleared his throat and resumed his narrative. "Well, anyway, when Grace married Drake, she was already a brilliant businesswoman, not to mention a natural at all games of chance. And when Morgan was born less than a year later, I agreed to be his godfather. Morgan was barely five when Drake was killed in a riverboat accident."

Sam nodded. She'd learned about Drake from Grace and Morgan. But they hadn't mentioned Storey or Deacon. However, that wasn't so surprising considering only about ten months had passed since the crash.

"Grace took the money Drake left her and some of hers from selling her first gaming house and moved to Eden Ridge to open the Golden Crown. Deacon and I moved with her and Morgan. Grace and I always worked well together, and she and Morgan were good for Deacon. He'd never had much of a home and he missed his mother."

Sam noticed Storey didn't explain about Deacon's mother. Judging by the sorrow in his eyes—she supposed it was private.

"Though Grace and I never had a romantic relationship, it was good business for people to think I was more than her partner. If there ever was a mutual attraction between us, those feelings transformed into a rare friendship few men achieve with a woman.

"Not long after the Golden Crown began to prosper, Grace met and married your papa, Chase. Things were good until your papa was killed in that bank robbery. For a time, I worried your broken heart wouldn't mend, but when you began spending time with me and challenging your brothers, I knew you'd be all right.

"As you children matured and Grace didn't depend on me as much, I got restless and traveled to other houses to work, only returning to Eden Ridge for a part of each year, typically in the warmer months. At first, I followed the settlements that attracted railroad workers, miners, and cowboys, who needed all manner of things, including sporting houses, saloons, and games of chance. In recent years, I've worked in the Canadian providences. I didn't return to visit Eden Ridge often because Grace had Mac and because you and Morgan no longer lived there. Deacon left about the time you turned eighteen.

"I visited Prosperity once while you and Morgan were building Gracelyn Palace. I considered becoming a partner but decided against it because I believed it was something you and Morgan needed to do on your own. I met Jackson when I was here, though, and saw the sparks fly between you. I'm pleased you married him. Morgan told me you're happy."

"I am happy. Jackson is right for me."

"Before that visit, I never seriously considered owning my own place—I preferred the footloose life of being a plugger for whatever gaming house took my fancy. I make lots of money while risking little, and it gives me the freedom to come and go as I please. When you're as good as I am, you earn more by accepting a percentage of house business. Though, lately, I confess I've begun to see the comforts to be gained by settling in one place.

"I wasn't cut out to be a judge, or a rancher, or a regular family man. I've had a good life. My son and your family get most of the credit for that. Most professional gamblers don't have my talent. Every so often one gets religion and dedicates his life to preaching against vice, but the majority either succumb to alcohol or opium or commit suicide.

"Though I can switch cards better than most muckers, I don't condone the practice. While I know to watch for bags fastened to the underside of a table, sleeve holdouts in a player's jacket, marked cards, and shaved decks, I don't use them. Gamers who are as good as us don't need to cheat. And cheating isn't how to make a good living in this business. To be honest, most of the tricks are so easy, they bore me.

"I've been successful because I have a reputation for playing an honest game. The most successful gamblers aren't the ones good at manipulating cards but those that are good at manipulating the other players' minds. It requires a rare skill few have. It's the part of the game I enjoy most.

"Mind you, I'm not saying I'm above using sleight of hand or other tricks when I'm in a game with someone cheating. If they start it, I'll use it to my advantage, as you did with Briggs." Storey paused to chuckle. "Damn, if you didn't lift Briggs's hole card better than a magician disappears a rabbit from a hat."

Something shifted in Sam's mind, opening a crack in the mortared brick wall imprisoning her memories. Suddenly she saw herself at eight years old sitting across from Storey at their favorite table in the Golden Crown, her mother's gaming salon, practicing her shuffle. She sat with one leg tucked under her, while her arms rested on the table. Her feet were bare. Because her free leg didn't quite reach the floor, she gently swung it back and forth while concentrating on shuffling a deck of cards. She wore her favorite blue dress, the one she thought made her look several years older, and a string of Grace's pearls. Her hair was tied back with a ribbon matching her dress.

Every so often, her hands would lose the rhythm of the shuffle, causing cards to spill out on the table. Each time it happened, she swallowed a sigh, determined to hide the frustration and shame she felt over her failure. With her eyes cast down, she would gather the cards and begin again. After the shuffle went right five times in a row, she looked up shyly at Storey, seeking his approval. Though she'd known he'd watched her every move, she was disappointed nothing in his expression told her what he thought of her performance.

She hated making mistakes. She wanted to do things perfectly. Sensing displeasure, she put the cards down and folded one hand over the other. Storey's expression didn't change. Nor did he comment when he noticed her rubbing the lightning bolt scar on the back of her right hand. Her troubled, slate blue gaze held Storey's brilliant green gaze as they studied each other. She dropped her eyes first.

She became aware Storey had come to stand beside her when his shadow fell over her. A part of her hoped he'd scoop her up in his arms and hug her. She didn't ask for the hug because she believed it was wrong to ask for something she hadn't earned.

Silent, Storey had gazed down at her honey-gold curls. He knew how important it was to her to do things right. Then he gently placed his hand on her shoulder and said, "Look at me, Sammy." His voice was kind, so she'd done as he'd asked. "Do you know I could see in your face how you felt? I knew you were angry you didn't shuffle perfect every time."

In denial, Sam moved her head from side to side until understanding stopped her. She'd thought she'd kept her frustration and disappointment hidden. But Storey had seen the truth. How would she learn to bluff if she couldn't hide what she felt about things?

Storey hoisted her from the chair onto his left hip, his arm supporting her bottom, while his right hand freed the strand of pearls caught on a button of his vest. Then he smoothed her skirt around her bare legs.

Wrapping her arms around his neck, she hugged him, soaking up the reassurance and affection she always felt when she was in his arms. He returned her hug tenfold. She and Morgan didn't have a papa. They had Mac, though, and Deacon shared Storey with them. She hugged Storey again, just because she could.

Storey slipped a finger under her chin to raise her head. "Sammy, it's all right to let others see what you feel. It's all right not to do things as well as you'd like to do them. And it's all right for you to ask for what you want. The rules I teach you for playing cards aren't rules for how to live your life, sweetheart. Do you understand?"

She didn't answer because she needed to think about what he'd said. She didn't know if she understood. "I'll tell you tomorrow after I study on it. Will that be all right?"

Storey had nodded and tweaked her nose. "Sure, Sammy, and while you study on it, think about how I'll love you even when you don't understand something or can't do things as well as you want."

Her heart lifted and she promised. "I'll study on that part most of all."

"Good." Pecking her cheek, Storey set her on her feet, turned her toward the stairs, and tapped her bottom to send her on her way. "Now, run upstairs and change out of that dress and Grace's pearls before your brothers catch you in that rig. You know they won't let you ride to the ranch in that getup."

When the memory faded, Sam lifted her eyes to find Storey watching her expectantly. She smiled shyly. "I just remembered I've been studying a few things over the years—things like it's all right to let others see what I feel. It's all right not to do things as well as I want to do them. And it's all right to ask for what I want."

Storey's eyes turned soft with understanding.

"Since the crash, I've learned memories can't return a hug or kiss—or give me love." Reaching to squeeze Storey's hand, she added, "People make memories. I'm fortunate to have Jackson, Grace and Mac, Morgan and Alexa, and, now, you and Deacon."

Favoring her sore ribs, Sam stood and reached for her hat. "Just so you know, I haven't mastered those things, though you set me studying them when I was little. But I do take comfort from realizing I might not have tried to learn about them if you hadn't pointed them out to me."

***

Despite her aching ribs, Sam placed a hand on Sheriff Rem Cooley's desk and leaned down to put her face in a direct line with his. She'd come to see him after leaving Storey. "I know you've talked to Deacon and Storey, Rem—and probably every other person in Gracelyn Palace that night, so don't think I'll stand here and let you blame my temper for what happened with Briggs."

Rem glared at Sam while waiting a full three seconds before responding. "With your disposition, Sam—"

From the fault-finding tenor of the sheriff's tone, Sam knew he was setting her up for an insult. Enunciating clearly, she cut him off. "And just what's wrong with my disposition?"

Recognizing the outraged indignation in Sam's eyes as she slowly rose to her full height, Rem was reminded of a female grizzly bear standing tall, claws ready to slash across a man's chest to flay open flesh. He refused to be intimidated. It was his duty to reprimand her for her part in the trouble, but that didn't mean he couldn't have fun doing it.

"As I recollect, Sam, we've had this conversation before."

Had it not been so early in their "discussion," Sam would have laughed, because, yeah, from what she'd been told, she and Rem had a conversation like this one *every time* she was involved in a fracas in Prosperity. Watching the lawman negligently rub his jaw, pretending he was more interested in finding evidence of whether he needed a shave than continuing their discussion, Sam waited for him to launch his ambush.

"You know you can't deny that when you're riled, the words *reasonable* and *patient* jump out of your body as if you were trying to poison 'em."

With a raised eyebrow and in a deceivingly calm tone, Sam bated him. "And when I'm not riled, Rem?"

"You're about the kindest, sweetest, and most generous woman God ever put on this earth, and I get so envious I'm tempted to railroad Jackson into prison so I can claim you for my own." Lips curved in a wry smile, Rem leaned back, fingers tented. She was sure he was waiting to see if she could best his response.

Biting back a chuckle, eyes sparkling with admiration, Sam moved her right hand to cradle her left side. "I'd laugh, Rem, if it wouldn't pain my ribs so bad I wouldn't have the strength to stay standing." Feeling weak in the knees, she added in a drained voice, "I give up."

Surprised by her quick capitulation, Rem leaned forward to assess Sam's sincerity. The surge of triumph he'd been experiencing over her surrender quickly transformed into guilt. She looked as if air stirred by the gentle wave of a fan would knock her down. Her face was so pale it made her skin appear as translucent as parchment paper.

Jumping to his feet, Rem rounded the desk to grasp Sam's arm and guide her to a chair. "Here, sit down before you fall." Patting her shoulder, he added, "I'm sorry. I should have gone easier on you. But your bein' hurt is why I'm making such a point of telling you that you took on too much. I don't want to see you or some innocent bystander killed. No cardsharp is worth dyin' over."

Feeling stronger now that she was sitting, Sam came back at him. "I understand, but it was more than that. He was—"

"I know, Sam," Rem interrupted, sympathy evident in his gentled tone. "The man doesn't respect women. Storey and Deacon explained. I expect Briggs had plans to get you alone later. Still, you should have waited and let me handle it."

"I did intend to let you handle it, Rem. I saw Alexa send the barkeep's assistant to get you. I intended to hold Briggs until you arrived and could witness the evidence of his cheating." She refrained from saying more because she realized Storey and Deacon hadn't considered it their civic duty to apprise the sheriff of how she'd lifted Briggs's hole card.

"One of the reasons I chose those marble tables for the gaming room was because they aren't easy to overturn to send cards flying. I admit it never crossed my mind anyone would use one as a battering ram. Been thinking I'll talk to Morgan about the practicality of bolting them to the floor."

Pausing, she eyed Rem while considering her next words. "So, what are you going to do about Briggs?"

"Already done it, Sam."

"What do you mean?"

"Now, don't get riled. The way things went down, I didn't have much choice, so don't waste your breath giving me grief. The law says if a man is convicted of cheating, he's to be fined not less than three hundred and not more than one thousand dollars—or imprisoned not less than thirty days or more than one year."

"So—"

"So, the jury would acquit Briggs because the evidence was lost when he flipped the table. You, Deacon, and Storey aren't credible witnesses because each of you had something to gain. I might have charged him with assault, but you pulled your gun first. Briggs would claim he was defending himself."

"So—"

"So, I fined him a hundred dollars and put him on a train early this morning for parts unknown. That's the best I can do."

"The best you could do," Sam repeated, "when that varmint—"

Rem cut her off. "Oh, and because I can't prove who did what, I'm fining you a hundred dollars too."

"Why you ol' tarnished son of a tin star, I ought to—"

Rem was all but beaming when he interrupted. "See what I mean about that disposition of yours, Sam? It flies right out the window when you get riled."

***

The creaking hinges of the hotel's kitchen back door brought Deacon's head around to see Jessa step onto the stoop and fling an irritated scowl in his direction. It was easy to see she

174

wasn't happy to see him. Ignoring her obvious displeasure, Deacon admired her looks. She was a beautiful woman, but with the flare of temper in her eyes, she was magnificent.

"What are you doing here?" Jessa snapped, letting the door snick closed behind her. She shouldn't be surprised to find him waiting, but she was. She watched him slowly push away from the stack of crates on which he'd been leaning. He wore all black—shirt, trousers, silk vest—the perfect color to draw attention to his brilliant emerald eyes glowing with a bright flame of mischief.

As he started toward her, Jessa willed her limbs not to give ground to his masculinity. Their eyes locked, and before she realized it, he'd grasped her elbow to propel her down the steps and through the alley.

Upon reaching the boardwalk, Jessa tried to tug her arm free but couldn't without making a scene. A slight drop of her shoulders signaled consent before she matched her steps to his, while ignoring the curious eyes following their progress.

When they arrived at her house, Deacon released her arm to push on the latch and swing open the gate. His other hand pressed against the hollow of her spine, gently urging her forward. She shot him an irritated sideways glance. He countered with an admiring smile, so disconcerting she almost missed his low murmur about returning in the morning. By the time Jessa recovered her senses, he was too far away to hear her tell him not to call again.

Jessa needed to put a stop to the handsome gambler's attention. His dogging her every step endangered her and Peter Jack, as well as Jackson and Sam. Though Sheriff Cooley had sent her husband packing, she knew he'd find a way to make good his threats. Common sense demanded she use the limited time before he reappeared to gather supplies, put her son under Jackson Knight's protection, and make her escape. For as sure as the sun sets and the moon rises, Colter Brogan would come. The man was a ruthless, unconscionable, cold-blooded killer.

Chapter 17

To Sam, five days had seemed a lifetime. Looking up from the green baize of the table where she was dealing twenty-one, her gaze found Jackson's. Tall and handsome, his shirt open at his throat revealing bronzed skin and muscle, he drew the eye of every female in the room. Sam's heart leaped at the sight of him, and her body ached to touch him—to feel the heat and power of his body covering hers.

Returning Sam's gaze, Jackson's eyes traveled from her tantalizing mouth to the creamy skin at the hollow of her throat and the hint of cleavage peeking from her lace-edged bodice before moving back to her luminous slate blue eyes. He saw so much in those eyes—her wildness, her generous spirit, her intelligence, her desire—for him. There was a shyness there, too, a certain vulnerability. Yes, she was beautiful, but so much more than that, and she was his.

Aware of Sam's run-in with the cardsharp, Jackson studied her movements. Though the cards leaped to life in her nimble hands, he noticed she kept her arms near her waist and didn't twist her upper body. She also supported her rib cage by pressing her forearm beneath her left breast. He surmised her left side must hurt more than her right. Frowning, he knew she wouldn't complain because she felt it was a sign of weakness.

Deacon's attention was drawn to Sammy while she studied the tall, dark-haired man who stared at her possessively. So, this man returning her gaze as if worshipping an angel was Jackson Knight, the husband with the power to overcome demons, instill trust, and arouse passion. This man had won Sammy's heart and crushed Deacon's dream.

Sammy's eyes were shining with happiness—and wanting. Jealousy and regret rolled through Deacon, but it wasn't so consuming he couldn't feel gladness she'd conquered the fear that'd kept her from pursuing love.

Sam didn't lift her gaze from Jackson's—refusing to acknowledge Deacon's presence despite his crowding in close to her side. When his hand pressed into the curve of her waist and urged her to move aside, she didn't budge—not even to alter the tilt of her head. "What do you want, Deacon?"

Nodding toward Jackson, Deacon answered. "It's time for a break. I'll take over for you." Confident Sam would be grateful for the opportunity to relinquish the table, he directed a friendly smile at the three players. "I'm sure you gentlemen will agree the lady deserves a rest."

One of the players objected. "The lady stays, gent. I'm winning, so I say the hell with another dealer—especially one that ain't got the right equipment to appeal to me."

Surprised at hearing crude talk from Ben Stockton, Sam's gaze flicked to his face. Ben visited Gracelyn Palace twice a week, and she'd never seen him act anything other than a gentleman, though Alexa and Miss Angie, Alexa's assistant, had warned her he could turn mean when he drank too much.

Sam clamped down on her temper. She was in no shape to handle a fracas. Darting a glance at Jackson, she was relieved to see a sardonic lift of an eyebrow and a wry twist of his lips, signifying he wouldn't interfere. Unfortunately, Deacon didn't share the same view. His fists and angry scowl were clear indications he thought it his duty to teach Ben manners. Erring on the side of caution, Sam pulled twice on the crystal in her left earlobe, signaling the barkeep to send for the sheriff.

Putting herself between Deacon and Ben, Sam placed her hand on the rancher's arm and gave him a conspiratorial wink. "Now, Ben, if you were a lady, you'd say the opposite." Then she appreciatively ran her eyes up and down Deacon's frame. "Why, if you were to ask me, I'd say Deacon, here, looks real good to the ladies. If you'll tolerate the man for a bit, I promise to send Miss Laurie over as soon as I can free her up. You know you like brunettes better than blondes, anyway."

Amused by Sam's boldness, Ben slapped his thigh and laughed with appreciation. The two other players joined in, though they sounded a bit nervous.

Accepting Ben's response for acquiescence, Sam took a step back from the table but halted when Ben's gruff, hard-edged tone challenged her. "Yeah, Sam, but Laurie don't have big ti—" He stopped short of saying the word.

Swinging around, Sam was able to elbow Deacon in his midsection in time enough to stop him from slamming a fist into Ben's jaw. The last thing she wanted was for the situation to escalate into a brawl or gunplay. Before facing Ben, she shot Deacon a glare, warning him to stay out of it.

Keeping her expression friendly and her tone pleasant, Sam dismissed Ben's remark and Deacon's reaction. "Don't mind Deacon, Ben. He's new in town. He doesn't know you mean no disrespect. Everyone hereabouts knows you're not a man to forget his manners around a lady."

Red circles stained Ben's cheeks.

Deacon felt as if he were being asked to swallow poison. If anyone other than Sammy had tried to stop him from smashing

Ben's jaw, he would've spit in his eye. Because she wanted him to back off, he'd let her handle it her way. Standing woodenly to the side, he gave Ben a half nod of apology.

From the bar, Morgan watched Jackson observing the altercation. When he saw Jackson's jaw tighten, he deemed it prudent to move closer in case things got out of hand. Joining Jackson, he commented, "Appears Sam found more trouble, but she's handling it."

Jackson raised one eyebrow but didn't lift his gaze from Sam's table. "What do you mean *more* trouble?"

Morgan was surprised by the question. "I know Rem Cooley sent you a telegram about that cardsharp pinning her under a table, same as I did. Are you claiming you didn't get our messages?"

"I got the telegrams—one from Doc Baxter, too. I'm asking if she did something I haven't heard about."

Morgan grinned. "No, nothing else. Her ribs keep reminding her to walk softly."

While viewing the drama at Sam's table, Storey crossed the room to join Morgan and Jackson. Extending his hand, he greeted Jackson. "It's good to see you again, Jackson. Let me congratulate you. I'm sorry I missed the wedding."

"Thank you, Storey. It's good to see you, too." Jackson's eyes moved back to Sam just as Deacon shifted his weight, taking a gunman's stance while tucking his jacket behind his holster. Jackson assumed Deacon was a new employee, though he thought he looked more gunman than professional gambler. "Who's the new dealer with Sam?"

Morgan's gaze flicked to Storey before answering. "That's Storey's son, Deacon. You've heard us mention him. He arrived the day after you left."

"He's visiting," Storey interjected. "Thinks he needs to look after Sammy whether she needs his help or not."

Jackson pushed down the twinge of jealousy nudging his gut at seeing Deacon's protectiveness toward Sam. He'd thought about interceding when it looked as though Deacon would smash Ben's jaw. But Deacon had backed off after Sam sunk her elbow into his gut. Jackson had once witnessed that elbow make a man lose the contents of his stomach. Because Deacon had looked more surprised than green, Sam must've gone easy on him. Anyone stepping in to help Sam at this point was likely to be the spark that set off the powder keg.

His attention on Sam and Deacon, Jackson barely noticed Storey excuse himself to stand near Deacon. If needed, Storey could put a restraining hand on his son's shoulder.

Meanwhile, speaking as though nothing unusual had happened, Sam drew Ben's attention away from Deacon. "It occurs to me you have a point about switching dealers before using the remaining cards in the dealer's box. It's not professional, so let's forget about it and go on about business."

"That's fine, Sam," Ben nodded curtly.

Sam smiled and let her gaze touch all three players. "Place your bets, gentlemen. Lady Luck's not gonna wait all night."

After all the bets were down, she dealt one card face up to each player, then one face down to herself. Quickly reviewing in her mind which cards had been played, she concluded the odds favored the players. If she were correct and the players' points remained under twenty-one, each would be paid one times his bet. If a player's points added up to exactly twenty-one, he'd win one-and-one-half times his bet.

Glancing in Jackson's direction, Sam didn't rush the pace of the game, reminding herself her goal was to keep a lid on things until Sheriff Cooley could arrive.

On her second pass, she dealt each player, including herself, a face-up card. Her tension eased as she saw the cards were running true to her prediction. The first player had a queen and a ten, their value worth twenty points. Ben had a king and an ace, an automatic twenty-one, making him a winner unless her cards equaled his. Should that happen, it would be a push, meaning Ben wouldn't lose his bet—but he wouldn't win anything either. The third player had a jack and an eight, adding up to eighteen.

Sam turned her facedown card to reveal a deuce. When added to her other card, a four of spades, she had six points. Her next card was a ten, upping her total to sixteen. According to the rules, the dealer must draw cards until the sum at least reached seventeen. Considering the tension at the table and Ben's surliness, Sam hoped the house would lose. When her next card turned out to be a nine, she beamed at the players. "Dealer busts with twenty-five points, gentlemen. Congratulations. You're all winners." While she paid the players, Sheriff Cooley sauntered in and quietly made his way across the room to stand behind Ben.

Relieved to see the sheriff, Jackson turned to Morgan. "So how long has Deacon been in love with Sam?"

After a moment of silence, Morgan replied, "It didn't take you long to figure that out. How did you know?"

"He looks at her the way I do."

Morgan nodded. "He forgets himself and lets it show every now and then."

Jackson ignored the remark. "So, how long, Morgan?"

Morgan sighed. "Deacon started falling for her when she was twelve. He wasn't in a hurry—waited patiently for her to grow up—tried not to let on how he felt. He'd planned to ask her to marry him when she turned sixteen, but you know what happened. She couldn't recover from McBride raping her. It got to be too much for Deacon, so he left home when she was eighteen, hoping she'd heal. But he left it too long."

"Did she know he was in love with her?"

"She knew; but, as damaged as she was, she didn't understand. Nor did she understand how it was near torture for Deacon to be around her. She treated his leaving more like a big brother deserting his little sister."

"Does she remember him?"

"When I asked her, she said she remembered he once got her in trouble with Mac by teaching her to say 'hell no.'"

Jackson grinned. "I doubt he taught her that. I'd wager Sam said those exact words when the doctor smacked her on the bottom at her birth and told her to cry."

Morgan laughed.

Jackson turned serious. "Did Deacon come here to take up where he left off?"

Morgan hesitated before answering. "I want to believe he cares too much for her and the rest of us to do that, but—"

"But what?" Jackson prompted.

"But I know how I feel about Alexa, so I understand how a man could give in to his feelings for a woman, no matter how honorable he is."

Jackson knew how that felt. He flexed the fingers of his gun hand to keep it from balling into a fist. "You know something you haven't told me?"

"Deacon stayed with her the night she was hurt. I know because he was there when I went to talk to her in the morning. I assumed the worst and belted him without giving him a chance to explain. I intended to beat the hell out of him until I realized he wasn't fighting back. Once I calmed down, he told me Doc didn't give him a choice. Sam needed looking after and she was upset, talking about someone watching her—he swore he didn't touch her."

"Do you believe him?"

"Yes—but later I realized I *wanted* to believe him because we were raised together, as if we were brothers. I needed to be sure I wasn't fooling myself, so I verified a few facts with Sam—couldn't talk to Doc because he's at his sister's place in Mercer, Nebraska."

Jackson was reading between the lines. "Are you saying if you allow a hungry man near his favorite pie, sooner or later, he's bound to take a bite?"

Morgan nodded, adding wryly, "Hell, if he's hungry enough, he'll eat the whole pie."

Several seconds passed while Jackson recovered from what felt like a sucker punch to his gut. "What did Sam say?"

"She admitted she accepted Deacon's help and that he sent for Doc Baxter. He wanted to wake Alexa and me, but Sam convinced him not to do it. When I asked who was watching her, Sam blamed the laudanum Doc gave her for talking nonsense. I didn't believe her but decided to drop it and let you figure it out. You should also know she admitted to Alexa she's been having headaches since before you left."

While they talked, both men's eyes stayed on Sam's table, so they tensed when Ben opened his mouth to say something after Sam offered Deacon the cards to switch dealers. They relaxed when Sheriff Cooley put a warning hand on Ben's shoulder and spoke a few quiet words near his ear. The rancher clamped his mouth shut. After rising from his stool and settling his hat on his head, he tersely wished Sam a good evening. Glancing sideways at the sheriff, he started for the door.

Rem Cooley smiled and touched the brim of his hat. "You did right well tonight, Sam. It's good to see you benefitted from our little chat."

To hide her smile, Sam turned her back to him.

Chuckling, Rem caught up with Ben and slapped him companionably on the back. "C'mon, Ben. We both could use some coffee."

Mumbling an excuse to Morgan, Jackson went to lean against the post railing at the foot of the stairs. Capturing Sam's gaze, he gave her a slow, wicked smile.

Crossing the room, her eyes fastened on Jackson, Sam was aware of nothing but him. When she reached him, he straightened and offered his arm. She took it, swallowing her disappointment in not being offered his mouth. He bent to brush his lips across the sensitive spot below her ear.

Jackson felt the shiver of Sam's response to his caress. She angled her head to bring her lips within an inch of his. His breath caught in his throat. Then she flashed a smile that made his heart swell and his groin heavy. Dropping his arm to her waist, he tucked her against his side, where she fit so perfectly.

Deacon concentrated on dealing cards, refusing to subject himself to the pain of watching Sammy ascend the stairs, pressed against another man's body, seeking a bed where she'd sleep in Jackson's arms.

***

While Jackson studied the mound of pillows on the chaise longue in their bedroom, Sam raised her arms to unfasten the line of buttons at the back of her dress. She quickly lowered them when the sharp tug on her rib cage reminded her why it wasn't a good idea.

Hearing Sam make a sound of frustration, Jackson saw what she needed. A surge of tenderness filled him. It wasn't in her nature to ask for help. Crossing silently to stand behind her, he deftly released buttons before gently turning her to face him. "It looks as though you've been sleeping on the chaise, darlin'."

Sam's eyes searched Jackson's while she considered whether she could answer without resorting to a lie. It didn't matter where she'd been sleeping. Jackson was home, and she *wanted* to sleep in the bed with him.

Awaiting Sam's answer, Jackson imagined he saw her consider and discard a hundred possible responses before choosing one. He decided to help her. "I know about the cardsharp and how you hurt your ribs."

Sam wasn't surprised Jackson knew and suspected her brother was the source of his knowledge. "It's not that I *couldn't* sleep in the bed, but without you, it felt empty." It *was* one of the reasons—just not the main one.

"I see." Jackson's tone was flat, communicating skepticism.

"Oh, all right," Sam huffed. "It's been more comfortable to sleep sitting up—but I don't want to sleep there anymore."

Jackson moved closer, his lips so near Sam's mouth their breaths mingled. "Why not ask for what you want?" He'd do anything for her. She was everything to him, and she stirred him, not just his body but his heart.

Against his mouth, Sam murmured, "I want to sleep with you." She felt his lips curve into a smile. Running her hands up his arms, then to the center of his chest, she admitted, "I want to feel your arms around me." Pausing, she lowered a hand searching for the waistband of his trousers. "And I want *other* things." There was a seductive, purring quality to her voice. Then, her lips teased his.

Jackson groaned, desire flaring, he took over the kiss until he remembered she wasn't in any condition to engage in *other things*. Pulling back, he said, "I'd like nothing more, but—"

Knowing he was concerned he'd hurt her if they made love, Sam interrupted. "You won't hurt me. That's what you were going to say, isn't it?" She wanted him too much to care, convinced the pleasure was worth the discomfort.

He nodded. "I'd do or give you anything in this world within my power—but I won't hurt you."

"If we're careful not to put pressure on my ribs, you wouldn't hurt me." She was eager and ardent, unwilling to be honest with herself.

Temptation sent a bolt of heat to Jackson's groin, but he repressed it. There was no way to love her without causing pain. He drew a measured breath to calm his heartbeat. "You know I want it as much as you, darlin', but—it's not a matter of position. You forget that I've had busted ribs."

She argued. "My ribs aren't busted."

"Cracked then," he countered.

"How do you know they aren't just bruised?"

"Because Doc Baxter wired me. And you may as well know I heard from Rem, too."

"So, you're well informed," she shot back.

"I am."

"I love you, but I hate you."

"I know," he answered, his tone patient, understanding.

"I didn't mean it."

"Mean what?"

"I don't hate you," Sam admitted.

"I imagine there are times you do, darlin'. It's only natural." Touching the pad of his index finger to her bottom lip, he added, "Because you love me so much."

"So, can we—?"

"Sam, darlin', it's about breathing."

"No, it's not." Capturing his hands, she placed them on her chest to cover her breasts. "Feel? I'm breathing just fine."

Jackson's mouth went dry. Yeah, she was breathing, and her breasts were soft, and her nipples were hard. Though she was making him ache, one of them had to keep their reason. If she chose to play it this way, he needed to fight fire with fire—so to speak.

Sliding her dress forward and off her shoulders, he said, "Allow me to demonstrate." Then he brushed back her hair to kiss her throat and the swell of her breasts.

Responding with a soft "Mmm," her breathing quickened.

Though her sound of pleasure made him harder, Jackson ignored the ache of his own desire. He lifted his mouth from her breasts. "Did that bring pleasure or pain?"

"Pleasure," Sam whispered, refusing to acknowledge the sharp jabs accompanying her breaths. She was determined to think of them as nothing more than a niggling annoyance.

Jackson laughed low and soft, causing something in her to quiver, like vibrations along a tautly strung wire. He opened her chemise to expose a nipple and covered it with his mouth, circling the tender point with his tongue.

Sam arched her neck to give him better access. They both were breathing hard.

Moving to the valley between her breasts, he licked hungrily before lifting his head and asking, "Pleasure or pain?"

Finding air, Sam managed to answer. "You're a devil."

"And you're avoiding the question. Pleasure or pain?"

Her breathing unsteady, coming in short gasps, Sam lied. "Pleasure."

Jackson scowled before lowering his mouth to suckle the nipple of her other breast while his hands moved her hips to rub against his hardness.

Straining to hold on to the pleasure, Sam tried arching her back to push her hips closer.

Jackson knew she lost the battle when she gasped from what must have been a sharp spasm of pain. Trembling, strength sapped, she slumped against him, his strong arms easily supporting her. "Relax, darlin', let it pass. I've got you," he crooned while cradling her body and soothingly running his hand from the center of her back to her waist.

"You win," she whispered when she could speak, her head resting on his chest, waiting for her breathing to even out.

Jackson placed a tender kiss on her temple. "Wrong, darlin', we both lose." Letting out a long slow breath to control his breathing, he inched back from her. "Let me help you change into a nightdress."

After guiding her to the bed, he made quick work of stripping away Sam's dress and undergarments. Still supporting her in the circle of one arm, he patted the mattress and urged her to sit. "Rest here, darlin', while I get a gown."

After some impatient rummaging in a drawer, he returned to Sam, a cotton gown in hand, his eyes sparkling with appreciation. His gaze wandered the gentle hills and valleys of her bared form. "You're too tempting to sleep with when you're naked."

While he threaded her arms through the gown's sleeves, Sam complained. "I could say the same about you. You always sleep naked."

Jackson smiled. "Are you just now catching on to why I do that?" Then, as the hem of the gown fluttered to her chest, his grin vanished and his hand seized a fistful of the fabric to halt its descent—his eyes riveted to the dark, angry bruises extending from beneath her left breast down to her hip and round to the bottom curve of her derriere. Skimming his fingertips over the mottled discoloration, his voice tight, he asked, "Where did you get this?"

"The same place I got the cracked ribs."

I could have lost her. An icy shiver rippled through him. He lowered his head to sprinkle soft kisses over the hurt, needing to touch her as much as he needed to hide his face so she wouldn't see his fear.

Sam sighed, instantly caught up in a new wave of wanting. "Jackson, what are you doing? I'm not up to another demonstration. I gave up, remember?"

"This isn't a demonstration." His tone was soft with concern.

"Then it would be?"

Hearing her tone rise and linger on the last word of her inquiry, Jackson answered honestly. "Me kissing your lovely bottom."

Curiosity got the better of her. "Out of respect?"

"No. Pure worship."

Chapter 18

June 1876

Awake before Sam, Jackson strode naked to the bedroom windows overlooking the road to Trinity's main house. Having spent more than three weeks in town, he and Sam had returned the previous day to their ranch house.

He watched three cowhands mount up, undoubtedly on their way to check fences and round up strays. While his eyes followed the activity outside, his mind was occupied with thoughts of his wife.

When he'd suggested to Sam they stay in town, she'd surprised him. She'd listened patiently to his arguments, especially those he'd learned from Doc Baxter warning of pneumonia—a common complication of rib injuries—and the inevitable setbacks she'd experience if she didn't avoid bone-jarring carriage rides and restrict physical activities. Jackson had also pointed out the rudeness of abandoning Storey and Deacon. And lastly, he'd stressed their responsibility to ready the firing range for the contest and complete the bank renovations before Brigham's gang arrived—Morgan couldn't do it alone. Sam agreed with all he said so quickly he suspected she'd decided before he proposed it.

Though he'd used Storey's and Deacon's visit as part of his argument, Jackson wasn't happy about giving Deacon the opportunity to spend time with Sam. Despite Deacon's obvious interest in Jessa Nolan, hardly a day passed the green-eyed monster hadn't raged in Jackson's blood. He was damn near worn out fighting the impulse to plant a fist in Deacon's teeth whenever the man got within twenty feet of Sam.

Dust billowing behind a supply wagon passing beneath the arch bearing the ranch's name interrupted Jackson's thoughts. He knew the wagon was headed for the east timber grove, the same place he'd be visiting the day after tomorrow with Grant Johnson. He needed to facilitate Johnson negotiating the final contract terms with John Landis, the mill owner. They would also determine a site for erecting an office from which to command the logging operation. Johnson wanted to approve the route Jackson had chosen for the half-mile stretch of road they would clear for hauling logs to the mill. Since the grove was two hours away, traveling back and forth was a waste of time, so he'd arranged to bunk down in the mill workers' quarters. Staying there reduced the risk Johnson would accidentally encounter Sam.

As the dust settled behind the retreating wagon, Jackson glanced over his shoulder to where Sam still slept. He'd deliberately delayed telling her about Johnson's visit and going to the grove because he suspected his absences contributed to whatever was bothering her. But last night, after enjoying a pleasant supper with Parker and Becky and returning to their house, he'd known he couldn't put it off any longer. He'd be gone three days.

Sam had taken the news calmly, nodding her understanding, giving no outward sign she was upset, but he'd known she didn't like it. The fact she'd clung to his side through the night was a clear indication she was troubled over it. His leaving increased her worry.

Jackson's gaze wandered back to the windows. While they'd resided in town, he and Sam had settled into a comfortable routine, with him riding back and forth to Trinity to shoulder the day-to-day responsibilities of running the ranch. He and Parker also prepared for Johnson's visit, though Jackson hadn't mentioned that aspect to Sam.

With him at the ranch most days, Sam had pushed to accomplish twice as much as a normal person, not always careful to give her body the care it needed to heal. Exhausted at day's end, she would fall quickly into a dead sleep. But, after an hour or so, she'd wake and move from the bed to the chaise, where he'd hear her shift restlessly, sleeping in short, fitful dribs and drabs. Shortly before it was time for him to get up, she'd slip back into bed, pretending she'd spent the entire night there. It wasn't until the latter part of the third week, she abandoned the chaise.

Most mornings Sam spent a few hours with Morgan at the bank. Afternoons, she'd go to the firing range. Workers clearing obstructions, installing target frames, and measuring and marking distances needed guidance. And who better to give it than Sam?

While there, she tested a new type of trap and glass ball target. Captain Adam Bogardus had developed "Bogardus balls"—hollow, feather-filled, glass-ball targets with exterior ridges to ensure shotgun pellets and rifle bullets would shatter them rather than glance off. He'd also invented a practical, spring-loaded trap for launching the glass balls 28 to 35 yards low into the sky. Bogardus intended to patent and manufacture the improved trap and glass targets after the new year.

Because trapshooting required a marksman to load, lift, sight, and fire at a fast rate, the exertion from loading and lifting her rifle as well as absorbing the recoil caused Sam significant pain. But by the end of the third week, the pain had faded to tolerable discomfort, so both her speed and stamina improved.

Since Morgan and Deacon had received the same training from Mac as Sam, she respected their expertise and gladly accepted their offers to direct several of the projects at the range. On days when the weather didn't cooperate or Sam's recovery warranted rest, her brothers conspired with Storey and Alexa to draw her into impromptu gaming sessions, when invariably they'd abandon the game and instead teach one another new tricks. Interested in the layout, variety of games, and amenities offered in Gracelyn's gaming rooms, Storey would compare other gaming establishments and differences in house rules and practices.

Evenings, they would dine with Deacon and Storey. When other responsibilities didn't interfere, Alexa and Morgan joined them. After supper, Sam and the others would adjourn to a reserved gaming room for a private poker game; though, occasionally, they'd choose to run games or deal cards in the salon. Jackson would go to the bank, where he toiled to install a revised version of Wharton's Robber Trap. Depending on schedules and skills required, Morgan, Parker, Cal Ennis, and Davis Wilson would meet him there to help.

On rare evenings when he wasn't at the bank, Jackson would enjoy a drink and friendly conversation with Wade Harper. Their friendship had been more rivalry than friendship until Wade's amorous interest had turned from Sam to Charity Rawlins. It was Wade who told Jackson the gossip whispered about Deacon and Jessa. Wade's mercantile was the most convenient location for the town's tongue-wagging citizens to gather and exchange real and fabricated tidbits, so of course, Wade was privy to learning every rumor whispered. The gossipers could transform the most benign conversation or innocent behavior into a scandalous tale. Unfortunately, malicious lies were more satisfying than truth. Delvinia Dalrymple was the most vocal regarding Deacon and Jessa. She embellished the stories she recounted so even a chance meeting between gambler and baker became an illicit tryst.

The gossip alleviated some of Jackson's jealousy while it amplified his protective instincts regarding Jessa. Though Jackson tended to believe Deacon was a decent, honorable man, he wasn't convinced. Experience taught him a man who gave vague and reserved answers when asked a direct question was hiding something. And a man with secrets was a difficult man to trust. Jackson wouldn't countenance Deacon playing Jessa false. She was too good a woman and had already experienced more than her share of heartbreak.

Jackson noticed Deacon was careful to treat Sam with brotherly affection, to which she responded with teasing humor and questions about their childhood. On the surface, their relationship appeared to be as Morgan had described, a younger sister admiring an older brother. However, on several occasions, Jackson saw a puzzled expression flit across Sam's face when in Deacon's company, as if something about him troubled her. Was she doubting Deacon's character or subconsciously sensing romantic undercurrents?

***

Drinking in her husband's nakedness as he stood brazenly in front of their bedroom windows, Sam detected an uncharacteristic stiffness in his posture. She'd practically glued herself to his side during the night. Was he wondering why his going to the timber grove upset her?

She needed to explain. But would he understand?

She was ashamed she'd allowed fear to rule her. Her failure to conquer it meant Ferguson was winning the battle to take part of her. She wouldn't surrender. Parker had told her Jackson had doubts about her trusting him, and she couldn't let Ferguson come between them.

But were there other watchers like Ferguson?

Flinging the bedcovers back, Sam swung her feet to the floor while impatiently unfastening the buttons of her nightdress. Once undone, her arms freed from the sleeves, a gentle shimmy of her hips sent the gown slithering to the floor.

Recognizing the soft rustle of bedclothes and the whisper of fine cotton gliding against bare skin, Jackson shifted his attention to Sam. Though he didn't turn to see or touch her, his skin tingled with stirrings of desire. He visualized silky, bare skin—lush breasts—creamy thighs. He swore he could feel her eyes running over his body, stringing him tight, his need heightened by the sexual frustration of having engaged in nothing more than affectionate caresses and light kissing while she'd healed.

While admiring the magnificent lines—architecture—of Jackson's body, Sam dipped her knees to grasp a corner of the bedsheet in each hand. Trailing it behind her, she went to him but stopped short of molding her breasts to his muscled back and her belly to his firm buttocks.

Hearing the soft pad of bare feet approaching, Jackson held his breath, waiting expectantly for the press of Sam's body. She was so near he could feel the heat radiating from her skin. Resisting the urge to step back, he pictured sleep-tousled hair, pink, pebbled nipples straining to rub against him, and damp, glistening thighs.

The erotic images made his erection weep in anticipation.

The sheet still within her grasp, Sam spread her arms wide and wrapped them around Jackson, partially enveloping their bodies in soft cotton.

Jackson didn't turn as she'd expected. Instead, he bent his elbows, his hands finding hers, and plucked the pointed corners from her clasp to bring them together—completing the circle. Wrapped together, Sam's soft curves molded to his hard, masculine planes.

Sam pressed her lips to the center of Jackson's spine, reveling in his scent and his heat. For a few moments, they stood quietly, their senses savoring the pleasure of bodies pressed together—until Sam's words could wait no longer.

"I'm afraid someone else—like Ferguson—watches me."

Sam felt Jackson's body tense. Then he released the sheet corners and let it float, as if in slow motion, to crumple into uneven folds at their feet. The body heat entrapped within its circle dissipated, allowing discomfiting coolness to take its place. He turned in her arms. Trembling, Sam tried to step back and turn so he couldn't see the shame she felt.

Jackson's arm wrapped around Sam's backside and pulled her close, while his other hand reached up to tangle in the hair at her nape and gently tug to raise her face. Gazing down, he caught a glimpse of a shadow in her eyes—a shadow he'd seen a hundred times. He'd begun to think of it as a predatory animal. With cunning it stalked her, waiting for vulnerable moments to pounce. He'd caught glimpses of it but hadn't realized its power. Hidden in her subconscious, it had been gnawing away her sanity while she'd fought against it alone.

Meeting Jackson's assessing gaze, Sam recalled Ferguson bragging about watching her. Crudely, he'd accused her of inviting him to bed her. He'd sworn she'd touched herself to arouse him; then, on the brink of release, she'd reject him and choose Jackson instead. He'd ranted Jackson's prowess was pitiable when compared with Ferguson's mastery.

She was tired of being afraid, tired of inventing reasons to leave her house, tired of feeling shame because she couldn't rid herself of the debasing terror. Held in the protective shelter of Jackson's arms, drawing from his strength, Sam fastened her eyes to his and quietly released all the words she'd held inside.

Then she stood silent, her forehead resting on his chest, waiting—not sure why.

Perhaps she did it because it was the wisest course of action after purging—should anything else ugly want to come out.

Chapter 19

I'm *afraid someone else—like Ferguson—watches me.* The words echoed in Jackson's head. Christ, he should have guessed. Now that she'd confessed, it was inconceivable he hadn't figured it out. Though, on some level, he had, or he wouldn't have imagined the predatory shadow he'd glimpsed in her eyes.

Clasping her upper arms, Jackson gave Sam a gentle shake. Then, turning to face the windows, he swept his arm in an expansive gesture, as if inviting the outside world into their bedroom. "Look out there, darlin', and tell me why it matters if someone watches us."

Sam angled her head to see beyond the panes of glass. Several ranch hands were gathering the reins of their horses, presumably preparing to mount and ride to wherever they'd been ordered to work. One of the men glanced in their direction. His eyes narrowed. Then opening them wide, they boldly roved over her nakedness before he caught himself and turned away. Oddly, she didn't try to hide herself. She wasn't embarrassed. Nor did she feel fear.

She shifted her gaze to Jackson. "Why doesn't it upset me that ranch hand looked at us? Is it because you're here?"

"It's not me who gives you courage. Hell, you can shoot a gnat off a pin head. If Mac's bullet hadn't reached

Ferguson first, yours would've killed him. You didn't need me or Mac."

He was right. She would've killed Ferguson. She felt some relief for having shared her fear with Jackson, but it wasn't enough. Though a fabrication of her mind, Reed Ferguson's disciple had captured a part of her—weakened her confidence and undermined her equanimity. She needed to obliterate him—sever his power—recover what he'd stolen.

Studying her face, Jackson recognized banishing a conjured stalker wasn't as simple as casting a symbolic wax figurine of Ferguson into a fire. But there might be a way to do the equivalent. "A watcher has an innate need for his victim to be unaware of his presence. He believes ignorance exposes his victim's vulnerability, thereby empowering the watcher to fulfill fantasies of pleasure, unachievable on his own. He relies on observing rather than personal participation. Imagine his other senses degraded or blocked. He can't hear your cries of pleasure, detect your scent, taste your mouth, touch your soft skin, feel the heat of your body, the expansion of your channel, the contractions of your release. With only his eyes to bring him gratification, he can experience nothing substantive."

Grasping Sam's wrist, Jackson pulled her into the hallway and guided her to the room Ferguson had used to sneak into the house to watch her. Halting outside the closed door, he reached around Sam to open it. As the door swung inward, Sam took an involuntary step back. Gently, Jackson urged her forward.

As though another person were there to see them, Sam moved her hands to cover her nudity. Standing behind her, Jackson's arms loosely circled her waist while his lips nibbled her shoulder where it met the column of her neck.

"Don't cover yourself, darlin'. Let him see you. Take away his power."

Take away his power. The words echoed through Sam. Jackson knew she could do this. She reached to capture one of his hands and guide it to cover her left breast.

Brushing his lips along the column of Sam's neck to the sensitive spot behind her lobe, Jackson pressed a kiss there. "What will you show him, darlin'?" His tone was curious, yet laced with an undertone of sensuality, inviting desire and eroticism into the room.

Savoring the pleasure of his lips on her neck and his hand kneading her breast, Sam slowly raised her gaze to the armoire she was facing. *What would she show him?* After a moment of silence, she stepped forward to open the armoire's embossed doors, revealing the full-length mirrors mounted on the inside panels. When she stepped back, she rested against Jackson's chest, studying their reflections as she answered with a shrug. "This is what I will show him. And I'll watch to see what he sees. But seeing without partaking can't fulfill desires. And unrealized pleasure depletes power."

Understanding flared between them. This was as much about reclaiming as banishing. At least it was if one understood the ability to live without the paralysis of fear was an act of reclamation. For most people, believing peril could be averted was a delusional necessity—because without that belief, free will and controlling one's destiny couldn't exist.

In the mirror, Jackson's eyes studied Sam's movements. He saw her turn from her reflection to face him, her arms lifting with the palms of her hands open to press against the hard slabs of his chest. But with the mirror at her back, she couldn't watch.

"You said you needed to see what he sees, darlin'," he reminded her.

Yes, she did need to see. Even as she thought it, Jackson's strong arms turned her with him until they stood face to face, sides to the mirror, their heads angled toward their reflections, their eyes following every caress exchanged between them.

Jackson ran his hand over the curve of her buttock, up the line of her back, to the side of her neck, to the delicate jut of her jaw, and finally around to the back of her head. Responding to his touch, Sam lifted her face as she arched her body against his. "Do to me what you wish to withhold from him—and remember, he can't feel—any of this," Jackson instructed, and with those words, his hand slid down her back, past the indentation of her waist, and over the swell of her bottom to cup her cheek and hold her softness against his hardness.

In the depths of the reflection, Sam's eyes locked with Jackson's. The beginning curve of a smile touched her lips, hinting at wanton prospects, as if she were deliberating the merits of each sinful delicacy one could sample when feasting at passion's table. Straining closer, her warm breath brushed his shoulder as she issued an invitation. "Watch with me—and feel me touch you."

Watching the pads of her fingers circle and drag across his male nipples, a sizzle of current, spiraling in waves of erogenous sensation, surged and receded with the variance of pressure she administered through her clever, tactile seduction. His nipples turned to pebbled knobs, her manipulations sending quakes of molten fire traveling through his belly to draw him up, taut, hot, and aching, against the apex of his stiff rod. Seeing himself with her, he felt as if there were two of him, one trapped within the cool glass, while the other was drowning in the pleasures of being loved, experiencing the fiery, hot sensations and decadence of the carnal act. He saw Sam's eyes grow heavy-lidded with need as she watched herself make love to him, as if she, too, had divided into two women, one a skilled seductress and the other a lustful bystander.

Watching her hands move over Jackson's body, reveling in the physical enjoyment of exploring his maleness, Sam realized the mirror reflected but a fraction of the truth it saw, for the images playing on its surface were nothing more than a false copy of the real world—the same—but different— for they lacked substance—while her touch was real.

For an instant, she glanced down before returning to the reflection to follow the path her splayed fingers took as they skimmed sensuously down the center of Jackson's chest, over the muscled ridges of his abdomen, seeking his hard shaft. Once found, she glided her palm along the hot, velvet skin. Then curving her fingers to form an incomplete circle around his girth, she stroked up and down his length. Entranced, she saw and felt the steel of him leap in response to her caresses, growing even hotter, harder in her grasp. Cradled in her other hand, his stones were full and heavy, straining with the pulse of his desire.

A bead of his essence formed at the slit on its tip as if begging to be sampled. She wanted to taste him, to put her tongue out to capture it. Slowly, she sank to her knees before him. In the mirror, she resembled a concubine, kneeling before her overlord. Then she leaned forward, the point of her tongue collecting the drop, savoring it, before taking him into her mouth, her tongue flicking and swirling and drawing.

Jackson had never seen anything so erotic. But it was the sensation and tenderness of her lips and tongue surrounding him that made him groan from pleasure so intense it was akin to pain. Fearing his knees would buckle, he closed his eyes and willed himself to maintain control, not crest too soon. When he opened them, his gaze didn't return to the mirror, for it put too much distance between them. He needed the flesh and blood woman, not the cool glass image of her.

God, he loved her. Sweeping her hair from her face, he saw her pulse beat in rhythm with his—that's what she did to him—brought their bodies into perfect synchronicity. Unable to bear more, he slid his hand from her silken hair around to cup her chin. "Stop, Sam. Not like this, not without you."

Releasing him, her eyes flew to his, and she raised her arms to capture his wrists, urging him to come down to her.

Sinking next to her, his mouth captured hers as he eased her onto her back and positioned himself between her legs. Breaking the kiss, he turned her head back to the mirror.

What Sam saw made her gasp. Poised to take her, desire hooding his eyes, muscles bulging, his manhood straining at her entrance, Jackson was magnificent, and she was his willing vassal, arranged to take him inside her as if she were an offering for her conqueror, his reward given in a ritualized rite. Seductress, temptress, and wanton, she looked as if she were created for this purpose. Perhaps it was true, and in giving, he would exorcise the fear.

When her eyes found Jackson's in the reflection, they were as passion-filled as hers. Slowly, he pressed forward, allowing his engorged tip to enter her. Then he gave her a little more and drew back. He bent his head to suckle a nipple leisurely, then the other one. Her hips rose, seeking more. When he didn't press forward, little sounds of disappointment escaped her. He advanced again. His withdrawals were as agonizingly slow as his advances. She turned her head from the mirror, whimpering her frustration.

"Watch, Sam," he commanded, and she obeyed.

She saw her knees fall farther apart, her stomach dipping as she sucked in an anticipatory breath. Then he thrust into her center, giving her all of him with one powerful thrust. Her hips rose to meet him, the heat and friction of his claiming bringing a sweet ecstasy of tingling fullness. The pleasure of receiving him was almost more than she could bear, except it wasn't enough to have him fill her, she needed more.

Staring at their joined image in the reflection, she saw him withdraw and immediately thrust forward, fascinated by his flesh disappearing into hers. But as arousing as it was to watch, it didn't convey a tenth of what she felt—his skin hot against hers, his flesh pressing against the front wall of her channel, stimulating the pleasure spot that would bring release, her inner flesh closing around him, surrounding him with her moist heat. The figures in the mirror were mimicking their movements, but the performance she watched was nothing more than a lifeless parody of their loving.

Then as one, they lost themselves in the all-consuming pleasures of mating. Sight alone wasn't enough. To experience this, she needed all her senses. Abandoning the images in the mirror, her body arching and bucking beneath Jackson's, she felt as if something indescribably dark was separating and lifting from her. The images and motion became nothing more than reflected flashes of light and color, blurs of movement that vanished the instant they registered on the cool, flat surface—for time was more powerful than fractured light—and with no discernment, gobbled them up—making them forever disappear—as if they had never been.

Free of her fear, triumphant, Sam's fervor rose. Her hands moved over the shifting muscles of Jackson's back and buttocks, kneading, urging him to drive himself as hard and deep into her as a man could go. The fiery sensations evoked by his long strokes were hurtling her toward the sweet throes of a bucking, cataclysmic orgasm. When she cried out, Jackson tensed, gave a guttural cry, and delved deep, flooding her with his life's force as her inner muscles convulsed around him.

Minutes passed before they moved—minutes during which Sam felt as if they'd been rescued from the fate of their twins watching within the mirrored glass, entities destined to disappear into the flat, cold, one-dimensional reflections, where they'd engaged in the real world through the trick of fractioned light from a place where touch, emotion, ecstasy could only be viewed—never attained— and, most certainly, never felt.

Still entwined, her face pressed into the curve of his shoulder, her arms tight around his middle, Jackson felt Sam's smile against his skin.

"Jackson?"

He kissed the valley between her breasts.

"I feel like we just cheated the devil." She felt the rumble of his mirth vibrate in his chest.

"The devil's loss is our gain," he murmured.

Then Jackson's mouth covered hers once more to tempt her. "Give me a few minutes of feasting on your sweet lips, darlin', and we'll cheat him again."

Chapter 20

Waking in the quiet aloneness of her and Jackson's bed, unease blossomed—the first since Jackson left for the timber grove. Sam consciously inhaled a deep breath before sitting up and focusing on her surroundings. Whatever woke her felt different from the fear of being watched. That fear had settled on her chest like the trunk of a felled tree, crushing her lungs until she could barely breathe. This didn't feel like that. Besides, she and Jackson had exorcised the imagined watcher.

Sam's ears caught the sound of wood pressing rhythmically against bare boards on the front porch. Someone was in the rocking chair. She reached for her gun belt hanging from the bedpost and drew her Colt before easing her feet to the floor. Perhaps Parker had ordered Wilson to stand guard. But it wasn't usual for him to do something like that without telling her. Cautiously, she crept through the shadows, pausing every few steps to listen. After reaching the door, she lifted the bar. While inching the door open, the rocking stopped.

The moon was full and bright, slanting slivers of silvery light beneath the porch roof. A short pair of legs stuck straight out from the seat of the rocking chair. The eyes of the boy sitting there appeared as enormous black hollows. Was his lower lip trembling? Sam shifted her gaze to surveil the shadows beyond the porch, searching for whoever brought the child. She saw no one. Turning back to the boy, she saw his lower lip quivering.

She smiled reassuringly as she knelt in front of him. Placing her gun at her side, she raised her hands and, palms down, rested them on Peter Jack's knees. His eyes followed her movements. "Peter Jack, sweetheart, are you here all by yourself?"

His head bobbed up and down. "Yes, ma'am." He barely whispered the words.

Sam slid her hands up his legs to find his hands and wrap hers around them. They were cold. "Sweetheart, it's chilly out here. Wouldn't you like to come along inside with me?"

Her smile was kind and her voice soft, soothing his fear. He was trying to be brave. His mama said she'd take care of him, but he hadn't been sure 'til now. "Yes, Missus Sam." He hesitated. He didn't know if she wanted him to scoot down from the chair now or wait until she stood.

Seeing his uncertainty, Sam picked up her Colt and gently clasped her other hand around one of Peter Jack's, urging him from the rocker, then to the door. After entering the house, she turned to search the deep shadows again. Still seeing no sign of anyone, she closed the door and dropped the bar into place. Peter Jack was staring up at her. The trust in his eyes was unnerving, especially since she had no idea how to proceed.

"Jackson's out at the east timber grove. Come into the bedroom. We can sit in the bed while we talk." After lighting a lamp, Sam grasped his hand to lead the way.

When they reached the bed, Peter Jack hesitated. He knew to take his shoes off, but then what? While Missus Sam turned the bedding back, he untied his laces and removed his shoes. Glancing up, he noticed her nightdress. "Mama didn't send any of my things with me. You s'pose it would be proper to take off my su'penders and sleep in my clothes?"

"I don't see why not," she answered. "Will that be all right with you?"

Nodding, he stripped off his socks. As he attacked the front hooks of his suspenders, Missus Sam tended to the ones in the back. Then he yanked his shirt from his pants and scrambled up onto the big bed.

"You're on my side, Peter Jack," Missus Sam said with a smile, waving her hand as if shooing chickens from her path. "Scoot over. You can sleep on Jackson's side."

Peter Jack was worried about occupying Mister Jackson's place in the bed. "Maybe Mister Jackson won't like me sleepin' in his spot. I see him get a riled look on his face when other fellas stare at you. I reckon he might get real mad about another fella sleepin' next to you."

Sam kept a straight face. "Well, since it's you that's gonna sleep there, I'm sure he'll consider you're doing him a favor by watching out for me while he's gone. You're his friend, and he trusts you." Though he had a doubtful look on his face, Peter Jack scooted over.

As Sam settled herself onto the bed and reached for the covers, she said, "It's late, Peter Jack. Who brought you here?"

His voice was low when he answered. "My mama." Then, she thought he must have remembered instructions from his mother because he dug deep into a pocket and pulled out a crumpled piece of paper, which he thrust into her hand. "Mama said I was to give this to Mister Jackson, but since he's not here, I 'spect it's all right to give it to you."

Sam read the note.

Jackson,

Peter Jack is your son. I'm sorry I lied to you. I'm confessing the truth now because I must go away and place our son in your care. I trust you and Sam will keep him safe and love him.

Jessa

Jackson and Jessa had made this beautiful, engaging boy. The truth cut deeper into Sam's heart than she was prepared for. Jessa had been able to give Jackson the one thing Sam couldn't. When she could think past her hurt, she found Peter Jack anxiously watching her. This child was depending on her and needed reassurance. Smiling, she patted his hand.

"Do you know what this says?"

"Yes. Mama said Mister Jackson is my papa and would take care of me until she comes for me. I asked her some questions, but she said she couldn't 'splain ever'thin' now."

"Do you know where your mother went, Peter Jack?"

"Mama said it was better for me not to know."

"Do you know why she had to go away?"

Peter Jack lowered his eyes and shook his head. He couldn't tell her about the bad man. Mama said the man would hurt her if he told her.

Sam suspected he knew something but wasn't comfortable telling her. To keep him from becoming more upset than he already was, she let it drop. "Well, it's after two in the morning. We'll sort things out tomorrow. We should go to sleep." Pretending to yawn, she fluffed her pillow. "I'm tired. How about you?"

Relieved she wouldn't ask more questions, Peter Jack replied, "I reckon I am, too."

Sam patted the boy's cheek and drew the covers up around his shoulders. As she turned to douse the lamp on the bedside table, Peter Jack's wavering voice asked, "You won't let Mister Jackson send me to the orphans' home, will you? My friend Tommy lives there, and he don't like it much." Sam's heart swelled with compassion. He knew the orphan's home was where children lived when they didn't have a mother and a father.

Sam's mind suddenly skipped backward, recalling a memory of when she was six, shortly after her papa had been killed in the Eden Ridge bank robbery. She'd been in the great room at her ranch, Highbreeze, sitting on a stool while listening to Mac read a story about a little girl sent to live in an orphanage. The headmistress didn't like the little girl, so she didn't give her much food, made her work harder than the other children, and gave her patched dresses to wear. Associating with the abused girl, she'd turned her face away from Mac to hide the silent tears sliding over her cheeks.

When Mac noticed, he'd laid the book down and lifted her onto his lap, his strong arms wrapping around her in a comforting embrace. She'd buried her face in his shirt, breathing in the leather and soap scent of him, trying to calm herself, not wanting her voice to shake. "I don't have a mama or papa, Mac. Please don't let them take me away. I want to stay with you, Grace, Uncle Storey, and my brothers. You won't let anyone be mean to me, will you?"

"No one will ever take you away from me, sweetheart, or mistreat you," Mac said, crooning the words she needed to hear. "Grace and I love you. Do you remember I promised your papa I would love and protect you?" She didn't answer because she wasn't sure she knew about the promise. He put his crooked index finger under her chin to tilt her head up to look at him. "I want you to always remember this, Sam.

You're my girl, and I'll always take care of you. So will Grace and your Uncle Storey—Morgan and Deacon, too."

As her eyes searched his face, Mac had smiled a gentle smile. "Wasn't it you who told me when you were only three that Grace is the angel your mama in heaven sent to take care of you?" Sam nodded. She'd known Grace was an angel as soon as she saw her platinum hair shining in the sunlight across the street from where she and her papa had been walking in town. Shortly after that, her papa married Grace.

"Well, it turned out true what you said. Grace is *our* angel, so I don't want you to worry about this ever again. If you let me finish the story, you'll see the little girl finds a new mama and papa who love her very much, and the bad lady doesn't get away with treatin' the little girl so mean." Mac smoothed the last of her tears away with the callused pads of his thumbs, and she reached her arms up to hug him around the neck.

Then the memory was gone. Jolted back into the present, Sam blinked.

Peter Jack had moved close and was gripping the material of her nightdress in his hand. Impulsively, Sam wrapped her arms around him and pulled his little body against hers in a warm embrace. "You're not to worry Peter Jack, sweetheart. Jackson will be a good papa. He already loves you." She believed what she said was true. Jackson was a good man.

Peter Jack relaxed against her. He'd been holding back tears, blinking away the moisture before it spilled from his eyes. "I mostly was worried about the orphanage and my mama." He rested his head on her chest.

Sam swallowed around a lump of emotion swelling in her throat. This child was accepting her reassurances and giving her his trust. It was humbling. Exhaling shakily, she snuggled deeper into the soft mattress, the boy in her arms. She strove to keep her voice even and calm when she spoke. "Let's go to sleep. Tomorrow, after JB makes us a fine breakfast up at the main house, we'll go to town and get your things. I bet Mr. Evans will drive us in the buckboard, so we'll have room to bring back whatever you want. Becky might even go with us if we promise she can buy some new ribbons at the mercantile. You'll see. Everything will be just fine." She gently stroked his hair until she was sure he was asleep. Then she listened to his even breathing while wondering whether the things that she'd told him were true.

She didn't let herself think about Jessa and Jackson—the important thing was to make sure Peter Jack felt loved and wanted. But before sleep took her, it occurred to her to wonder why a mother as loving as Jessa would ask them to keep Peter Jack safe first and to love him second.

Wouldn't the natural order have been first to love him and second to keep him safe?

Chapter 21

The thumping and scraping of a wooden chest lashed loosely in the wagon bed made it difficult for Sam to sleep. Jackson should have tied it down tighter. Sighing, she groggily stroked the hair on the head resting on her breast, intending to tell him. But then she realized the hair was too fine and the body too small and soft. Jackson wasn't here and there was no wagon or chest. She and Peter Jack were snuggled in the bed, and the sounds she'd heard in her dream were real.

Someone was in the house.

Careful not to wake Peter Jack as she slid from bed, Sam reached for her Colt for the second time that night and quietly drew back the hammer. After first checking to make sure the bolt was secure on the door to her office, she crossed to the opposite wall to put her ear against the hallway door panel. While listening, she briefly reviewed her options.

If she exited the bedroom through the office door, there was a chance she could sneak up on the prowler from behind. But if she did that, she might expose Peter Jack to more danger than if she were between him and the intruder—*and she was damn sure someone* was in the back part of the house. The noises that woke her had given him away.

She considered waking the sleeping child and taking him with her but quickly discarded the idea. If bullets started to fly, especially in the dark, the odds of his being hurt were high. Nor could she chance sneaking him out the front door or through one of the bedroom windows, because she didn't know whether the intruder was alone or had accomplices outside the house.

The intruder probably didn't know the boy was with her. If she hid him, the trespasser might accept the room was empty. But if he searched the room looking for her and found Peter Jack instead? No, her best bet was to confront and eliminate the threat the intruder posed while leaving the boy here.

Making no sound, she unlatched the door and eased it open a crack. Hearing nothing, she risked another inch. Still nothing. Opening the door wider, she peeked around the doorframe. She couldn't see much, but nothing stirred.

Pulling back, she considered the other doors along the hallway. Three rooms were on the other side of the hall. The one directly across from her and Jackson's was a large guest bedroom, connected by a bathing room to a smaller bedroom. At the far end of the hall was the room that Ferguson had used to gain entry to the house. On the same side as her room, was a private space, designed for her brother, although he hadn't used it since marrying Alexa. His suite had a bedroom, office, and small sitting room. An exterior door opened directly into the sitting room. From the dining room, another door opened into the office. Morgan's bedroom, like hers and Jackson's, could be accessed from the hallway or his office. That put his bedroom door opposite the corner bedroom, the one Ferguson had used. She'd made love with Jackson in front of the armoire mirrors in that room.

During Jackson's absence, she'd pored over the plans for the bank, made two trips to town to help Morgan, and checked progress at the firing range. She'd also been regularly grooming her black stallion, Hooker, taking walks, and doing some light lifting, trying to build her stamina and core strength. Each day, she'd grown stronger and less tolerant of her physical limitations. Though her ribs were much better, her energy ebbed by the middle of the afternoon, leaving her drained and listless. Yesterday, she'd fallen asleep at her desk for two hours. Jackson was coming home tomorrow. No, wait. It was past three in the morning. Jackson would be home today.

Grant Johnson would likely stay the night and return to Cheyenne the following day. It wouldn't be soon enough for her—especially now that Peter Jack was here, although she hadn't had time to consider how she would tell Jackson about being a father or figure out what she'd do after that. Her immediate concern was eliminating the threat inside her house.

When a drawn-out, high-pitched creak reached her ears, she recognized the sound. She'd heard it the other day while opening the armoire doors in the corner bedroom. The hinges needed oil. Sam exhaled a slow breath, reminding herself whoever was in that room wasn't an imaginary watcher conjured by her fear. Since neither she nor Jackson had bothered to tidy the room after they'd "cheated the devil," the unknown intruder must've brushed against one of the doors.

Hugging the wall opposite her bedroom, crouched low, gun ready, Sam groped her way along the hall. There were no windows or open doors to provide light, so she navigated strictly by touch. A few seconds after her fingers found the corner bedroom doorframe, she discovered the intruder hadn't latched the door. It swung inward from the slight pressure of her hand running along the panel seeking the doorknob.

The glow of moonlight filtering through the room's sole window revealed the armoire door near her was all but closed. The mirror on the other door reflected the dark image of a tall, broad-shouldered man—holding a gun.

Casting the image of Ferguson from her mind, Sam made herself step around the door to point the barrel of her Colt at the intruder's chest. He didn't raise his gun or move.

"If you're not going to shoot me, Sammy, would you point that gun somewhere else?"

Though there wasn't enough light to make out features, Sam recognized the voice. But why would he break into her house when he could have knocked and been invited in?

"While I'm deciding, Deacon, put your gun on the floor and shove it my way. I think much better when a man I didn't invite into my house doesn't have a gun in his hand, which reminds me that you need to send your derringer over here, too."

"Now, Sammy—" Deacon began.

That's all she allowed him to say before cutting him off. "Raise your gun hand and bend your knees to put that Colt on the floor with your left hand—hold the barrel with your thumb and index finger." Encouraging him, she added, "That's right. You know how to do it."

Bracing the front of her bared foot, she trapped the barrel of the Colt to halt its slide. "Now, take your derringer out with your left hand and send it over here like you did your Colt."

Holding his jacket open, Deacon protested. "Sammy, this is ridiculous. You know I wouldn't hurt you."

"I wouldn't have thought so, Deacon, but me finding you here like this doesn't provide much evidence to support that kind of thinkin' on my part. And if you'll remember, I don't have much in the way of memory to go by."

It was difficult to see in the dim light, but she thought she saw him roll his eyes before setting the derringer on the floor and sending it in her direction. Not taking her eyes off him, she stooped to pick up both guns before motioning for him to stand.

She thought it odd he placed a hand on the wall to steady himself. After straightening, he wedged his back against the wall, as if he needed it to hold him up. Sam craned her neck forward to get a better look, but in the dim light, it was impossible to see.

Suspicious he was playing a trick, she motioned toward the bed. "Sit down and light the lamp on the bedside table. There are matches in the top drawer."

Deacon took three unsteady steps before pausing and patting the bed surface as if he needed to make certain where the edge was. With his hand still on the bed, he turned and dropped down, within easy reach of the lamp.

His weapons in her left hand, Sam kept her gun trained on Deacon, although she was beginning to think it unnecessary. Something was wrong with him. Usually, his movements were deliberate and fluid, not hesitant and jerky. Was he drunk?

Fumbling in the drawer, Deacon found the matches, but it took him two tries to light one, the flame circling the wick before it made contact and caught. The match burned down too far. Forced to pitch it to the floor, he popped the tip of his finger in his mouth to soothe the burn.

In the lamplight, Sam saw he was a mess. His clothes were dusty and rumpled. There were dark stains on the right shoulder of his jacket. Then she saw the crimson on his white shirt collar. Her eyes moved to his face and she noted the unhealthy gray color of his skin. Their gazes held while he cautiously raised a hand to explore the back of his head with his fingers.

"How bad are you hurt?" Sam asked.

Instead of answering, Deacon inquired, "Is Jessa here?"

"Is Jessa here?" Sam repeated, confused by the question. "Why would Jessa be here?" Tensing, she worried about Peter Jack. Was Deacon looking for him, too?

"I trailed a wagon here after Jessa and Peter Jack disappeared from Jessa's house. I thought their kidnapper was in here doing God-knows-what to you, Jessa, and Peter Jack." Wearily, he pressed a hand over his eyes. "Trust me, it sure as hell wasn't you I expected to see come through that door." Circling back to his original question, his voice sounding strained, he asked again. "So, Jessa's not here?"

"No, Jessa's not here." It was the truth, and Sam felt no obligation to volunteer anything about Peter Jack. Before Deacon could ask anything else, she managed a question of her own. "How did you get hurt?"

"Someone hit me from behind while I was at Jessa's." *More like while I was lost in the pleasure of kissing Jessa. Lord, what had he been thinking? The truth was, he hadn't been thinking—at least not with his head.*

"I don't know who hit me." *That was a lie.* "I was unconscious for about an hour. When I came to, Jessa and Peter Jack were gone. The house was mussed up, but not ransacked. I don't think there was a struggle. But Jessa had been acting nervous." *And she was as stiff as a broom handle while I kissed her.* "I don't believe she and Peter Jack went voluntarily."

Sam tried to piece together what Deacon said with what she read in Jessa's note and learned from Peter Jack. She couldn't see how kidnapping fit in. "Why didn't you go to the sheriff?"

Because Jessa's wanted by the law, and I don't want her hurt. But Deacon couldn't tell Sam that, so he lied again. "I guess I should have, but I didn't think about it at first. I followed my instincts, which told me to look for a trail. I thought if I moved fast enough, I could find them."

Correctly interpreting the dubious expression in Sam's unblinking gaze, Deacon considered exaggerating the severity of his injury to distract her. As a girl when she was roughhousing with him and Morgan, they'd sometimes pretend she'd accidentally hurt one of them to trick her. She had a tender heart when it came to those she loved.

He didn't need to pretend this time, though. Dizziness washed over him in a sickening wave, and he clutched a handful of bedcovers to keep from toppling over. Jessa hadn't held back when she'd hit him. His head hurt so bad he couldn't have play-acted if his life depended on it. It was a wonder he'd made it to Trinity without falling off his horse. If he hadn't been so wobbly, Sammy wouldn't have heard him break in. His god-awful balance and blurred vision were what caused him to stumble after breaking in through the coal chute doors. Then later, he'd bumped into several pieces of furniture. Hell, he hadn't even been aware the armoire doors were standing open before he heard one creaking. Giving his head a little shake, he made himself concentrate on Sammy's voice.

"How would you be able to track them, Deacon? If you didn't see them leave, how do you know which way they went? You wouldn't know if they took a buggy, wagon, or horse. Hell, they may have walked to the railroad depot and boarded the train. Did you think of that?"

Relaxing his clamped jaw, Deacon answered. "I know the train schedule, Sammy. That's one of the things I check when I first arrive in a new town—the stage schedule too. It's standard practice for a professional gambler. You know that. Grace and Storey taught you the same rules they taught me."

"Fair enough, Deacon." His answer was what she'd expected. "So how *did* you track them here?"

"I saw a tarp-covered wagon behind Jessa's house when I tied up my horse. I knew it wasn't hers. When I regained my senses, it was gone, but one of Peter Jack's precious marbles was on the ground where the wagon had been.

"I took careful measure of the width between the wheels and noticed it has wider-than-normal, metal rims. There's enough moon out tonight to follow sign. It didn't take me long to recognize it was headed here. Whenever the tracks got mixed up with those of something else, I kept riding toward Trinity and would find them again."

It was a plausible explanation, well within his skills, assuming Mac had taught him how to track.

Deacon's hand moved to shield his eyes from the lamplight, and suddenly he looked paler. Sam put all three guns on the floor at the foot of the bed before going to his side. Reaching to the back of his head, she urged him to lean forward so she could examine his wound.

Embarrassed, Deacon pulled back. For years, he'd dreamed of Sam's touch, but not like this. Things were different now.

"I'm all right, Sammy. Leave it."

Deciding to tend to Deacon in the kitchen, away from Peter Jack, Sam asked, "Can you get to the kitchen if I help you? I'll clean up the gash and put in some stitches."

"I expect I can get to your kitchen without keeling over. But I can't promise not to bleed while I do it."

Feigning an excuse so she could check on Peter Jack, Sam ran a hand up and down her left arm, pretending to be cold. "Wait here while I get my wrapper and slippers." Then she slid open the top drawer of the bedside table, retrieved a candle mounted in a holder, and quickly flared a match to light the wick. Leaving the lit candle on the table, she kept her eyes on Deacon while moving to the foot of the bed to collect the three guns on the floor. With the weapons clutched in one arm, she darted back to the bedside table to pick up the candle holder with her free hand. Heading for the door, she called over her shoulder, "Rest here. I'll be right back."

Sammy wasn't gone but a few seconds when Deacon remembered Jackson teasing her about the huge tub in their fancy bathing room. So why wouldn't she take him there? Was she embarrassed to invite a man into a private room she shared with her husband or was she hiding someone? And, sonofabitch, if Jessa and Peter Jack weren't here, where were they?

Sammy had gotten the drop on him too easily. And she had his guns. Wearily he passed a hand over his eyes, hoisted himself up, and went to the bedroom door to peek into the hallway. Candlelight cutting the hall's blackness identified which bedroom was Sammy's. Oddly, she'd placed the candleholder on the hallway floor next to the partially open door.

It made following her incredibly simple.

Chapter 22

Careful not to wake Peter Jack, Sam backed from her bedroom and eased the door closed. Half a turn and two steps later, she plowed into Deacon's chest. He caught her upper arms and kept her from falling. Angry she hadn't sensed his presence and concerned he might have glimpsed Peter Jack, she shoved at his shoulder. "I told you to wait for me," she hissed in a loud whisper.

Deacon mustered a wan smile. "I know, but I'm feeling worse. I remembered your bathing room is closer than the kitchen, so I decided to come to you." Between his aching head and the frustration over her shutting the door before he could see inside, it was the best excuse he could fabricate. He was certain she was hiding something or someone in there.

"Why are you whispering?" he asked. When Sammy hesitated, he decided patience wasn't a virtue. He needed to do something to get her away from the door. Though he didn't like doing it, he bent his head close, his lips a few inches from hers.

Sammy's eyes widened and she backed away quicker than a jackrabbit hops, but not far enough to put the door within Deacon's reach.

Hoping a slow advance would force further retreat, he edged forward. But after an inch or two, Sammy planted her feet, raised her palms to his chest, and pushed back—hard—though she lacked the muscle to make him fall back.

He didn't want to hurt her, so he tried more trickery. Pretending to come at her from a different angle, he feinted to her left. Sam reflexively sidestepped, leaving the goal Deacon sought undefended. Moving fast, he covered the distance, twisted the knob, and pushed the door open to find Peter Jack curled on his side in a large bed, one arm flung out and the other tucked under his pillow. Deep in sleep, the boy was blissfully unaware of his presence.

Sam watched several emotions flit in quick succession across Deacon's face before he returned to the hallway, shutting the door behind him. When he pinned his icy glare on her, she imagined it could freeze water in the middle of a desert. Scowling, arms crossed over her chest, she returned his glare.

Deacon's hand shot out to capture her elbow and forcibly scuttle her to the far end of the corridor. When his grip loosened, she jerked her arm free and spewed her fury. "If you came to hurt that boy, you'd better pray for a quick death because I've about made up my mind to shoot off tender bits of your anatomy so the devil can roast them over hell's flames for that cheap trick you pulled to get me away from the door."

It wasn't until then Deacon noticed her holster strapped over her robe. Now he was the one retreating. "Calm down, Sammy. I'd never hurt Peter Jack or Jessa—I care about them." Unexpectedly, a wave of weakness swept through him, leaving him drained. He swiped an unsteady hand across his forehead, and, for the second time that night, sagged against the wall.

"Deacon?" Sam murmured, alarmed at his faintness.

"I'm all right, but I need to ask again about Jessa. Are you hiding her, too?"

"No! She's not here. Peter Jack said she brought him. And she sent Jackson a note."

"What does it say?"

Instead of answering, Sam started back toward her bedroom. Deacon rallied to scramble after her. "Dammit, Sammy. Turn around and talk to me."

Sam slowed, allowing him to fall into step beside her. "The note said Jackson is Peter Jack's father and Jessa had to go away. She left Peter Jack in our care."

"Do you believe it?"

"I don't know." Having reached her bedroom door, she paused and looked up at Deacon. "Go on in. The bathing room is the door to your right. There are matches and a lamp on the table to the left of the door. I'll fetch a bottle of bourbon for cleaning up that gash."

***

Though dizzy and bleary-eyed, Deacon grinned at the bathing room's splendor. Most upper-class homes had a tub stored in the pantry, a chamber pot under the bed, and a privy out back. Wealthy homes in the West had a washbasin in the bedroom and a tub hidden behind a screen. Heated water was hauled in to fill the tub. Instead of an outdoor privy, there was a water closet, usually located beneath the stairs in a two-story house.

Sam's washroom exceeded anything Deacon had seen, except in a Chicago luxury-class hotel, where the miracle of indoor plumbing first appeared in the 1850s after someone finally figured out how to deliver pressurized water with enough force to flush waste outside through a system of pipes. Deacon knew the water supplying Sam's bathing room was stored in a huge tank elevated on a tower at roof level. Pulling the chain hanging from the cistern mounted on the wall near the ceiling would run water through pipes to a lidded bowl anchored on the floor. The pedestaled commode resembled a rimmed funnel with its narrowed end crimped back to attach to a pipe disappearing into the wall behind the base. Attached to the bowl was a hinged lid to cover the rimmed opening.

The tub, washbasin, commode bowl, and cistern were blush-rose-colored granite, rubbed to such a high polish they gleamed in the lamplight. The deep granite tub was big enough for two people to bathe together. The fittings were copper and connected to two copper pipes running from the outside tank. One pipe carried cold water. Deacon assumed the other pipe drew hot water from a boiler. The floor was white marble. Three rectangular-shaped windows were set high on the outer wall to vent steam and moisture and provide natural light.

Deacon recalled Jackson recounting how he'd met John Randall Mann, an American entrepreneur who'd invented a three-pipe, siphonic closet for which he'd been granted a patent. Impressed by the design, Jackson invested in Mann's company. He'd also encouraged Morgan and Sam to study the technology and projected sales figures. Eventually, they made substantial investments. While the product wasn't one people talked about in polite circles, it did provide an attractive solution to an age-old human problem; thus, it all but guaranteed netting a good return on their investment, especially if the problems of drainage could be conquered in cities. Out here, where space and land were plentiful, it wasn't a challenge.

Frowning at Deacon's frank admiration, Sam deposited a bottle of bourbon on a small nearby table. She waved him to the chair situated between the table and the bathtub before retrieving a needle and thread from the cabinet mounted over the washbasin. Supplies in hand, she turned and nodded toward the bourbon bottle. "Take a few pulls of that."

Deacon arched an eyebrow, clearly asking a question.

"What?" Sam teased, impressed his manners prodded him to seek permission before imbibing directly from the bottle. "Do you expect me to offer you a glass?"

One corner of Deacon's mouth twitched. "Won't it shock your tender sensibilities to see me drink from the bottle?"

Sam grinned. "Hardly. Jackson and Morgan tell me proper has never been a big concern." Proving her point, she tugged the bottle from his grip and took a half-swallow. Swiping the back of her hand across her lips, she stoically ignored the bilious twist in her gut when the evil-tasting stuff hit bottom. "I don't care for bourbon, so it goes down best when I guzzle it. I'm convinced, it's only good for medicinal purposes and bucking up courage." Extending her arm, she passed Deacon the bottle. "Best drink up. I expect you'll need it."

Ignoring the tremor in his hand, Deacon raised the bottle to his lips and drank deeply. Sammy moved behind his chair to draw hot water from the tub spigot into a basin. He could feel the heat of her skin. While suffering her ministrations he concentrated on the light citrus fragrance clinging to her skin. Thankfully, she made quick work of cleaning the dried blood away; otherwise, encouraged by the bourbon he'd consumed, he might have been tempted to notice other things.

Sam pressed her hand against Deacon's neck, urging him to lower his head over the side of the tub. Holding a dry cloth to his forehead to protect his eyes, she flooded the wound with alcohol. He made no sound but couldn't control the jerk of his shoulders. His forearms taut, knuckles white, Sam half expected he'd rip the chair arms from their joints. As he dragged in a steadying breath, she gently patted the drips before motioning he should straighten. "Better take a couple more pulls," she advised, pressing the bourbon bottle into his hand. "It'll take three or four stitches to close this up."

Grateful for the offer, Deacon took another gulp. Eyes closed and jaw clenched, he made himself focus on the needle piercing his skin and the drag of the thread rather than the woman doing the stitching.

After tying the last stitch, Sam rubbed at her temple. Lord, but she was tired. Dealing with Peter Jack and Deacon had taken its toll. Sunrise was all but here—and when Jackson arrived home in the afternoon, they would need to talk about Deacon and Peter Jack being here and Jessa's note. Beyond that, she wouldn't let herself think.

She poured the bloodied water from the basin over the stained cloths mounded in the bottom of the tub. Then, bent low, she wrung them out, stoppered the drain, and twisted the spigot to run cold water to soak the cloths.

Satisfied with the depth of the water, she turned the spigot counterclockwise and started to straighten. Flickering spots and a whooshing sound filled her head. Her hands scrambled for the tub rim.

Deacon saw Sammy's frantic grab and sprang forward. Catching her at her hips, he towed her backward, momentum pressing the soft contours of her rump against his face. The back of his head clipped the hard edge of the chair seat as they slid to the floor, Sam's bottom intimately following the hard lines of his torso before settling heavily on his lap— make that, crushing his tender male anatomy. Widening his legs, he gingerly scooted back, letting gravity sink her backside to the floor. Unconscious, her head lolled against his bicep.

If she were any paler, Deacon doubted he'd be able to distinguish her from the white marble beneath them. Gently he moved her head to the center of his chest. After turning her upper torso so his arm supported her back, he lifted her legs to rest over his thigh. With her side curled against his chest, and his shoulder cushioning her head, the glow of the lamp accentuated the dark smudges beneath her eyes.

"What's wrong with Missus Sam?" Peter Jack asked, his voice low and anxious.

Deacon's head jerked up. He hadn't noticed the boy's approach. He stood in the doorway gripping the doorframe with one hand while rubbing his eyes with a balled-up fist.

Careful to keep his tone reassuring, Deacon answered with a bald-faced lie. "She fainted after doctoring my head. She's never been good with the sight of blood, and it was too much for her." Suddenly inspired, he tacked on, "You know how girls are. I guess I was lucky she held up as long as she did." He curved his lips into what he hoped was a comforting smile, and recklessly added, "She'll wake in a minute or two." Of course, that was another lie. He had no idea when she would regain consciousness. Moments later, though, Sammy stirred weakly in his arms, turning his lie into truth.

Confused, Sam wondered why she was in the dark with her backside resting on something cold and hard when the rest of her was warm and floating weightless. Slowly gaining awareness, she realized strong arms held her. When she opened her eyes, Deacon was studying her face. He was so close his breath brushed her skin.

Memory flared.

***

Deacon's lips came down on hers, and his tongue swept over the fullness of her lower lip, urging her to open for him. His embrace tightened—and she felt trapped. Despite wanting to break free, she tried to push the panic down. But it kept rising. Oh please, God, she prayed, don't let me hurt

229

Deacon's feelings. *He loves me. I wish his kisses thrilled me. I wish his touch excited me. I wish I felt desire.* But she didn't—couldn't.

Fear overwhelmed her. She pushed him away and covered her face with her hands. "I'm sorry! So sorry. I can't do this. I can't! Please, f-forgive me."

The memory bore a hole in her chest so deep the pain hurled her back to the present.

***

Sam's fingers flew to her lips as if the sear of Deacon's lips still burned there. "You kissed me—and—said you were in love with me. I remember."

Deacon's heart soared because she'd recalled something of their feelings for each other, then nearly stopped as he realized how much the memory must hurt. Though he'd tried to show her how good love could be between them, his kisses and caresses had failed abysmally. She'd been too frightened—too damaged. She was the dream he'd chased and could never catch. And her rejection had hurt so much, he'd gone away.

Sam recognized the pain in Deacon's expression. He'd known that long-ago kiss had brought back her terror. While he'd held her, kissed her, caressed her—she hadn't been able to keep away the ugly memories of McBride. It hadn't mattered how gentle he'd been or how much she cared for him. She hadn't been able to love him—not like that.

Because of her love for Jackson, she understood she'd hurt Deacon deeply. She'd felt shame and guilt over not being able to return his kisses. And here in the present, she knew she could never have loved him that way. Though she felt a tenderness for him, it wasn't love—not the kind he'd sought—deserved. Jackson was the man who completed her—the man she desired—the man she loved with all her heart.

Unaware of Peter Jack's presence, Sam was startled when he laid his hand on her cheek. Was there anything in the world more tender and comforting than the gentle touch of a child's hand? Turning to him, she was dismayed to see the quiver of his lower lip and shining, unshed tears in his eyes.

"Why did you kiss him?" Peter Jack demanded. "You're not supposed to love him—only Mister Jackson—and—and me," he accused, so much anguish and hurt in his voice.

Taking his hand in hers, Sam tried to explain. "You know how I don't remember things because of hurting my head in the stage wreck?"

Peter Jack let his hand rest in hers and nodded.

"Well, sometimes a memory comes to me. And when it comes, it surprises me."

While explaining, Sammy was looking at Peter Jack, but Deacon was aware her words were for him as much as they were for the boy.

"I remembered a kiss Deacon gave me a long time ago before I came to Prosperity—before I knew you or Jackson. Deacon left home soon after because I made him sad. You see, I was raised with Deacon. He is my brother, like Morgan is my brother. You remember me telling you about Morgan's mama, Grace, being my mother, too?"

Peter Jack reluctantly nodded again.

"Deacon shared his papa, Storey, with me and Morgan, just as Morgan shared his mama, Grace, with me and Deacon. Storey and Grace had room in their hearts for us all. When we got older, Deacon started to care about me— different from a brother's caring, and I just now remembered a time when he told me. But back then, I didn't understand and that made me—afraid. I do love Deacon, Peter Jack, but my love for him isn't the same as what I feel for Jackson—

or you. Think of your mama and Mrs. Chambers. Because each is special and touches your life in different ways, your love for each is different. Do you understand?"

Deacon knew the question wasn't truly about understanding. She was asking if he could accept sisterly love and friendship. He saw it in her eyes. And yes, he did understand. *She would never love him—and he would never love her—not as he had once dreamed.*

In a moment of clarity, he realized there may have been a moment—if things had been different—when love might have had a chance—might have flourished, but the moment hadn't been allowed—because of McBride, the difference in their ages, and countless other misaligned variables. Seeing her happiness now, he could understand—forgive her— more important—himself. With understanding, came acceptance. And with acceptance came relief—for with it, doors to possibilities opened—freeing him to search for something else—*no*—*for someone else*—a special someone. *Jessa.* Thoughts of her flowed over him like waves curling over a sandy beach, advancing and receding to leave unblemished sand on the shore.

Sam, making a weak effort to sit up, brought Deacon's thoughts back to her. Quickly exhausted, her body went lax and her eyelids drifted closed. Uncertain if she was conscious, he said her name. "Sammy?"

Sam heard Deacon but was too weary to open her eyes when she answered. "Let me rest a minute. I should have eaten more today—and it's been a long night." Peter Jack's little fingers stroked her arm. She patted his hand, not wanting him to be frightened.

Seeing Sammy's gesture and correctly assessing the anxiety evident in the shadowed eyes and paleness of Peter Jack's face, Deacon's heart went out to the kid. Christ, his mother was who-knew-where, and the woman charged with his care was weak as a kitten. The boy was probably terrified he would lose her too. "Peter Jack, you take Missus Sam's hand. It's time we got off this floor."

Sam felt Peter Jack grasp her hand as if he could pull her up all on his own. But she knew it was Deacon's strength bringing her to her feet and keeping her upright. Her head felt as if it were detached from her shoulders. This was ridiculous. She was supposed to be nursing Deacon and taking care of Peter Jack. Moving as if in a fog, trusting the voice issuing instructions, she did her best to cooperate— surprisingly, content to drift along.

When Sam felt the soft brush of Peter Jack's lips on her cheek, she fought the drowsiness weighting her eyelids. Until then, she hadn't realized she was tucked into bed. She didn't recall removing her gun belt or her wrapper. Deacon must've done it.

Settling her head into the pillow, sleep near, she saw Deacon extinguish the lamp and heard Peter Jack wish her goodnight.

She wondered if she answered.

Chapter 23

"**W**hat're you doing here?" Jackson demanded, unable to keep the irritation from his tone. He'd been on his way to take care of his and Grant Johnson's horses when he spotted Deacon Storey settled on a bench, carving away at a piece of wood, with Peter Jack peering over his elbow.

Putting aside the wood, Deacon stood, slipped the knife into his pocket, and reached to take the reins of the horses from Jackson's grip. "We're whittling a cat for a game Peter Jack invented. But we're ready for a break." Peter Jack scrambled down from the bench to slip his hand into the gambler's free hand. "How about if we take care of the horses for you?" Deacon suggested, nodding meaningfully at Peter Jack, who was listening with wide-eyed attention.

Aware of the boy's interest, Jackson nodded before bending to scoop Peter Jack up and tuck him beneath one arm like a sack of flour. Ignoring Peter Jack's squeals and squirms, Jackson's dark eyes raised to question the cool emerald ones holding his. Nodding toward Jackson's house, Deacon waved him off. "We can talk later."

Jackson's concern immediately refocused. "Is Sam all right?"

"Yes, but if you're free from Grant Johnson, you need to talk to her."

"Johnson is upstairs gathering his things. Now that he's satisfied with the arrangements and settled the mill contract, he decided to catch the evening train to Cheyenne."

"Good. Can Parker see him to town?"

Approaching from behind Jackson, Parker answered. "I've already told Johnson you're needed to take care of a problem with the windmill. I'll see him to the station."

"What the hell is going on?" Jackson growled, unable to contain his mounting apprehension. "*Is* there a problem with the windmill?"

"No," Parker said, laying a hand on Jackson's shoulder. "Nothing's going on that can't be handled, but it's complicated, too complicated to explain before Johnson comes down. And Sam needs to tell you a good part of it." While speaking, he plucked Peter Jack from under Jackson's arm, right-sided the writhing five-year-old, and hitched him on his hip.

"Where's Sam?" Jackson asked.

"At your house," Parker replied.

With one last sweep of Parker's face, Jackson turned away, anxious to see Sam. Behind him, Parker set Peter Jack next to Deacon and started for the main house. Deacon laid his hand on the boy's shoulder, urging him toward the stable, the horses trailing them.

Nearing the front porch, Jackson noticed the movement of a curtain settling into place. Sam had been watching.

***

After letting himself in, Jackson reached around the door for Sam, knowing she was waiting there, out of sight, should Johnson happen to glance at the house. Not allowing her time to speak, he wrapped his arms around her waist, walked her back to the wall, and crowded against her—reveling in her scent and softness pressed against him.

"Are you all right?" he asked, his lips near her ear. "You didn't worry about the watcher? Parker and Deacon said—" Sam didn't let him finish.

"I'm fine," she murmured. "Now that the watcher is fueling hell's fires, Satan won't give him up." Rubbing her breasts against the hard planes of Jackson's chest, she brushed her lips over his. She needed him. "Mmm. Don't talk, just kiss me."

Kisses were what Jackson wanted, too. His mouth covered hers and she opened to him. Losing his awareness of anything but the woman in his arms, savoring her sweet taste, the pleasure of her, he forgot he was supposed to be listening, learning why Deacon and Peter Jack were at Trinity. His cock demanded he move his leg between Sam's and press his thigh to her apex, rubbing his arousal against her inner thigh. "Kissing you always makes me want more, Sam. When I'm near you, my head forgets practically everything I ever knew."

The raw, visceral tone of his voice evoked a reciprocal primal need in Sam, inciting, igniting, inflaming every particle in her being to strain toward him, to answer the demand—to give and take—of each other's bodies—to sate desire. Her arms tightened around his neck. The scent of pine, leather, and male amplified her arousal. Rough stubble rasped her lips. "Just kiss me for now. We'll take our time with the 'more' later."

Her clever hands pulled his shirt from his pants and slid beneath to find his nipples. He groaned in pleasure and his tongue surged against hers in deep, hungry thrusts. Wild, molten desire shot through him. He was a weak man, and she drove him crazy. His fingers opened the buttons on her shirt as his mouth claimed hers again, in kiss after kiss, each deeper, more erotic, more demanding, until he lifted his head and groaned. "Let's take the 'more' into the bedroom, Sam." He was hard for her, so hard.

"Yes." Her desire matched his. They needed each other now—because after they talked, "more" would be different. And everything would change.

***

Later, studying Sam while she slept, Jackson wondered about the faint smudges beneath her eyes. Something had upset her while he was away. At first, he'd suspected her fear of a phantom watcher had returned, but her teasing earlier, saying the devil wouldn't release the fiend, had freed him of that worry. Then he'd allowed his desire to overpower his good sense and ceased probing, so he'd no clue what was wrong.

He felt guilty for taking her to bed instead of talking. Then after their loving, reluctant to let the interlude end, they'd nestled together and she'd fallen asleep in his arms. He'd almost succumbed to the bone-melting languor that descended after loving her, but concerns about why Deacon and Peter Jack were at Trinity and what Parker meant when he'd said things could be handled had kept him awake.

Quietly leaving the bed, he retrieved his discarded clothes and dressed. He'd talk to Sam later. Before the others returned, he'd find Deacon and get some answers. *Ah, but would Deacon's answers be truthful?* He couldn't dismiss his suspicion Deacon was hiding something. And though he proscribed to a man's right to protect his secrets, he wouldn't be forgiving if Deacon were hiding something that threatened Sam or anyone he held dear. Brother or not, he'd break the man into pieces with his bare hands before he'd let that happen.

***

Pacing on the front porch, Deacon watched Jackson's long, purposeful strides eating up the distance to the main house. His disheveled ebony hair and hastily donned clothes were evidence husband and wife hadn't spent much time talking.

Jackson's dark eyes were pinned on Deacon's face, and he didn't miss the set of his rival's jaw, the wrinkle between his brows, or the quizzical lift of his brows.

"I assume Sammy told you about Jessa and Peter Jack," Deacon said, despite having seen evidence to the contrary.

Sammy. Inwardly, Jackson cringed at Deacon using that pet name. But his gaze contained no hint of his irritation—or jealousy. He'd be damned before he allowed anything the cool gambler said or intimated to goad him into divulging he and Sam had bypassed talking for loving. "Not yet. She's sleeping. And by the look of the smudges beneath her eyes, I'd say she needs it, so I decided to come and talk to you."

After loving her, Deacon added silently, as he scratched the stubble on his jaw. He hadn't shaved since yesterday morning. This was damn awkward. It wasn't his place to pass judgment or to tell Jackson that Jessa had named him Peter Jack's father.

Studying Deacon, Jackson noted his defensive stance. An irrational thought, birthed from jealousy, flared. Had Deacon come knowing that he was away, hoping in his absence… An image of Deacon touching Sam seized him, and he battled to suppress the urge to beat the living hell out of the man.

Recognizing the jealousy shooting from Jackson's eyes, Deacon rushed to quell it. "Sonofabitch, Jackson, it's not what you think. Would I be here with Peter Jack if I'd come to seduce Sammy? She loves you—not me, and I'm smart enough to accept she's found the right man. What she needs to tell you has nothing to do with me."

"Then what's going on? Why are you and Peter Jack here—and where's Jessa?"

As he turned toward the front door, Deacon replied, "Let's go inside. Becky went to town with Peter Jack, Parker, and Johnson."

Jackson headed for the bourbon decanter in Parker's study, while Deacon settled into one of the high-back leather chairs in front of Parker's desk. After perching a hip on the corner of the desk, Jackson poured two drinks.

Nodding, Deacon accepted the bourbon Jackson offered and downed it in one toss. With one brow raised, Jackson took the glass from Deacon's hand, refilled it, and handed it back. "That's the last liquid courage you'll get from me until you explain what's going on."

Deacon took a measured sip before he began his explanation. By the time he finished, his glass was empty and Jackson was draining his second drink.

"Did you see Jessa's note saying I was Peter Jack's father?"

Deacon shook his head. "No. Sammy told me about it after I discovered the boy asleep in your bed." He paused, half expecting a fist in his face for mentioning he'd been in their bedroom. When it didn't come, he added, "I asked Sammy if she believed it, but she didn't answer me."

Silence.

"*Are* you Peter Jack's father?"

"I don't think so—but—"

Impatient and practically growling, Deacon interrupted. "Dammit, Jackson, *but what?* Either you were with Jessa or you weren't." He jerked to his feet, his hands balling into fists at his side. "I've only known you for a short time, but I would've expected you to take responsibility for a woman you loved and a child you made, so answer my question."

While waiting, Deacon questioned why he thought it so all-fired important to learn the truth. Something more than curiosity was driving him. Then, in a place deep inside him—the same place where he kept the memory of Jessa held in his arms at the top of Gracelyn's staircase—he felt a stab of jealousy. Was he angry because he couldn't stand the thought of Jackson being with Jessa?

Hell yes, he was jealous—no, it was more than that. Jackson had not only captured Sam's heart but had also known physically the body of the woman Deacon was coming to love. *Wait. Did he use the word love? Was he falling in love with Jessa? Damned if he wasn't one sorry bastard.*

Jackson set his glass on the desk before he stood and positioned his face within inches of Deacon's. "The answer is I don't know if I was with Jessa. Before this, she was adamant we weren't together in that way. She said her dead husband was Peter Jack's sire. If her note says different, I don't know why she changed her story."

"But how could you not know? Did you lose your memory, too, you lyin' piece of—?"

"Don't finish that!" Jackson commanded. "I'm realizing you have feelings for Jessa, so instead of slugging you, I'll try explaining, so shut up and listen!"

Eyeing each other like two predators preparing to fight to the death over a kill brought down together, Jackson told Deacon about South Pass, his parents' deaths, and being ambushed by Jessa's husband and his thieving, murdering brother. He also explained he'd been out of his mind with fever and chills. Jessa had nursed him, going so far as to sleep with him one night when she'd feared he'd die if she couldn't warm him. Her being in his bed had caused him to have an explicit sexual dream—even now, it seemed real.

Deacon didn't like the explanation, but he recognized the ring of truth in it. "Then why did you bring Jessa and Peter Jack to Prosperity?"

"Because when I discovered she was living hand to mouth with that little boy and being hounded by every rough miner left in that God-forsaken tent town, I couldn't leave her there. She'd been good to me—saved my life. I couldn't allow her or her son to be mistreated."

Jackson's eyes blazed with anger and frustration. "If Jessa left Peter Jack here in the dead of the night with only a note and without talking to me or Sam, something is wrong. She wouldn't leave Peter Jack willingly. But if forced to give him up, she might change her story to bind Peter Jack to me. She'd do or say anything to protect her son."

Deacon nodded. "Agreed. And she's in trouble. I know a few things I can't tell you. Will you accept that without asking me more? I need your help, and we'll have to figure out how to keep Sammy out of it. Can I count on you?"

"Yes, but you know we won't be able to keep Sam out of it. She can help."

"Normally, I'd agree, but she isn't well."

"What're you saying? Her ribs may still be tender, but they're nothing to worry over," Jackson assured him.

"If she's such a picture of health, then why did she faint last night after she sewed up the gash on my head? She said it was because she didn't eat much and had been up all night, but I have my doubts."

***

241

After talking to Deacon, Jackson returned to Sam, who was still sleeping. Because it made him feel close to her, he left the bedroom door ajar. She'd barely stirred when he adjusted the bedding around her bare shoulders. Normally, she had a sixth sense that woke her when anyone approached, but she must've relaxed it, trusting he'd keep her safe.

Glancing at the desk, he considered making a minor adjustment to the drawing he'd drafted for their thief trap but decided to hold off. His mind was too full of Peter Jack and Jessa to concentrate. He moved one of the wing chairs opposite the desk so he could see into the bedroom and sank into its soft cushions. Lord, but he was tired. He wished the chair was a tub of hot water. A bath, shave, and decent meal would do much to restore his energy. Because of what Deacon said about Sam fainting, he didn't want to disturb her.

It had been a long three days, and Grant Johnson had been a demanding swine, complaining and arguing about everything, just because he could. Johnson had taken great satisfaction in tossing out veiled insults about Sam. The man harbored unnatural resentment over Sam's rejection of his son and extended it to include Jackson. Men like Johnson hated being thwarted, thought their money and power should bend people to their will—especially women.

Every chance Johnson got, he'd made it clear Jackson and Parker should be groveling at his feet, grateful he was willing to do business with them. And he reveled in the fact he could demand Sam be kept from his sight as if she were unworthy of socializing with her betters. Jackson's right hand ached from clenching his fist to keep from pummeling the bastard's face into a bloody pulp. Only his friendship and regard for Parker had kept him from killing the son of a bitch. He'd gladly live the rest of his life never earning another dollar rather than do business with Johnson, but Parker didn't have that option. He had a daughter to provide for and loans to repay from before the time Jackson and Sam had become his partners. Parker needed this deal, so Jackson and Sam had agreed to Johnson's terms. Otherwise, Jackson would've set fire to the timber rather than sell it to the bastard.

Then to return home and learn what he had from Deacon—was a shock. Jessa wouldn't leave Peter Jack unless keeping him with her was dangerous—which meant she was in danger.

Jackson wondered what additional things Deacon knew about Jessa. He'd agreed to Deacon's request not to pry; however, sooner or later, he would insist Deacon come clean.

Dammit, he should have talked to Sam.

And they needed to figure out how to protect Peter Jack. God only knew how scared the kid was. Though Sam would've reassured him, he must feel as if the ground had disappeared beneath his feet. How could he keep the boy—*his son?*—safe when he was uncertain of the magnitude of danger? The only place Jackson could think to look for Jessa was in South Pass, the mining town where he'd first met her.

Sam's voice interrupted Jackson's thoughts.

"Did you talk to Deacon while I was sleeping?"

"Yes," Jackson replied, his eyes devouring her. Propped naked, with one hip wedged against the doorframe, eyelids half lowered, lips still swollen from his rough kisses, and hair tumbling wildly over her right shoulder to her waist, she was the picture of temptation.

"I'm sorry you had to hear it from him. I should have told you right away. But when we kissed, and—well, I didn't intend to fall asleep afterward."

"I know, darlin'. Parker told me we needed to talk. But I wanted the same as you." Then with a wicked leer, he added, "And if you don't put something on, I'll want it again."

Having forgotten her nakedness, Sam blushed and hastily retreated into the bedroom. When she reappeared, she'd donned a pair of trousers and a plain blue cotton shirt, though she hadn't taken time to fasten the buttons on either garment.

From the flashes of bare skin visible, Jackson realized she hadn't bothered with undergarments. Desire heated hot in his blood. What the hell was wrong with him that he wanted her again so soon?

Seeing Jackson's gaze weld to the gaps in her clothing, Sam flashed a guilty smile and scrambled to guide buttons through openings. Then positioning the other chair to face him, she sank into soft cushions. She would've preferred Jackson's lap.

"Is Parker back yet?" she asked, gathering her long tresses and tying them with a ribbon she fished from her shirt pocket.

"No."

"Did Parker say he'd talk to Morgan and Storey while he's in town?"

"No, but I'm certain he will. Deacon expects Storey will come back with them."

"Where's Deacon?"

"In the barn getting outfitted with what we'll need to search for Jessa," Jackson replied.

"I don't think any of us will be going anywhere."

"I don't understand, Sam."

"I think Jessa planned her disappearance because she's running from the law. Mac can check Brigham's hideout. It's the nearest outlaw stronghold. She may have gone there."

"Why do you think Jessa is wanted?" Jackson asked.

"Get Deacon and I'll explain. I'm sure he knows more than I do. There's no sense in telling it twice," Sam said.

Sam was right. Deacon knew things they didn't. He'd admitted it earlier. "All right," Jackson agreed. "But while I'm gone, put on some undergarments. I won't sit here and watch him pretend not to notice your breasts straining against the front of your shirt."

"But, Jackson—"

"Please, Sam, just do it."

Chapter 24

Deacon waved Jackson off when he held up the bourbon decanter sitting on a side table in their office. "Thanks, but it's time to start clearing my head. Where's Sammy?"

"She'll be here in a minute."

"Do you know what this is about?" Deacon asked.

"Only part of it. Sam said something about Jessa being wanted by the law and that she'd explain when you arrived."

"I suspect Deacon knows Jessa is wanted," Sam announced. Both men's heads swiveled in Sam's direction. Jackson's eyes flicked to her bust before lifting to her face. Deacon's eyes were wary. She'd ambushed him. He was probably wondering how to retreat and retrench without divulging too much.

Silence.

Earlier, Sam had ransacked the office and bedroom looking for old Wanted posters that Price Hardin gave her as a joke before leaving Prosperity after they'd resolved things with Webster and Ferguson. He'd asked her to consider banding with him and Mac to hunt fugitives. After rifling through drawers and her armoire, she'd found them stuffed at the back of her stocking drawer. Among them was a poster of Jessa, though it wasn't a good likeness. Issued before Peter Jack was born, the name printed beneath the picture was Jessa Brogan.

Sam didn't appreciate Deacon's silence. "You've already seen her Wanted poster, haven't you? I doubt it's surprise clamping your lips so tight."

Deacon consciously relaxed his expression. "Yes. I know about it." *No sense lying.*

"You're not *just* a gambler are you, Deacon?" Sam accused. Cutting air with her hand, she commanded, "Wait. Let me guess." Her eyes raked him up and down while considering her next words. "No, definitely not a bounty hunter. You don't fit the profile of a U.S. Marshal." Pausing, she tapped a finger to her chin as if it helped her think. "Let's see, that leaves the rangers—no, they're too rough—not your style." She wouldn't get a rise out of him if she went too easy with her goading.

Other than a slow pulsing of muscle in his jaw, Deacon didn't react to her derisive tone or conjecturing. Sam admired his control, though she didn't let it stop her. "Sooo, I'm guessing you work for a private agency—and not some back-alley one. My money is on Pinkerton's. With your skill and reputation, you could open doors for finding answers to questions few people would think twice about your asking. Yup, I'd bet on Allan Pinkerton's outfit." *Was that a flash of anger she saw cross Deacon's face?*

She pressed on. "Should I ask Morgan to send a telegram to confirm it or will you save us the trouble? You do remember Morgan is personally acquainted with Pinkerton—or has that slipped your recollection?"

Though he stood stiff and unmoving through her inquisition, Deacon was pissed. She'd seen through everything, something no one had ever done before. Was he losing his touch or was she that good? And it didn't slip his notice Jackson wasn't showing surprise.

Deacon let the respect and admiration he felt for Sam's intelligence sound in his tone. "Yes. I work for Pinkerton, and Jessa is *one* of the reasons I came to Prosperity. She's my assignment. Jessa's father, Rafferty Nolan, wants to find her and his grandson. He served five years of a seven-year prison sentence before it was overturned. Jessa's husband was responsible for the trumped-up charges that got him convicted. Upon his release, Rafferty married his lawyer's rich, widowed sister. Rafferty and his wife tried to find Jessa and failed. When they learned she'd married Brogan and was wanted for participating in a stage robbery in which the driver was shot and killed, they went to Pinkerton."

"That's a good start, but don't stop there," Sam prodded when Deacon paused.

Though annoyed, Deacon didn't let it show in his voice. "While incarcerated, Rafferty didn't know Brogan married Jessa. The first year of her father's incarceration, Jessa wrote positive letters telling him she missed him but was doing well with her baking business. She didn't mention Brogan or using whatever money she earned or siphoned from Brogan to hire the lawyer working to win her father's release. In the second year, her letters stopped." Pausing, he nodded toward Jackson.

"Jackson did a good job secreting Jessa away to Prosperity. But, as you said, Sammy, people will talk when they think it's with one of their own. Once I began my search in South Pass, I pieced facts together, filtered through gossip about Brogan and Jackson, factored in the probability she'd revert to using her maiden name, and decided to visit Prosperity. I already had plans to meet Dad here. The morning after your run-in with Briggs, I met Jessa and Peter Jack. Later at the jailhouse, I saw evidence she feared someone more than the law arresting her."

Jackson held his hand out to Sam. "I'd like to see that poster, darlin'." Sam slipped it from her pocket and gave it to him. Jackson knew Nolan was Jessa's maiden name and had advised her to use it. He'd also counseled her to quit writing her father and sever connections with the few friends she'd made in South Pass. He hadn't known she'd hired a lawyer or that she was wanted. "I don't believe Jessa helped her husband rob a stage. If she was there, I'd wager she didn't have a choice. Brogan set her up for control."

Jackson passed the poster back to Sam. "Jessa had been married to Brogan less than three months when I met her. Brogan would leave her on her own for days at a time. Then he'd suddenly return to lay low and make her life miserable before taking off again. A couple of decent women and their husbands befriended her—helped her start a baking business. Some of the miners protected her because a woman who can bake bread and pies is worth her weight in gold—and because they feared Brogan."

Deacon extracted the clean-face drawing he'd sketched of Colby Briggs from his jacket pocket and smoothed it before offering it to Jackson. "Take a look at that." An operative from the Denver office had visited Deacon in Prosperity to inform him they'd found a name to go with the drawings.

Sam had been watching Deacon. The tightness of his jaw and shallow furrows lining his forehead spoke volumes. She swung her gaze to Jackson.

Jackson was stunned. He recognized Colter Brogan's face, but the name beneath his picture said Colson Brigham. He pried his eyes from the drawing to lock gazes with Deacon.

Deacon shrugged before speaking. "I don't know how he did it, Jackson, but Colter Brogan didn't die in that mine.

He escaped, changed his name to Colson Brigham, and has been leading a band of outlaws for almost five years."

"Colson Brigham!" Sam, couldn't believe her ears.

Jackson didn't give Sam or Deacon a chance to say more. "I thought I killed Colter Brogan years ago, in South Pass, Sam. That's one of the reasons I feel responsible for Jessa and Peter Jack. We haven't talked about Jessa since the crash—"

Recognizing the regret in Jackson's tone, Sam interrupted, "But I know a few things and guessed the rest. On the train when you were delirious from the stab wound from Webster's thugs, you talked about lots of things, including killing two men who ambushed you in South Pass. I guessed that they murdered your father and that one of the men was Jessa's husband."

Jackson plowed a hand through his ebony hair. "I don't know much about Brogan's past before South Pass, but I've heard whispers. He and his younger brother, Jeremy, were former Confederate soldiers, who rode with Quantrill's raiders under George Todd's command. When the war ended, they split from William Quantrill, resenting the small percentage they received for the booty they stole. Between 1865 and 1868 the seriousness of their offenses escalated. In South Pass, they took to claim jumping and murder. They murdered three men to steal their mines, and one of those men was my father.

"I tracked them through towns most decent people would call hell's outposts for murder and mayhem before I realized they were circling back to South Pass. Of course, I followed, but before I could get them, they ambushed me—drilled a bullet in my back and left me for dead. They'd planned to bury my body in an abandoned mine shaft, but I managed to set off a charge collapsing most of the mine with them in it.

"Later, while Jessa nursed me, I learned Jessa's father put his claim in Jessa's name to ward off claim jumpers. If he'd known Jessa was coming to South Pass, he wouldn't have done it. He hadn't known Jessa's aunt had passed away from a heart attack or that Jessa had decided to find him. Before Jessa arrived, the Brogan brothers framed Rafferty Nolan for the murder of another miner, expecting a judge would sentence him to hang. With Rafferty out of the way, they planned to take over his claim. The evidence at trial was circumstantial. Rather than hanging, the judge sentenced Jessa's father to seven years in prison. Forcing Jessa to marry him was the simplest way for Brogan to get the claim—her property became his." Jackson paused to draw a deep breath. "I'm shocked the bastard isn't dead, but I have no trouble believing he's the gang's leader."

Recognizing the strain in Jackson's voice, Deacon hesitated to divulge another revelation. Sammy, especially, would suffer from learning her actions had inadvertently allowed Brigham to learn Jessa's whereabouts. But they had a right to know. Too much was at stake, and they were too deeply involved. "Brigham uses another alias."

Sam's gaze jerked to Deacon's face. "How do you know?"

"Colson Brigham, disguised and using the name Colby Briggs, came to Prosperity looking for Jackson and to scout the layout of the town. While he was here, he signed up a team to compete in the Centennial Rifle Shoot. I'm guessing he plans to use the occasion to rob the bank. When he learned Jackson was out of town, he took the opportunity to size you up, Sammy. But you were more than he expected and got him arrested. I don't think he had any idea Jessa lived here and had a son until she and Peter Jack brought his lunch to the jailhouse. Storey and I were there when Jessa and Peter Jack arrived. Jessa took one look at Briggs and stepped in front of the boy. It was clear she was frightened. She couldn't leave fast enough."

"Wait," Sam broke in, thinking she'd misunderstood some part of his explanation. "Colby Briggs is Colson Brigham?"

"Yes," Deacon replied, nodding. "That's right."

Sam exchanged glances with Jackson before moving to his side to study Deacon's drawing. Minus facial hair, it was difficult at first to recognize Colson Brigham *was* Colby Briggs. Once she accepted it, though, she realized Deacon was right. Brigham as Briggs had come to Prosperity because Price Hardin had done his job convincing Brigham the shooting match was an opportunity to gain fame while it provided cover for robbing the bank. They hadn't known they were inviting Jackson's worst enemy to Prosperity.

Watching Sam and Jackson study the drawing, Deacon said, "Why did Sheriff Cooley free Briggs—Brigham? It's a sure bet he's seen Brigham's Wanted poster."

Jackson offered his opinion. "The likeness isn't good. If you never saw Brogan—Brigham in the flesh, recognizing him disguised as Colby Briggs would be near impossible."

Sam nodded. "If you hadn't told me they were the same man, I wouldn't have recognized Colby Briggs was the same person depicted in that Wanted poster." She turned questioning eyes to Jackson, who understood what she wanted because he nodded as if giving permission. When she swung her gaze back to Deacon, she said, "Price Hardin, Mac's former partner, is a Deputy U.S. Marshal now and asked Mac, Jackson, and me to help capture Brigham's gang. The Centennial Rifle Shoot is the lure. That's why Jackson and I are promoting it. Of course, we didn't know Brigham's past with Jackson."

"Good Lord! You've invited Satan's pet disciple to supper," Deacon growled. "He'll swallow Peter Jack in one gulp and devour Jessa in three. He'll cut Jackson into bite-size pieces to munch on between belches." His imagination painted horrific pictures to accompany his words. Swiping a hand down his face, he drew a deep breath to calm his churning gut.

When he glanced at Sammy, her face looked as if she'd imagined the same horrific pictures he had. But Jackson stood tall, resolute, defiant. His eyes blazed—every muscle in his body bulged as if anticipating ripping open his enemy's throat.

"Brigham won't be dining in Prosperity," Jackson pronounced, articulating each word solemnly as if quoting scripture. "It's amazing how quickly the mighty lose their appetite when they *fall*."

Deacon suspected there was a hidden meaning in Jackson's words, but he didn't ask—not even when Sammy turned away to hide the amusement sparkling in her eyes. Instead, he asked about Jessa. "Do you think Jessa is with Brigham?" He needed affirmation his feelings weren't clouding his judgment.

Sam and Jackson shook their heads before Sam volunteered, "I don't think so, but we need to confirm it. Mac's the best person for that job. Every brigand in the West has heard of him and knows Price rode with him. They're practically legends in outlaw circles. Price Hardin is at Brigham's hideout, pretending to be one of the gang. No one questions Mac's presence visiting a friend. Mac will tell Price about Brigham's past trouble with Jackson."

Agreeing with Sam, Jackson turned to Deacon. "We'll count on you to search for Jessa. I suspect she's hiding close to home to stay out of Brigham's clutches and to watch over her son. Sam and I will protect him from any plan Brigham may have for using him. This situation will be especially hard on him. When you're not looking for his mother, we'd appreciate any time you can spend with him."

Jackson glanced at Sam before continuing, "I'll talk to Sheriff Cooley. He won't like any of this, but he's honest and will stand with us. We need his backing. Rem also needs to know about Jessa and that Peter Jack is with us. I'll make sure he knows all our plans, especially the details for nabbing Brigham and his men. Meanwhile, Morgan needs me to finish the bank renovations before Brigham's gang arrives. Those renovations are key to our ensuring innocent bystanders aren't hurt when we take Brigham."

Deacon wondered about the renovations and what they'd planned but decided not to pursue it. There'd be plenty of time later. "What story will you tell to cover Jessa's absence? I know two women won't be easy to fool. Each owns a house flanking Jessa's. Jessa and Peter Jack think the world of the one who takes care of Peter Jack when Jessa works, but the other, Delvinia Dalrymple, is a mean-spirited, sharp-tongued gossip."

Jackson nodded. "You're right about Delvinia. However, the other neighbor, Mrs. Chambers, is a good soul. She'll be worried. Inventing a tale to satisfy her and the rest of the town won't be easy. Folks know Jessa has no family, so we can't say a relative fell ill suddenly. Let me think—as her employer, it wouldn't be unreasonable to ask her to travel somewhere on business—would that suit? It must be something that came up unexpectedly to explain the suddenness of her departure and yet be within the realm of Jessa's talents to handle."

Sam snorted her disapproval. "Too complicated. I talked to Parker, and we decided to say Jessa went to help Parker's younger sister because she's needed to nurse her husband's mother. Of course, her three children are much too young for Becky to manage. Though we couldn't consult Jackson because he was away with Grant Johnson at the east grove, we determined Jessa was the perfect person to send. She was reluctant because of Peter Jack, but we offered a huge salary and promised to look after him for her. Deacon brought Jessa and Peter Jack here before he took her to Red Buttes, where Jessa could board the train. There wasn't time for anything else." Flashing a smug smile, Sam dusted her palms together. "And that, gentlemen, will take care of that. Remember to thank Parker—most of it was his idea."

Her mind racing, Sam moved on to other issues. "We need to attend to a few things as soon as possible. I propose we send Cal Ennis to explain the situation to Mac and ask him to visit Price. Cal can wait at Highbreeze until Mac returns so he can tell us what Mac learns. I plan to ask Cal's mother, Laurel, to stay here with us. She knows how to run a house and take care of a little boy's needs." Sam stopped to pull her lips into a wry, self-effacing smile. "Lord knows I don't have those abilities. And Cal won't mind because he won't want Laurel staying at their ranch with only their one hired hand to look after her. We'll also need to talk to Parker about making sure we button up Trinity so tight no one will be able to come or go without our knowing."

Clatter from the buckboard coming up the drive halted conversation. Deacon started for the door, eager to talk to his father. His stomach was churning. So much depended on everyone doing their job and protecting one another's backs. His mind flashed an image of Jessa and Peter Jack looking happy and safe.

They deserved a story with a happy ending.

For that matter, so did he.

Chapter 25

Having put a pot of coffee on the stove after Deacon left, Jackson turned to watch Sam drag her hand across the kitchen tabletop and frown at the dust clinging to her fingers as if unable to fathom how it got there. While rubbing the offending particles against the rough weave of the trousers hugging her hips, she lifted her gaze to meet his.

"Have you eaten today?" Jackson asked, instead of commenting on her behavior. The paleness of her skin had him recalling what Deacon said about her fainting.

"Deacon and Peter Jack brought coffee and biscuits stuffed with ham from the main house earlier."

"And I can see you did everything but lick the crumbs," Jackson replied with a wry smile, nodding toward a plate of barely touched food abandoned on the sideboard.

"I ate some—all I wanted."

"Well, I'm hungry, so I'll fix something. I imagine Parker treated Becky and Peter Jack to supper while they were in town. He'd see it a good opportunity to spread the story you and he concocted. I fetched a few supplies from the main house after talking with Deacon. How about pancakes? As I recall you brought home a jug of maple syrup that hasn't found its way to JB's kitchen yet. Would you find it while I throw some bacon in a skillet and stir up the batter?"

"All right. I—I'll set out plates, too."

While he worked, he could hear Sam rummaging through the pantry. After a bit, he recognized the grating of plates sliding against wood, followed by the clank of cutlery. The distinctive thunk of an earthenware object plopped on the table made him smile. Without verifying it, he knew she'd plunked the heavy syrup jug directly on the table rather than pour some of its contents into a serving pitcher. Curious when no sounds followed, he turned to see her leaning with arms braced on the tabletop, staring at nothing.

"Sam?" he questioned, puzzled over her apparent preoccupation. Hearing her name, she straightened but didn't speak. "What're you thinking?" Jackson prompted.

"That I don't even know how to heat water, let alone cook a simple meal on that stove." She swallowed around the catch in her voice. "How can I be a mother to Peter Jack or a true wife to you now that you have a son?"

"The same way your stepmother, Grace, is a true mother to you." His voice was warm and reassuring. "She loves you no different from Morgan. He is the son of her body, but you're the daughter of her heart. No one who sees you with her or Morgan would question whether their blood flows in your veins." He paused to chuckle.

"And I know for a fact Grace can't light a stove. For the love of God, Sam, being a wife and mother have nothing to do with domestic talents. Cooking isn't what Peter Jack and I need from you. Hell, we can hire a cook and a housekeeper." Moving around the table, he stepped close to wrap an arm around her and placed a finger under her chin, tilting her head up to see into her eyes. "Your job is just to love us, darlin', and you're damn good at that. No one can love us like you can."

The love and sincerity shining softly in Jackson's eyes made her shortcomings seem insignificant. But then she remembered how Peter Jack had turned to Deacon earlier in the day to ask about breakfast.

Little boys couldn't live on love alone. Neither could grown ones.

***

Though Jackson had once harbored doubt about Jessa's honesty regarding her pregnancy, his uncertainty had dissipated as their friendship blossomed. He'd told Deacon the truth. He'd believed what Jessa had said in the past rather than what she'd written in that damnable note.

Deacon revealing Jessa's husband, Colter Brogan, was alive and using the aliases Colby Briggs and Colson Brigham provided a motive for Jessa to change her story about Peter Jack's parentage.

Back in the office, seated comfortably in wing chairs, only a few feet separated Jackson from Sam—she was close, but not close enough. He sensed she used the distance to hold a part of herself from him. He felt as though something vital was slipping away, stripping a layer of the happiness and contentment he'd known since they'd married. If he were to pull her into his arms right now, would it make it easier to tell her all he needed to say? He wasn't sure, so he didn't risk closing the distance.

Wrestling with her emotions, Sam struggled to accept a situation created from past events about which she knew little. She saw doubt and vulnerability in Jackson's eyes—and it frightened her. He was always so confident, so strong. He deserved more from a wife than what she could give. He should have married a woman who could bear a son or daughter to continue his legacy. He said he didn't need children, but deep in her heart, she believed he wasn't honest.

"I've been thinking you should have chosen someone else for your wife." Sam kept the hurt she was feeling from sounding in her voice. "Jessa bore you a son."

"Before this, Jessa swore Peter Jack wasn't my son," Jackson replied. *What the hell was Sam saying? He'd made no mistake in his choosing.* He closed the distance between them, drew his wife up from her chair, and kissed her. And for a heartbeat, she responded—to being in his embrace and the passion of his kiss—until she found the strength to step back.

"But why would Jessa need to say anything to you about Peter Jack's parentage if you and she hadn't been—intimate?"

There it was. Before her amnesia, when she'd been battling fears of sexual intimacy and questioning whether her feelings for him could be love, he'd told her everything, and to his great relief, she'd accepted all he'd said. But now he questioned if he'd convinced himself she believed him because he needed to believe it. Since the crash, had he avoided the subject because they'd moved forward and he'd been afraid it might change her feelings for him? This time when he told her, would she question his love for her?

He'd tell her the truth and pray she wouldn't believe it a lie. "First, I need you to know we talked about this in the past—early on when I first told you I loved you."

"I thought we might have. I'm sorry I don't remember." The pain of having to admit it stung deep.

Jackson blew out a breath, somewhat reassured. "As I explained earlier, Jessa nursed me after her husband and his brother shot me. I came close to dying. Infection set in and I was out of my head with fever and chills, much worse than from the stab wound from Webster's henchman. You've never said much, but I know I was delusional on the train. I saw the bruises on your wrists and arms later. When I tried to apologize, you made light of it—teased me I'd mistaken you for one of the bullies who tormented me about my name when I was a boy."

"You didn't intend to hurt me, Jackson. You didn't know what was real. I understood."

He took her hands in his. "For several days while Jessa tended me, I either burned from fever or shook from bone-numbing chills. My mind had me reliving events, enacting fantasies, and participating in crazed dreams. I couldn't distinguish truth from fiction. There was a night my chills were so violent that Jessa feared I was dying. She'd used all the blankets and couldn't heat bricks fast enough to make a difference, so she used her body. She told me later I thought she was there for pleasure, but I stopped when she said differently. She swore nothing more than a few kisses passed between us and that she was already pregnant with Peter Jack.

"I believed her, Sam—maybe because I wanted to believe her. I confess, in my delirium, I did think we were both willing, and I thought—but I must have imagined it— that we—I mean, that we took it to its natural conclusion. But Jessa said we didn't."

"Would she have a reason to lie about it?"

"I don't know. I've always believed she's hidden things about her past. Lying would save Peter Jack from being labeled a bastard. Although most people were afraid of Brogan and glad he was dead, they judged Jessa for nursing the man who killed him. Think how much worse they would've treated her if they believed I was the father of the child she carried. She didn't know me back then—maybe she feared if she didn't lie, I'd take her baby away from her. I realize accepting her explanation lifted guilt and responsibility from my shoulders. And I won't lie. Once or twice, early on, I did wonder if she'd been truthful."

The ache in Sam's heart bored deeper. Jackson might have never been hers because he'd already belonged to Jessa and Peter Jack. "And now Jessa's missing and given Peter Jack to us, *to you*, to keep safe," she said. The ache turned to sharp pain. She couldn't let it out—at least, not now, not while Jackson and Peter Jack still needed her.

"Until we find Jessa and finish with Brigham, we'll protect Peter Jack. Jessa told him what she wrote in the letter, and he's afraid you won't want him. He asked me if you'll send him to the orphanage."

"What did you tell him?" Jackson asked.

"The truth—that you love him and will be a good papa."

Chapter 26

Though relatively safe in Doc Baxter's carriage house, Jessa was bored, lonely, and terrified her very-much-alive husband would find her or figure a way to take Peter Jack.

If Doc hadn't left for an extended visit with his sister's family in Mercer, Nebraska, she had no clue where she might have gone to hide. According to town gossip, this was the first time in ten years he'd gone anywhere for more than two days. Because he'd arranged with her to watch his house, she knew he wouldn't return for another month.

Jessa had begun storing supplies in Doc's buckboard the night after confronting her husband at the jailhouse. At one time, Doc had used the buckboard to visit patients. These days he used a carriage, while the buckboard stayed in the carriage house. Jessa was thankful Deacon had never seen Doc driving the wagon because it would have led him to her hiding place.

The physician filling in for Doc was the brother of Mayor Windbag's wife, Alberta. He used Doc's office and surgery, but he didn't stay there. Each day before returning to the luxuries of the mayor's house, he posted a notice directing anyone who called after hours to find him at his sister's.

Several years ago, Doc Baxter had temporarily hired a sickly widower as a caretaker and furnished a small room in the back corner of the carriage house with a cot, table and chairs, armchair, and cabinets. There were no windows, and when Jessa examined it, she'd checked to make certain no lantern light would show through cracks to betray her residence.

For personal needs, she used a chamber pot and emptied it at night in the privy behind Doc's house. Tall bushes lining the backyard fencing kept neighbors from seeing activity within. Twice, she risked sneaking into the house to borrow a book and replace a knife she broke while opening a can of peaches. She'd begun a list so she'd remember to reimburse Doc. She had a month's supply of canned goods, soda crackers, dried fruits, and dried meat. She couldn't risk a fire to heat water or cook. For now, she and her son were as safe as she could manage.

***

After again spending the night with Peter Jack in Sam and Jackson's guest bedroom, Deacon rose when the boy did, eager to start searching for Jessa. Having had the evening to consider the facts, he was as certain as Sam and Jackson that Jessa wouldn't abandon her son and go willingly with Brigham to his hideout. If Brigham had threatened to use her and Peter Jack to his advantage, a woman of Jessa's intelligence would devise a plan to protect herself and her son.

As he'd reviewed Jessa's behavior before her disappearance, he recognized he'd unknowingly slowed her preparations and made her plans difficult to execute. His unexpected visit the evening she'd vanished undoubtedly delayed her taking Peter Jack to Sam and Jackson.

The facts supported the conclusions he'd drawn. Jessa would feel putting her son in Sam and Jackson's care would ensure his safety. It must be agonizing for her to be parted from her son. And given the rumors Jackson was Peter

Jack's sire, Brigham wouldn't think it out of character for Jessa to abandon her child, especially when he knew how much Jessa feared him.

Deacon doubted Jessa knew the man she'd married, Colter Brogan, masquerading as Colby Briggs, was also the outlaw gang leader, Colson Brigham. But no matter the name he chose, she harbored no misconceptions about the danger he posed. She'd suffered his abuse in the past and had witnessed, firsthand, the pleasure he derived from it.

Deacon suspected the wagon behind Jessa's house was full of supplies. He reasoned she wouldn't shelter on Trinity because the probability of discovery was high. Knowing Jessa's love for her son, he believed she'd choose a place from which she might catch a glimpse of him. That narrowed hiding places to abandoned shelters near Trinity or in town.

Reviewing the events from the night Jessa took Peter Jack to Trinity, Deacon could easily imagine her watching Sam's house to ensure Peter Jack was taken safely inside. She probably hadn't known Jackson was away. Nor would she have expected Deacon to regain consciousness and track her to Sam's. It wouldn't shock him to learn she'd seen him arrive and break into Sammy's house through the coal chute doors. She probably hadn't left until she was confident Sam and Peter Jack were safe.

Believing they'd find Jessa in an empty structure where she and the wagon could remain out of sight, Deacon and Storey would begin searching in town. If they didn't find her there, they'd search nearby areas. Father and son were naturally methodical and doggedly persistent—good at following clues. They'd find her. And if Deacon's prayers were answered and she were unhurt, he'd kiss her senseless—then wring her lovely neck for subtracting years from his life.

Chapter 27

Shirtwaist open, Jessa mopped the rivulets of perspiration sliding down her body. This was only her fourth day hiding out. Though the day nudged early evening, the temperature in Doc's airless carriage room was still climbing, expelling moisture faster than she could remove it. Wearily lifting a sodden linen from a basin of tepid water, she dabbed at the droplets beaded on her forehead and upper lip. Her other hand plucked at the center of her camisole, unsticking the clinging cotton in anticipation of traversing the valley between her breasts.

"Is this your imitation of basting meat?"

Jessa recognized Deacon's voice before her eyes found him. He was leaning casually against the doorjamb, the bunched muscles in his arms and shoulders radiating repressed ire held precariously in check. The creases in his brow and the hard slash of his mouth were disapproving. And his eyes, wending a smoldering journey over her bared skin, scorched the top of her shoulders, column of her neck, delicate hollow of her throat. At the naked swell of her breasts, they blazed into flame. Already overheated, Jessa's temperature rose, her skin burning each place his eyes touched.

"You look like hell," he pronounced, forcing his gaze from Jessa's half-bared breasts.

Bravely rallying her composure, Jessa let the dripping cloth slip from her grasp before swallowing to moisten her throat. "Thank you for the compliment. If I'd known you were coming, I would have donned my white gloves and ball gown and arranged for the servants to serve high tea." She was pleased she managed the perfect tinge of haughty sarcasm.

Deacon's relief at finding her unharmed and not Brigham's captive vanished as completely as a shadow at high noon. One corner of his mouth lifted into a mocking smile. "I don't much care for tea. Champagne, however, would do the trick, if chilled. Regrettably, in this oven, the only source of a chilled libation would be to drink from your cold lips." The anger resonating in the clipped cut of his words was an attempt to conceal his impulse to test their exact degree of chill by covering her mouth with his. But if he yielded to temptation, he'd undoubtedly do something even more stupid, like haul her to his chest and ravage more than her smart mouth. This was not the moment for that.

The thought of Deacon's mouth on hers sent Jessa's temperature ratcheting up another degree. He was a treat to behold—all of him, from wide shoulders to mounded chest, trim waist, and powerful legs encased in well-fitting trousers hugging his thighs and calves. With his vest undone, his shirt open at the throat, clinging damply to his chest, defining impressive contours of hard muscle, and the muted color of dusky brown male nipples, it was difficult to do anything other than admire him. When she could force her gaze up, she concentrated on the soft waves of dark hair brushing his collar, framing masculine features—so much safer to look at than the anger glinting in his emerald eyes.

Though his words stung, Deacon's condescending tone, so like a master admonishing a servant, hurt more. Wishing she could escape, Jessa's eyes flicked to the door.

Watching closely, Deacon saw everything—the admiring assessment of his body, her hands clutching the folds of her skirt, her desperate glance to the door behind him.

"There's no way you can get past me."

Jessa backed a step, all too aware there was no other exit, not even a window. Willing her body to relax, she stood in place, unclenched her fists, and asked, "Is Peter Jack safe?"

The quaver in her voice shattered Deacon's anger. He couldn't deny her comfort. "He's fine, but he misses you and is a little afraid—although he doesn't admit it. He's trying to be brave."

Jessa turned her head to hide the sudden tears gathering in her eyes.

"He's a good kid, Jessa."

"I knew I could count on Jackson and Sam to keep him safe," she murmured, without looking up, as if she'd forgotten he was there.

"Yeah, you could trust them, but not me," Deacon commented, his tone resentful. He rubbed the back of his head as if re-experiencing the pain from the vase she'd slammed against his skull. "I guess that's how you justified walloping me senseless the other night—or did I deserve that because my kisses weren't up to your standards?"

How could she possibly answer that question? Especially since there was nothing wrong with his kisses. But some things didn't add up. What if he was a lawman—or a bounty hunter—or a gunman her husband sent? The world favored men, and a husband had the power to lock up his wife. She had no legal redress. If a couple separated, the husband had first claim to the children. And her husband was a merciless devil.

Jessa wanted to trust Deacon—and much more. But then, she'd wanted many things in her life she'd never gotten. She acknowledged some of her past choices limited future ones. Too bad. Deacon would be an easy man to love. Hell, she was already half in love with him.

"I've asked you before, Jessa. From whom do you need protection?" Her response was an exasperated huff. Well, he was done cajoling.

"I know your husband is alive," Deacon announced. *That captured her attention.*

Jessa's eyes flew back to his. But his gaze had already moved to her shaking hands. *Was he guessing? If he knew Colter Brogan was alive, he must also know she was wanted.* "Jackson Knight blew my husband and his brother to perdition in South Pass before my son was born. And I bless him for it."

"I know you thought your husband was dead. But it wasn't a ghost glaring at you from that jail cell." Though his voice wasn't harsh, his tone made it clear he meant to pursue answers. "He was using the name Colby Briggs, but that bastard was Colter Brogan." He paused for the equivalent of two heartbeats. "Your husband has another alias. He's Colson Brigham."

"Wh-what did you say?" Fear and disbelief weakened Jessa's knees. She gripped the table edge for support. *Dear God, I must have misunderstood.*

"He's Colson Brigham, leader of the notorious Brigham Gang," Deacon repeated, moving closer. Whether from shock or heat, he was concerned she might faint. "Is he Peter Jack's father or did you say otherwise to ensure Jackson and Sam would protect him?"

Staring into the brilliant green of Deacon's eyes, Jessa couldn't look away or find her voice. Long ago, she'd made a mistake choosing her first man—though twenty-five, he had a boyish maturity—a winsome charm—enough to convince her he loved her and no harm would come from them giving in to the desire surging through their bodies. He hadn't meant to make a child or to hurt her. She believed he'd intended to marry her. But he was dead. He and his parents died when the raft transporting them across the swollen North Platte River capsized. Shortly after arriving in South Pass, she'd realized she was pregnant. Colter Brogan had threatened to kill her unborn child if she didn't agree to marry him. But she couldn't tell Deacon that— couldn't tell anyone that. Nor could she risk her son's life, so she didn't answer.

Deacon didn't know who moved first, but suddenly Jessa was in his embrace, her hands sliding up his arms to circle his neck. When his lips covered hers, he felt the shock of it throughout his body. His breath wedged in his throat, his heart beat wildly. A low sound rumbled from his chest to his throat. She filled him, especially the empty place in his heart.

Jessa pressed herself against Deacon and kissed him as she'd never kissed a man before—not even Peter Jack's father. Yet from somewhere she found the strength to lift her lips from his, though she stayed in his embrace.

Breathless, each studied the other. Deacon noticed the dark smudges, signs of worry, and sleepless nights, staining the hollows beneath her gray eyes. Loving Jessa was easy. Convincing her to trust him was damn hard. "Peter Jack has Sam and Jackson to keep him safe. You are done hiding here alone and unprotected. Beginning now, you're under my protection."

He stepped back, gently pulled the edges of her shirtwaist together, and fastened the buttons. Now that he'd found her, he needed to hide her where no one would accidentally discover her, yet give him easy access to take care of her. But with his breath still uneven and his cock hard, he conceded he was a danger. When she was near, self-discipline was difficult. He'd entrust her care to his father. His lips quirked into an amused smile thinking of Storey as a proper chaperone protecting a thirty-year-old mother from his thirty-something son.

Deacon couldn't promise Jessa happiness, but he could promise to protect her, care for her son, and clear her name. Price Hardin's trap would capture her husband. The law would judge and execute him. And Jessa would be free.

Then he'd do his damnedest to make her his.

*****

Four days after Cal Ennis arrived in Eden Ridge with a letter from Sam explaining the new developments concerning Brigham, Mac Covington wearily climbed the boardwalk in front of the Golden Crown gambling salon, his thoughts full of his wife.

As if she'd had a premonition of his arrival, Grace slipped through the outer batwing doors—a pleasing eye full of womanly curves and platinum angel hair. Her gaze found his.

"I missed you," hers said.

"And I missed you more," his answered.

Grace sighed as if he'd said the words aloud and glided into his arms. Her head tilted up, his down, and he drank from her lips. Water never gave life to his body as much as this woman's kisses did. They were a fine pair—an aging gunman and a beautiful and too-intelligent gambling palace proprietress.

Though Grace suspected her husband was presently feeling his years, he didn't look them. A big man, an inch taller than her son-in-law, Jackson, the silver threads in

Mac's dark hair and mustache took nothing away from the air of danger he wore like a second skin. True, the blue in his eyes was a little less vivid and the lines cut in his rugged features were a little deeper, but rather than detract, they testified to his considerable experience and augmented the power and authority he exuded.

Widowed twice, Grace's first husband, Drake Garner, her son Morgan's father, and her second husband, Chase Stone, Sam's father, had been cut from the same cloth as Mac—handsome, gifted, perceptive, commanding.

"Were we right?" Grace asked, searching her husband's face.

"Jessa wasn't with Brigham. He'd give a fortune to get his hands on her, though I expect Deacon and Storey have found her by now. Brigham's a real piece of work. Either God forgot to give him a soul or the devil stole it."

"Well, God doesn't make mistakes, husband, so it's the latter. I've packed our things. We'll leave tomorrow to travel with Annie and Frank to Prosperity. Sam and Jackson need us."

Mac smiled, not the least surprised Grace had divined his plan before he'd voiced it. For a quick second, he pondered whether God gave all angels the ability to read people's minds and hearts.

Grace, who'd been watching his face, planted a kiss on Mac's cheek and leaned in close to murmur, "Some of us see more than others, but don't let that get around or some of the other angels will get jealous."

Mac was still chuckling when his lips covered hers.

Chapter 28

"He's not going to take my son, is he?" Jessa blurted out, unable to contain her worry.

Shock blossomed on Storey Deale's famous poker face. "No, of course not. Why would you think that?"

"I didn't until he left me here with you last night." Jessa's hands swept up and out to indicate Jackson's private hotel suite. It was spacious: two bedrooms connected by a comfortable parlor, no kitchen, but a four-place table to take meals. Deacon's one-bedroom suite was across the hall.

While Jessa was dressing, breakfast had arrived from the hotel kitchen and Storey had wheeled in the cart. When she approached the table, he held her chair. Her hesitancy before sliding onto its velvet cushion didn't pass his notice. He poured her a cup of coffee. Raising a questioning brow, his hand hovered over a rose-patterned sugar and creamer set.

"No, thank you," Jessa declined politely, dropping her eyes to her cup. Taking a sip, she savored the heat and slightly nutty flavor. While hiding, each day had seemed like a month, and she'd had no coffee. It hadn't taken Deacon much time to locate her. At first, she'd been thankful it was Deacon and not her husband who'd found her. However, after a few hours of rest, her mind was working well enough to recognize she and Peter Jack were still in danger. She put her cup down and cast troubled gray eyes on Storey.

"Deacon said he'd protect me, but he left after I fell asleep. How do I know he didn't take Peter Jack and leave town? Maybe he works for Brogan, my—my husband, not Pinkerton as he claims. Has he tricked me, Storey? Are you helping him?"

"No, Jessa, he's not tricked you. But I am helping him keep you safe while he helps Sam and Jackson protect your son and deal with your husband. I swear it's the truth. Deacon won't be here much, but I will be. I promise you'll know everything we know. And Deacon will see Peter Jack every day and tell you about him." While reassuring her, Storey's ears recognized his son's footsteps approaching in the hall, then the metallic grating of the key turning in the lock.

The distinct click of the bolt released from the frame captured Jessa's attention. Deacon's eyes briefly touched hers as he sidled through the narrow space he'd allowed for entry. After closing the door and re-engaging the bolt, he approached the table, picked up his father's half-full coffee cup, and drained it.

"Don't trust us, yet, Jessa?" he asked, handing the empty cup to Storey, who refilled it before rising and excusing himself to run a quick errand. Deacon locked the door behind him.

Watching, Jessa felt the heat flaming in her cheeks. He hadn't heard her conversation with Storey; yet, he knew she doubted him. Remorse assaulted her conscience until she remembered her suspicion sprang from her love and duty to protect her child. Of course, she should be suspicious.

"It's all right, Jessa," Deacon murmured, getting lost in worried gray eyes too expressive for him not to be able to read her thoughts. "I'd have doubts, too, and not be half as civil about it." He smiled. "I left last night because your son has insisted Miss Kitty and I be his roommates." Internally, he acknowledged staying with Peter Jack removed the opportunity to share Jessa's bed. Quickly burying that thought, he added, "When I left Trinity this morning, Jackson and Peter Jack were busy making a place in his room for Miss Kitty to sleep. Sammy ruled no pets on the bed—insisted fleas would eat us up. I can't say I'm sorry about that." He grinned, his eyes sparkling like the emerald gems they resembled. "I could see Peter Jack wanted to argue the point, but he didn't. He doesn't do anything to displease Sam or Jackson."

Seeing moisture gather in Jessa's eyes, Deacon silently cursed himself. Damn, instead of assuring her Peter Jack was relatively happy and settling in, he'd made it sound as if the boy were afraid he'd be homeless if he wasn't on his best behavior. "Jessa, it's not what you're thinking. I said it wrong. Peter Jack is safe and happy—the only thing that would make his world perfect would be to have his mama with him. You know your son best. Can we trust him not to give you away if I tell him I've seen you and you'll be coming for him soon?"

Jessa blinked to clear the welling tears before nodding. "Yes—and tell him I miss him and love him."

"Of course," Deacon mumbled—his voice whisper soft. He'd turned his head from Jessa to study the pillows on the sofa because the emotion in her loving words reminded him of his mother on the day Storey came for him.

When he turned back to Jessa, she asked, "Are you angry with me?"

"No."

"But you were yesterday when you found me."

"I wasn't really angry. What I was feeling came out sounding like anger."

"Wh—what were you feeling?"

"Frustration—relief—perhaps a little anger, but not for you—for those in your life who didn't care for you enough to protect you."

"Oh." Jessa couldn't imagine Deacon not safeguarding what he viewed as his. What was this between them? She'd experienced the love of a long-distance father and a winsome man who'd given her pleasure and a son, but was this another kind of love she was feeling for Deacon? She acceded it must be—and it felt right.

Deacon was watching her. "I think you're a loyal and courageous woman who was caught in events over which you had no control."

"And an innocent one?" she asked, wondering how she could prove she wasn't a thief and accomplice to murder. She was a woman with a past that could poison everything she touched. She needed to be free from that before she could offer Deacon anything.

Deacon didn't hesitate. "As innocent as your circumstances allow. But it's what we can prove that will keep you out of jail and restore you to your son—and your father."

"My father?" Jessa murmured. "What do you know about my father?"

He told her then about her father's release from prison and marriage. He outlined their plan to capture her husband. He also assured her they were doing all they could to protect her and Peter Jack. He pulled her onto his lap. His lips brushed her cheek. "Be patient, Jessa. Trust us—trust me."

Was she setting herself up for heartache again? She didn't think so. "I'm nothing like Sam," she ventured, hoping to gain some inkling of his feelings. If he still loved Sam, he wouldn't be able to open his heart to her and Peter Jack.

"You're more like her than you think. You both fight for what's right, even when you're afraid. And like Sammy, you won't be afraid to grab on to love with everything that's in you once we take care of Brigham." *And neither will I.*

Jessa was back on her chair watching Deacon settle his hat on his head when Storey returned. Deacon took a few steps toward the door before swinging around to face her. "You remember what to do if anyone should come in when Dad and I aren't here?"

"Yes, I'm to escape using the door to Sam and Jackson's suite." She gave him a cheeky grin. "I'll be fine, though. Storey promised to teach me to play poker."

***

Having seen to his horse, Deacon found Sam and Jackson lounging on the steps of their front porch. Peter Jack wasn't with them. He stepped over Jackson's legs blocking his way to the front door before turning to ask, "Where's Peter Jack? I brought him some peppermint sticks."

"He's baking molasses cookies with Laurel and Becky," Jackson said with a chuckle.

"Why is that funny?"

"It's not," Sam replied. "Cal's mother is doing an excellent job caring for him, but according to Peter Jack, she doesn't measure up to Jessa. I'm afraid if he tells Laurel one more time *his* mama does this or that better—or that her cookies aren't as good as *his* mama's—she'll send him out to play in El Toro's bullpen."

"That's not good."

"I explained his saying those things hurt Laurel's feelings," Sam replied. "But he just looked at me with his big brown eyes all wide and innocent and said he didn't understand. He claimed his mama told him to always tell the truth and that's exactly what he'd done. Then he asked if I was tellin' him his mama shouldn't have learned him that." She paused to swallow her amusement. "I knew the little wrangler was deliberately twisting things, but he was so damn cute about it, I forgot myself and laughed."

"And you let him get away with it?" Deacon asked.

Sam shrugged. "Jackson didn't back me up. He'd turned away so we couldn't see his face, but his shoulders were shaking. Peter Jack knew he'd got past us and scampered back to the kitchen, so we let it go."

"Well, you two make pretty sorry guardians," Deacon scolded, shaking his head in disgust. "Mac and Storey wouldn't have let us get away with that." He saw Sammy suck in a breath, preparing to launch into one of her "but" arguments, so he cut her off before she could start. "I don't want to hear it, Sammy. I'll talk to him. Jessa won't like hearing he hurt Laurel's feelings and dodged responsibility for it."

Jackson's head jerked up, and he shot to his feet. "You found Jessa? Is she all right?"

"Yes," Deacon admitted.

"And she's explained everything?"

"Not everything," Deacon hedged, "but enough. It's what we worked out on our own. We didn't discuss Peter Jack's parentage."

"Where is she?"

"She's in a place where Dad and I can keep her safe without anyone becoming suspicious. Brigham won't find her."

"You won't say where?"

"No."

"You son of—" Jackson growled before clamping his mouth shut. Nodding to Deacon, he apologized. "Sorry. I'm not angry with you."

His anger was directed at himself—for daring to hope Jessa had withdrawn her claim he was Peter Jack's father.

Chapter 29

On the second to last day of June, Sam and Jackson stood together on Prosperity's railway depot platform watching a barely five-foot woman step from the midafternoon train. Although she had a woman's body—full bust, tiny waist, and shapely hips—she looked no more than sixteen. They'd never met her, but they knew who she was. Though it sounded too big for her, Phoebe Ann Mosey was her given name. Perhaps that was why she preferred Annie Oakley.

The tall man assisting Annie toted a heavy rifle wedged in the crook of his elbow before offering his other arm to his diminutive companion, who with a shy smile cast liquid brown eyes up at him before accepting it. Sam recognized Frank Butler, a professional traveling show marksman from a handbill Jackson had shown her. Jackson had explained they'd once watched him compete in a contest in a small Nebraska town. But, of course, she didn't remember.

"She's tiny, isn't she?" Jackson commented in Sam's ear. "That rifle Butler's toting for her looks bigger than she is. She can't weigh more than a hundred pounds." His arm slid around Sam's waist as he spoke. "He's ten years older and divorced with two children. I read Annie beat him by one point when they competed in a turkey shooting contest in Cincinnati. From the way he looks at her, I'd wager she won his heart as well as the contest."

Sam smiled. "It was smart of Mac to ask for their help. If Annie's skill is anywhere near the level it's purported to be, she and Frank Butler will be credible opponents. They made their decision to compete quickly, despite Mac's warning about *you know what*—because of—*you know who*." She'd whispered *you know what* for the word danger and *you know who* rather than utter Brigham's name. "Their acceptance letter, with entry fees enclosed, arrived less than a week after Mac's visit."

"Perhaps," Jackson suggested, "they accepted because Butler advised Annie winning against you would grow her reputation. He's been in the business a long while and understands how to promote new talent. With Morgan on their team, they could beat us."

"I don't care why they signed up," Sam replied, "I'm just glad they're competing. And if they're good enough to win, it's fine by me. You, me, and Mac don't need to add to our reputations."

Jackson pecked Sam's cheek. "I agree, darlin'. And to tell the truth, I wish them luck."

Sam caught sight of a handsome older couple approaching the disembarking shootists. "Mac and Grace are here!" Excitement and relief were evident in her tone. "With Mac doing—er—our errands, I didn't expect they'd be able to travel with Annie and Frank."

Sam's gaze met Mac's. Blue and piercing, his eyes reflected strength and determination. His body, exceptionally fit, was still straight and powerful. There was a quality of danger about him, an assuredness that said he was expert in taking care of himself and others, while warning he wasn't a man to cross. Yet there was kindness in his expression.

Nodding a greeting to Jackson, Mac was mostly pleased with what he saw in his daughter's gaze. His girl was a fine woman, determined, courageous, intelligent, capable—and as vulnerable as she was beautiful—if one knew where to look—and he did—because he'd failed to protect her as well as he should have when she was a girl. As he guided Frank and Annie across the scuffed planks of the train platform to where his girl and Jackson waited to welcome them, he saw Sam's eyes catch and hold her stepmother's warm gaze.

Grace Garner Stone Covington was a woman for whom age refused to collect a toll. Her beauty matured rather than dimmed. Intelligence and serenity shone from her eyes. And kindness shaped the mirthful contour of her lips. Her hair, so pale that time couldn't alter its shade, reflected light in a luminous half-circle, remarkably reminiscent of an angel's aurora.

After Grace hugged Sam, Mac watched Jackson envelop her in his strong, but careful arms. Grace had never been able to convince him her bones wouldn't break. His wife was much stronger than she looked. Mac sighed, sorry for the things in life that had made Grace that way.

Grace hadn't missed Mac's calculating assessment of Sam. When his eyes met hers, she saw their opinions were the same. Their daughter, though happy, was once again assuming responsibility for things beyond her control and blaming herself for her imperfections.

Grace sighed. It was difficult for Sam not to hold herself to a higher standard than a person could achieve. Though blessed with many talents, she'd never learned to accept her shortcomings. Nor could she understand others, especially those who loved her, forgave them—because she, herself, couldn't forgive them.

After Grace completed introductions, Mac remarked, "We've invited Annie and Frank to your suite for supper this evening. It'll be private and allow us to explain—things." Catching Sam's eye, he added, "I'll make sure your brother and Alexa can attend. Would you send word to Deacon and Storey to join us after we've finished eating? Tomorrow, we'll visit the range and settle the contest rules."

Sam nodded, relieved her stepparents were comfortable assuming the role of host and hostess. Grace and Mac would stay with her and Jackson in their suite's second bedroom. Frank and Annie would have separate rooms at the hotel, near Deacon and Storey.

Jackson gestured to the buggy, explaining they should go on ahead while he stayed behind with Eddie and Charley, two of the hotel's employees, to collect baggage and oversee its delivery to their rooms. He'd also visit the hotel kitchen and arrange to have supper sent up.

***

Although the living area of Sam and Jackson's suite was roomy enough to accommodate Mac and Grace, Morgan and Alexa, and the two visiting shootists, the arrival of Storey and Deacon pushed its limits. To an outsider, the evening gathering would have appeared to be nothing more than an ordinary family get-together to welcome new friends. Of course, it was much more.

Plates had been cleared and stacked on the cart from which the meal had been served. Sam and Jackson remained seated at the dining table, but Jackson had shifted his chair so he could wrap an arm around Sam's shoulders. Morgan, next to Alexa on the divan, was holding her hand. Storey and Deacon were lounging against the wall near a window, their gazes occasionally darting from Mac to check the activity on the street. Annie Oakley and Frank Butler sat across the table from Sam and Jackson, looking more curious than concerned. Grace was in the wing chair near the desk on which Mac perched.

Mac's eyes, searching the faces turned in his direction, stopped when they reached Sam's. "I've warned Brigham you're moving the award money, rifles, and depositor's money from McKinley Trust and Savings Bank to your start-up bank. He's suspicious by nature, so he's sending Price and his chief lieutenant, Sedge Cannon, to scout things out. I expect they'll arrive tomorrow. We need Sedge to see evidence you're trying to pull a fast one."

Morgan frowned. "McKinley's not going to be comfortable with that, but he'll help us. I'll talk to him." With a raised brow, he glanced at Jackson and Deacon to receive affirmative nods. "Jackson and Deacon will arrange with Sheriff Cooley to have guards in place to oversee the transfer."

Jackson added, "And we'll make a plan to ensure we've enough guards and deputies to make it appear McKinley's bank is well protected and to maintain order during the festivities."

Mac chose his next words carefully. "I've told Brigham we've discussed security and I advised assigning only one guard until after the celebration is over to support the myth you have nothing valuable in your bank vault to protect. I've also told him I'll be the guard on duty the night of the robbery."

All but Frank and Annie nodded in agreement. With Mac inside, the robbers would have no reason to damage the building or the vault.

Morgan wanted some clarification. "As the 'inside man,' I assume you'll let his men in the bank and work the combination to open the vault for them?"

Mac nodded. "Yes. I've assured him you'll trust me with the combination." Mac turned to Jackson. "This time when I visited the hideout, because I know about Brigham's—er, Brogan's—past with you, Jackson, I could see he's hellbent on vengeance, though Price and I are positive that his men don't know it. He didn't mention any specific plans for you, but he's been open about getting even with Sam for exposing his cheating and getting him arrested. Once he sees you with Sam, he'll follow through because hurting her will hurt you."

Sam spoke up. "Except for Annie, Frank, Morgan, and Grace, we'll recognize Brigham. That should help. Deacon made a good drawing we can show the others."

Mac disagreed. "It won't help. Brigham will wear a disguise and separate himself from his gang. He'll arrive at least a day after his men do. He's normally clean-shaven, but he's good at disguises. He won't show up with the mustache and beard he used for his Colby Briggs alias. Not even Sedge Cannon knows what he'll look like or when he intends to arrive."

"Has he said when they'll hit the bank?" Jackson inquired.

"He wants nothing to interfere with the match, so he won't do anything until after the winners are declared," Mac replied. "Same with the bank. They'll wait and rob it during the fireworks display."

Mac could see that Jackson hadn't expected Brigham to choose such a busy time. "But the town will be full of people," Jackson said. "At the first shot, every man with a gun will shoot to kill."

"Most people will watch the display from the community fairgrounds," Mac reminded him. "Besides, Brigham figures there won't be a need for gunplay with me on the inside. And if there is, between rocket bursts and the usual celebratory gunfire from revelers, folks will ignore it. Should anyone get curious and investigate, they'll presume McKinley's bank is the target. Brigham thinks he holds all the cards."

Exchanging frowns with Morgan, Frank Butler asked, "Do Annie, Morgan, and I need to worry about Brigham sabotaging our team? It's something I didn't think to consider until you explained earlier that Brigham ordered you to shoot poorly to ensure Sam and Jackson's team lose the competition."

"I don't think so," Mac answered. "But Deacon will keep a close watch just in case. The bast—er, I mean, the bandit is cocksure his team—Price Hardin, Larkin Johns, and Digger Crane—can outshoot anyone competing. He'll think differently once he sees your qualifying performances. In his mind, coming in second to a team with two professional marksmen is almost as good as winning first place. Either place will bolster his gang's reputation. Stealing the prize money before it's awarded makes it his, regardless of who wins."

***

Later that evening as Alexa, Morgan, Annie, and Frank said their good nights and filed out the door, Sam was surprised Storey and Deacon didn't follow. Glancing first at Jackson, then at Mac, she saw no indication they regarded it odd that father and son weren't leaving with the others.

In silence, Storey moved to the divan, while Deacon claimed a corner of the desk. From her chair, Grace raised her hand in Mac's direction offering a glass of bourbon.

Accepting the drink, Mac raised his eyes to meet Deacon's and broke the silence. "So, what's on your mind?"

"We need to talk about my job in this plan of yours."

Sam spoke before Mac. "This isn't your fight, Deacon. You didn't volunteer for it." She waved at Jackson and Mac. "We did. Your job is Jessa."

Deacon held Mac's gaze while he spoke. "I'm family. That makes it my fight, too, so I'm not asking—I'm informing. I'll be watching your outlaws and your backs. I'll also be scouting around to find Brigham. I need to make sure Jessa and Peter Jack get free of him."

A slow smile worked its way across Jackson's lips. "You have plans regarding Jessa?"

Deacon pinned his eyes to Jackson's. "I do. Any objections?"

"None, as long as the lady is amenable."

Breaking the tension between the two men, Storey interrupted. "It seems my son is crazy about Jessa's pancakes. And I can't resist her cinnamon rolls."

"Well, that's one way to put it," Grace commented dryly. Her eyes laughing, she caught Storey's eye. "Guess you've decided to deal yourself the grandfather card."

"Deacon dealt this hand, Grace. I'm just here to see that he wins."

Chapter 30

The following evening, an hour before midnight in the alley behind McKinley Trust and Savings Bank, well aware Price Hardin and Sedge Cannon were watching and listening, Sam poked her brother's bulging bicep with her index finger, and spoke in a loud whisper, playing her role to the hilt. "Use those muscles to lower that rifle crate quietly or every bank robber in the Territory will hear us. I swear you're trying to get us caught."

Morgan groaned. "Hell's bells, Sis, lay off."

"Not a chance, Brother. You're moving at a snail's pace and making too much noise because you don't like this plan."

"Guilty as charged," he snapped. "This loot and the rifles won't be any safer in our vault than it is here in McKinley's."

"Thieves can't steal what they can't find," Sam growled. "You just refuse to accept it. Our bank won't open officially until mid-July, so all any bank robber will get from robbing this one is a backside full of lead."

Morgan grumbled, "We're only leaving enough cash in McKinley's bank for him to conduct business for the next few days. If his customers' withdrawals exceed what he's estimated, his tellers will stall while sending word to me to bring the cash. I'll be the one at his beck and call."

"Tough," Sam barked, not lowering her volume. "At least, being an errand boy won't cost *you* a fortune. To appease McKinley's misgivings about moving the contents of his vault to ours, I had to sign a personal note promising to repay depositors should anything happen to the money."

Mac's authoritative voice cut in. "Sam, quit exercising your jaw. Morgan, Son, move your tail. We need to get everything back under lock and key before the whole town figures out what we're doing."

***

Price Hardin and Brigham's lieutenant, Sedge Cannon, watched the activity in the alley from the second-story, back bedroom that Price rented from Widow McCarthy. The boarding house was behind McKinley's Savings and Loan. Sound from the alley filtered up to the partially raised window in the darkened room so they could hear most of what passed between the five people loading the wagon.

They'd been watching Sam, Jackson, Morgan, Deacon, and Mac traipsing in and out of the bank's back door for about thirty minutes, while the bank president, McKinley, made entries into a leather-bound ledger. Two guards were inside the bank. Sheriff Cooley was stationed at one end of the alley, while his deputy, Phil Thompson, was at the other. There was one guard on the roof overhead, another on the bank's roof, and two more on Main Street watching the bank's front doors—one at ground level, the other on a roof. Earlier, they'd heard Knight, McKinley, and the sheriff agree they would station guards in the same locations for several days before and during the Independence holiday.

"Mac told us true when he said they'd move the loot from the bank," Sedge whispered. Thumbing toward his vantage point, lust thickening his tone, he added, "The woman's more of a looker than what you said, but she's got a mouth on her." He cupped his crotch. "I'd like to stuff it with what I'm packin'."

Price's voice, cold as the reptile it resembled, hissed back, "Her gun is a hundred times more deadly than her mouth, fool. She'll shoot your pecker off before it can get half hard for her. And if she don't, I will. She's my plum. Anyone, including you, makes a play in my game will greet the devil—pronto—and notice I ain't winkin'."

Though Sedge was a skilled gunman, his blood chilled in his veins at hearing the deadly threat in Price's words. Uncertain his fast draw was equal to the former lawman's, he quickly backtracked. "I was just talkin', *compadre*. No offense. She's an uncommon beauty and I forgot myself." Though he wasn't certain it could be seen in the unlit room, he stretched his lips into an unnatural smile, and added, "Soon, because of you and Mac, I'll be a rich man. Far as I'm concerned, the woman is yours, and anything else you want out of this deal."

Satisfied he'd put a scare into the outlaw, Price turned away to resume watching the activity in the alley.

"They'll waste lots of manpower guarding a vault with nothing in it," Sedge commented, wisely changing the subject.

"Yup," Price agreed, "but they don't know Mac's a snitch. Brigham is one smart *hombre*. I reckon he has a plan for hitting the other bank." In the dim light, Price squinted to see Sedge's features. Though good-looking, his lips tended to slant up into one cheek in a perpetual smirk. His black eyes could bore a hole through a man almost as well as the bullets fired from his .44 Colt. He carried himself with a callous arrogance and wore his shooting iron tied low on his leg, within easy reach of a hand so smooth it obviously had never done manual labor.

Recognizing Hardin's tone had warmed, Sedge nodded and let his breathing settle back into regular rhythm. "You can bet your last double eagle on it. We'll get everything when we rob that new bank instead of only a few thousand from cashier drawers. With Mac being the only guard and knowing the vault combination, it'll be the easiest job we ever pull."

***

Twenty-five feet wide and sixty feet front to back, the Commerce Bank of Prosperity was an impressive, two-story, brick building. With Second Street to its right and City Hall to its left, it anchored a prominent corner of Prosperity's Main Street.

The large plate window to the left of the recessed front entrance displayed the bank's name in elegant black-and-gold lettering. Eight windows, evenly spaced and protected by iron bars, watched over the town jail on the adjacent corner of Main and Second Streets.

Inside, marble flooring and a cage of iron bars with bisecting crosspieces set every two feet rose from ceiling to floor, safeguarding the teller's workspace and vault. Outside business hours, steel-grated panels set in deep channels at the front and rear entrances were rolled into place to provide a second barrier should an exterior door be breached.

The second floor was divided into office spaces, though none were currently used. The first floor, exclusively devoted to banking, was sectioned into four distinct areas: customer lobby; teller counter and workspace; an impressive walk-in vault adjacent to a room for customers to handle safe deposit boxes privately; and two offices at the back, the smaller for an assistant and the larger, corner office for the bank manager.

Accessible to customers and employees, the corridor on the City Hall side of the bank spanned the entire length of the building. Another, on the Second Street wall, extended from the teller counter to the cross-corridor separating the offices from the stairs leading to the basement and second floor.

Six feet wide, eight feet high, and eight feet deep, the vault had survived the Great Chicago Fire of 1871. It was surrounded on three sides by two-foot-thick masonry walls and ventilated by concealed air shafts. Sheets of boilerplate wrought iron incorporated in the ceiling and floor above and below the vault would prevent break-ins from the basement or second floor.

The bank's concrete basement walls were a foot thick. The floor space within those walls was open, except for critical, weight-bearing, support columns and the ten-by-twelve rectangular jail cell constructed directly beneath the double trapdoors in the ceiling. When tripped, the braces supporting the doors would slide back to drop them and anything or anyone on them into the holding cell.

Consequently, robbing the Commerce Bank of Prosperity wouldn't be the pushover Brigham anticipated.

Chapter 31

Late in the afternoon on the first day of July, Grace was startled to find four of her family members, stationed two to a window, in her daughter's Gracelyn Palace suite bedroom, avidly watching something or someone down on the street. Mac, paired with her son, motioned her over.

Fairly certain she already knew what she'd see, she crossed to Mac and let him tuck her in front of him. Her gaze dropped to a group of men dismounting in front of the Fortune Queen saloon. They resembled a prowling pack of coyotes approaching a henhouse.

"I assume that's Brigham's gang?" Grace murmured, directing her inquiry to Mac, who nodded his answer.

Watching with Jackson at the other window, Sam shifted her attention from the troublemakers to Jackson's face. The smile that was there moments before had vanished.

"Brigham's not with 'em," Jackson remarked to no one specifically, his gaze glued to the troop of outlaws who were greeting Price Hardin and Sedge Cannon.

"Mac said he wouldn't be," Sam reminded him. "He knows we'd recognize him. He, especially, doesn't want you to see him because you'd realize Colter Brogan didn't die in South Pass. He wants to witness your shock. Seeing your reaction is as important to him as watching you die."

"I don't like any of this, darlin'. When we agreed to this scheme, none of us, including Price, knew Colson Brigham's real identity or his link to me or Jessa."

Sam tried to make the best of it. "I'm glad we found out or he'd have a bigger advantage. It would've made it easy for him to surprise you and Jessa."

"Don't forget, he's looking to get even with you, too."

"We won't let him," Sam said, but not as confidently as she'd intended. Her emotions were in a hopeless muddle. She held them on a short rein, but with each passing day, her grip slipped a little. And she was tired—physically and mentally.

"Dammit, Sam, you're too brave!" Jackson blurted, having forgotten the others could hear. "I can't stand to think—" He clamped his jaw tight, cutting off the rest. Getting control, he continued in a calmer, quieter tone. "You make me so crazy, darlin', I sometimes pray I'll never be sane again. And other times, like now, I'm *crazy afraid* for you."

***

Contrary to expectations, Colson Brigham had arrived in Prosperity on the same morning as his men. With hardly anyone glancing up to notice him, he'd guided his rickety wagon to an unclaimed campsite on the fringe of the community fairgrounds.

Initially, he'd planned to attend to his personal business with Jackson and Jessa while his gang cleaned out the bank. Though he'd seen no evidence of betrayal, a sense of something being not right with Mac Covington induced him to revise his plans. Nor could he rid himself of the feeling Price Hardin had an agenda separate from his own. Consequently, he decided he'd lure Sam and Jackson to the bank while his gang pulled off the robbery. That way, he could keep an eye on Mac and Price while he dealt with them.

After much consideration, he'd decided to take care of Jessa and her son on another occasion. In fact, it would be easier once Knight was out of the picture.

***

Two days before the holiday, Sam and Jackson were to meet Mac, Annie, Frank, and Morgan after breakfast at the shooting range to engage in some target practice. Jackson left before Sam, saying he would meet her at the hotel stable after he spoke with Wade Harper about ordering some additional supplies for Trinity.

Rather than cut through the hotel, Sam elected to use the alley alongside it to avoid morning patrons milling in the lobby. Concerned Jackson would arrive at the stable early, she accelerated her pace. She didn't want him to feel obligated to saddle her temperamental stallion. Phrased politely, Hooker was spirited and possessive. He preferred women and was aggressive toward male handlers, especially Jackson.

With most of the alley behind her, Sam was surprised when two men rounded the back corner of the hotel. She recognized Digger Crane and Larkin Johns from having watched them from her suite yesterday when they arrived. Crane grabbed her arm in an iron grip, while Johns, starting at her feet, worked his gaze up to her breasts. She recalled thinking he looked more like a starving, traveling minister than an outlaw. But now, reassessing his skeletal frame and gaunt face set with pale, gold-ringed eyes, she revised her opinion to *Death Come to Call*—except he carried a handgun rather than a scythe.

She didn't struggle to free herself, nor did she show fear. The only indicator of her emotions glittered in the cold depths of her eyes, but Crane, like Johns, was too preoccupied with appraising her attributes to notice.

294

Mac had told her Crane liked women and they liked him back. Tall, well built, in his early thirties, he wore a pair of ivory-handled pistols in holsters and carried a sawed-off shotgun in the sling wedged at an angle under his left armpit. His dark beard and mustache, neatly trimmed, suited his chiseled features. His pomaded hair was carefully slicked back from his forehead. His eyes, a peculiar green, reminded her of the green scum on stagnant pond water—no doubt a physical reflection of his rotten soul. Over his black shirt, he wore a black leather vest. Infamous for his quick draw and volatile temper, his skill with a rifle purportedly matched that of Larkin Johns.

Crane tightened his grip, and Sam's eyes flickered like gray-blue storm clouds backlit by lightning. The muscles in her left shoulder and arm contracted, eager to do her bidding. Though she could kill him easily, she held back. Neither man had attempted to take her gun. If they tried, both would die. Her lips curved into a derisive smile.

"You can't outshoot her," cautioned a male voice coming from a few yards behind and to her right. Sam recognized Price Hardin's drawl and imagined him lounging lazily against the rear wall of the newspaper building enjoying the show.

"You seen her shoot, Hardin?" Crane asked with open curiosity.

"Yup."

"She fast?"

"Makes lightning look slow."

"She got the guts to kill a man?"

"Ask the undertaker. He's buried a whole graveyard full of 'em."

Crane shifted from one foot to the other, the only sign Price's words affected him. "Can she take all three of us?"

"Not sure about three, but she can take two easy." His speech was slow, distinct—letting his message sink in. Just to make sure, though, he stepped into plain view. Hooking his thumbs in his gun belt, he propped his back against faded clapboards. "I ain't in this, boys." His eyes, wrinkled at the corners, and his lips curved in an unrepentant smile directed at Sam. "I may have turned to outlawin', sweetheart, but I don't draw on friends and I ain't stupid. I came here to win a shooting contest—not die in this alley." Then he glanced over to the hotel kitchen stoop, where Jackson stood watching everything, hand poised to draw. "Her husband, there, don't seem none too happy with your manners."

Two sets of eyes flicked to Jackson and stayed there, sizing him up. "That Providence Jackson Knight?" Larkin Johns asked. The unnatural rasp in his voice made Sam's skin crawl.

"Yup."

"Thought so. Saw him once—long time back. He's fast."

Sam remembered Mac saying Johns was fast with a pistol and so good with a rifle he could pick off small targets at half a mile or more. No doubt he'd shoot on Brigham's team.

After a short, considering pause, Johns asked another question. "Is he faster than she is?"

"Never knew him to test it out," Price answered conversationally. "But I'd have to put my money on her if I was riskin' my life." He winked at Sam and tossed an apology in Jackson's direction. "Sorry, Jackson, no offense intended."

"None taken, Price. Damned if I know myself which way I'd call it."

Sam spoke up. "I'm sorely disappointed you went back to outlawin', Price. I like your confidence in me, not to mention your sense of humor. Heard you were shootin' with these two—uh—gentlemen—in the contest."

"Yeah, I do what the boss tells me. We got a better than fair chance of winnin'."

Sam shrugged. "Well, if you want to lose your money, Storey's takin' bets."

"I might just do that. No hard feelings, sweetheart?"

Sam shrugged again. "I'll think on it and let you know." A fraction of a second later, she turned cold, questioning eyes back to her captor, who glanced at Price before shifting his gaze to Jackson, standing tall, silent—ready.

Finally, he released Sam's arm and stepped back. Lifting his hat in a mock salute, he snapped his fingers at Johns to fall in next to him before executing a crisp about-face and tramping toward the boardwalk.

Sam turned to watch Price take his time separating from the clapboard wall. His eyes followed the retreating outlaws before dropping away to meet her gaze. Raising a delicately arched eyebrow, she spoke in an undertone so her words wouldn't carry. "I can't believe you said it without winkin'."

"What?" Price asked, with the false innocence of a five-year-old caught stuffing cookies in his pockets.

"Ask the undertaker. He's buried a whole graveyard full of 'em," Sam quoted, imitating his drawl.

Price nodded. "I guarantee every man buried in that there graveyard is dead." Then with an exaggerated wink, he respectfully touched a crooked finger to his hat brim and murmured, "You sure as hell are Mac's girl, sweetheart. See you at the shootin' match."

From behind Sam, Jackson's arms circled her waist, his breath stirring her hair. "Crazy, darlin'—plumb, raving mad, crazy."

Sam could tell from the strain in his voice he was only half-teasing. Before she could murmur words of reassurance, he turned her in his arms and slanted his lips over hers.

Chapter 32

With the qualifying event of the shooting contest scheduled for tomorrow and the final event on the Independence holiday, the one loose end Colson Brigham intended to address this afternoon was arranging a little show to ensure Sam Knight's presence when he and his men robbed the bank.

He'd briefly weighed and dismissed the idea of staging an accidental encounter with her but discarded it almost as soon as it came to mind. A woman of Sam's intelligence wouldn't be fooled by such an obvious ploy. However, overhearing a conversation filled with clues hinting at his disguise would inspire her to use the brain in her pretty little head to spot him and follow him. And Jackson Knight wouldn't be far behind. It would never occur to her that Brigham had manipulated her into being exactly where he needed her when the time came.

As he traversed the town's boardwalks, he noted the obvious security measures at McKinley Trust and Savings. Extra guards armed with rifles and revolvers were stationed around the exterior and several more on the inside, just as Sedge and Price had reported. Brigham laughed at their play-acting, well aware they pretended to guard a fortune that wasn't there while leaving its actual location barely protected.

Hunched over his cane and limping pathetically, Brigham slowly threaded his way through riders, buckboards, and carriages on Main Street to reach the boardwalk in front of Harper's Mercantile. Turning to his left, he hobbled across Third Street and entered the Fortune Queen saloon. The two men he sought would be swigging rotgut or ruttin' with whores in the brothel behind the saloon.

He would've preferred to charge Digger and Larkin with the errand he had in mind, but couldn't because of the confrontation they'd instigated earlier that day with Sam and Jackson Knight in the alley. Juice Jenson and Cross Wolcott wouldn't exactly be welcome in Gracelyn Palace, but they'd be tolerated so long as they minded their manners. Sedge and Price would keep an eye on them. Their mission wasn't difficult. All they had to do was order a drink and drop a few clues to enable Sam Knight, or someone close to her, to figure out his disguise.

***

"Sedge and Price are headed here to Gracelyn Palace," Mac reported to Grace, who was waiting patiently for him to abandon his post at an upstairs window and drive her in Sam's carriage to Trinity to pay a call on Parker Evans and his daughter.

"Good. They'll keep those other two men you're worried about in line." Rising from her chair, she smoothed the folds of her dress and straightened her hat. Mac passed her parasol and offered his arm. "You're enjoying this thing you're doing to help Price capture Brigham, aren't you, Mac?"

"I am," he answered, nodding.

"Except what?" Grace prodded, certain he was holding something back.

"I didn't say anything about 'except what.'"

Grace smiled. "Your expression did. I've been reading faces for a living since before I was fourteen when my papa took me on my first riverboat to play cards."

Mac sighed his capitulation and voiced his concern. "Except us not being able to flush Brigham out into the open is dangerous, and I can't fully enjoy myself when I know that puts our girl and Jackson in more danger. Price and I thought we would've spotted him by now."

Grace studied his face. She knew him well. "You're going to disobey Brigham's order to throw the shooting match."

"'Course I am."

"But you're not going to tell Sam and the others."

"No—better they don't know."

"I'm not certain it will keep them safe. Brigham's a wild card," Grace cautioned.

"I know. But we didn't know the deck was missing a couple of cards when we started this. Our girl and Jackson could lose if I don't cheat a little. And Price and I can't put a rope around Brigham's neck if we can't find him," Mac explained.

"True," Grace sighed. "I know Price is looking out for us, but we need to remember his working undercover could hinder his ability to act. If Brigham discovers Price is a Deputy U.S. Marshal, he'll kill you both. If you talk to Jackson, he can step in to help. He needs to know your plans in case something prevents you or Price from playing this out."

After a moment of hesitation, Mac gave a curt nod. "You're right. We need Jackson."

Grace smiled her relief. "One more thing, husband. Keep in mind Sam is *our* girl. We've raised her to be courageous and skilled—with weapons and games of chance. She's also fiercely protective of those she loves and better than good when it comes to figuring out who holds what, which means she could decide to make an unexpected play."

Mac sighed. "You're right about that, too."

***

"Brigham's men have nerve coming to Gracelyn Palace," Sam grumbled to Jackson, while frowning at the glass of brandy she lifted from the bar before setting it back down. For some reason, it didn't appeal to her. The summer heat and worry over Brigham, Jessa, and Peter Jack were playing havoc with her appetite and energy.

"Maybe they'll mind their manners," Jackson responded, not any more pleased than Sam to see two of Brigham's crew leaning over their whiskey at Gracelyn Palace's bar. The outlaws were speaking in normal tones enabling anyone within eight feet of them to hear everything they said.

Keeping his voice low, Jackson commented, "Brigham will have ordered them to keep a low profile. If they disobey, he'll have their heads." Then he nodded discreetly toward the front entrance. "I expect that's why Price and Sedge are here."

Instead of turning her head to follow Jackson's gaze, Sam watched Price and Brigham's lieutenant in the gilded mirror situated on the wall behind the bar. Price claimed the space next to Cross Wolcott, while Sedge wedged in next to Juice Jenson. Raising two fingers to catch the barkeep's attention, Sedge gestured between Price and himself before slapping a gold eagle on the bar top and covering it with his palm.

"What?" Juice Jenson sneered from the side of his mouth. "We're good 'nough to stand next to but not to buy a drink?"

The half-inebriated outlaw was corncob-rough and looked like a backwoodsman—had been one long ago. Though his demeanor was generally mild when sober, Mac had warned them that he could transform into a possessed demon when drunk. Noting the Peacemaker in his holster, Sam also recalled that he was, at best, a fair shot with a six-gun and a rifle. Supposedly, Juice's first name originated from his dependency on rot gut whiskey, commonly called bug juice. And if he had another name, no one recalled it.

"No need to get nasty," Price said, attempting to smooth Juice's ruffled feathers. "Give me an' Sedge a long minute to catch up with you, an' I'll stand the next round of tonsil varnish. We got nothin' but time to kill 'til tomorrow when the qualifying event for the shootin' contest begins."

"That's right," Cross Wolcott chimed in, recalling Brigham's order to do their jobs and keep their weapons in their holsters. "We might as well enjoy what the town has to offer." Sending his eyes on an admiring circle of Gracelyn Palace's elegance, he added, "Don't reckon I ever seen a fancier waterin' hole, and the liquor is first-rate. If'n we temper our imbibin', we might could get lucky at the faro table. Been awhile since I had me a chance to buck the tiger."

Surprised at Cross's geniality, Sam raised a questioning eyebrow in Jackson's direction. He answered with a shrug of his shoulders, indicating he had no idea what game Cross was playing. According to Mac, Cross Wolcott was the oldest of the gang members. Though solidly built, his barrel-shaped body, dark hair touched with gray, and heavily lined face showed the evidence of his age. He'd earned his nickname from his proficiency in drawing his six-gun from the cross-draw holster he wore on his left hip. Some gunmen favored a cross draw over a side draw because it required less shoulder rotation to pull a gun. The unexpected motion could capture an adversary's attention and provide an extra split second to gain the advantage or opportunity to pull a backup weapon.

Though Sam was capable of handling trouble if needed, she didn't feel like doing it. She was weary of the situation and would have preferred to collect Alexa and retire to the office. Jackson could handle things if the need arose, and he wouldn't stand alone. Deacon and Storey were playing cards at a nearby table while keeping a watchful eye. They'd back him, as would Morgan, who was watching warily from the end of the bar.

Shocked by her thoughts, Sam shook off her lethargy. Of course, she wouldn't desert, but it would be wise to get Alexa out of harm's way. Swinging around to locate her sister-in-law, she saw Morgan was already escorting his wife to her office. When Sam redirected her attention to Price and his outlaw companions, she was pleasantly surprised to see Juice's disposition had sweetened. Instead of growling, he was eyeballing the tables. Sam thought it a fine pastime until his interest switched to Miss Angie, who was running a nearby roulette wheel.

Recognizing the lust firing in Juice's eye, Price sent a warning nod to Sedge, who leaned into Juice and murmured, "Remember the reason we're here. The women aren't for sale. Once our business is done, we'll mosey back to the Fortune Queen where our coin buys somethin' besides liquor."

Picturing his guts spillin' out should he dare disobey Brigham's orders, Juice reined himself in. But then he caught his first glimpse of Sam and couldn't contain his admiration. "Look to yore right, Sedge. Whoo-eee! Ain't that honey-haired gal about the finest piece of calico you ever seen?"

Without looking, Sedge knew Juice had spotted Sam Knight. Darting a nervous glance in Price's direction, he agreed. "Yeah, I saw her. She's the prime article, all right." He was careful to keep his volume low and tone respectful. "That's Sam Knight, and that black-haired powerhouse with her is her husband, Jackson. If you think on it a minute, you'll recall who the lady's promised to."

Juice nudged Cross's side with his elbow and whispered, "It's story time. Do you reckon she can hear us?"

"No reason to think she's deaf. I been watchin'. She's heard ever'thin' we've said 'cept what we kept low. Just to be sure, tell Sedge to come round us next to Price." Spreading out after Sedge moved, less than two feet separated them from Sam.

Sam saw Cross toss an annoyed glance over his shoulder, as if angry his conversation had been interrupted. When he turned to Juice, he looked eager to pick up where he left off.

"Pard, you recall we was talkin' about that ol' gimp with the cane we see'd crossin' the street 'fore we come in here?" Cross asked.

"Nothin' wrong with my memory," Juice replied irritably.

"That geezer reminds me of an outlaw, name of John Hurley. They call him Lame Johnny 'cause he limps, maybe from polio or somethin' else, I dunno for sure. Lame Johnny ain't ol', tho'—just a few years younger than Jesse James."

"Why you bringin' Jesse into this?" Juice asked, sounding more annoyed than curious.

"'Cause Jesse James likes disguises. Sometimes he walks with a limp and a cane, pretendin' to be an ol' cripple.

"You sayin' that gimp we seen is Jesse James?" Juice was obviously skeptical.

"Hell no! I'm sayin' maybe Jesse met Lame Johnny and figured walkin' gimp-legged would keep people from recognizing him. It's a good disguise—make his hair white, maybe glue on bushy eyebrows and mutton-chop whiskers, and hobble hunchbacked with a cane."

"Reckon it would do the trick, al'right," Juice agreed.

"I read in one of those dime novels that when Jesse rode with Quantrill's Raiders he dressed up as a young girl to visit a bawdy house. Told the madame that *she* and a couple of lady friends would call that evenin' so she'd pass the word to soldiers new doves was avail'ble. Ruse worked. Twelve soldiers visitin' that night was picked off easy—carried out feet first, boots on."

"The hell you say! That's quite a tale." Juice exclaimed, highly entertained. "Know any others?"

"None so good as that one." Thinking for a moment, Cross started up again. "Jesse uses aliases—Thomas Howard and John D. Howard are a couple I recollect. He's been known to pass himself off as a Texas cattleman by using the name of William Campbell. Sometimes he claims to be an English gentleman—calls himself Charles Lawson."

"That last one's a whopper," Juice bristled. He knocked back the rest of his whiskey and swiped the back of his hand across his lips. "Not a soul west of the Mississippi would swallow Jesse James talkin' like one of them English gents."

Momentarily forgetting about possible trouble, Jackson's gaze connected with Sam's, his lips twitching with suppressed laughter. He saw an answering twinkle in her eyes, but it faded as a frown pinched her brows.

Minutes later, the outlaws filed out, Cross Wolcott leading, Juice Jenson two steps behind, Sedge traipsing after Juice, and Price, last in line, nodding in Sam's direction as he pushed through the external batwing doors.

Jackson heard Sam mumble, "Why?"

"What do you mean?" Jackson replied. "They were just passing time."

"It was more than that," Sam insisted. She turned away to watch Storey and Deacon pocket their winnings and move to the bar.

Storey reached around Jackson to accept two glasses of bourbon from the barkeep and passed one to Deacon. "That was interesting," he commented to no one specifically.

"You hear something I didn't?" Jackson asked, suspicion beginning to nibble at his gut.

Silent, Storey's quick mind was busy sorting through possibilities—examining the who, what, and why of it.

The fact Storey sought a hidden agenda made Sam even more certain Brigham sent his men to Gracelyn to make sure she heard those Jesse James' tales.

Having figured it out, Deacon locked eyes with his father, intending to explain; but, Sam spoke first. "Brigham's already here and disguised as a white-haired cripple who uses a cane."

"Why would he go to so much trouble to provide clues for figuring out his disguise?" Jackson asked, hoping the answer would be different from the one in his head. But it wasn't.

"Brigham needs Sam to be able to recognize him," Storey explained. "He knows she's smart. If he simply revealed himself to her, it would put her on guard and jeopardize his plans; whereas, feeding her clues to use her deductive powers to figure it out would lull her into believing she has the advantage, unaware he's controlling her."

Sam agreed. "That's his game, but he's forgotten, we're cardsharps. Brigham's already proven he's not good at manipulating cards. This proves he's not any better at it with people. He didn't know I stole that ace hidden in his trouser cuff until he couldn't find it. Then he lost his temper and went to jail for it."

"True," Deacon agreed. "But you're forgetting you lost your temper, too, Sammy, and he pinned you under a table. If Dad and I hadn't backed you, he could've done about anything he wanted, including kill you."

Jackson felt himself going to that crazy place again. He wanted to tear out of Gracelyn and put six bullets in the first white-haired, limping, old man he spied. Instead, he cupped Sam's cheek and pressed a fierce, hot kiss to her lips. Then he strode away, making for the loft in the hotel stable—not that he expected to find sanity there. But it would offer privacy.

At least, Sam and the others wouldn't be able to watch him fall apart.

***

Quietly closing the door of their suite, Jackson was surprised to find Mac waiting for him. Nodding in his father-in-law's direction, he sought the bourbon decanter and poured two tumblers of the topaz spirit. After handing one to Mac, he savored a swallow before asking, "Where's Sam?"

"In bed, sleeping." Mac's voice was low so it wouldn't carry. "It's prit near midnight."

Jackson set his glass down and pressed the heels of his palms against his eyelids. "I can't let her be hurt, Mac. You've raised her to be too confident—too brave."

"A woman as beautiful and true of heart as Sam must be brave, Son. There are too many in this world who'd use her beauty and destroy that goodness. Her father knew that. Grace and I know that. You know it, too."

"I hate that it's like that." His heart was in his voice, the gravel tone he used when emotion swelled his throat. He plowed his fingers through his hair. "I know Brigham, Mac."

"I've known lots of men like Brigham, Son. We can beat him." Mac waved to a chair. "Before you go to Sam, I'd like for us to have a little talk. I have a plan and I'll need your help."

Half an hour later, Mac's "little talk" had Jackson's head spinning. He grasped the brilliance of the strategy Mac had proposed and recognized this was Mac at his best: cunning, resolute, invincible. They *could* beat Brigham.

Having won Jackson's support, Mac offered comfort when he saw his son-in-law's attention wander to the door of the bedroom where Sam was sleeping. "She's not angry with you. She understands. Now, go and get some rest. You'll need it."

Chapter 33

When Sam awoke hours later in their Gracelyn Palace bedroom, Jackson was asleep beside her. She'd spent most of the hours before midnight thinking about Jackson and the things that needed to go right with the contest and the bank. She'd heard him come home and had drifted into a deep sleep while listening to the low, comforting murmur of his and Mac's voices.

"What are you thinking, darlin'?" At the sound of Jackson's morning voice, low and raspy, Sam raised her head from her pillow to smile at him. She would never love anyone the way she loved him.

"That I'm happy you came to bed last night."

"Only a foolish man would sleep anywhere else—and I'm no fool," he teased. He'd stayed away until he'd calmed his fear—regained his equilibrium. He loved every inch of her but controlled none. She was her own woman, but she was also his wife, and she filled a part of him he hadn't even known was missing until he'd loved her.

And today they would engage the enemy.

He didn't want her to be brave.

***

Though early morning the day before the Independence holiday, Sheriff Rem Cooley didn't hesitate to offer the first of the hundred prayers he'd mutter before the celebration ended.

The Fourth of July was the hardest day in the year for a lawman to keep the peace. Citizens were usually awakened between three and four in the morning by cannon and small-arms fire. Whistles and bells joined the din shortly before dawn. Amid the display of flags and red, white, and blue bunting, there were always too many drunks, too many guns, and too many hot tempers firing off as loud and recklessly as rockets exploding in the fireworks display.

And of course, there were accidents. Only last year, during the reading of the Declaration of Independence, a whirlwind struck the ladies' stand, bringing down the awning and its supports and injuring several women.

This year, because Rem had agreed to back Price's scheme to capture Brigham and his gang, he was dreading the holiday more than ever before. Between rockets bursting into white-blue sprays of brilliant light in the night sky and a murderin' band of outlaws pulling a bank job, he'd be lucky if the whole town didn't go up in flames.

***

Sam and Jackson guided their horses around the wagon and tent town growing larger by the hour on the outskirts of Prosperity, west of the community fairgrounds. Since there weren't enough accommodations in town, most visitors and neighbors would shelter there over the holiday.

The day had dawned still and clear. By ten o'clock an oppressing heat haze had formed and there wasn't a hint of breeze to dispel it. As they approached the shooting range, Sam noted the audience bleachers were a quarter full. Apparently, few spectators considered today's qualifying event worthy of their time.

After dismounting, they tied their horses to the wagon Mac and Morgan had driven to transport Frank and Annie, as well as everyone's ammunition and rifles. As Sam gave a final pat to Hooker's shoulder, Jackson's gaze swept over her. The divided skirt she wore—brown and practical—emphasized her small waist and the pleasing curves of her hips and thighs. She'd chosen her cream-colored blouse for the soft gathers in the back yoke that wouldn't pull tight across her shoulders when raising her arms to shoot, unaware its front complimented the full shape of her breasts. And though she'd sensibly braided her hair into a single, thick, golden rope, she had no inkling it swung provocatively from one firm derriere cheek to the other in a mesmerizing rhythm. Were he to tell her, she'd be dismayed to hear her modest choices and plain grooming did nothing to mask her beauty.

Taking Sam's arm, Jackson cleared a path to the registration booth, where Mayor Windbag's spinster sister, Anita, dressed in an eggplant-hued gown, too snug for plump curves, stood tapping her foot while rolling a lead pencil between her palms. When he touched his hat brim in a gentlemanly greeting, she responded with a disapproving huff of impatience before reporting that he and Sam were the last of the contestants to check in. Jackson chose not to take offense. Believing everyone was entitled to show a little attitude now and then, he accepted the pencil she offered and signed the roll.

Evidently, not in a forgiving mood, Sam wasn't willing to let Anita's comment pass. "Thank you for mentioning that insignificant fact, Miss Bagley," she ground out, her tone carrying an unmistakable sting of reprimand. She then scrawled her name, and without glancing up to see her victim's wide eyes and stunned expression, abruptly turned her back.

Sam's uncharacteristic rudeness impelled Jackson to dart an apologetic smile in Anita's direction while tucking Sam's hand into the crook of his elbow.

Already regretting her outburst, Sam let him escort her to the audience bleachers, where they paused to scan the tiered rows for Mac and Morgan, who'd be sitting with Annie and Frank. A moment later, when she tilted her face up to Jackson's while pointing to a place in the roped-off contestant section, she could still feel the warmth of embarrassment in her cheeks.

"Is something wrong, darlin'?" Jackson asked, keeping his gaze on her face rather than the direction she'd indicated.

Sam lowered her head before answering. "I shouldn't have spoken to Anita like I did." Owning up to her rudeness, she added, "We were late. She probably had plans to join her family, expecting she would finish her duties earlier. She's actually a sweet woman." Sam hated she wasn't perfect. She tried, but obviously, she didn't try hard enough.

Jackson nodded kindly. This was his Sam—sorry for her flare of temper—censuring herself for not being a better person. "I'm sure Anita will understand. We'll look for her later and you can apologize." His understanding response brought a weak smile to Sam's lips and a nod acknowledging she would do just that.

As they climbed the aisle stairs to reach Mac and the others, Jackson scowled at the sea of male eyes watching Sam. Men from the area knew better, but the visitors who were currently enjoying the scenery were outsiders, unaware they risked their lives should they dare anything more than look from afar. If Sam had glanced back and noticed his expression, she would have accused him of jealousy. He, however, attributed his feelings to a deep-seated need to protect her, although he'd be a liar if he claimed jealousy had no part in it.

Looking around, Jackson counted only a few women present in the audience. Tomorrow, many more would attend. Sam and Annie were the only females competing. The male competitors he'd observed thus far appeared eager, radiating confidence their skill would win their team a place in tomorrow's final event.

He and Sam greeted Annie, Frank, and Morgan before sitting on the bench next to Mac. Once seated, Jackson leaned back and looked to his left where he spotted Price, Sedge, and the other gang members grouped at the end of the row, taking up more space than was polite. He searched the area near the outlaws for Brigham, then the rest of the stands with no success. When his gaze returned to Mac and Sam, he saw they'd been doing the same with no more success than he.

"I don't see Storey or Deacon, either," Sam commented.

"I expect Deacon is with Jessa while Storey's taking wagers and helping your mother and Alexa. Business was already brisk when we left."

Heads turning toward the stage signaled the contest was about to start. Winchell Abbott, one of the three contest judges and officiating host, stood behind the podium waiting for contestants and spectators to quiet before welcoming everyone. After that, he would segue to the contest rules and close with announcing the order in which teams would shoot.

In his mid-thirties, wearing a black frock coat and string tie, Abbott looked the man for the role. A well-liked local attorney, he was respected for his fair-mindedness, honesty, and polished, concise speech. Jackson predicted he would campaign for the mayor's job in a few years.

Today, they'd weed out the amateur sharpshooters. The three teams with the best scores would advance to the final event tomorrow on the holiday. Though scores would be reported during the qualifying and final events, Mayor Bagley wouldn't officially announce the prize winners until after the Independence Day potluck supper. Because the bank would be closed for the holiday, contest winners would collect their cash prizes and Winchester rifles the following morning.

Jackson watched Brigham's men for their reaction to that bit of news. Later, he joked to Sam their tongues licked their lips like starving men scenting fried chicken sizzling in the kitchen. The information assured the outlaws the money and rifles would still be in the bank when they robbed it.

As Abbott moved on to the contest rules, spectators were more interested than contestants, since they'd either read or listened to them being read earlier.

The contest rules supported the one-target-one-bullet principle, meaning a fresh target was required for each discharged shot. Canvas targets, mounted vertically on identical wood frames sized for distance to target, were painted with six concentric circles, radiating from a solid black center, on which a white-on-black "X" designated the bullseye. The diameter and thickness of the circles, "X," and bullseye were also sized for distance to the target, while numbers on the targets equated to points earned. The unique serial number in the left, bottom corner of each target tied it to a specific shooter.

Range assistants at each of the three firing distance stages were responsible for attaching, detaching, and carrying the targets to judges for scoring. Judges could debate among themselves whether a hit was on the inside or outside a target circle, but once agreed, the score was final. Shooters weren't allowed to argue or offer opinions.

In today's qualifying event and tomorrow's final event, each shooter would be required to discharge twelve record shots from behind the firing line—one series of four shots for each of the three stages: 300, 500, and 600-yard firing distance or their team would forfeit the contest.

Shooters would use their weapons and ammunition. Sights not incorporated by the manufacturer as standard to the weapon weren't allowed.

Shooters could choose their firing position: stand, sit, kneel, lie on their belly, or lie on their back, as well as choose whether to learn their score after the discharge of each shot in a specific stage series or wait until after the discharge of all four shots in a specific stage series.

After concluding his remarks, Abbott, on behalf of the judges, mayor, town council, and good citizens of Prosperity, wished the teams good luck.

Astonishingly, the competition went smoothly. Everyone, including the outlaws, minded their manners. By three o'clock, the contest qualifying event was over. And no one was surprised by the results. Team One—Mac, Jackson, and Sam—had the highest collective score. Team Two— Annie, Frank, and Morgan—earned only one point less. Team Three, whose members were rumored to ride with Colson Brigham's gang—Price Hardin, Larkin Johns, and Digger Crane—qualified with a score of three points less than Team One.

Throughout the day, Jackson, Sam, Mac, and Morgan took whatever opportunity presented itself to continue the search for Brigham, but no one saw him. However, Mac felt certain he'd been there watching.

Later that evening, when Mac met with Price, the lawman confirmed Brigham had attended wearing a different disguise. He'd discarded his cane and dressed in clothing appropriate for a farmer—faded-blue cotton shirt, braces to secure baggy twill trousers, and a wide-brimmed felt hat, pulled low to shade his eyes. He'd removed the mutton-chop whiskers worn by his lame-old-man character and exchanged a salt-and-pepper full beard for the white one. Price also reported Brigham hadn't liked what he'd seen and was planning something to turn the odds of winning back in his favor.

***

While observing the teams compete for a place in the next day's Fourth of July final event, Brigham had been impressed Mac Covington was every bit as good a marksman as Price Hardin had claimed. No wonder his progeny were crack shots.

And though Brigham had been prepared for one or two professional marksmen to enter the competition and was familiar with Frank Butler's reputation, his not-quite-sixteen-year-old teammate's performance had shocked him. *Where the hell had that Annie, gal come from?* He would never have predicted Annie's skill would surpass Butler's and equal Mac Covington's and Sam Knight's. The same was true of Morgan Garner, whose score had matched Sam's, though it had taken him more time to line up his shots. As for Brigham's team, Price Hardin had turned in a perfect score, but Digger's and Larkin's scores were a half tick short of the others.

Though Brigham had no choice but to accept his team placing third in today's event, he needed insurance to guarantee they'd win first or second place in tomorrow's showdown contest. Price had described polite tolerance masking deep-seated resentment between Mac and Sam, but Brigham saw no evidence of it. In fact, after witnessing Mac's interaction with his daughter and son-in-law, he seriously doubted Mac would follow orders to sabotage

Knight's team. Nor could he depend on Digger and Larkin being able to improve their scores.

After several minutes of thought, the solution came to him—simple to arrange, it would get him what he wanted.

Chapter 34

The Independence Day celebration turned Prosperity into a circus. Horses and wagons and carriages of every description littered the streets. In the empty lot next to City Hall, the mayor and several city councilmen sat on the platform built for town dignitaries, watching folks cluster around.

Once the rows of chairs reserved to seat the elderly and infirm were nearly full, Mayor Windbag, wearing a fawn-colored suit with wide, tapered lapels—which he tended to clutch when striking his favorite politician's pose—rose to deliver his speech in dry, loquacious sentences. His audience paid polite attention. Unfortunately, the embroidered pattern on his red vest—worn in homage to the patriotic holiday— was more interesting than his speech. A smattering of applause, accompanied by grateful sighs, broke out when he finished.

Now that the fun could begin, people scurried toward the community fairgrounds or the Prosperity Gun Club. All chores and responsibilities forgotten, pleasure was the byword for the remainder of the day.

And while most folks celebrating the country's one-hundredth birthday expected it would be one of the most memorable days of their lives, there were at least a dozen individuals who prayed they survived to remember it as the day the Colson Brigham Gang was brought to justice.

But justice wasn't what Jackson Knight prayed for. While he would settle for Brigham's incarceration, he preferred a more permanent state—for everyone's sake— dead and buried would rid the world of Brigham's blight.

***

With the 300 and 500-yard stages of the shooting contest behind them, Winchell Abbott announced a three-hour break, after which, the teams would reconvene to complete the third and last, 600-yard stage. The break was to allow folks time to enjoy a noonday meal and participate in the Winchester rifle charity auction benefitting the Prosperity Children's Home. Endeavoring to raise funds to purchase a church organ, the Christian Woman's Aid Society was conducting a baked goods sale and had weighted down three long tables with pies, cakes, cookies, and cobblers.

So far, teams one and two had accumulated scores identical to those in yesterday's qualifying event. However, two of the outlaws competing for Team Three—Larkin Johns and Digger Crane—had managed to improve their scores, so only two points were separating Team Three from Team One. With scores that close, a fraction of an inch in the placement of one or two shots by any of the shooters in the last and most challenging stage of the competition's final event could change the outcome of the match.

***

When Jackson went to check the horses, Sam watched him take the dirt path cutting through a grove of trees. Disliking how the outlaws' eyes also tracked his progress, she decided if any of them pursued him, she'd get Mac and go after them. But they stayed where they were—in plain sight, while looking every inch the predators they were, full of suppressed violence and aggression—trying to blend with decent folks and failing. They stood out like hawks attempting to hide in a flock of chickens.

Sam patted beads of perspiration on her brow and the back of her neck. The heat and humidity were worse than yesterday. She raised a jar of water to her lips and took several deep swallows. Pushing aside her barely touched plate of fried chicken, green beans, and buttered bread, she reached for the ginger cookies she'd purchased at the baked goods sale.

Unfortunately, she savored only a couple of bites before folks started stopping by to comment on the contest, inquire about the rifle auction, or ask after Jessa and a dozen other things. As the minutes dragged by and Jackson didn't return, she couldn't shake the feeling something was wrong.

She tried to think about something else, but what came to mind were her concerns regarding Jackson, Jessa, and Peter Jack. When she resolutely pushed that subject away, the door opened to worrying about what would happen tonight with Brigham at the bank.

***

Sheriff Cooley was wrapping up another prayer beseeching the Almighty Father to keep blood and guts away from his jurisdiction when the sounds of men fighting cut through the air from the grove of trees separating the creek from the picnicking area.

Rem pulled his shotgun from its scabbard, checked the cartridge load, and dug his heels into his mount's sides.

So much for prayers.

***

There were three men waiting to jump him.

Although Jackson didn't recognize any of them, they knew him. Their eyes never left him. They wore the simple

321

clothing of cowhands. The largest was equal to his height and had a powerful frame. The other two were four inches shorter, but healthy specimens—wide shoulders and thick chests.

Bent at the waist, head and shoulders straining, the big one surged forward on brawny legs, aiming for Jackson's midsection. He resembled an incensed bull charging a matador.

Jackson cursed and dodged to the side. Grabbing the charging man by the scruff of his neck, he used momentum to help his attacker find the trunk of a nearby tree—with his head.

One of the others picked up a club-sized branch from the ground. Raising it over his head, he brought it down on Jackson's back. Stunned, Jackson managed to stay on his feet and swing around to slam his fist into his assailant's face. Unfortunately, the third foe rushed forward to ram the stock of a rifle into his temple. Arms reflexively rising to protect his head, the blow hit him before they were in place.

Jackson thought he heard a shotgun blast. More likely it was his head colliding with the ground. And that was his last conscious thought before blackness pulled him into oblivion.

Mission accomplished, two of Jackson's opponents jerked their half-conscious, felled-bull *compadre* to his feet and made their escape.

***

The roar of Rem Cooley's shotgun firing into the cloudless blue Wyoming sky drove every thought from Sam's head except for her concern for Jackson. An abnormal silence followed the report. Then people began murmuring to one another as they went to investigate.

By the time Sam arrived, a small crowd of curious onlookers had gathered, and more were on their way. Some migrated toward Sheriff Cooley, while others focused on a form sprawled on the ground. Sam found

Annie and Frank standing among them. She didn't see Mac anywhere. As she drew closer, she realized Morgan was kneeling next to Jackson.

The churning emotion Sam had been fighting for days pushed into her throat. Only the hand she pressed against her mouth kept it from escaping. Jackson had agreed to help Price because she'd insisted—never dreaming it would precipitate a battle with an old enemy. And now he was hurt.

Kneeling at his side, Sam brought her face close to his. "Jackson, can you hear me?" His breath feathered against her cheek. His left eye was swollen and beginning to color. Blood flowed from a cut on his temple. Morgan placed a folded handkerchief into her hand and guided it to put pressure on the wound. Jackson groaned when Morgan's hands prodded the back of his right shoulder.

"Jackson?" Sam entreated.

Sounding a great distance away, Jackson heard Sam's voice and willed himself to escape the blackness, but with consciousness, came pain. He raised his hand to cover Sam's hand gently exploring the side of his face that felt as if a horse had stomped it. Cautiously, he opened his eyes, but his left one wasn't cooperating, and his right one wouldn't focus.

"Sam?"

"I'm here. So is Morgan. Can you tell us what hurts?"

"My head," he admitted, moved by the tenderness in her voice. He could imagine her slate blue eyes searching over him, but his vision was so blurred he couldn't see her clearly. "One of them rammed me with his rifle stock. Another one clubbed my shoulder."

"Nothing's broken," Morgan interjected. "They ran off just as Sheriff Cooley arrived. Were they trying to rob you?"

"They bet a month's pay on Annie and Frank," Jackson joked. "They didn't intend to kill me, only rough me up enough to make sure your team wins."

His reply provoked a reluctant smile from Sam. "But you're going to shoot anyway, aren't you?"

"Damn right, I am." The set of his jaw backed up the determination in his words. "Brigham hired 'em, Sam," he added in a low voice so others couldn't hear. "He doesn't want to settle for third place."

"But—" was all she could say before Jackson stopped her.

"No buts, darlin'. I'll take my turn."

***

When the final, 600-yard stage of the Rifle Shoot Contest resumed, the shooters from Team Two—Annie, Frank, and Morgan—each stepped to the line and matched their scores from the previous day. Team Three—Price, Larkin, and Digger—was only one point behind Team Two. If Team One—Mac, Sam, and Jackson—all hit their marks, the outlaw team would take third place again. But with Jackson having taken that beating, the outlaws figured they were a shoo-in to move up to second place.

When Team One was called, to give Jackson as much time as possible to pull himself together, Sam shot first. Mac watched his girl discharge her weapon with uncommon speed and precision. Each of her rounds passed through the center of its target's bullseye within a hair's breadth of the others. Had the canvases been stacked, they could have fooled a person into believing one bullet had pierced all four. If not for the unique serial number imprinted on the left-bottom corner, the judges wouldn't have been able to distinguish one from another.

Mac shot next. Each of his rounds pierced a target bullseye. If examined collectively, the area they spanned could've been covered by a silver dollar. He sighed over that fact. His age was beginning to catch up with him. There'd been a time when his targets would've matched Sam's.

Mac's gaze moved to Jackson, who was moving toward the firing line. He didn't look in any shape to compete.

***

Adamant he would take his turn, Sam watched Jackson weave on unsteady legs to the shooting line. Despite fearing he'd suffer more injury, she did nothing to stop him.

However, Mac must have formed a different opinion, because he moved in front of Jackson, blocking his path.

Sam shot from her seat and hurried to join them. Halting before she reached Jackson's side, she let her presence show Mac she supported her husband's decision.

Having turned his head toward her, Mac hastily turned it back when Jackson growled, "Let me pass." Mac let Jackson brush off the hold he had on his arm but didn't move.

"Dammit! We'll forfeit the contest if I don't fire these rounds," Jackson declared before sucking in a ragged breath. "If I can pull the trigger four times, we'll place third. If I'm lucky and put a bullet anywhere in the bullseye of two targets, we'll snatch second place away from Brigham's team."

Mac's eyes dropped to run up and down his son-in-law's beat-all-to-hell body.

Defiant, Jackson pressed, "Don't make me use the last of whatever's keepin' me on my feet to take a swing at you, Mac."

Sam didn't release the breath she'd been holding until Mac stepped aside.

***

Despite the pain, Jackson raised his rifle and concentrated on sighting the target. For several long seconds, with his vision impaired as it was, he feared he wouldn't find it, but years of experience aided him. Gently he squeezed the trigger. The recoil sent him staggering back a step and ripped bolts of agony through his bruised shoulder and battered head.

While waiting for the judges' official result, he took several deep breaths. When announced, he learned the round had drilled through the target at the lower edge of the bullseye. Doggedly, he shifted the rifle back to his shoulder, taking his time to position his body. Sighting through his blurred vision, he consciously blocked the pain, endeavoring to visualize what his eyes couldn't see. This time, the recoil didn't stagger him, though his chin ended up resting on his chest. He didn't waste energy lifting it. When the score came, he thought it a God-blessed miracle. The bullet had pierced the bullseye's center.

He'd fired only two rounds, but they'd taken a toll. His stomach was queasy and his clothes wet with perspiration. He caught himself swaying and staved off a sudden craving for cool water. If he gave in to his body's weaknesses, he wouldn't last to fire two more bullets.

Briefly, he contemplated changing his firing position. He could sit, kneel, lie on his belly, or even his back. Fearing he wouldn't get up once he lowered himself, he elected to remain on his feet. It afforded the greatest visibility of the target, though it offered no support other than his muscle strength.

Standing perpendicular to the target with his feet spread the width of his shoulders, he brought the butt of the rifle snug against his shoulder, his right hand holding the grip, his elbow pointing out, but not exaggerated. He could make out the shape of the target frame but not the circular bands on the target canvas. Once again, he relied on visualizing the center. He took a breath and slowly expelled it as he squeezed the trigger.

The recoil knocked him backward, and he would've fallen on his ass if Mac hadn't moved behind him, supplying a wall of flesh to brace against. When he felt Mac's hands close around his upper arms, he let his head drop forward. His grip on his rifle loosened, but he tightened his hold bringing it closer to his body. What seemed like seconds later, Mac spoke near his ear. "That was a bullseye, Son. Only one more round to go."

Eyes closed, Jackson lifted his head heavenward, as if offering prayer—*or making a deal?* He inhaled deeply and from somewhere deep inside summoned the will to stand unassisted. His vision remained blurred, but the spots in his head weren't whirling quite as fast. He blinked several times. It helped very little, but he didn't let it erode his determination to persevere. Slowly he raised the rifle and snugged it against his shoulder. Again, aiming more by instinct than eyesight, he inhaled. Upon exhaling, he squeezed the trigger.

When his ass slammed into the ground, he didn't care—because he didn't need to muster the energy to get up. He was still sitting there when the judges announced the bullet went to the left of center, half in and half out. Decent enough. In his dazed state, he gave God the credit for his willingness to perform four miracles.

The crowd was quiet as they watched Sam and Mac crouch next to Jackson and help him to his feet, Mac straining to take most of his son-in-law's weight. From the stands, murmurs of encouragement reached Jackson as he gamely shuffled his feet forward. The crowd's encouragement, though, changed to a collective gasp when his knees buckled. Morgan came to take Sam's place. Then, Cal Ennis maneuvered a buckboard nearby. Once Mac and Morgan settled Sam and Jackson in the straw-lined bed, the wagon rolled forward. Spectators heralded its departure with raucous cheers, applause, whistles, and heavy stomping that swelled into a wild, discordant anthem of praise and admiration.

***

Brigham swore. This wasn't how it was supposed to go. He'd not only lost bragging rights to first and second place in the shooting contest but also lost a reliable inside man for the robbery. All deals with Mac were off.

It took him less than a minute to debate with himself over Price Hardin. Though the former lawman had warned him Knight would move the money from bank to bank, he had a powerful motive for pulling a double-cross. Price wanted Sam Knight and her fortune.

Brigham intended to take what Price wanted. Because the former partners were probably in each other's pockets, he couldn't trust them. They were both expendable.

***

"We need to revise our plan, Son," Mac announced.

Jackson shifted his bruised shoulder against the mound of pillows piled behind him. Swallowing the pain the effort cost him, he scowled at Mac, who sat calmly on the chair angled close to the bed as if he'd said nothing upsetting. Jackson's lip curled in disgust.

Earlier, while Grace and Mac had attended to his injuries, Deacon had checked in with Mac to inform them he and Storey were keeping tabs on Brigham's gang. He had also reported that Cal took care of the horses and buckboard before joining Parker in Jackson's hotel suite to watch over Jessa and Peter Jack.

Jackson had almost groaned when he heard that revelation. So that's where those two cardsharps were hiding Jessa. He should have guessed it'd be right under his nose.

Soon after Deacon left, Trinity's current and former foremen, Davis Wilson and Jim Ryder, had visited to inform Morgan and Mac they'd be downstairs with Grace, Alexa, and Ryder's wife, Miss Jenny, until it was time for Wilson to take up his post in the bank basement. Ryder would stay at Gracelyn and Cal would leave Parker to go with Wilson to the bank.

Relieved Jackson's injuries weren't serious enough to warrant the services of a doctor, especially since the doctor wouldn't be Doc Baxter, Sam had allowed Grace to convince her to bathe and take a short rest in the other bedroom. No one believed she'd stay there. Consequently, Morgan was standing guard, prepared to signal should she approach.

Jackson swiped a hand down his face, trying to dislodge the wisps of cotton clinging to his brain. "What do you mean about changing the plan, Mac?"

"Before this, Brigham *thought* he might need Sam. Now, he *knows* it for certain." Mac's open betrayal of Brigham meant he was living on borrowed time. Even so, he intended to be at the bank at the appointed time to admit the outlaws.

"So, Brigham's lookin' to take you down, too," Jackson stated. "What about Price?"

"We don't know, Son."

Jackson interpreted that to mean Price had already been measured for a coffin.

"Since you are a tad indisposed," Mac added, "I've decided Morgan will hide in the closet of the room next to the vault, the one where customers open safe deposit boxes. Those hidey-holes drilled in the back wall work well for spying on the teller's workspace. They're practically invisible in that wallpaper pattern Sam selected for the outer wall. He'll pull the lever you installed to spring the trapdoors when he sees the time is right."

"Brigham's deranged, Mac. He wants all of us. The way I see it, he plans for us to die easier than what he intends for Sam. We're sending her after him blind."

"We need her as much as Brigham does. But we can't tell her everything we've planned. If her reaction isn't genuine, it'll tip Brigham off and we'll fail. We'll just have to pray she'll forgive us later."

Jackson detected regret in Mac's voice. That's when he began to wonder if Mac had shared all his plans.

Sonofabitch.

Chapter 35

Brigham's plan was working. Sam Knight had followed him to the bank as if he'd led her on a long leash.

She was his hole card—the strongest weapon for foiling whatever Mac and Knight had cooked up to capture him and his gang. Though a hellcat, she loved her husband and family, which made her easy to manipulate. Through her, he'd finally get rid of Knight.

When Knight and the others were dead—and the bank cleaned out—he'd enjoy keeping her for a while. Her brother and mother would pay a ransom to get her back. Tied to his bed, he'd use her for his pleasure—until he tired of her. Then he'd kill her.

***

Sam watched Larkin Johns approach the bank's back door and disappear inside. Several minutes later, Digger Crane followed. Within ten minutes, the rest of the gang, except for Juice Jenson, entered the building. She'd spied Juice loitering at the back of the pool hall, next to the empty corner lot behind the jailhouse, holding the horses until needed. With so many other visitors' animals there because of the holiday, theirs blended perfectly.

Since Brigham had gone to so much trouble to lure her to the bank, Sam wondered why he wasn't going in. A sick feeling churned in her gut as she watched and waited. Ten slow minutes crawled by before Brigham separated from the shadows, still wearing mutton-chop whiskers and a full beard, but no longer limping or carrying a cane. He darted to the door and vanished inside.

Now that he'd made his move, Sam hesitated. Should she wait before following? While deciding, she reviewed the location of the others. Of course, Deputy Thompson with a contingent of guards were staked out at McKinley's bank as a precaution. Sheriff Cooley, with Deacon, Wilson, Wade Harper, and Cal, all of whom he'd deputized, were hidden behind sand-filled packing crates in the basement waiting for the robbers to plummet from the floor above into the holding cell. Morgan would be watching for the right moment to pull the lever. Price would probably be somewhere near the vault. Mac could be anywhere. Sam scowled, just now realizing she had no idea where Jackson would be. Nor did she know where Storey was.

Cautiously, Sam moved forward. Though it would probably do no good, she'd try to stay hidden. After all, Brigham knew she'd follow him. After cracking the back door to ascertain whether anyone was on the other side, she widened the space and slipped through. Crouched low, she angled left to avoid being seen by whoever was posted as the lookout in the lobby to watch the front entrance and the City Hall corridor.

Easing open the door to Morgan's corner office, Sam peered inside, her ears cocked for any sign of Brigham or his men. Dim light from the jailhouse spilled from the opposite side of Second Street, revealing the office was unoccupied. Having locked the door behind her, as well as the door from the assistant's office, she crossed to the northeast corner door.

Thankful for her dark clothing, Sam pulled a black scarf from the pocket of her trousers and used it to cover her hair and the lower half of her face before opening the door and checking the outside corridors. Seeing they were empty, Colt in hand, she darted to the base of the second-floor staircase.

After sucking in a deep breath, she squatted and peeked around the corner. From the light cast by lanterns lit every night as part of the bank's standard security precautions, she saw the barred door at the end of the corridor into the lobby was open. So was the door midway in the corridor for access in and out of the teller workspace. Mac must've opened them before he let in Brigham's men.

Despite hearing the murmur of low voices, she didn't see a lookout or anyone else. Then cocking her head, she thought she recognized Mac's and Price's voices, pitched low and sharp-edged as if they were angry. They must be in the lobby.

Dropping to her belly, her Colt gripped in her right hand, Sam slithered forward, blending with the dark shadow beneath the corridor windows. Having reached the open barred door adjacent to the vault's front wall, she was disappointed she couldn't see more than a quarter wedge of the teller's workspace. The counter blocked her view of everything in the lobby except the barren patch of marble floor from the front corner of the lobby to the open barred door into the workspace.

The voices were louder now, definitely angry, and distorted from echoing off the high ceiling and lobby walls. Straining to understand the words, Sam was confident the terse, deeper-pitched words were Mac's. The other voice, Price's, spoke in a smooth baritone drawl. Reaching up, she removed the scarf covering her face and hair. From this point forward, it wasn't needed because she'd run out of shadows in which to hide.

Unexpectedly, Mac strode to the open-barred door next to the counter and swung around to face Price, who'd moved to the front corner of the lobby, out of sight of anyone who might look in from the street. Then Sedge Cannon came into view, sliding along the teller's side of the counter, obviously soaking up every word exchanged between Mac and Price as if watching actors on a stage. Sam saw the barrel of Sedge's pistol peeking from his side, aimed at Mac. But Mac's full attention was on Price, and she doubted he had any idea Sedge was there. Sam could clearly hear the argument now.

"You haven't fooled me," Mac shouted. "You want Sam, her money, and Highbreeze."

"Look who's talkin'," Price shot back. "How many times have I heard you say Highbreeze should be yours—that you've given twenty-five years of your sweat to earn it?"

"Sure, I've said that. But I care about Sam and won't allow anyone to hurt her or Jackson. Hell, Sam would give me Highbreeze if I asked her for it."

"Why did you agree to this plan if you're so damned loyal?" Price asked.

"To protect her, you fool," Mac answered. "I failed my girl once. I won't do it again, not even to save myself. I knew from the beginning you hooked up with Brigham to set me up—knowin' I'd stand by Sam. You did it so Brigham would pull the trigger to take me out instead of you, and so Sam wouldn't guess how you played her false so you could step in after Jackson and I are out of your way. Well, I'm here to tell you, you won't live to see that day."

***

Sedge was grinning. He should have killed Mac and Price before now as Brigham had ordered, but the show was just too good. Price Hardin was a cold-hearted bastard. He'd pretend to throw his arm around you in friendship while pointing a revolver at the back of your head and calmly pulling the trigger.

Judging by the words exchanged between the long-time friends, things were about to explode. They'd probably kill each other any second, saving him the trouble. Just in case, though, he'd drawn his weapon and was prepared to fire. Though Brigham would be arriving soon and Sam Knight would follow, he decided to give the angry pair another minute.

*****

Suddenly, the deafening boom of gunfire colliding with the thunderous blast of a rocket from the fireworks display shook the building. Wide stripes of orange light pulsed crazily between the bars protecting the lobby windows, creating an illusion of slowed motion. Shocked, Sam couldn't tear her eyes from the tableau playing out in front of her.

The force of Price's bullet drove Mac backward into the iron bars of the unlocked door. Collapsing to his knees, .45 Colt in one hand, the other splayed over his gut, blood streamed through his fingers. Slowly, he pitched forward, his face smacking the marble floor, a dark river flowing from his center.

Price Hardin, torso half-turned as he'd fired his gun, jerked oddly—first forward, then back, as if struck twice, before stumbling, foot-over-foot, and dropping heavily on his side—facing the front wall.

Neither man moved.

"Maaaaccc...!" Sam's anguished wail reverberated as if bounced from one canyon wall to another.

Having emerged earlier from the customer safe deposit room into the back of the teller workspace, Brigham pressed flat against the front of the vault and crept toward Sam. Stunned by Mac's and Price's dying in front of her, she was oblivious to his presence. When he boldly lunged into the corridor, he stripped her Colt from her loose grip and tossed it to Sedge.

It wasn't until bruising hands wrapped around her upper arms and hauled her to her feet, that a part of Sam's mind comprehended what was happening. With her back pinned to Brigham's chest, she reflexively kicked back and down, aiming for his shin; but, with her arms restrained, the angle was wrong. Ignoring her ineffectual attempts to break free, Brigham flung her face first into the vault door.

Dazed from the blow and drowning in the horror and grief of Mac's death, Sam barely registered what Brigham was doing to her. She didn't feel the gun barrel poke her spine, nor did she see the fist that drove into her temple. Mercifully, instead of Brigham capturing her attention, a suffocating black curtain dropped over her consciousness.

***

By nature, Price Hardin was a patient man. However, his having to play dead in the bank's lobby while exercising said patience was pure torture.

Christ, it'd been a miserable night.

Thank God, he and Mac had been in motion reaching for their weapons, acting out the gunfight they'd staged to convince Brigham and his band of cut-throats they'd killed each other, or Cross Wolcott's aim might have been better.

Because Price had made it his business to eavesdrop when Brigham designated Sedge Cannon their executioner, neither he nor Mac expected Cross, stationed as lookout in the City Hall corner of the bank's lobby, to be a danger. Brigham must've ordered Cross to step in if Sedge dragged his feet.

Price had seen Cross's first bullet graze Mac's head just before he'd felt a second rip a fiery path through his left shoulder. Though his wound wasn't serious, the blood he was losing because of playing dead was a concern. Blood loss made a man weak and dizzy.

With Mac unconscious, only Price was left to ensure Sam came out of this thing alive. Until Sam opened the vault, he couldn't do anything to prevent Brigham's abuse.

***

Locked inside the vault, Jackson heard muffled gunshots followed by a banshee-like wail. Then nothing reached his ears—until a dull thump sounded from something striking the vault door.

What the hell—?

Five minutes crawled by while he strained to detect other sounds to determine what was transpiring on the other side of the thick, steel door. Any second, he expected to hear the first series of clicks from Sam manipulating the dial.

***

"Wake up, bitch, and open the vault," Brigham growled.

A soft moan spiraled from Sam's throat as Brigham's guttural command penetrated the dark curtain around her. She struggled to get her bearings, but her brain responded slowly. Lifting her hand, her fingers gingerly explored the raised bump on the side of her head.

The cold metal of a revolver pressed into her cheek. Using the vault wall to brace against, Sam struggled to her feet. While sucking in a steadying breath, she met Brigham's glare. With eyes full of menace, he poked the gun barrel into her side before motioning to the vault. Turning slightly, Sam's right hand traveled to the dial while her left reached for the eighteen-inch, perpendicular lever that would retract the door's side bolts once she entered the combination.

***

By the time the first cylinder disk completed one of the three full rotations required before Sam stopped at the first number of the combination, Jackson was wound tighter than catgut string on the bow of a fiddle. Already kneeling, weapon in hand, he stretched out flat on his belly and wedged himself in the floor space beneath the bottom shelf of the safe deposit boxes on his right. Because the vault door opened to the right from the outside, the wall opposite his hiding place would be exposed first.

He prayed Morgan would pull the lever to trigger the weights and pulleys to drop the trapdoors before Brigham or any of his men spotted him or hurt Sam. He envisioned the smoothly planed support braces sliding in greased tracks. There would be no betraying grating sounds to warn the outlaws the floor beneath their feet was about to disappear.

***

While Cross Wolcott remained in the lobby watching Main Street and the City-Hall corridor, the rest of the gang, including Sedge Cannon, eager to see the vault's treasures, had moved onto the expensive carpet camouflaging the trapdoors.

With the barrel of his gun still aimed at her, Brigham stood next to Sam, both feet planted safely on the two-foot strip of solid flooring in front of the vault. Unfortunately, Sam was positioned with only the ball of her left foot resting on the stable flooring. And with Brigham's boot wedged in front of it, she couldn't slide her foot forward—not that it mattered—because when the vault door swung outward after she worked the combination, she'd be forced to step back onto the ten-by-eleven Persian carpet covering the trapdoors. How the hell could she save herself from dropping into the holding cell when the trapdoors collapsed?

If she could keep hold of the steel handle and draw up her knees to swing with the vault door when she opened it, she might be able to pass over the trapdoors. More importantly, the door would act as a shield to deflect bullets should Brigham, Cross, or any of his gang manage to get off a shot or two.

Having manipulated the dial to the first and second numbers of the combination, Sam swiped her sweating palm on her trouser leg. Brigham growled, "Quit stalling," and, again, viciously jabbed her side with his gun.

Sam's fingers moved back to the dial. She spun it counterclockwise one full revolution before slowing to stop on the third combination number. Listening carefully, she heard the click of the nose lever drop firmly into the cutout on the third cylinder disk.

"Is that it?" Brigham asked, having watched her hand move from the dial to the handle.

"Yes."

He swatted her hands away and pulled. The door didn't budge. "Why doesn't it open?"

"Move your hand, and I'll show you."

"No tricks," he warned.

"Watch," she commanded while turning the lever handle from a vertical position to a horizontal one, her other hand hovering close to grasp it. The side bolts retracted with a distinctive, metallic clunk.

As Sam slowly pulled the heavy door toward her, she was forced back to accommodate the door's width.

Brigham's feet inched sideways in the same direction as the door as more of the vault's interior became visible, while the outlaws behind her leaned forward to peer inside. She prayed their attention stayed on the vault's contents and that the handle and hinges could bear her weight. In the fractional second before the trapdoors yawned open, she tightened her hold, preparing to dangle like a monkey clinging to a fragile limb.

Like the gunfire earlier, the trapdoors dropped in tandem with a rocket explosion, the boom so thunderous, it was akin to God presaging hell's doors to open wide and swallow the wicked. The only element missing from the scene were the flames of hell's fires shooting from the chasm.

Outraged curses and anguished howls rose from the pit, simulating the cries of lost souls burning in eternal damnation.

Soon after that, the war of the damned broke out.

***

In the seconds before the trapdoors opened, Jackson studied the face of his father's killer. Brigham had never had a conscience, nor suffered a tick of remorse for the horrible acts he'd committed. And Jackson needed him to pay. God willing, he was about to get revenge.

Watching his enemy's eyes sweeping the shelves and cubbyholes on the vault's opposite and back walls, Jackson recognized the instant Brigham's expression began registering shock. There was nothing to see.

The shelves were—bare.

***

Despite the mayhem erupting behind him, Brigham's head continued bobbing up and down, his eyes raking over empty spaces in disbelief. When he finally turned to investigate the pandemonium, he ignored the shelves lining the opposite wall, intuitively discerning the safe deposit boxes would be as empty as everything else. The truth of it slapped him in the face. He'd fallen for a brazen hoax.

Then he discovered the deep cavern in the floor.

Recovering his senses, the blasts of bullets biting into sand-filled packing crates in the battle his men waged to free themselves from their prison in the building's basement sent his head turning side-to-side, searching for targets. His face a mask of ferocity, he was nearly blind from the red rage flaring in his eyes. *Where the hell was Jackson Knight?*

His fury bordering on the maniacal, Brigham reached around the vault door to drag Sam from behind its protection.

Knight would show himself to save his woman.

***

Amazingly, wedged as she was between the heavy door and the front wall of the vault, Sam recognized the pounding of boot soles on marble before they moved to hardwood. Hope flared. *Was Jackson coming for her?*

Suddenly, Brigham reached around the door, presumably to drag her out into the open. But he withdrew almost as quickly. Cross Wolcott's appearance to Sam's left explained his retreat. Wolcott had her dead to rights. Out of habit, her hand went to her hip for a gun that wasn't there.

A gun barked.

Sam crouched, waiting for the punch of a bullet that didn't come. Instead, Cross's body slumped to the floor, his gun finding it before he did.

Sam caught a blurred glimpse of someone darting to the lobby side of the counter. She stretched her neck to get a better look, but whoever had been standing there didn't show himself. The possibility it was Jackson renewed her hope of rescue.

With Wolcott down, only Brigham was left.

***

After killing Cross Wolcott, Price darted back behind the lobby counter where a bout of dizziness staggered him. Unable to keep his legs under him, he slid to the floor. Resting with his legs stretched out in front of him, he cradled his left arm with his right and prayed silently Jackson wouldn't need his help sending Brigham to hell.

***

Sam anchored her heels against the steel wall at her back. With both arms raised, she threw her body against the heavy door. If she toppled Brigham, she'd have an opportunity to dive for Wolcott's gun.

She did hit Brigham, but not with much force. Then, from out of nowhere she heard her brother's voice.

"Drop it," Morgan ordered, his diction tight as whipcord, "or you're dead where you stand."

Sam risked a peek. Morgan stood eight feet beyond Brigham, legs locked, the muzzle of his pistol pointed at the gang leader's chest.

Brigham was about to ignore Morgan's warning, despite not having recovered fully from Knight's hellcat of a wife slamming the vault door into his back, when the unmistakable sound of a gun's hammer being thumbed back captured his attention.

Heart pounding madly, Sam angled her head in the same direction as Brigham's. Then she blinked, not believing her eyes.

Hellbent on vengeance, Jackson's imposing frame filled the vault's doorframe. The icy shards glistening in the green flecks of his dark eyes and the chilling caress of his finger on the trigger of his Colt cemented Brigham in place.

"You!" Brigham hissed, sounding much like the venomous serpent he resembled. "Where the hell is the money—the rifles?" he demanded, eyes blazing with fury, flecks of spittle flying from his lips.

Jackson gave no indication he heard a word.

"No one plays me for a fool and lives to gloat over it," Brigham shouted, raising the barrel of his revolver, apparently oblivious to the fact Jackson's and Morgan's weapons were cocked—ready to fire.

"Don't do it," Jackson warned. "Drop your weapon, or you'll die for certain this time."

"I'll take you with me!" Brigham bellowed, his finger tightening on the trigger.

In the low light, the muzzle of Jackson's single-action revolver flashed fire. The force of the bullet slammed through Brigham's chest, lifting his feet from the floor as if he weighed nothing, and launched him backward into the gaping void behind him.

Brigham's body hit bottom with a bone-cracking thump.

Guns boomed in retaliation, their bullets plowing into the ceiling above the pit.

***

When the gunfire ceased, Morgan cautiously sidled near to the crater's edge, while Jackson stepped from the vault, his eyes searching for Sam. When her gaze met his, some of the tightness in his gut eased. Eyes too round, face too pale, he'd never seen her look as frail as she did at this moment. When she stooped to retrieve Wolcott's gun, he noticed the tremor in her hand. He reminded himself that he still had unfinished business and reluctantly pulled his gaze away.

"Rem," Jackson shouted, "are you and the others all right down there?"

"Yeah, just pinned down. Reckon you noticed they're not out of bullets." As if to lend credence to his words, a gun barked and another bullet bit into the ceiling.

"Toss your weapons out and grab for the bars, boys," Jackson ordered, his head tucked safely out of the path of more flying lead, "or we'll send down a barrage of bullets. We don't need to expose ourselves to do it. Sooner or later, one of our slugs will find you."

And that's all it took for hell's pit to fall silent permanently.

***

Juice Jensen, followed by Storey Deale, holding a Colt to the outlaw's back, traipsed into the teller workspace from the Second Street corridor and halted. Cross Wolcott's body blocked the way. Storey administered a none-too-gentle jab to Juice's spine and nodded in Jackson's direction. "Keep moving if you don't want to end up like your friend."

Casting a black scowl in the gambler's direction, Juice pivoted and moved toward Jackson. Though armed with Cross's weapon, Sam warily backed to the vault, wisely putting as much distance between her and Juice as possible.

"Appears I missed quite a ruckus," Storey remarked after running out of flooring on which to advance. The amused glint in his eyes disappeared as he peered into the holding cell. Brigham's body wasn't a pretty sight.

"Deacon, Son," he called down, "got room for one more polecat?"

"Sure, Dad. His friends have been waitin' for him to drop in—so to speak."

"Far be it for me to keep a man from his friends," Storey quipped, humor back in his voice.

Moving behind Juice, Storey planted his boot sole firmly in the hollow at the back of the outlaw's knee. Juice dropped like a giant buzzard stripped of its wings.

Storey was dusting the palms of his hands together as if he'd just completed a full day's labor when Deacon's voice reached him. "Why do things the hard way when an easy one works just as well? Right Dad?"

"Exactly Son."

***

While Storey expedited Juice's descent to the basement lockup, Sam fought to hold herself together. There were two of her—the one made of flesh and blood struggled to do what had to be done, while the other, comprised of grief, battled to wrest control from the functioning one.

***

As Jackson approached Sam, he noticed the bruising on her cheek and the dullness of her pupils. When he eased his arms around her shoulders and touched his lips to her hair, her fingers clutched the folds of his shirt as if the material twisted in her fists would anchor her to the world. Jackson doubted she was half aware of anything transpiring around her.

"Sam, darlin'," he murmured. Something in his voice reached her because she lifted her face from the notch between his shoulder and his arm.

"Jackson—" she managed before her mind flashed the gruesome image of Mac's body on the marble floor. Grief rushed in—raw and overwhelming—spilling tears from her eyes. *Mac! Oh, Mac!*

Morgan, standing a step behind Jackson, spoke the awful words she couldn't say.

"She saw Mac and Price kill each other."

Chapter 36

Once able to think past the pounding in his skull, Mac blessed Cross's bad aim; otherwise, the bullet that had plowed a shallow crease above his left ear would have been fatal.

His second thought superseded the first.

Is my girl all right?

As if Mac had voiced his question aloud, Price spoke from somewhere nearby in the bank's lobby. "Sam's safe."

"How bad are you hurt?" Mac shot back, concern heavy in his tone. His friend's voice had sounded strange.

"My shoulder, but not bad—lost too much blood while I played possum. Worth it, though. I got Cross before he could get your girl." Price paused to swallow a groan. "Trapdoors worked like a charm. Jackson nailed Brigham—Rem's got the rest of the gang in the basement."

"Good."

"Not everything is," Price warned. "Sam thinks we're dead."

***

As Storey veered off to check Price, Morgan dropped to a crouch next to Mac. Aware most of the blood around his stepfather came from slaughtered chickens, he examined Mac's head wound. "Another inch to the right, Mac, and—"

"I know, Son," Mac interrupted. "Brigham ordered Cross to step in if Sedge hesitated."

While pressing a handkerchief to Mac's head, Morgan called to Storey, "How's Price?"

"Shoulder wound. Not too bad, but still bleeding. He just passed out."

Upon hearing Mac's voice, relief flooded through Jackson, and he started to guide Sam toward the lobby.

Already beyond comprehension, Sam's mind, protecting her from the pain and grief shredding her consciousness, shut down her senses.

When Sam suddenly sagged against him, Jackson caught her. With his head angled toward the open trapdoors, he shouted to get Sheriff Cooley's attention again. "Rem, can you spare Cal and Deacon? We got a little situation up here."

"They're already on their way."

When Cal popped into sight, Jackson, with Sam in his arms, began issuing orders. "Round up the sawbones Doc Baxter brought in to take care of folks in his absence and herd him over to Gracelyn Palace. Take two of the nags tied up out back—Brigham's crew won't be needing 'em. And, later, would you see all their horses get to the hotel livery?"

Nodding, Cal darted his eyes to Mac—then back to Jackson. "Price?" he questioned.

Jackson's clipped reply came fast. "With Storey—other side of the counter. He needs the doctor, too."

"Right," Cal replied, already turning away.

Jackson glanced down at Sam. She didn't stir. When he looked up to meet Deacon's gaze, he asked, "Would you get the buckboard?" Hesitating a fraction of a second, he added, "And bring Grace."

Deacon's eyes swept over Sam before he nodded. "Be right back."

***

Sam slept with Jackson's arms sheltering her, her face burrowed against his throat. Last night she'd been incapable of understanding words, so he'd given up trying to convince her that Mac and Price were alive. Several times during the night she'd moved fitfully against him as soft sounds escaped her lips. Each time, he pressed his body closer to hers and moved his hand on her back in long, reassuring strokes until she calmed.

Raising his head now, he assessed the pulse throbbing in the slim column of Sam's throat. Moving his gaze up, he saw the angry, dark bruise along her cheekbone that bled into a faint purple stain circling her eye, bearing evidence of Brigham's abuse. Tenderly, Jackson skimmed a fingertip over the bump on her temple. Her eyelids fluttered briefly, and the lovely arch of her brows puckered, but she didn't wake.

The blow Jackson was most concerned with was the one that didn't leave a visible mark. Keeping Sam in the dark about what they'd planned in the bank had wounded her emotionally.

***

Cradled in Jackson's arms, sleep was a haven from the sorrow and grief of last night's horrors, and Sam wanted to hide in its comforting cloak. But the insistent throbbing in her temple invaded her sanctuary and was soon joined by the pain of loss. She clenched her eyes against the tears threatening to fall.

"Sam, darlin'," Jackson murmured, "don't cry."

"I'm not," Sam mumbled, denying the wetness pooled on her lashes.

Jackson framed her face with his hands, his palms holding her so she had to look at him. She lifted her fingers stroking along his jaw, rasping over the stubble where the black-blue bruises from yesterday's beating were darkest.

Jackson felt the trembling in her touch.

"You're hurt and Mac and Price are dead," she lamented, her voice faltering as a shudder ran through her.

Jackson drew a sharp breath. He had to tell her—make her understand. Their gazes locked, and he spoke softly, solemnly. "Mac is alive. So is Price."

"But I saw—" she began before her breath caught in her throat. Her breasts rose as she inhaled and fell as she exhaled.

"You saw the show they put on to convince Sedge Cannon they'd killed each other so he wouldn't shoot them." *They should have warned her—saved her this anguish.*

"*Show?*" she repeated, struggling to comprehend the meaning of his words. "*Faked?*" she muttered. "You mean Mac and Price *pretended* to die?"

"Yes," he confirmed, his dark eyes holding hers squarely. "They're alive. I'm sorry we didn't tell you what we planned. I should have—"

"*Sorry?*" she repeated, cutting him off. Though profound relief washed through her, a powerful surge of anger followed. Her eyes filled with sparks; her body shook with anger. She pushed him away and wiggled out of bed.

"Dammit," Jackson swore under his breath, reaching for her and capturing her wrist.

Sam didn't notice because the floor slanted precariously beneath her feet. Then instead of standing, she was sitting on the edge of the mattress. *How had that happened?*

"Sam?" Jackson was beside her. "What's wrong?" His arm was at her waist and his hand swept up to cradle her cheek. "Are you dizzy?"

Confused, she drew a deep breath, but dots swirled in her vision—so many, they ate up the light. "I'm not going to faint." Her words came out in a whisper.

"You already have. I'll send for the doctor."

"No! I don't need a doctor."

"The hell you don't!" he snapped, a muscle working in his jaw.

Sam felt the battle of wills ignite between them, sweeping away the dots, clearing her head, and bolstering her strength. "It was the shock—I thought they were dead—and now you say they're all right—and I'm so happy—and so, so—" *Angry.*

She lifted her head to glare at him. "I'm really, *really* angry—so angry I'm picturing what parts of your and Mac's and Price's anatomy would suffer the most from my bullets. You put me through too much!"

Then as quickly as her strength had returned, it dissipated, leaving weariness in its wake. She didn't want to fight, didn't want to be angry. But she couldn't bear the thought of a doctor. She glanced at the bedpost, relieved to see her Colt in her holster. If that doctor came, she'd put a bullet in his behind.

Watching her closely, Jackson didn't miss the glance at her gun. She was afraid of doctors. Before losing her memory, she'd told him the intimate, invasive examinations of the physicians and specialists who tried to repair the damage from McBride's abuse had been almost as horrifying and painful as what McBride had done to her.

"I don't need the doctor," Sam said, the querulous note in her voice and pleading look in her eyes stirring his compassion. "I only trust you—and Doc Baxter." Jackson's hands moved to her shoulders and drew her close against him.

"All right. No doctor," he conceded. With a sigh, Sam closed her eyes and let him settle her back into the bed. "But you'll rest today."

"Yes," she murmured, already drifting into sleep's comforting arms.

***

The doctor who had stitched Mac's head warned his headache would last several days and advised him to limit his activity. Mac listened with half an ear, more concerned about Sam's emotional state than his or Price's wounds.

When Jackson reported Sam's reaction and fainting spell to him and Grace, he also informed them she'd agreed to spend the day resting. Her state of mind and ill health weren't surprising considering the worry, physical demands, and emotional strain she'd undergone. Concerned, they'd accepted she needed time to recover and work through her feelings.

Mac had waited until early afternoon the following day to approach Sam. Now, pausing in the open doorway of her suite, he was surprised to find her sleeping, her head resting on her crossed arms and her honey-gold hair streaming in thick strands over the dark, polished surface of the desk.

Remembrances of other times he'd found her similarly tugged at his heart. He'd been given such a gift when she'd come into his care. Unable to resist, he moved to her side and stroked a silky curl.

Lifting her head, Sam's eyes opened wider as she examined the bandage on his head. "Mac?" she breathed, as if doubting he was real.

"When you were a little thing," Mac reminisced, "you'd cuddle in my lap after I combed out the tangles. It's the same color as your father's. Your eyes, too."

She'd always looked at him as if he could whip the world and had all the answers. This time, he'd come up with the wrong one. Though his and Price's plan had worked, he suspected from what Jackson told him that it had undermined her trust in him—maybe in herself, too.

"I shouldn't have done it, sweetheart," Mac apologized, his tone full of regret. "I knew things would get bad in the bank. We knew Brigham ordered Sedge to kill us, but we never guessed he'd issue the same order to one of the others. He intended to kill Jackson, then keep you for ransom." *And other things.* Mac thought it but didn't say it. "We had a chance to stop him if we could fool him, but I believed we couldn't fool him if we didn't fool you, too. I should've told you. If Cross had killed us, no one would have been there to help you."

"Price saved me from Cross. I was trapped behind the vault door and didn't have a gun. There was no place to go."

"The doctor said Price will be fine, but it'll be another day or two before he's strong enough to get out of bed," Mac said to reassure her. "When I saw him earlier today, he joked he was pretendin' to be in worse shape than he was so Jackson wouldn't make good on his threat to bury him alive for putting you in harm's way."

Sam grinned. "If he winked after that joke, he's for sure on the mend." A moment passed between them before Sam spoke again. "I was—afraid, Mac." Her eyes and her voice dropped on the last word. "I couldn't think of anything except what I would do without you."

Mac sighed, suddenly feeling older than the Earth. Fate could be kind or cruel. Would his brave girl ever accept she had little power to influence it?

"You'd go on, sweetheart. It's what we all do when we lose someone we love. It's what I did when my wife, Lorena, and baby boy, Andrew, were killed. It's what Grace did when she lost her first husband, Drake. It's what your father did when he lost your mother. It's what you, me, Morgan, and Grace did when we lost your father. That's how God made the world. I'm sorry you had to face losing us when it wasn't true. Can you forgive me?"

"Of course, I forgive you. All of us came through this because of you and Price. Though I can't remember most of the things between us from the past, my heart knows. You love me and I love you."

Mac recognized the soft sheen of forgiveness in her eyes. Then she was hugging him—the same way she had when she was a little girl.

***

Restless after Mac left but determined to bring some normalcy back to her life, Sam ventured downstairs to Gracelyn's gaming room. Patronage was light, not unusual for a Thursday afternoon, especially when most people were probably working feverishly to complete work left undone because of the holiday only two days past.

Having chosen a quiet corner table, Sam played solitaire, letting her attention wander from the cards to listen with half an ear to Alexa and Miss Jenny commiserate on their pregnancies. Alexa would deliver a week or two after Jenny.

353

"Where's your head, Sis?" her brother's voice teased, while privately noting she looked more fragile than he'd expected. "There are two places to play that red queen you've been holding in your hand for the last five minutes."

Sam placed the queen on a black king before looking up and smiling. Morgan was hard to resist when he was being playful. "The train must be on schedule," she murmured, aware Morgan and Jackson had accompanied Annie and Frank to the train station to see them off. She'd said her goodbyes privately the night before.

"It was," Morgan confirmed as he dropped onto the chair next to hers. "Jackson will be here shortly. He went to Abbott's office with Rem and Price."

"Price?" Sam questioned. "Mac said he needed to rest. I hope Jackson and Rem didn't drag him from his sick bed to set his affairs in order before they kill him for putting us through our paces with Brigham's gang."

Morgan laughed. "It probably crossed their minds, but they didn't do it. Price got up first thing this morning under his own steam and had his Deputy U.S. Marshal star pinned to his vest and his arm in a sling when he left. By the time I finished breakfast in the restaurant, he'd given up his room at the boarding house, taken the room next to Deacon's at the hotel, and was on his way to the telegraph office. Later, he arrived at the train station to thank Annie and Frank for all their help. And he did it without making one joke."

Sam laughed. "Everything went smoothly at the station?"

"Yes. Even Mac looked good. With his hat on, his bandage barely shows. I'd been worrying Alexa and I would need to step in as chaperones if he weren't up to traveling. Grace insisted Annie be chaperoned to protect her reputation and quell gossip regarding her relationship with Frank

Butler. With the baby coming soon, I don't think it wise for Alexa to travel. She tires easily and suffers from backaches."

Having just heard Alexa and Jenny discussing those very things, plus food cravings, mood swings, breast sensitivity, and darkening nipples, Sam understood her brother's concerns.

"Grace and Mac will return Saturday and stay until after the baby comes," Sam sympathized. "Mother and I will assume Alexa's responsibilities here at Gracelyn to help out."

As if possessing a special perception for sensing his presence, Sam turned her gaze from her brother to watch Jackson make his way across the salon. Once he reached their table, his eyes swept over her in appreciation before he lowered his tall frame onto the empty, straight-backed chair closest to hers. She smiled into his eyes.

For no other reason than wanting to touch her, Jackson placed his hand over one of hers. "Are you checking up on me?" he teased, nodding toward Morgan.

"Though you're an interesting subject," Sam drawled, undisguised laughter in her tone, "not everything is about you." Then contradicting her words, she boldly dropped her eyes to admire his chest and the breadth of his shoulders. "However, I must admit Morgan mentioned a meeting with Winchell Abbott."

Jackson chuckled. "The mayor and city councilmen met last night and suggested we donate the third-place prize money to the orphanage. Since Price had already declined his share and Abbott saw no legal problem with that solution, I agreed. I also asked the mayor to auction Larkin Johns's and Digger Crane's rifles at the Fall Harvest Festival and use the funds to purchase Christmas gifts for the children."

"Am I right in assuming Price decided to keep his rifle?"

Jackson grinned. "You called it, darlin'. He did it with a big wink at the mayor and a joke about never riding with a posse again because outlaws would search him out just to get a gander at a rifle with the 'One of One Thousand' inscription."

Sam laughed, picturing it in her mind. Then sobering, she asked, "Did Price or Rem say anything about what will happen to the rest of the gang?"

"Three Deputy U.S. Marshals are coming tomorrow to transport them to Cheyenne for trial," Jackson replied, understanding the reason for the question. The outlaws had friends who wouldn't be afraid to try a jailbreak.

Morgan lit a thin cigar and leaned back in his chair, squinting through the curl of smoke while watching Sam's face. "Sis," he murmured, pulling her attention from Jackson. "Alexa and I would like to sell our shares in Gracelyn Palace to Storey and Deacon. We purchased land near Windbag's place and intend to build a house suitable for a bank president's family."

Because they'd discussed the possibility before, Sam was neither surprised nor opposed to her brother's plans. "I have no objections." A smile lifted the corners of her mouth. "I told you once before, I like the idea of my niece or nephew having a banker for a papa." As she finished speaking, she wrinkled her nose and fanned away a wisp of smoke.

Morgan immediately transferred his cigar to his other hand. "Storey wants to take over our suite when we move out."

"That makes sense," Sam replied, nodding her approval while endeavoring to ignore the bitter taste gathering at the back of her throat.

Catching Sam's eye, Jackson said, "Storey and Deacon approached me about purchasing partnerships in the hotel and restaurant. I agreed if they accepted the day-to-day headaches of managing the businesses. I want more time with you, the ranch, and one or two other investments that interest me."

"Like opening a company to manufacture porcelain commodes?" Morgan interjected, unable to resist the opportunity to poke fun at Jackson.

"There's money in it," Jackson responded, taking the bait. He'd recently read William Smith had obtained a patent for an improved jet siphon bowl. "Someday all houses will have indoor plumbing. As a banker, you should have the vision to recognize the potential."

Morgan held back his laughter. Jackson was preaching to the choir.

Preoccupied with wondering whether Jackson had talked with Jessa to learn the truth about Peter Jack's parentage, Sam barely noticed Morgan and Jackson's playful argument. Just as she decided to wait and ask Jackson privately, Morgan inquired about it.

"Were you surprised when Jessa explained about Peter Jack's real father?" Focused on satisfying his curiosity, he stabbed his cigar in Jackson's direction, unmindful of the cloud of pungent smoke he released in Sam's face.

Learning Peter Jack wasn't his or Brigham's son didn't bring Jackson as much relief as he'd expected. In fact, the truth was accompanied by a little sadness. And because he hadn't had an opportunity to share Jessa's revelations with Sam, Jackson was slow to answer. Cornered, so to speak, he locked his gaze with Sam's and chose his words carefully.

"Jessa apologized for naming me her son's father. She did it out of fear, explaining she fell in love with a man who perished in an accident before she arrived in South Pass. Peter Jack is his son, and Jessa made no apologies for loving the man. She swore she wouldn't have married Brigham had there been a way to avoid it." Pausing, he cleared his throat before continuing.

"Jessa truly believed her husband, Colter Brogan—Brigham—was dead. When she saw him in Rem's jailhouse, she couldn't believe her eyes. To protect Peter Jack from being hurt or used as a weapon against us, she wrote the lie in that letter and brought him to us, confident we would protect him."

"In Jessa's place, I would probably do the same," Sam admitted, with a touch of regret in her voice. Then smiling shyly, she added, "She was wise to trust you."

Jackson hoped his cheeks didn't show the warmth he felt from the compliment. "Well, now that Jessa's free of Brigham, Deacon is hellbent on clearing her of the charges on that Wanted poster. Price sent wires to a judge and some marshal friends asking for help."

"And Deacon and Jessa married this afternoon," Morgan interjected. Fully aware he was the bearer of surprising news, he leaned back in his chair, puffing his cigar, watching Jackson and Sam share an amazed moment.

"Would you please put that thing out?" Sam choked, her hand flying up to press against her lips.

Recognizing her distress, both men bolted from their chairs to each grasp an arm and ease her gently to her feet.

"Take a deep breath, Sis, and try to hold on," Morgan murmured, as Jackson pointed them toward the stairs. However, upon hearing Morgan call, "No time," he scooped her up and headed for Alexa's office.

Morgan thrust open the door and snapped it shut once they passed through. By the time he turned to face the room, Jackson was kneeling on the floor supporting Sam as she emptied her stomach into a tin waste paper receptacle.

Morgan strode to the desk and removed a napkin from one of the drawers. After filling a glass with water, he squatted next to his sister and thrust the glass into her hand. "Here, sip it." Then tossing the napkin in her lap, he added, "Choke down a few of those soda crackers." Noticing her grimace at the word choke, he softened his tone. "Try, Sis. Alexa suffered through this kind of thing every morning for three months and it helped her."

While both men watched in silence, Sam forced down a few sips of water and several crackers.

"Feeling better?" Jackson asked, observing some color returning to her face.

Sam nodded, offering a tremulous smile. "Yes. I'm sorry. For some reason, the cigar bothered me—maybe because I'm not fully recovered from everything that's happened lately." The indignity of not being able to control her stomach was embarrassing—stupid cigar!

Morgan agreed with Jackson. Sam did look better. When she drew her legs beneath her to sit unaided, he was sure of it.

Thankful her stomach was calmer and the awful taste at the back of her throat had dissipated, Sam peered up at Morgan. "Check the salon to make sure no one is smoking. Then order some ginger tea and toast and have it sent upstairs."

"You must be feeling better or you wouldn't be issuing orders like a drill sergeant," Morgan replied dryly. "But since it was my cigar that made you sick, I'll obey—this time."

"Darlin'," Jackson admonished when they were alone, "he's your brother—not your servant."

Sam's eyes twinkled. "Next time he puts a match to one of those foul things around me, I'll make sure the smoke blows up his—"

Laughing, Jackson clamped his hand over her mouth to cut off the rest of her threat while his other arm snaked around her waist to haul her up against him. "I'm helping you not say something you'll regret later, darlin'," he crooned against the column of her throat, pretending to save her from her temper.

Sam understood his motives exactly. Slipping her arm through his, she countered, "Come on, Galahad. Escort me upstairs or the tea will arrive before we do."

Proffering a slight bow, Jackson conceded gallantly, "Your wish is my command."

Chapter 37

The next morning, Sam woke before Jackson, wanting him—his body and his heart.

A sleeping husband was such a waste.

Sam's hand wandered down the center of Jackson's chest, seeking a more intimate place. Roused from sleep, Jackson fleetingly wondered what man wouldn't give up sleep for what his wife was promising. He turned his head to lock his gaze with hers and felt his heart swell as quickly as his sex.

Recognizing the desire and emotion swirling in the depths of his green-flecked, brown eyes, Sam's breath caught in her throat. He hardened in her hand—long and thick and hot.

Sam's touch turned his insides to molten lava and his cock to pile-driving steel. Though every muscle in his body was taut with his desire for her, Jackson needed the feelings between them even more. The passion she called from him blossomed from the power of the tenderness he felt for her— his beloved wife.

Jackson reached for Sam. And she arched to kiss him. His mouth locked on hers, telling her with his thrusting tongue of the love deep inside him—for her—only her. Then covering her, he rubbed his chest against her breasts while pressing his erection against her inner thigh.

Aching for him, Sam reached to guide him to her center.

"Not yet," he murmured before settling his open mouth on her breast to suckle. Then he tasted her other breast, licking the nipple as if savoring a drizzle of honey on its pebbled tip, while his fingertips explored the petals of her intimate flesh—dipping, retreating, promising.

Sam's hips rocked in response. His hands stroked down her legs and drew up her knees. Poised at her entrance, he lifted his lips from the mound of her breast to ask, "Yes, darlin'?"

"Yes," she responded, breathing the word, closing her eyes against the waves of emotion washing over her.

He entered in one thrust, hard and deep, and held himself there, her slick heat wrapping him tightly.

"Yes," she breathed against his skin, clenching her internal muscles around him. He groaned before moving. She met him, stroke for stroke. The friction was so good between them that their bodies slicked with perspiration and trembled from the pleasure. The sparking fissions and flames rose higher as they sought the ultimate peak. Then hovering on the brink of release, they cried out together as they hurtled over the edge, her convulsions drawing him deep—milking him in powerful bursts.

***

On Monday, Price Hardin received replies to his telegrams regarding Jessa's Wanted poster. As it turned out, Brigham, using one of his aliases, promulgated the poster. Though Jessa was present at the stage robbery, she hadn't gone willingly. Thankfully, there were no witnesses to contest that defense. Nor was there evidence she'd carried a weapon or aided the gang. However, for Jessa's and the court's protection, the judge reviewing the case advised Jessa to appear before him, present testimony, and assist the court with making an official record justifying the ruling. Eager to comply, Deacon and Jessa left Peter Jack in Sam and Jackson's care while they traveled to Cheyenne to resolve the issue.

On Wednesday, Deacon wired that Jessa was cleared of all charges. When the couple returned Friday morning, they spent several hours in business discussions with Storey, Alexa and Morgan, and Sam and Jackson before hastily packing and arranging to have their belongings carted to the train depot. Then, after collecting Peter Jack and stopping briefly at the telegraph office to wire Deacon's resignation to Allan Pinkerton, they boarded the last train of the day. Upon their return from visiting Jessa's father, Rafferty Nolan, they planned to reside in Jessa's house. The location was good and, though small, there was plenty of room on the lot to add on.

***

Although the days that followed settled into a comfortable routine, Sam experienced an uncharacteristic lethargy between bouts of sharp-edged anticipation, as if at any moment something was about to happen. Though she doubted the feeling was associated with something bad, it wreaked havoc with her state of mind and emotions. Shockingly, within a few hours, her mood could bounce from anxious to sad to joyous.

She was napping at odd times of the day, and she wasn't eating well. In her opinion, she looked far too pale. However, Jackson claimed she'd grown so blindingly beautiful that men's eyes followed her everywhere. On several occasions, she'd cried for reasons she couldn't explain.

Jackson grumbled the more he tried to draw her out of her moods, the further she withdrew from him. He said he felt as though she were doing it to distance herself from him emotionally.

Sam didn't understand how that could be true when her physical need for him had increased. In their joining, she found respite from whatever was deviling her. While she was in his arms, all things in her world felt as if they were in their rightful place. Outside his embrace, her anticipation returned, and with it the lethargy and fluctuating emotions. And each time they visited, she found them more difficult to bear.

***

"Are you not talking to me because you realize you love Deacon and regret marrying me?" Jackson blurted the accusation before he was fully aware his patience had deserted him and he'd asked something that made no sense.

Sam opened her mouth to give him a facetious answer but instead settled on a dignified one. "My silence isn't about Deacon. He has a bride. You said that to shock me."

"True, but now that you're answering, would you please tell me if your behavior is about *me* or about *you*?" It was a legitimate question.

Staring blankly into Jackson's gaze early in the morning before he left for Trinity, Sam struggled to explain feelings that she didn't understand. Rarely had she felt so unsure of herself.

"Dammit, don't just stand there, Sam. Please talk to me."

"I can't answer, Jackson, because I don't know," she ground out. As inadequate as her answer was, it was the truth. But she could see that Jackson couldn't accept it.

"When you agreed to marry me, darlin'," he replied, "you said memories don't matter because our future together is what's important. You said you love me. When a woman like you gives her heart, she gives her whole heart. If you've convinced yourself differently, you're lying to yourself. I need you to see the truth. This thing between us hurts too much."

Sam started to turn away, but Jackson caught her wrist and tugged gently to bring her back to him. "We've talked this through before," he said, his voice gentler, "but I'll say these words once more because you must not have understood. *I don't want what you can't give.* I never have. I never will. I want you for who you are and the love you can give."

Sam made an effort to offer some explanation Jackson could understand. "My emotions are all over the place. I won't lie and tell you I haven't wondered if I did the right thing marrying you. I do believe deep inside my heart that you deserve a woman who can give you a family. I wish I didn't have so many flaws. Why I am plagued with so many self-doubts now, I don't know. I think there must be something wrong with me."

"Is this your way of telling me you don't love me?" Jackson asked, his voice strained, raw with hurt. Fearing she was on the verge of leaving him, he was desperate to make her understand there was no circumstance under which he'd give her up or sanction a divorce.

"We. Are. Married." *Dammit! It wasn't possible for him to love any other woman.* In his mind, he believed Jessa had unintentionally reopened a wound he'd believed healed.

After holding his gaze for several seconds, Sam dropped her eyes. Confused and overwhelmed, she feared she'd give into tears or accidentally say something hurtful. She needed to get away before she fell apart. She didn't have the strength to debate with him—not now.

Jackson watched emotions, one after the other, flit across Sam's face. Then, to his amazement, shoulders squared, back straight, she purposefully strode toward the door.

"Are you too much of a coward to admit you don't love me?" Jackson called after her, expecting she'd spin around and hotly deny her cowardice. Instead, she resolutely continued her march to the door, opened it, and stepped through, leaving him primed for a battle she didn't stay to fight.

The sound of the latch settling in place spurred him to action. But halfway to the door he questioned the wisdom of following her and halted. In his present frame of mind, he'd likely make things worse. The better strategy was to give her time to adjust her thinking.

He had no idea his decision was an egregious mistake.

Then, cocksure fool that he was, he compounded it by staying away the rest of the day—believing he was being wise to give her time to sort out her feelings, to understand nothing could come between them.

Later, that evening, he faced the reality of his flawed thinking and was appalled at how easily he'd deceived himself.

In the hours he'd stayed away, Sam left him.

Chapter 38

Jackson's preliminary inquiries to find his wife revealed where she was not.

When he discovered Sam's private railroad car was gone, he was certain she'd run to Chicago. But a day later, after receiving replies to the telegrams he'd sent to the caretakers of Sam's townhouse, Clare and Madison Hadley; Sam's lawyer, Thomas Miles; and Sam's second cousin, Tanner Roberts; his certainty turned to gut-wrenching worry. Not only was Sam not there, they hadn't heard from her and could offer no suggestions as to where she might be.

Jackson's subsequent efforts produced results.

Desperate to find her, he used his influence with the railroad to trace her private train car and was rewarded with the news it had been uncoupled and sidetracked in Mercer, Nebraska. He was able to learn she'd hired railroad security to guard it, but could find no information about where she'd gone from there—not even a clue of what means of transportation, if any, she'd arranged from that point.

The pain of her leaving sliced deep. He wouldn't accept the possibility he might never see her again.

***

Before heading to the train station to catch the eastbound train, Jackson searched for Mac. He knew Alexa and Grace were at the bank with Morgan, which was fine. He'd get away with fewer questions if he only involved Mac.

Jackson found his father-in-law outside Gracelyn Palace, saying his goodbyes to Price Hardin, whose shoulder had healed well enough he could return to business. Anxious to start on his journey, he kept the conversation brief. "Sam's in Mercer, Nebraska. At least, that's where her train car is."

"Do you know why?" Mac asked.

"No—she didn't even tell me she was going," Jackson responded, deliberately not disclosing the fact Doc Baxter was visiting family in Mercer. To throw Mac a bone, he added, "Before she left, she expressed doubts about how good she is for me because of her inability to have a child. Before she agreed to marry me, she'd say she was too damaged for anyone to love."

"More likely she meant for a man like you to love," Mac said bluntly. "She thinks you deserve everything a woman can give, including children. Since she doesn't have the ability, she may have convinced herself that the right thing to do is bow out. Though how that fits in with Mercer is a puzzle."

"If that's in her head, it's not true," Jackson replied, hoping to put a stop to questions.

"I know that, but I'll bet my girl adds her tally sheet differently than we do."

Jackson agreed. Though he'd believed marriage was his ace in the hole for holding on to Sam, it now appeared her rules said a wild queen who couldn't bear a child trounced an ace. "I'm going after her, Mac, but I have no idea what to say when I catch up with her."

Mac clapped his son-in-law's shoulder. "I'll pass along what an angel taught me. If you listen with your heart, it'll come to you."

***

"Why did you let him get away with lying about Mercer?" Price asked after Jackson left.

Mac slanted his old friend a sly grin. "You noticed that, did you? Why do you think I did it, *ol' pard?*"

Turning his back to Mac, Price lifted his foot into the stirrup and swung up onto his saddle. "Ain't no thinkin' needed," Price quipped. "You already know all you need to know about where and why that girl of yours lit out of here." Holding the reins, he smiled down at his friend. "You gonna tell me?"

"Not yet, but I will soon," Mac promised.

"And when you do, *ol' pard*, we'll celebrate the news with a good cigar." Then with one last wink Price Hardin reined his horse around and galloped out of town.

***

When Eva Gibson, Doc Baxter's sister, showed Sam Knight into the parlor of her home, her brother not only looked shocked but alarmed over the young woman's paleness and anxious expression.

"What in God's name are you doing here, Sam?" Doc demanded.

Sam hesitated, not sure what to say. Knots of anxiety roiled in her stomach—or was that the bland oatmeal she'd forced down after the train car was finally uncoupled? Her stomach had been upset most of the trip.

"Let the poor girl sit down before you yell at her Roy," Eva admonished, guiding the distressed young woman to a wingback chair. "She's traveled quite a distance to see you, so I suggest you discuss things calmly while I arrange for tea." Shooting a warning look at her brother, she patted Sam's shoulder and left the room.

"Where's Jackson?" Doc asked, his tone quieter, though still insistent.

"I—I left him in Prosperity," Sam stammered, having found her voice.

"Did you at least tell him where you were going?"

"I left a note," she snapped, offended he thought it necessary to ask. "I hadn't planned to come, but I got a crazy idea—then there was barely enough time to get my railcar coupled let alone find Jackson—especially since I wasn't sure where he was, so I—" she stopped abruptly, recognizing she was rambling.

After taking a steadying breath, she met Doc Baxter's gaze. "I came because I need you, Doc. I only trust you for this. Jackson will understand."

Sam Hilliard Stone Knight had always had Doc's heart. And her trust humbled him. Despite her incredible strength of will, she'd graciously yield when intellect proved her wrong or her generous spirit urged her to do so out of kindness. She disconcerted and enchanted, hence captivated and conquered. He'd do anything for her.

"All right, Sam. You talk and I'll listen." Leaning back in his chair, he folded his hands in front of him. "Don't leave anything out."

Less than an hour later, Doc Baxter concluded Sam wasn't crazy.

***

"Did you show Jackson the note Sam left?" Grace asked later while pouring them both a cup of coffee upstairs in their daughter's Gracelyn Palace suite. "Miss Angie had no idea she'd scooped it up in the pile of invoices she took from the desk."

"No," Mac admitted. "He'd already traced her railcar and was on his way to the train station."

"Too bad he worried," Grace said. "At least Sam is all right."

"She will be—once Jackson gets there," Mac agreed.

"Does he know how to handle things when he talks to her?"

Mac grinned. "I told him what you taught me about listening with your heart."

Grace smiled, the love she felt for her husband shining softly in her eyes. "Are you going to ask me, Mac?"

"I would if I knew what question you had in mind," he answered. "Is there any chance you'd save me breath and just tell me the answer?"

Grace nodded, mischief mixing with the tenderness in her gaze. "The answer is, 'Yes, I would sell the Golden Crown and move here to Prosperity with you.'"

Mac searched her face for regret and found none.

When Grace saw he understood, she volunteered a second answer. "And, no, Sam won't mind if you turn Highbreeze over to someone else to run."

Holding his wife's gaze, Mac nodded and waited, certain there was more.

There was.

Grace stepped close and slid her arms around Mac's waist. "Ready?"

He managed to nod, once again.

"We need to take a nap so you can share some of that breath I've been helping you save."

Chapter 39

After three days of visiting Sam's railcar, Doc Baxter was both irritated and puzzled over the fact her husband hadn't shown up to collect her. It wasn't good for her to worry. When after bidding Sam goodbye and descending the railcar stairs, he looked up and spotted Jackson watching him, he didn't hesitate to show his ire.

"'Bout time you got here," Doc growled, glaring at the younger man. "What took you so long?"

"It's hard to catch the wind, especially when you don't know in what direction it's blowing," Jackson shot back, annoyed at Doc's criticism.

Doc fought the smile lurking around his mouth, before giving into it. "She is that—the wind, the rain, and the sun." Then stabbing a finger into the center of Jackson's chest, he added, "But make no mistake, you're the earth anchoring her to this world. Remember that when you talk to her."

Jackson heard it as an order, not advice. "Is she ill?" Jackson asked, his voice tight, controlled. "Is that why she came to see you?"

"No, but she needs to be looked after. She expected you several days ago, so be prepared to deal with her temper."

Jackson frowned. "Her temper?" he repeated. "She's the one that left without telling me where she was going."

"That's not the story I heard. Besides, it's irrelevant, even if it's true. You love the woman, so you'll listen. In fact, that's my prescription for you both."

Having ambled past Jackson to climb into his carriage, Doc added, "I'll look in on you when I get back to town, end of next week." Then, before flicking the reins, he muttered, "If I'd known physicians have to patch up marriages, I'd have become a veterinarian."

After Doc left, Jackson stood outside her railcar, tamping down his hurt and reminding himself Sam must be hurting too.

***

Sam sighed after Doc left. Three days and still no Jackson. Beyond her yearning for him, she was concerned. She didn't understand why it was taking so long for him to come for her. While she'd waited, her mind had replayed the discussion between them on the day she left, and she'd realized, when viewed from his perspective, he might have misinterpreted the few things she'd said, especially when she'd followed them with her walking out. *Did he think she'd left him?*

Recalling she heard the eastbound train pull into the station shortly before Doc Baxter left, she was suddenly certain if Jackson were coming, he would have been on that train. She needed to go home—as soon as possible. Impatient to make the arrangements, she flung open the railcar door.

"Jackson," Sam breathed, hardly believing he was standing there. His hands were planted on his lean hips, long, powerful legs spread apart, his eyes watching her every breath. She wanted to step into him, glide her hands over his strong shoulders, feel muscles shift beneath her touch. Instead, stunned, she just stood there.

Jackson's eyes swept over Sam's face before moving down to notice her blue gown of lightweight lawn. The skirt, narrow with a soft drape in the front and back, was unevenly gathered beneath the tooled leather gun belt cinching its folds. Though she appeared more delicate than he'd last seen her, her skin was glowing and the fullness of her breasts challenged the tiny buttons fastened over them.

"Hell," he croaked roughly, the muscles of his throat contracting. After swallowing deeply, he managed huskily, "I was worried, Sam." His heart was racing. What he wanted to do was sweep her in his arms and kiss her.

To Sam's humiliation, her bottom lip quivered and tears burned behind her lids. She hated weakness. Fighting it, she took a deep breath.

Jackson could no more stop himself from going to her than he could stop breathing. He folded her in his arms and held her. His hands stroked her back, his jaw pressed tightly to her forehead as he rocked her.

Resolutely following instructions to listen, he hesitated to speak. Perhaps a well-mannered question was appropriate. "Were you going somewhere, darlin'?"

Sam moved her head back to study his face. Perplexed to hear his polite words while expressions of caring and anger warred on his face, she retreated a step before answering. "I was on my way to talk to the station manager about coupling the railcar tomorrow when the train comes."

"The train to Chicago?" Jackson inquired, a line appearing between his brows. He advanced a step, recovering the distance she'd put between them.

Sam stepped back once more. She was inside the railcar and Jackson was on the threshold. "Chicago?" she repeated, making it a question. The destination confused her. "Do— do we need to go to Chicago for some reason?"

Jackson edged closer. "I don't know. I thought—" he stopped, recognizing he'd started down a dangerous path. Inhaling a quick breath, he murmured, "I thought *you* might have a reason to go there." He reached an arm behind him to close the door.

"Why would you think that?" Sam's tone was soft, but perplexed. "I meant the westbound train home," she clarified, the frown between her brows deepening. The padded arm of the chair behind her halted her cautious retreat. Jackson's eyes never left hers. There was something there she didn't understand. Her hand moved to cover her stomach.

Careful to keep his tone even, Jackson reminded himself he was there to listen, not judge. "You were gone when I came to find you, and I had no idea where you were. I followed as soon as I learned you were here with Doc. I assumed you'd be traveling on to Chicago to see your lawyer because you're leaving me. I don't want you to go." Sam's other hand moved to stroke the scar on the hand pressed to her middle, a sure sign of her agitation.

"I left a letter explaining I was coming here," Sam insisted. "I left it on the desk. I'm not leaving you." There was no artifice in her tone, only incredulity that he would believe her guilty of such a thing. Jackson's black brows relaxed and his gaze softened. Seeing he believed her, she leaned toward him. "Did you talk to Doc outside? You must've seen him."

With tenderness flowing through him as his fear ebbed, Jackson gave no thought as to why she'd asked about Doc. He answered with a dismissive shrug. "I saw him, but we didn't say much of anything."

He didn't know.

Jackson reached for Sam's hand and she came willingly. Her other hand lifted to his face, her fingertips smoothing his cheek, skimming the blade of his nose, the seam of his lips.

At that moment, he was certain she loved him still. He saw it in the soft shimmer of her eyes, felt it in her loving caresses.

Then her eyes held his and she said, "You're a father."

Everything good he'd been feeling evaporated in an instant. One second ago, he'd believed in her love; and in the next, it vanished.

"You know Peter Jack isn't my son." His voice was flat because he had lost hope. He expected to see sadness in her eyes—regret—desire for something that could never be—but, it wasn't there.

"Not Peter Jack. Doc says *we're* going to have a child."

"But you can't," he murmured, softly, his dark eyes filled with compassion. "The doctors said you can't, darlin'." As soon as the words left his mouth, he regretted them. *What were the right words?*

In the moment Jackson hesitated, Sam spoke, giving him the opportunity to listen—as Mac had advised. And what he understood made the floor tip crazily under his feet.

"The doctors were wrong." Sam's eyes fluttered closed, and when she opened them, they were brimming with tears. "I didn't know. But when I overheard Alexa complain Morgan's cigars made her ill, too, the thought popped into my head. Suddenly I recalled things I heard Alexa and Miss Jenny say about their pregnancies. And as extraordinary and improbable as the thought was, I couldn't help wondering. I needed Doc. You know I couldn't trust anyone else." Suddenly shy, heat warming her cheeks, her eyes dropped away.

"You're pregnant," Jackson whispered, testing the words. Miracles were possible. Seeing her blush, he was touched she could make love with him so freely yet feel shy about this. They'd made a child. There weren't words enough in the world to tell her how he felt. Their eyes met and emotions wrapped around them like golden strands of spun silk.

"Doc said everything appears normal." She was proud and uncertain and a little afraid.

Jackson saw the joy and the fears. His mouth pulled into a teasing smile. "As usual, darlin', when told you can't do something, you make it your business to prove you can."

She had to ask. "What if something happens to the baby?"

"What if the sun doesn't rise tomorrow or some other catastrophe happens?" Jackson asked in return. "We didn't promise to love each other so long as we don't face any bad times. We'll persevere, darlin'." She was everything to him, and if God were to take this child before it could be born, it would be a devastating blow. But not insurmountable. They'd weep, grieve, mourn, and go on—together. He wouldn't let it tear them apart.

"I love you with all my heart. You're everything—"

"Everything?" Sam echoed, interrupting, her intonation making it a question. Then she waited expectantly for him to finish. Instead, he smiled that slow smile that always melted her insides.

"There is no more, darlin'—only you. You are everything. When a man has everything, he doesn't need anything more."

She blinked before leaning into him, her lips close to his ear. "Neither does a woman. I love you, Jackson. With everything I am—and am not."

And they understood with a clarity of mind that buried itself deep in their hearts, there wasn't a gift greater in the world than *everything*.

Epilogue

"**G**imme back my pancake, Peter Jack Storey, or I'll tell Papa and he'll tell Mama to come and fix your wagon but good."

In their ranch house kitchen, pouring batter into the skillet on the stove, Jackson pretended not to hear his four-year-old daughter's threat. He knew if he turned, he'd see Jack Morgan's fists resting on her hips and her storm-blue eyes blazing brighter than her honey-blonde hair. She had her mama's beauty and temper.

"And by wagon, you low-down 'cake thief, I mean your bu—"

"Jack Morgan," Jackson warned, "I suggest you don't finish that sentence unless you want to eat your pancakes with molasses instead of maple syrup. You know that's not a fittin' word for a lady to use."

"But I don't want to be a lady, Papa. Ladies have to talk all prissy-like. Besides, Mama says bu—er, I mean, Mama says that word."

She had him there. He drew his brows together endeavoring to look stern before moving from the stove to peer into the dining room, where Sam was nursing a cup of coffee. "Darlin', our daughter and nephew need a firm hand—and I do mean on their bu—er, backsides. Peter

378

Jack's up to his old pancake-stealing, syrup-slurping tricks and Jack Morgan isn't in a forgivin' mood."

"Why must I be the disciplinarian?"

"Because you still can't cook, that's why." Lowering his voice, Jackson added, "And because she can wrap me around her finger." He lowered his head in mock shame. "Face it, darlin'. You married a weak man. I'm good in the kitchen—and the bedroom."

Sam grinned. "I'll be there in a minute."

Jack Morgan's eyes moved from her papa back to her cousin, who was brazenly draining the syrup jug. "If you don't leave some for Mama, she's gonna tan your…bottom."

"There's more," Peter Jack retorted. "I heard my papa say your papa always stocks up when it's Uncle Morgan's and Aunt Alexa's week to take us to church. Mama said he does it 'cause a woman is extra accommodating when her husband does nice things for her."

"What does 'commodatin' mean?"

"Don't know for sure," Peter Jack replied. "I think it means she'll do whatever he asks."

Jackson was back at the stove, trying like hell to keep his shoulders from shaking.

"Besides our folks haven't ever spanked us," Peter Jack added, backtracking to address his cousin's earlier warning.

"I know, but I feel bad when they look so sad over my bad 'havior," Jack Morgan confessed.

"Sometimes, I feel bad, too," Peter Jack admitted while nudging the syrup jug to the center of the table.

"Well, just so you know," Jack Morgan warned, "I keep a list of the mean things you do to devil me. Papa helps me 'cause I don't know but a few of the words. When I'm bigger, I'm gonna take a little notch out of one of your ears for each thing on my list."

"Not if I can shoot better than you!" Peter Jack declared. After all, he was six years older.

Jack Morgan giggled. "You can try, but Mama promised I'm gonna shoot better than her and Grandpa Mac."

"How many things are on that list?" Peter Jack asked, ignoring Jack Morgan's threat.

"Well, none right now, 'cept this pancake-slurpin' meanness from today," she answered honestly.

"How can that be? I've been devilin' you since you were born."

"Papa makes me cross somethin' off when you do somethin' nice. Up to now, you're 'bout even." Wily as a coyote, she added, "'Course, I don't mind. I like it when you're nice."

"That so?" Peter Jack commented, intrigued by the concept of keeping a list. "Don't your papa get tired of tending that list?"

"Papa likes lists, 'specially the Do List Mama keeps for him. That's where she writes the nice things she wants Papa to do for her."

Curious, Peter Jack asked, "What things?"

"I don't know. But Papa checks it every night after supper."

Jackson leaned in close to Sam's ear. "Lord, darlin', you'd better stop keepin' *that list of chores*. Jack Morgan isn't that far from being able to read, you know."

"Hmm. Maybe I should whisper one or two in your ear during dessert."

"Not if you want me to get up from the table. You could tell me in the morning while we're still in bed. It'd give me something to think about all day."

"If I do that, we'll never get out of bed."

Jackson took her in his arms. "Well, then, darlin', we'll just have to trust we'll eventually cover everything—at least once."

"Mmm," Sam agreed, imagining the pleasures implied in the word *everything*.

Recognizing the desire sparking in Sam's eyes, Jackson murmured, "And nothing's better than *everything, darlin'*—except, of course, covering it *twice*."

Historical Notes

Throughout its early years, *Scientific American* articles reported news from the U.S. Patent Office. Patent No. 193,790 for William E. Wharton's Robber Trap was granted on July 31, 1877. The article was published in *Scientific American*, Volume 37, Number 14, October 6, 1877. The three figures referenced in the patent description (Figures 1, 2, and 3) are accredited to N. Peters, Photo-Lithographer, Washington, D.C.

Adam Bogardus, sharpshooter and inventor of the Bogardus glass balls and trap target thrower, is regarded as one of the best marksmen in history. In 1877 at Patrick Gilmore's Garden (predecessor to Madison Square Garden) in New York City, he shot at 5,000 glass balls in 8 hours and 20 minutes, breaking 4,844.

Historians are uncertain what Annie Oakley did between 1875 and 1880. Annie claimed she married Frank Butler on August 23, 1876; however, the date on their marriage certificate is June 20, 1882.

The whirlwind on a Fourth of July in 1875 recalled by Sheriff Cooley happened in Laramie in 1876. Striking the ladies' stand, it toppled the awning and its supports, inflicting several scalp wounds.

Excerpt From

Book 1—Prosperity Series

Lost in Prosperity

Chapter 1

August 1875, Wyoming Territory

The stagecoach should have already arrived in Prosperity. Because the driver took extra time at each stop to check the left rear axle, it was more than an hour late.

A man and woman, the stage's only passengers, were returning from business in Laramie. At the start of their journey, the male passenger had been both amused and disappointed when his traveling companion made a point of saying he was a "distraction" and chose not to sit next to him. He was amused because he knew she was strongly attracted to him and found it difficult to concentrate when he was nearby. He was disappointed because he'd hoped to "distract" her all the way home. So here they were, on opposite sides and corners of the coach, riding in silence, while the only distraction he dared was studying her when he thought she wouldn't notice.

Bored, he crossed his arms over his chest and stretched his long legs in the space between the seats. From under the brim of his black Stetson, he surreptitiously watched his companion.

He liked looking at her. Almost any man would. She had a graceful neck, slender shoulders, and a long-legged frame blessed with curves that fit against him in all the right places. He admired how easily those curves swayed with the motion of the coach. The symmetry of her face was pleasing but upstaged by the arresting boldness of her slate blue, widely spaced, and oh-so-very expressive eyes. He'd seen them clouded with suspicion, sparking with anger, and darkened with passion. Men caught in her unblinking gaze, depending on insecurities and confidence, would either lose their conviction and courage or become trapped in the mesmerizing power of her allure.

Shifting in his seat, the man lifted a corner of the heavy leather flap that served as a window curtain. The sky's purple and gold autumn colors were fading, anticipating the surrender of day to sunset.

Inside the coach, the dim light revealed that his companion continued her reflection. Seeing her drop her gaze to the jagged lightning bolt scar near the curve of her thumb on the back of her right hand, he recalled the pleasure of feeling its imprint pressed against his lips. Outwardly, she appeared composed, but he wasn't fooled. He knew she was disappointed with how she'd handled the unwelcome, crass advances from the owner of the Bar W Ranch the day before.

When she leaned back in her seat, she tucked an escaped, honey-tinged curl behind her ear before raising her hand to examine the bruise on her left cheek.

He hadn't been present when the rancher had backhanded her. But when he'd arrived soon after, he'd enjoyed watching her make the sonofabitch pay for touching her. He would have pummeled the bastard to within an inch of his sorry life, except for having learned from experience she wouldn't welcome his interference. Had he dared to step in, his reward almost certainly would have been to sleep alone until her anger dissipated enough to forgive him.

She often accused him of being hot-tempered. He couldn't deny it, especially where she was concerned. He did, however, find it ironic she tended to ignore the trait in herself, which, in his opinion, made it a clear case of *it takes one to know one*, whether she cared to admit it or not.

Less than a minute later, her slate blue eyes turned to him, and a delicate brow arched in an unspoken question. The corners of her mouth curved in an inviting smile, signaling she'd set reflection aside and was ready to engage in a little "distracting" behavior.

God, he loved this woman.

Straightening, he leaned toward her, offering his assistance to help her change seats. She scooted forward and was reaching for his outstretched hand when the left rear axle separated from its hub, sending the wheel careening and the coach bed slamming into the road, stripping the door next to him from its frame.

Caught off balance, he pitched sideways out of the coach, sailing several feet above the ground down a steep incline until his shoulder plowed into loose gravel and rocks. He tumbled once before falling to his side and rolling. Fighting momentum, he grabbed onto a cone-shaped boulder halfway down the slope. The coach had already flown beyond his resting place, and he could hear it colliding with the ravine walls as it hurtled to the distant bottom.

***

The woman's back hit the coach wall with so much force she couldn't draw air into her lungs. Then the floor beneath her feet fell away, and she was propelled out of the gaping chasm created by the missing door.

When she woke, she didn't recall sailing through the air or striking the ground. Those memories were interred in the void of unconsciousness and the torture of sharp spears piercing her head, back, and shoulders. The pain was debilitating, offering but two choices: fight it or surrender to it. She elected to fight.

Willing her senses to assess her surroundings, she heard the high-pitched screams of a horse rising from somewhere down the steep incline. In her peripheral vision, she recognized the dark shape of the stagecoach's severed luggage rack. Careful not to move her head, she slowly fanned her arms, examining the granite beneath her.

She rolled to her side and swallowed the agony it triggered. Because she hadn't anticipated the waves of nausea and vertigo that accompanied it, she was forced to rest. Minutes later, she struggled to a sitting position by pushing against an outcropping of stone. With her legs dangling over the boulder's edge, she placed her palms on its surface, steadying herself. Then she waited motionless with her eyes closed while concentrating on breathing.

As the dizziness receded, her mind began to clear. She remembered the fading light and a few brief moments before the coach collapsed. Now, the stars and the moon were evidence dusk had come and gone. A man's strong hand had brushed against hers before he'd been pitched from the coach, but she couldn't recall his face or whether she knew him.

"Is anyone there?" she called into the night, concerned for the man's safety. "Can you hear me?"

She held her breath while listening for a response. But there was no answer. Even the horse she'd heard earlier was quiet. Then the faint scuff of boots scraping stone reached her ears, followed by footsteps and the clattering of dislodged gravel bouncing off boulders as it rolled down the incline toward her. Her eyes searched the embankment. A male silhouette separated from the night shadows and a voice answered.

"Is that you, Sam?"

He sounded anxious. The name Sam puzzled her until she realized he must have been searching for the stage driver. She raised her chin to answer, hoping her voice was strong enough to project up the slope.

"Be careful. We're not at the bottom of this hellhole," she warned.

Though she could hear him working his way down to her, he didn't reply. Perhaps he was hurt.

"Are you all right?" she asked.

"My shoulder's bruised, but nothing's busted," he replied. "Sam, I still can't see you. Say something else so I can find you. Are *you* hurt?"

Although relieved he'd answered, she wondered why he called her "Sam." Following his instructions, she admitted, "I hit my head. I caught a glimpse of you earlier, but I don't see you now." Each word was an effort, and she recognized her voice was weaker. "You sound close," she added, wanting to encourage him.

Seconds later, he quietly announced his arrival. "I'm behind you, but don't turn around."

Before she could respond, he added, "The ravine plunges at least another fifty feet from where you're sitting. Do you understand the danger?"

Sensing the alarm beneath the calmly spoken words, she nodded—but only once because of the pain. She was aware there wasn't any solid ground beneath her dangling feet but hadn't realized the drop was deadly.

Boots scraped against rock as the man knelt behind her. Strong arms encircled her waist, while his chest supported her back and head as he dragged her slowly back from the precipice. Shivering, her body molded to his, seeking his latent heat. After settling her head in the crook of his shoulder, he turned her hips and legs to the side.

With his torso wrapped around hers, his hand found her chin and tilted her head up before he lowered his mouth to cover hers. Surprised, she held very still—but only until his lips moved against hers in a tender, undemanding kiss. She responded with no hesitancy, giving back—right up to the moment she realized she shouldn't. Emitting a faint sound of protest, she pushed weakly against his chest.

Concerned, he withdrew immediately. "I'm sorry, darlin'. I didn't mean to hurt you," he apologized, his tone soothing. The backs of his curled fingers grazed her cheek before sliding into her hair to explore the bump on the crown of her head.

Reflexively, she clutched a handful of his vest and shirt. Though his touch was gentle, she couldn't muffle the gasp that escaped her lips.

"I know it's painful," he murmured near her ear. "It's a wonder you're conscious."

His warm breath against her neck sent a tremor through her, making her forget the pain and remember the kiss.

"I recall reaching for your hand, but I can't remember your face. Please, let me see you." She'd endure the pain for the reward of seeing the face that went with the voice and the kiss.

Supporting her head and upper body, he shifted, dipping his head so the moonlight illuminated his features. Unaware a muscle worked in his jaw, he watched her examine his face.

Uncommonly handsome, his eyes, filled with kindness, were almost as dark as his black hair, which was so thick it begged a woman to run her hands through it. The strong planes of his face were ruggedly, pleasingly male. His mouth was firm, pleasantly curved, and sinfully compelling. His square chin completed the composition of masculine good looks and sensuality.

When her eyes lowered, he drew her back against him.

"It's beginning to cloud up," she murmured, frowning her displeasure at losing the light.

"It's all right," he replied, gently stroking her arm. "I can see well enough to get us home. Your pain is what's stealing the moonlight. Soon, you won't be able to see anything at all."

Her eyelids drifted shut, and she whispered one last random thought before consciousness left her. "I bet you're kind to horses, too."

About the Author

Even before reading Owen Wister's, *The Virginian: A Horseman of the Plains*, in tenth grade, Judy Hannigan loved historical westerns.

In the Old West, where a good man and a good woman can prevail—together—the heroes and heroines in Judy's romance adventure novels persevere to find enduring love. They do what's right, instead of what they're told—and justice triumphs. And her supporting characters demonstrate blood isn't the primary factor that binds people to one another.

Raised in Southwest Michigan's "fruit belt" country near the shores of Lake Michigan, she earned a BA in Secondary Education (English and American History) and an MA in Reading at the Secondary Level from Western Michigan University.

She taught high school for more than six years before deciding technical editing was a better fit. Presently, she writes full-time and resides in Southern Maryland with her husband and the best neighbors in the world.

Judy loves to hear from her readers. Visit her website and sign up for her newsletter: *www.Judyhannigan.com*
And write to her at: *judy@judyhannigan.com*